OPIUM
AND
ABSINTHE

OTHER BOOKS BY LYDIA KANG

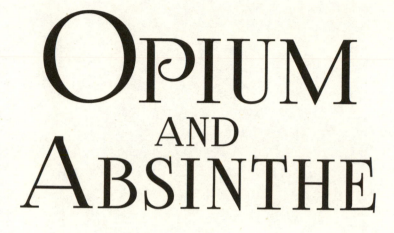

OPIUM AND ABSINTHE

A Novel

LYDIA KANG

LAKE UNION
PUBLISHING

Published by Lake Union Publishing, Seattle

www.apub.com

Amazon, the Amazon logo, and Lake Union Publishing are trademarks of Amazon.com, Inc., or its affiliates.

ISBN-13: 9781542017794
ISBN-10: 1542017793

Cover design and illustration by Edward Bettison

Printed in the United States of America

For Ama and Agon

I want you to believe . . .
To believe in things that you cannot.
—Van Helsing
Bram Stoker
Dracula

CHAPTER 1

I am all in a sea of wonders.

I doubt; I fear; I think strange things, which I dare not confess to my own soul.

—Jonathan Harker

June 8, 1899

Dear Miss Nellie Bly,
I'm not sure how best to address you. Miss Bly, by your pen name? Mrs. Seaman? Mrs. Elizabeth Cochrane Seaman? Mrs. Bly?

Well, I shan't bother you endlessly about your name.

I am writing to let you know how much I enjoy your newspaper articles, though lately I have not seen very many. I especially enjoyed the one you wrote about elephants. I imagine they were rather malodorous.

Please write back and let me know how badly they smelled. You left that out of the article, and I should like to know. I cannot find the information at the Lenox Library.

A devoted reader,
Miss Tillie Pembroke

———✦———

It is better to be a coward than a corpse.

The phrase was a cacophonous jingle in Tillie Pembroke's mind. She huffed uncomfortably and swiped at the veil irritating the edge of her cheek. Everything was conspiring against her today.

Coward, corpse. Coward, corpse.

"Tillie! Hurry, we're leaving soon!" Dorothy Harriman called from outside the stable. She was already on her mount, hat and veil perfectly in place, a swirl of chestnut hair at the nape of her neck. Her ebony mare was a glossy beauty in the sunlight. Dorothy always did everything perfectly, even nagged her friend with precision.

The clean scent of soil and moist greenery beckoned to Tillie. Here on Long Island, the sky was unmarred by buildings and church spires. The humidity of the June day was rising in a mist. Grand oak and maple trees arched around the riders gathering for the hunt.

Of course, Tillie would be the last rider to mount. And her riding habit didn't fit quite right, because she had torn hers yesterday and now wore her mother's old one. This heavy melton fabric smothered her. Her favorite antelope gloves had been misplaced by her maid, and the gold pin on her muslin cravat was slightly bent from the last time she'd fallen off her horse.

Only a few feet away, a barn cat tended a litter of new kittens. Upon seeing Tillie's lingering gaze, she immediately picked up one kitten in her jaws and carried it elsewhere for some quiet nursing. How was it that the cat didn't harm her babies with those teeth? How was it that the milk came only when the kittens needed it, instead of constantly pouring forth from her belly like a full watering can?

Tillie batted away the questions. She was eighteen now. She no longer had the luxury of her permissive childhood to pore over books and endlessly question the gardener, the cook, her sister, and all the maids in order to loosen the stewing questions that constantly simmered in her head. She wondered if Nellie Bly, the famous journalist, would write her back. The elephant-odor question was still fixed in her mind. Perhaps they smelled like horses.

"Miss Mathilda. Please pay more attention to your mount than the barn cat."

"Yes, Roderick," Tillie replied with a sigh.

Her groom was the age her father would have been, if he still lived. Roderick's teeth were brown from tobacco stains, and he smelled perpetually of old hay and horse sweat. A comforting scent.

She readied to mount Queenie, a somewhat vicious Thoroughbred that belonged to her sister. Tillie would have never dreamt of taking her, but her mother no longer rode and suffered to pay for only two horses here on Long Island. Tillie's horse was resting in her stall, nursing a bruised hoof that may or may not have been Tillie's fault.

"You ought to stop riding, Miss Mathilda," Roderick continued. "You've fallen once already this season, and you hardly come here to practice."

"That's because Lucy is always taking my best cane and has the best horse and the best teacher," Tillie said under her breath.

Roderick heard her well enough. "But I've taught you both!" he protested.

She blushed. "Yes, and yet she's so much better."

"She *listens* to me, Miss Mathilda. Instead of watching the anthills for an hour."

He didn't need to say more. Tillie was already nervous to ride, and she hadn't even climbed on the mare. But today, she must. Because Dorothy was here, and Tillie had heard a rumor. Dorothy had been overheard to say, "A rock could ride a horse better than Tillie Pembroke."

Oh, but she wished Lucy were here. Older by three years, Lucy looked like she belonged in a pinque coat like the other riders; Tillie was merely the mirage of one.

It was Lucy who would buffer Tillie from their family's disappointment when she made occasional gaffes in public, like asking the Courtlands' butler how their new toilet imported from France worked. Three months ago, she had vomited in front of Mrs. Astor at Lucy's engagement party, because she'd wondered if consuming an enormous quantity of cake would absorb the champagne like a sponge. Lucy told everyone that it was the pastry chef's fault—a bad recipe with too many wine-soaked cherries. Everyone was soothed (except the pastry chef, for whom Lucy found another position without a mention of the incident). At her coming-out party the year before, Tillie disappeared to the library to research the origins of the word *fuliginous* after her great-uncle had used it, then became distracted by a picture of a collared fruit bat before losing herself completely in the *F*s. It wasn't the first time she had been utterly consumed by the pages of *Webster's International Dictionary*. Lucy had lessened the embarrassment by explaining that her sister was quite modest and needed time to recover from all the attention.

Lucy, with her large brown eyes, her perfect pale-gold hair piled in loose curls upon her head, her swan's neck, was the very image of a Gibson Girl. And she had a perfect fiancé too. James Cutter, whose bloodline extended to the Dutch in the 1600s, like the Pembrokes'. In a city where the new-moneyed Rockefellers and Vanderbilts put up vulgar, showy mansions, drawing their wealth from disgraceful sources like the railroad, the marriage between Lucy Pembroke and James Cutter would be one for the ages—perhaps one of the last. It would be, as everyone murmured, the greatest New York wedding of the new century.

James himself was here for the hunt, but he'd hardly ever paid more than passing attention to his future sister-in-law. Lucy couldn't ride because she'd only recently recovered from a bout of typhus. She had of late been visiting the orphans at the Foundling Hospital, a few avenues away from their mansion in Manhattan. Sweet Lucy was always looking to help those less fortunate than her.

Tillie would tell her later all about the ride and how brilliantly it had gone. She would tell her how she had not gotten distracted by anything today.

Roderick helped hoist her into the saddle. She hooked her right knee around the pommel, nestled her other knee under the leaping head, and fit her left foot into the single stirrup. The groom tightened the girths and balance strap, the latter to keep the saddle from sagging on the more burdened left side, and offered her the cane for her right hand.

"Your sandwich box is filled, and there's a flask of tea in there as well."

Tillie unbuckled the leather box, pulled out the linen-wrapped sliced-cheese-and-lettuce sandwich, and gobbled half of it.

"But that is for during the hunt, Miss!"

"Oh. I'm sorry. I'm hungry when I'm nervous," Tillie said, delicately wiping her mouth with a handkerchief. She returned the rest of the sandwich to the box.

The food helped, but her heart was quivering like a cold chicken jelly. There were several jumps today that demanded confidence. Roderick advised her as he led Queenie out of the stable.

"Be careful of the rabbit holes in the north paddock. Remember, a lady must keep a clear head when the fox breaks cover. Keep within sight of the hounds. And for God's sake, if you aren't perfectly certain you can make a jump . . . do. Not. Jump. It's better to be a coward than a corpse."

Coward, corpse.

Tillie inhaled as deeply as her corset would allow, a mere cupful of air. "I'm ready."

No sooner had she said the words than Queenie rapidly entered a trot, wishing to catch up to the group of twelve riders ahead. Warm, wet air rose from the turf after the deep rainfall the day before, and it felt thick in Tillie's chest as she breathed. The oak and maple trees surrounding the barn seemed to curl, clawlike, toward their party. Dorothy, who'd been riding alongside a gentleman, slowed her horse, and together they brought up the rear of the company. The other riders in their scarlet riding coats shone like poppies against the greenery. Tillie's underarms were already swampy, and her drawers stuck to her thighs like wet paper.

"They're going to the field just north of here," Dorothy said.

"Yes." The less Tillie said, the less likely she would say something inappropriate.

"We are greatly looking forward to your sister's wedding. Only one more month! Have you seen her wedding gown yet? Did she order it from Paris, like Eleanor Van der Wiel did?" Dorothy was dangerously close to reaching old maid status. At the mention of weddings, her eyes widened with hunger. Despite Dorothy's having a shoddyite father who gathered his money from shipping, Tillie liked her. Dorothy was equally friendly with Tillie and Lucy, whereas most people simply ignored Tillie.

"I . . . I don't know." Tillie tried to move the skirt so it didn't bunch on her lap. "It's silk. And lace." She knew all about the extinction of Steller's sea cow in 1768. Nothing about lace.

"Of course, but what kind of silk? And lace?"

"Er . . . we're falling behind," Tillie said. She kicked her left boot against Queenie's side and pressed her cane into the animal's right flank. Queenie ignited at the suggestion and reared into a gallop.

"No! Whoa. Whoa! Queenie, slow down!" yelped Tillie as she swiftly surpassed two, then three, then five riders. They were already slowing in a line to jump a short stone fence into the next field. Tillie pulled harder on the reins, then gathered them again when her gloves loosened in the fingertips. The cane fell from her right hand. Feeling pressure only from the left side of her saddle now, Queenie abruptly turned in the opposite direction and cut in front of the stone fence, past the entire company of riders.

"Stop!" Tillie yelled. Behind her, James called to Tillie to slow, and she heard sounds of dismay from other riders. But Queenie went ever faster.

An old, unkempt stone fence stood before them. There wasn't time to turn. The horse leaped up, but Tillie had forgotten to give Queenie her head and held the reins tightly. Confused, Queenie jumped too low. Her front hooves went into a dip in the ground unseen beneath a cluster of raspberry brambles. And Tillie went flying.

It was an exquisite, unnatural sensation. She recognized that parting between herself and her horse, the feeling that the earth had momentarily released her from its eternally wanting clutches.

Tillie soared—and was terrified.

Her left shoulder hit the ground first. There was an audible snap and a white-hot pain that took her vision completely away. Then her jaw clanked painfully closed as her temple thudded against a large fallen branch.

She waited for the world to stop whirling in pinwheels of color and pain, but it didn't. Her long asymmetrical skirt was caught in Queenie's saddle, and the horse dragged her rag doll body a good fifteen feet. She heard sharp yells—"Goodness gracious!" "Miss Mathilda!" "Grab the reins, James!"—until finally the skirt came free. In a blur of horse legs Queenie galloped away, probably indignant, and probably back to her groom and stall. The world had blessedly stopped moving and pummeling Tillie like a pugilist.

Her ears were ringing, not like bells but more like the hissing of old street gaslights. Pain spiked through every part of her body—her head, her wrists, her back. But the pain in her collarbone marvelously outshone the others. Tillie had never known until then that bones could scream in her head.

Vaguely, she heard boots crunching the leaves nearby while the horses snorted and whooshed their commentary.

"Tillie! Dear Tillie! Can you speak?" It was Dorothy. Her voice sounded shaken.

Tillie felt a gloved hand on her cheek. She opened one eye, seeing Dorothy's wall of skirt, a hand, and a group of faces anxiously peering at her. James was gently lifting her, assisted by Alistair Sutton and his less attractive brother, the one with the face that reminded her of a turkey.

"Can you move your arms and legs?" James asked. He sounded rather irked.

The pain, after its initial blossom, had reintroduced itself as excruciating. Tillie tested herself and cried out.

"I can't move my left arm," she said, gasping.

There was a masculine huff of irritation. "Easy. We'll get you home," James said. Sweat glistened across his deeply cut cheekbones, which meant that her situation must be direr than she'd realized. The Cutters did not, by convention, perspire while in society. "Your sister will be furious with me for not looking after you, Mathilda."

Tillie, she wanted to say. Call me Tillie. Even in normal circumstances, she hardly had the bravery to enforce her preferred name.

A hand touched her injured shoulder, and the broken shards of collarbone scraped against each other. She cried out in pain.

"Fetch some laudanum," Dorothy urged a groom. While the gentlemen riders carried her, the ladies rode ahead. If only they would loosen her corset, then she could take a breath. She fainted repeatedly, only rousing when someone jostled her shoulder enough that the pain awoke her to fresh misery.

She was propped up in her carriage. Dorothy and her eternally present lady's companion, Hazel Dreyer, were at her side. Someone brought a wineglass to Tillie's lips.

"Laudanum," Roderick said in reply to Dorothy's glance. "An opium tincture. Enough to make the trip back tolerable." Tillie drank it down, suddenly thirsty. It was bitter and made her cough. But they had driven only a quarter of a mile when she felt the pain at her shoulder dull a little, and a soporific cloud settled over her mind. Dorothy and Hazel fussed over her until she fell into a jagged slumber muddied with moments of queasiness.

At some point in her dreams—or was she awake?—she heard Dorothy exhale irritably and whisper, "She is an utter disaster. Surely this will take her out of the events for the next month."

Tillie muttered, "Disaster." What was the origin of that word? she wondered. Did it have anything to do with the Astors? Maybe there was such a thing as a disvanderbilt. "Dis . . . disrockefeller," she murmured.

"More laudanum," Dorothy replied and dosed her again with a flask of medicine-laced wine. Tillie remembered Lucy telling her she ought to speak her mind. It was nearly the turn of the century. A lady could speak for herself sometimes. There were lady doctors, lady journalists. Even in their society, women had enormous amounts of power at their disposal. Look at Mrs. Astor.

"I have ssssssomething to say," Tillie said, blinking sleepily and trying to sit up. She winced at the pain of moving her body. "I have something to anna . . . annoo . . . *announce*."

"What is it, Tillie, dear?" Dorothy leaned in closer, probably hoping for a bit of indiscreet gossip, or complaints about her all-too-perfect sister, who seemed destined for the perfect marriage, for sainthood, for all of the best salons for the next decades to come.

"I ought . . . to have chosen cowardice," Tillie said in a groan, before vomiting her half sandwich all over Dorothy's lap and winking out of consciousness.

—✦—

It was the pain that awoke Tillie.

Her left arm was bound against her chest. The fluffy blankets confined her movements and made her insufferably hot. Her mouth was drier than a crust of toast and tasted something terrible—like a rancid sewer on Canal Street. She heard a low feminine voice murmuring nearby. Always, Lucy was there at her side. Through the measles and chicken pox, through fevers and the grippe—Lucy had been there. She would read to Tillie from the dictionary to keep her quiet. Her mother and maid didn't even bother answering her ring when she called from her sickbed. It was always her sister she wanted.

"Lucy," she mumbled.

"May I fetch you something, Miss Tillie?"

It wasn't Lucy's voice. They weren't Lucy's words. Tillie opened an eye, which took effort. Her eyelids were pasted together with a gluey substance. Her vision was blurry, but she saw an orange-haired figure hovering at her bedside.

"It's me, Miss Tillie. It's your Ada."

Her maid. A comfort, but not her sister. Ada was arranging her bed linens, a gentle smile spreading under her small snub nose.

"Where's Lucy?"

"Never mind your sister. How is your pain? Will you sit up and eat some porridge? Or toast? I have some beef tea for you, too, if you'd like. The doctor says you must eat something." Ada went to a table near the foot of the four-poster bed. On it sat several brown bottles and crystal glasses, a bowl, a ewer and basin—the old-fashioned kind they never used now that they had a proper washroom—and a stack of soft white cloths. There was also a small tray of toast, a teacup of broth, and a bowl of creamy porridge. Ada busied herself adding a spoonful of sugar to a glass of water and mixing in drops of a brown liquid. Her cap was neat and frilled, apron perfectly ironed, and she smiled kindly at Tillie. But the hand holding the medicine shook. The brown liquid quivered at the tip of the dropper, and a splash fell on the cloth laid out beneath the glass, spreading like muddy water on a clean petticoat.

"Where is Lucy?" Tillie repeated.

"Drink this, and I shall bring your mama. But not before you come with me to the bathroom suite to wash and tend to yourself."

"But Lucy—"

"She will let you know where Lucy is," Ada said.

The pain was beyond oppressive, so Tillie acquiesced. She drank the draught, noting the bitterness and the sugar's inability to mask the opium's presence. Then, Ada brought her to the room next door, where she relieved herself and let Ada bathe her puffy eyelids and wan face. Only after Tillie was back in bed, with a half piece of toast in her stomach, did Ada fetch her mother.

By the time her mother arrived, Tillie was growing drowsy from the medicine. Victoria Pembroke entered with a pause and a sigh. She seemed disappointed that Tillie was awake. Her mother's graying hair was tucked beneath the fine Parisian lace of her cap, and beneath her curls her eyes were piercing and lapis blue. Tillie's father's eyes had been a burnt-brown color, possibly a sign of his rumored Chinese ancestry. Now that he had been gone for over ten years, she supposed she'd never learn if the rumor was true—her mother abruptly changed the subject whenever Tillie asked. Tillie would far prefer to ask a lion to stop chewing on a gazelle carcass than query her grandmother on the subject.

"You're awake." Her mother smiled as she leaned forward to kiss Tillie on the cheek and grasp her unbound right hand.

Tillie pulled her fingers away. Her mother was never demonstrative. She did not embrace or kiss or squeeze hands, gloved or not. The break in routine alarmed Tillie.

"What's wrong, Mama?" she asked. The medicine had made her head cloudy. "And where is Lucy?"

Her mother brought a handkerchief to her mouth and turned away, unable to look at her second daughter.

"Lucy . . . Lucy is missing."

CHAPTER 2

Even if she be not harmed, her heart may fail her in so much
and so many horrors; and hereafter she may suffer—both in
waking, from her nerves, and in sleep, from her dreams.

—Van Helsing

"Missing?" Tillie asked. Her hands trembled on her coverlet. "What do you mean?"

Her mother took in a breath. "She went with Betty—ugh, I never liked that maid—to Dr. Erikkson's office. A good doctor, finally!" Tillie's mother was always looking for a better doctor, one who would open his doors to the family upon immediate request. So many other doctors were always out, delivering babies—so utterly inconvenient!—or attending to the rest of their rich clientele. Dr. Erikkson maintained an office and stayed there. "Betty said that afterward Lucy wished to go to the museum at the park for an hour. And Betty just let her go! Unaccompanied! I knew that woman was troublesome. Ada thinks she saw her stealing an entire box of groceries from the pantry the other day."

"Stealing? Lucy's last maid was let go for taking linens from the closet." She tapped her lips, thinking. "I know why Lucy wanted to go to the museum. To see the Joan of Arc painting."

"Is that so?" Her mother frowned.

"It's her favorite. The one by Jules . . . B-something or other. A French fellow." Lucy had seen it, oh, ten times already since they'd brought it to the museum last year. She'd even dragged Tillie there, who found paintings vastly boring. Paintings did not explain how the world worked.

"Well," her mother continued, "Lucy never arrived back home."

"Did she take the carriage?"

"No. She wished to walk, and she had been feeling so much better, so I allowed it. And Betty was supposedly with her."

"Such a long walk." Tillie imagined her sister walking all the way up Fifth Avenue to the museum alone. "Where is Betty now?"

"Let go, of course. She'll never set foot in this house again."

Tillie paused. Betty was a sweet maid and always doted on Lucy. But a thief was a thief, and one who didn't care properly for her mistress was intolerable. "When did this happen?"

"Two days ago, around eleven o'clock in the morning. Around the same time as your accident."

"Two days!" Tillie sat up straighter, then mewled a cry of pain at the sudden movement. "Why didn't anyone tell me? What's been done? Who's searching for her?"

"Lower your voice!" her mother hissed. "Don't make yourself more ill. We almost didn't tell you at all."

"But I don't understand. Where could she be?"

"I said to be calm!" Mama snapped. "You're not a child anymore. You cannot simply raise your voice at the slightest provocation."

Tillie shrank back into her usual reticence. Why wasn't her mother in absolute hysterics? Her daughter—her favorite daughter, at that—had been missing for two days. But her mother only leaned in and smoothed out the ridges that had formed in the lace coverlet. Everyone was always smoothing away the ripples that Tillie created.

"James confessed that they had a disagreement the day before she disappeared," her mother said, more calmly now. "The wedding is coming soon, and Lucy's nerves have been anything but peaceful. She is likely with one of her friends and ought to return soon."

"But . . . ," Tillie began, keeping her voice dulcet. "We should look for her. We could speak to other families to see if—"

"We have already made some inquiries."

"Then . . . perhaps . . . we could ask more people—"

"Oh, Mathilda! Don't be ridiculous. We'll not shout from the rooftops that she's gone. The last thing we need is gossip with the wedding imminent. All brides are silly and restless. Lucy will return soon. Tonight, even."

Ada had come in, and her freckled face startled in alarm at the sight of Tillie's strained expression. She went directly to the bottle of medicine.

"Miss Tillie, I'll get your drops ready."

"I don't like it," Tillie complained. "It makes my stomach feel like I'm on the *Campania* again." Her only trip across the Atlantic had nearly killed her with the relentless seasickness that would not stop roiling through her. The laudanum gave her the same sense of queasiness—as if her stomach were bobbing incessantly in a steadfast world.

"She's in a bad way," Ada remarked. "Not just the broken bone, you know." She gave Mama a knowing glance, and Tillie realized for the first time since she'd awoken that her belly felt knotted with pain. Muslin layers swathed her skin beneath her sleeping gown. Oh. Vaguely, she remembered Ada attending to her and realized she'd been bleeding from her monthlies.

Her mother sighed. "Very well."

Tillie said nothing, just looked toward the window.

"Drink it. And sleep, Miss," Ada urged. Tillie knew a maid's mistress was far easier to attend to when she was asleep most of the day. When Ada pushed the drink toward her, Tillie could not refuse. The pain was returning with a crescendo of inevitability. And her heart was full of Lucy—her absence. Tillie drank the cordial entirely.

Her mother moved to leave. "Do not worry about Lucy. She will be back. Just like . . ."

Tillie looked at her mother expectantly, but she did not finish the sentence, leaving Tillie to wonder if her mother had also had a three-day escape before she'd married Papa. Mama had said once, "A woman's heart is full of secrets." Apropos of her comment, she had refused to elaborate.

The door shut. Tillie felt some comfort that being ill meant less time spent with her mother and grandmother. There would be no chiding over how abominable her riding was, how embarrassing her fall had been, how weak her constitution was. The medicine churned in her belly, seeped into her bloodstream, numbed the nagging sensation that Tillie was just a splinter in their fingertips in comparison to Lucy. Before five minutes had elapsed, she'd fallen back asleep.

<hr />

When Tillie finally awoke from her opium-soaked stupor, her mind was thick like day-old raisin pudding and her bladder uncomfortably full. Her skin itched, her mouth was dry, and her hair was an abominable mess. The pain in her collarbone was still sharp and terrible, but other aches accompanied it.

She opened her eyes to see Ada laying out a day dress of blue poplin. Her hair was more of a riotous red than usual.

"Come, Miss. Wake up, and have a little something to eat. You're to see Dr. Erikkson soon."

"Can't he come here just this once?" Tillie attempted to stretch the stiffness from her limbs and was rewarded with what felt like a sword thrust to her shoulder. She moaned.

"You know he has an ill child of his own who needs constant attention. I'm to take you."

As Ada helped dress her, Tillie's memory awoke. "Lucy! Is she back?"

The ensuing silence settled bleakly in the room.

"I should like to speak to my mother before we go."

"Your mother and grandmother are out today. They will be back by supper."

She hoped they were searching for Lucy. Tillie felt a rising panic but stoppered it for later, after she could speak to them. Bathing and dressing with her left arm in its sling were immensely painful. Her eyes were dry and scratchy, she ached everywhere, and she wanted only to go back to sleep.

As she descended the oak-paneled stairway, the usual bustle of their Madison Avenue house was eerily quiet. Normally, there was someone showing flower arrangements for the wedding or visitors discussing whatever Mama's friends tended to discuss—the latest fashions from Paris, who'd built a new house in Newport, or who was likely to lose their fortune as the new century loomed. The absence of Lucy—her quick footsteps, her lively chatter—yawned before Tillie. Ada coaxed her to drink and eat the half cup of tea and triangle of dry toast the cook had set out, and they went to the carriage waiting at the curb.

The trip to Dr. Erikkson's was a short one. He occupied half of a modest limestone town house on Fifty-Ninth Street, down the block from the Bloomingdale Brothers' dry goods store and hemmed in between two much larger houses. Tillie hardly noticed the carriages rolling down the avenue or the pedestrians walking with their canes and umbrellas. She was cautiously extricated from the carriage and leaned heavily on Ada as they knocked on the door. Tillie had never been here before. Their previous doctors had all made house calls.

A maid in plain black livery answered, her wiry gray hair in a low twist.

"Miss Mathilda Pembroke, here to see the doctor," Ada informed her.

"Of course," the woman said, smiling. She opened the door farther, admitting them into a small dim foyer. "My husband will be with you in a few minutes. Please have a seat in his examination room, on your left. May I offer you some tea or water?"

Tillie and Ada exchanged glances; they had both assumed the petite, rounded lady dressed in neck-to-floor black woolens was a servant, not a wife. Mrs. Erikkson smiled again, her eyes crinkling merrily at the edges. She ushered them into a room with a large chaise and a fireplace with a brass brazier sitting beside it. Books lined the shelves on either side. Mrs. Erikkson stoked the fire—the room's only light, since the curtain over the window was closed—with a poker. "I shall return if you need anything. I need to go check on my boy," she said brightly and shut the door as she left.

Tillie was grateful for the fire; she felt a chill despite the warm day. She drew close to one of the shelves and scanned the titles.

Treatise on the Medicinal Leech
Surgical Exploration of the Face and Neck
Illustrations of Syphilitic Diseases

She reached for the leech book, thought twice (Lucy would have admonished her), and withdrew to the chaise. The door opened, and Dr. Erikkson entered. He was an extremely tall, spare man whose hair was a wheat color admixed with silver. He had light eyes that looked as if someone had pricked them with a hatpin and all the color had dribbled away. He studied Tillie's shivering and sling, then nodded.

"Miss Mathilda. Good day. I'll see to that break now."

Apparently, he was spare of words as well. Ada hovered near as Dr. Erikkson palpated the broken bone on either side while Tillie tried not to cry out. He examined her upper arm and neck, pulled her eyelids down, and looked at her throat and teeth. Had he examined Lucy this way before she'd disappeared? Had her typhus infection fully cleared? The grim expression on the doctor's visage squashed Tillie's ability to speak.

Finally, he felt her pulse for a long time. Tillie surreptitiously stole glances at him. His eyebrows seemed to grow straight out of his face instead of lying flat. It made her think of the greenery on the pathways of their garden. She'd looked the plants up in a botanical book. Creeping thyme.

"More rest, and walking only inside the home. She must not exert herself," he said, giving Ada a severe look. "Opium, eight drops, every four hours for pain. Everyone has laudanum or some version of opium tincture on the shelf, so be sure it's ten percent strength. My own brand is safe and always of excellent quality. If she's in pain, the muscles will contract, and the bone will not heal well. Wake her up for the medicine if necessary."

"Thank you, Doctor. Mrs. Pembroke requests a written prescription, if you may. She explicitly asked, as she is afraid I'll report the dosage incorrectly."

"Very well. I'll return in a moment."

Dr. Erikkson left, and Ada moved aside the curtain to look out the window. "Lord, he keeps it dark in here. There is a large wagon unloading, and the driver moved the carriage. He's gone down the block. I shall let him know we're ready."

When she was gone, Tillie stood to examine the brass brazier by the fireplace. It was shaped like a wide bowl perched on four squat feet, with a long handle so the entire thing could be placed directly upon the fire. It was etched with a decoration of swirls and flowers—such antithetical beauty for something created to aid in the scorching of human beings. Three cautery irons rested within it. She picked each one up by its wooden handle to examine it. One was shaped like the spade on a playing card, one was pointed, and one had an edge like a tiny ax. She lifted the pointed one and noticed a charred substance on the tip.

"I wonder if that was a piece of Mr. Carnegie's festering toe infection," Tillie said to herself.

"It probably was."

Tillie dropped the iron, and it clattered onto the slate hearth. She turned around, nearly losing her balance, since one arm was still bound to her rib cage.

A young man stood in the doorway, his shoulders draped in a blanket of gray wool. He was nearly as slight as Tillie. His hair was a mass of sandy curls—the same color as Dr. Erikkson's must have been before it had grayed. He had pale-blue eyes (though all the color had yet to drain away), and a muddy maroon shadowed the hollows beneath them. His cheekbones were sharp and angled.

"I'm sorry I startled you." His voice was unexpectedly deep and rich.

Tillie promptly picked up the iron and replaced it in the brazier. She blushed at being caught touching the instruments.

"I'm Tom. Dr. Erikkson's son," he said.

"Oh! I thought you'd be a little boy, not a grown man." She blurted out the words before she realized how rude they sounded.

"My mother would say the same. I will be twenty on September first."

"My birthday is September first too!" Tillie said, grinning.

"Well! It's like we are already acquaintances somehow." He leaned against the door, his arms crossed over a large book. "I'm sorry to disturb. I heard the door and thought the room was empty. I was returning this."

Tillie followed the tilt of his chin to a gap in the row of books. "May I fetch you a new one?"

"Thank you. But you're hurt—I wouldn't want to be a bother."

"I can lift a book with one hand," she said, smiling. She took a step closer to the boy. There was a playfulness about his mouth. With more food and less illness, he could be quite fine looking. She blushed deeper.

"Well, then. Here you go." He handed his tome to Tillie. "I hope it won't be the death of you."

"*On the Removal of Tumors Both Benign and Cancerous.* That must have quite a plot! What is it like to remove a tumor, I wonder? I hear there can be calcifications. Like cutting into a popcorn ball. Or is it anything like peeling a potato? Cutting a carrot?"

"Not nearly so vegetal," he said, laughing softly. "I would prefer something with more excitement, but alas. Father has me studying to be a physician when my aching head allows it."

"Maybe this is why your head is aching so." Tillie slid the book back in place. She pulled out another. "Here you go. *Vesicants and Blistering: A Primer.* Ah." She tapped the book. "This must include medicines with *Lytta vesicatoria.* I read all about it last summer."

Tom looked at her blankly.

"Spanish fly?" Tillie said helpfully.

He blinked and frowned.

"The blistering beetle?"

"Good God, that's what Father puts on my back?" Tom said. His face went a shade of yellow.

"Probably," Tillie said. She liked Tom. He didn't seem to judge her, as most others did, nor did he look at her the way other young men did, measuring her marital and societal utility, wondering about her fecundity as one might a prize sow's. She couldn't speak to Dorothy like this. Only Lucy. And Lucy was missing.

She was suddenly, achingly lonely—and worried about her sister all over again. Maybe when she returned home, Mama and Grandmama would have news. "I'm Mathilda Pembroke. Mathilda Cora Flint Pembroke, if I were to be more formal. But I prefer Tillie."

"Thomas, but as I said before, I like Tom. Oh, you're a Pembroke? Have you found your sister yet?"

Tillie dropped her mouth open in surprise. "How do you . . . ?"

"The police came to question Father and me and Mother." He shook his head. "It's a sad state of affairs."

Tillie looked at him sharply. "It's not sad yet."

"Of course! I just meant . . . you must be so frightened." He flushed deeply. "I'm out of practice when it comes to conversation. I apologize. You know, I saw her the day she went missing."

"You did? What was she like? Did she seem flustered?" she asked.

"She wasn't acting normal, if that's what you mean. Didn't they tell you?"

Tillie had started to ask what he meant when the front door opened, and Ada and Mrs. Erikkson bustled into the room, all exclamations and wide eyes.

"Tom! Why are you not in your chamber?" Mrs. Erikkson demanded. "I'm so very sorry, Miss Mathilda. He ought not to be around other people—he has such a frail constitution."

"Oh, Mother. I can walk a few steps to get a book." Tom winked at Tillie. "My mother will feed me gruel when I'm ninety, if I allowed it. You ought to rest yourself, Mother, looking after the two men in your life all the time."

Mrs. Erikkson affectionately shooed him through the doorway. "Get on with you. I've left your tea by the side table. Extra sugar."

Tillie opened her mouth again to ask what he'd meant about Lucy but remained silent. Had Lucy been upset during her visit? With Ada and Mrs. Erikkson present, her meekness had ricocheted back with a vengeance.

"Come along, Miss." Ada wrapped a shawl around her and directed her to the entranceway. The carriage was now waiting with the driver just outside. "Do you know," Ada asked quietly, "how angry your mother will be if I don't bring you back home immediately? After what happened to your sister?"

"I know. Of course, Ada. I wish I could ask the doctor one more question. About Lucy."

"By golly, there's nothing to ask that your grandmother hasn't asked already. You know how she is."

True. Grandmama Josephine would question a fly if a crumb were missing from the table. Ada began to help her into the carriage. A few feet away, a tall boy not much older than Tillie waved a newspaper at passersby.

"Pape! Get your *World* for one penny! Papes for sale! Brooklyn Trolley strike, day two! Fires set on Twenty-Second Street line! Man held as a slave in the Amazon! Papes, one penny! Vampire strikes Manhattan, kills lady near the museum!"

Tillie's arms erupted in gooseflesh. She halted her entrance into the carriage. Her mouth had gone dry.

Lucy had been headed for the museum.

"Ada. Fetch me a paper from that newsie."

"No, Miss! All that bad news—terrible for your nerves. We ought to be going home now."

Seeing their interest, the boy's face lit up, and he waved a paper more vigorously in their direction. "Only one cent to hear about the man held captive in the Amazon!"

"No, no, not that," Tillie said. "What did you say about the girl? Near the museum?"

"I'll say what I want, but you'll have to buy the paper to hear the truth," he said with a grin. He had a remarkably good set of teeth, for a street rat. "For you, a half penny and a kiss."

Ada stiffened with disgust and tried to step in front of her charge. Tillie ought to have hung back and let Ada perform the exchange, but she stepped forward.

"Never mind that. I don't need a kiss. I need a paper. Here." She prodded Ada, who procured a penny from her silk reticule. The boy's eyes were large and brown, with thick eyelashes that put Tillie's to shame. Wavy brown hair peeked out from under his hat, reminding her of dark chocolate icing on a cake. He handed over the paper as he pocketed the penny.

Tillie snatched it, scanning the front page. "Where is it? Where?"

The boy shuffled closer. "Here." He took the paper from her, carefully turned the page, and folded it. His hands appeared too large for his frame, as if the rest of him had forgotten to catch up and grow a few inches. But his clothes were neat, not as shabby as most of the newsies'. He looked as if he slept on a bed rather than the street. "Don't want the ink to soil your pretty dress, now." He handed the paper back to her and pointed to an item on the second page.

Tillie read the tiny headline greedily.

Woman Found Dead in Shadow of Metropolitan Museum of Art

Vampire-like Punctures Found on Neck

Empty Absinthe Bottle Found with Body

Identity of Victim Unknown

June 10, 1899—Yesterday, police recovered the body of a young woman near Fifth Avenue and Eighty-First Street, near the south wall of the Metropolitan Museum of Art. Puncture wounds were found on the victim's neck, and the cause of death appears to be exsanguination, though no blood was found at the scene. She appeared to have been deceased for twelve hours before being found.

The victim's identity is yet unknown, but police are seeking information on missing females in their early twenties, blonde, of slim physique, approximately five foot, five inches tall, and last seen wearing a lilac silk dress. An empty absinthe bottle was found next to the body.

Tillie dropped the paper and staggered back, her free hand clutching at the carriage for support.

"Miss Tillie! What is it?" Ada exclaimed. "Call the doctor! Call Dr. Erikkson!" Her voice sounded distant, as if shouted over miles and miles through a snowstorm.

Lucy. Lucy was five foot, five inches tall. Lucy had worn her lilac dress the day Tillie had gone to Long Island to ride in the hunt. The day she had disappeared.

"Lucy!" It was the last thing Tillie said. The newsie rushed forward, dropping his papers in a spreading whoosh, catching Tillie as her knees buckled and the world went sideways.

CHAPTER 3

Despair has its own calms.

—Jonathan Harker

It was a strange thing to be awake within a nightmare.

"Are you all right, Miss? Will you need help getting home?" The newsie leaned against the carriage door after laying Tillie out on the seat cushions.

"No, no," Ada said as she covered Tillie's ankles decently with a blanket. "She's had a shock."

"Say, does she know that dead lady?" he asked.

At this, Ada, too, went pale, and there was a brief danger of two swooning women. But Ada composed herself, and the carriage door was shut. The newsie's question went unanswered, and Tillie thought she saw him briefly speak to the driver—the newsie's hand slipping a coin into the driver's palm—before the horse leaped to a start.

The next hours were a blur. Tillie could hardly breathe, hardly stutter a word. The moment they arrived home, Ada fairly flew through the house to send word about the newspaper article. Tillie's head pounded as if driven full of iron nails, and her shoulder felt newly broken after her swoon. When one of the other maids prepared her medicine, Tillie drank it down and waved her hand.

"More. Another dose. I cannot abide being awake. I cannot . . ." She inhaled sharply, hyperventilating at the mere thought of finishing her sentence.

I cannot live without my Lucy.

The maid, shocked at her state, complied. Tillie groaned, feeling the bitter tincture warm her throat. Within minutes, a strange levity entered her body. She felt loose as goose down, and the pain in her body unscrewed itself to a tolerable level. Now she could close her eyes and think of Lucy, see her blonde curls drooping over her forehead, watch her hand pour another cup of tea. She could imagine Lucy's laugh, like the bells of Trinity Church were signaling for all to sing of that immutable grace that transcended despair. It was a grace Tillie could not touch. Numbness would do instead.

Tillie heard the front door open and close, and the exclamations of her grandmother, a sound that was sandpaper and vinegar. Silence followed. The house shook with the repeated opening and closing of the front door. Hallway chatter from the parlormaids bled into the room from time to time.

"They say it's just like in that book. *Dracula.*"

"I heard it's trash, but my sister loves such novelties. She only just bought it at Baker and Taylor, downtown."

And:

"A vampire! Here! Can you believe it?"

"What a sad affair. I liked Miss Lucy. She was a good lady."

"Aye. But she can't fix this heap of laundry, and I'd like some of that rarebit for luncheon, so let's get back to work, eh?"

Tillie squeezed her eyes shut. Vampires were just stories made up to frighten children. Tillie wasn't much of a novel reader; she preferred factual texts. But at the moment, she did not wish for her beloved dictionary or her father's library. She didn't want to move or think. All she wanted was gone, and the only explanation came from the smudged pages of a penny paper.

How blessedly convenient, this broken bone. She could stay in bed all day, frozen in her grief, instead of facing a funeral and mourners. She needed none of the extra smothering reminders that she was sisterless.

Oh, Lucy. Did he hurt you so very much? Her mind filled with fractured images—a large hand forcing Lucy's face to the side, pinning her to the ground, her silk-slippered feet kicking, blood spattering the ground. Tillie turned to howl into her pillow, but the movement sent pain bolting through her shoulder. All of this was utterly intolerable. She could, however, reach for her bell. Ada promptly opened her door, dressed in her crisp livery. Her eyes were lined with red.

"Good morning, Miss." Oh. It must be morning again. Ada's voice was scratchy. "Goodness, you're a sight. Your face has no color! Let's get you into the bath. I'll have the cook make a soft-boiled egg and tea. The dressmaker will be by shortly for measurements. You have a black bombazine gown that will do for now, but you'll need a parramatta silk to wear for your mourning period."

"No," Tillie said. "I don't want to be fitted."

"Now there. First, medicine. I woke you up last night for your dose. Do you remember?"

Tillie shook her head. She was glad not to recall. Being awake for any reason meant being despondent.

"Dr. Erikkson said you should take it regularly," Ada said. She went to the table at the foot of the bed. Tillie drank the medicine willingly. But her pain seemed so much worse than yesterday.

"Ada," Tillie said, handing the glass back. "Give me a few more drops. I can't bear today with this broken bone, on top of everything else."

"Well . . ." The maid hesitated.

"It's safe enough. They give it to little children all the time."

Ada's expression softened. Tillie saw her own puffy, forlorn face in the mirror over her maid's shoulder. Quite pathetic. Ada placed two more drops into the small crystal goblet and added water from a glass decanter.

The opium took effect quickly, and the next hours were a blur. Tillie was fitted for a proper mourning gown of matte silk and lace trim, with stiff crape ruffles along the skirt and sleeves. Someone handed her a locket of gold and jet with a curl of Lucy's beautiful flaxen hair inside. Which meant that someone must have snipped it off her corpse at the morgue. The very thought sent her into a fit of hyperventilation that required more laudanum and a six-hour nap. She ate something, possibly an egg or toast, and there was more sleep. There could never be enough sleep.

The wake tomorrow was to be a very short affair, given how long Lucy had already been deceased. Tillie suffered through dinner, seated across from her mother while her grandmother occupied the head of the table.

Josephine Pembroke was a stout sixty years old, silver of hair and with a face lined so deeply that she appeared to have bloodless knife gashes on either side of her patrician mouth. Like her daughter's, her eyes were dark blue, and they sparkled with intelligence. Dotage had not yet touched her. In fact, Grandmama had likely sent it sniffling away in abject fear.

Her imperious nature had allowed certain rules to be bent. After her son-in-law, Charles Flint, had died when Tillie was eight years old, she'd reverted the names of her daughter and granddaughters back to Pembroke so that the money could stay in the family. Luckily, the entailment had no specifications on sex, only legal names and bloodlines. Their previous surname was swept away.

Tillie and her father had always clung to the earth, wanting to trawl its meanings and explore its factual revelations. She still remembered his gift to her at age eight, a mere month before he'd died. A dictionary. They'd read through it together, learning odd words like *whorl* and *escamotage* and *numismatic*. She ached from his loss acutely now, as if mourning Lucy had created more space for heartbreak.

Grandmama tasted the soup—a creamed asparagus. Nausea gripped Tillie again. It never seemed to go away, probably from the medicine. Creamed asparagus soup should be made extinct, Tillie thought, staring at the bowl before her.

"I am glad to hear that you are resting well, Mathilda," her grandmother said in her scratchy voice. It had grown pricklier as every year passed, likely from her habit of secretly smoking a pipe in her chamber. She had a way of nodding genteelly at Tillie until Tillie did something untoward—loudly ponder the similarity between asparagus and hunting spears, for example—at which point she would incline her head toward Tillie's mother and say, "Victoria."

That was all that ever needed to be said. *Victoria* meant "if only you'd borne a child with a better figure." *Victoria* meant "if only you had chosen a husband who had not fathered such an awkward, graceless child." *Victoria* was never intoned in discussions of Lucy, however. As though they weren't sisters who shared the same father.

With this intonation of *Victoria*, her mother dabbed her mouth with her napkin and launched into a lesson on etiquette that Tillie already knew. It was not dinner unless Tillie was lectured in some way, and she usually bore it with quiet compliance. But not today. Tillie dropped her spoon into the bowl and began to moan.

"Lucy," she said softly, wiping away the pale-green cream that had splashed her nose. "Lucy would never drop her spoon. I miss her. I miss her not dropping her spoons."

Her mother waved a servant over.

"Miss Mathilda is unwell. Please call Ada. She needs to rest for tomorrow."

"It's that opium. It needs to be thrown out," Grandmama said. She and Tillie's mother were both charitable trustees of the Temperance

Society of Union Square. They perceived physical discomfort to be a personal failing rather than true sickness.

"But Dr. Erikkson said until the bone is healed—"

"Bones healed before opium was ever discovered," Grandmama declared. "Get rid of it by the end of the week."

"Are you not upset? What about Lucy?" blurted Tillie as she stood and swayed. Her voluminous skirt caught the edge of the spoon, which flipped out of her bowl and landed with a double thud on the Persian carpet. Soup slopped onto her skirt. "May I not even speak her name anymore?"

"Enough, Mathilda." Grandmama stood, eyes narrowed. "We are Pembrokes. Don't be a Flint."

Tillie could barely keep her face from contorting.

Her grandmother sighed. "You'll learn how to survive this, Mathilda. No woman lives a life unscathed. It's what makes us strong. We are broken and mended, remade every time. We must, or it destroys us."

Tillie gazed in wonder at her. Grandmama had never said anything so forthcoming, so personal—even as vague as her words were. How many heartaches had she endured? What love had she lost that had turned her into pure adamant? Perhaps those deep wrinkles in her face had been carved by more than just time.

The eldest Mrs. Pembroke glanced at Tillie's clothes and reverted back to practicalities. "That waist needs to be brought in, and her hair is atrocious. Be sure it looks suitable tomorrow, Victoria." She barked toward the servant at the door: "Clear the table."

The servant looked confused. "But we've only just brought the soup—"

"Supper is finished. We're to have a wake here tomorrow. Why are the floors not polished? Why is the cook not preparing dishes for tomorrow?" Grandmama exited the room, orders flying from her mouth like a bellows fueling a fire.

Ada appeared at Tillie's side and whisked her upstairs. Within a few minutes, Tillie's gown had been unbuttoned, her stays and underthings removed, and a nightgown swooshed over her head. Sleep came after yet another dose of medicine. Tillie heard Ada speaking to her mother—or her mother speaking to Ada; she was not entirely sure.

Perhaps she should not attend the wake or the funeral.

Perhaps only one or two more days of the opium.

Perhaps she should see Dr. Erikkson again.

Perhaps Tillie ought to be dead, instead of Lucy.

At that last murmuring, Tillie realized she wasn't really conscious anymore. At least, she hoped she wasn't conscious.

The next day, Tillie did, in fact, attend the wake. The other mourners were given strict orders to leave her alone, as she was still recovering from her equestrian accident. Really, it was all too much for such a young lady.

Ada kept her in a quiet corner. A large wreath of laurel hung from the grand front door; white crape and ribbons tied to the brass knocker signified that Lucy had been young and unmarried. There was no black to signify that she had any of the achievements she was supposed to have deserved—a husband or old age. In the parlor, the open coffin had been placed before the unlit fireplace, its Italian marble mantel laden with white gardenias and waxy greenery. The scent of flowers overwhelmed every breath.

Guests approached the casket, put their handkerchiefs to their lips, and gazed at its contents. Dorothy came, accompanied by the flaxen-haired Hazel.

"Oh, Tillie. Oh, our poor Lucy," Dorothy murmured, patting Tillie's unbound hand while Hazel held a handkerchief for her mistress—it wasn't Hazel's place to cry, only Dorothy's. James Cutter came by, too, and despite Ada's demurral, he insisted on sitting next to Tillie.

"You and I have lost something more precious than any other in this room. For them, she was but a friend, an acquaintance. Lucy was the love of our lives, was she not? We should not ignore each other in our sorrow."

"Thank you, James," Tillie said, hoping this would make him go away. But oddly, he stayed close by throughout the wake, as if guarding her from busybodies. Her mother and grandmother were busy presiding over the condolences from the Fishes, the Havemeyers, the Astors, the Webbs.

After the mourners had left, Grandmama retired to the library to discuss some matters with James's father. Mama was elsewhere in the house, making arrangements for the funeral cortege the next day.

Only Tillie had yet to pay her respects to Lucy. She'd wanted to wait until the house was quiet. The servants were gathering the soiled glasses and dishes. She leaned toward Ada.

"Can you please bring me some wine?"

"Of course. And then you can rest upstairs."

"Thank you, Ada."

Her last dose of laudanum had been four hours earlier, just before the wake had begun. Her body was becoming like a well-wound Longines, ticking away and letting her know precisely when her pain was scheduled to reappear. But before she could rest, she needed to see her Lucy, one last time. Alone.

Slowly, she rose, blinking away the stars that came after sitting in one attitude for hours. Across the parlor, the casket lay open, wreathed with more greenery and white blooms. The scent of gardenias nearly crushed her as she approached.

"Perfumes are created to mask the scent of something wretched," Lucy had whispered at a party once. And then they'd taken turns guessing which person nearest to them was hiding a terribly embarrassing odor, and giggling. So very unladylike. At the memory, Tillie's throat constricted. What if the gardenias had been brought to hide the scent of her sister's decaying body?

Only Lucy's upper body was visible. They had placed her in her wedding dress, of all things, as though Death were her betrothed. Cosmetics had been used to make her skin porcelain white. A blush of pink had been dusted onto her cheeks, and her lips were reddened with salve. Yet there were so many details askew. Her rosebud lips were flat. Tillie spied the tiniest stitch at the corner of her mouth to keep her forever silent. Around her neck was a wide band of ivory silk sewn with seed pearls.

Lucy owned no such ornament, and Tillie knew it was not part of her wedding parure. She had seen the set with Lucy during a private showing at Tiffany and Company. There had been a sapphire necklace with brilliants, a matching bracelet of glittering stones, and sapphire drop earrings with diamond florets.

Tillie looked behind her to confirm she was alone.

She leaned over to kiss her sister on the forehead, finding her cold and powdery dry. She smelled vaguely of aniseed, like licorice. This person was not her sister. There was no warmth in her, no smile with that particular crinkle in the space between her eyes. This was not the Lucy she knew.

A question entered her mind, itched and writhed there, begging to be answered. It forced Tillie to reach forward and hook a finger on the silk-and-pearl band. It came free easily.

The white makeup hadn't been applied beneath the silk. Lucy's true skin color was grayish, with a purpling from blood that had seeped under the skin. Her neck was mottled with bruises.

And in the middle of the right side were two puncture wounds, an inch and a half apart. They had been sewn shut. They reminded her of hands folded upon each other or a mouth closing primly. Someone had torn into her sister. An animalistic thing done to fell the pride of the Pembroke family and the only person who had ever loved Tillie without any correction, despite her bizarre curiosities, despite all her defects.

Inside herself, Tillie felt something rising, like a wind heralding a storm. Her hands opened and closed, as if trying to grasp the air and force it into extruding its truths. She would find the person who had committed this atrocity. She would learn all she could about what had happened to her sister, every detail. She knew how to find answers, how to ask questions. She would do whatever she could in her power to procure the truth. Even . . . even steal if she needed to. Even lie. Anything a lady wouldn't do.

The sound that came from her body was wretched and rageful, the sound of a rending, as when one's heart broke irreparably. Ada rushed into the room, alarmed.

"My goodness, Miss Tillie! What is it?" she said, her face ashen. "Is it your shoulder?"

Having released the howl, Tillie was utterly calm. "No, Ada. Not at all." She tenderly replaced the silk-and-pearl band around Lucy's neck.

"Come upstairs so you may lie down for a spell. Here is your wine. Come, come away, Miss."

"First, I would like my medicine," Tillie said, turning slowly. "Then I need to find Betty, Lucy's old maid. And to speak to Dr. Erikkson again."

"But Miss, you only just saw him—"

"I didn't ask the questions I needed to ask."

"Yes, Miss," Ada said, but her face was all astonishment. Usually, it was Ada telling Tillie what needed to be done.

"And Ada?"

"Yes?"

"I should like a copy of Bram Stoker's *Dracula*. Immediately."

CHAPTER 4

"Ah, well, poor girl, there is peace for her at last. It is the end!"

He turned to me, and said with grave solemnity: "Not so, alas! Not so. It is only the beginning!"

—Dr. Seward and Van Helsing

Ada, flustered, babbled about the impossibility of procuring *Dracula* that day or the next. It would be Lucy's funeral, after all.

On the day of the funeral, the opium made the preparations for the journey to the cemetery tolerable. From Grandmama's severe glances at her, Tillie knew she would not be taking it for much longer. The cortege was a large one. Lucy had been well loved in society, and the worst gossip that ever circulated about her was how intolerably *good* she was. James stayed close to Tillie's mother, looking solemn as he was bound to do. Yet he caught Tillie's eye whenever possible, as though they were the true kindred spirits in mourning.

Lucy's coffin was placed into the horse-drawn hearse, festooned with white gauze and rosettes, so much that it nearly looked matrimonial. If Tillie concentrated on the doings of the day, like not stepping on her hem, it was easy to forget what the pomp was all about. Then she would turn to say something to Lucy, as she was wont to do at public events ("Lucy, why is crape called crape? It sounds an awful lot like *scrape*. And then of course, *scape* is a leafless flower stem. Are they related etymologies?" And Lucy would say something like, "Tillie, hush. We can look it up in your dictionary later. Straighten your pin; it's crooked. You're a doll today—you look so fresh in that pink chiffon!"), but Lucy would not be at her side, and Tillie would crumble inwardly, the way a sugarloaf did under a torrent of cream.

Tillie felt like she ought to cry at these épée thrusts to her heart. But the opium had fogged her heart just so, and instead, she blinked languidly. Mama and Grandmama were already outside by the curb and motioned for her to follow them into the carriage.

"Ada. Can we bring the laudanum with us, in case I need more before we arrive back home?" Tillie asked.

Ada nodded. As she fetched the bottle, Tillie swayed near the door. Nearby was a three-legged table holding a vase choked with white roses. Several calling cards had been left throughout the day, carefully bent at the lower corner to denote a condolence visit. But a small piece of folded paper caught her eye. It appeared to be a wrinkled piece of newsprint instead of a thick card.

It was the article about Lucy's death, the one she had read after her visit to Dr. Erikkson. Pencil scrawl covered the back of the article.

Dear Miss Pembroke,
I hope you are feeling better. Ladies usually don't faint when I sell them a paper. Do you know her? The dead lady, that is? If you do, please write to me at the World.
Ian Metzger

Tillie stiffened. Oh. That was that boy, the one who'd sold her the paper. He must have gotten her name and address from her driver. What a terrible note. He didn't seem concerned, only curious if she knew poor Lucy. She crushed the paper in her fist and considered tossing it into the fireplace. Thinking again, she smoothed it out against her black skirt and folded it into her reticule.

Her reticule. Lucy had had one with her, a little silk sacque that usually contained a bit of rose salve, a few calling cards, and money. Where was Lucy's reticule? Did the police have it? As she wondered this, Ada fairly flew down the hallway and handed her the bottle of opium, which she nestled by the article. She would ask her mother later about Lucy's belongings. Perhaps there was something there that explained why her sister had felt the need to walk alone that day.

And why the absinthe? Lucy hardly touched alcohol, nor was she in the habit of drinking absinthe or bringing spirits with her on her excursions. It didn't make any sense.

The rest of the day was a disjointed conglomeration of happenings. The funeral cortege up Fifth Avenue; the verdant greenery of the park, looking bright and merry as if nothing bad could ever happen; the noise of the horse hooves on the street, which lent a cadence to the trip. Tillie would always remember one particular detail from that day: the cauldron of asphalt being poured on upper Fifth Avenue to pave the street so that the slow-going electric motorcars could roll along with more ease. No more dirt and cobblestones.

Streets, Tillie thought, should not be paved on the day of her sister's burial. Normally, she would wonder—how did they scoop the asphalt out of the earth? Was it really made of dead plants and creatures from eons ago, digested by the bowels of the earth and rendered into black pudding? But today, she thought only that Lucy would be underground soon. Making the earth—the beautiful, living earth—impermeable with a thick layer of noxious asphalt seemed terrible. Nothing should separate her sister from the heavens. Nothing should keep her from rising again, be it via the truth or an unholy reanimation. So her sister might be a vampire. Tillie would love her just the same, would she not?

They arrived at Woodlawn Cemetery, a picturesque expanse of rolling hills, lush evergreens and oaks, and stately marble obelisks and mausoleums. As Lucy's brass-trimmed, glossy chestnut coffin was low-ered into the loamy earth, Tillie stood between stolid Grandmama, her hair steely and perfectly curled, and Mama in her jet finery. She blinked sleepily in the breeze, her good shoulder bumping against her mother's poufed, mutton-sleeved polonaise. Mama cried as quietly as possible so as not to invite the glare of her own mother. Tillie had been five years old when Grandmama had last deigned a sniffle, over the stillbirth of Tillie's brother.

Tillie didn't cry either. Yes, there was a yawning absence where Lucy had been. Yes, her laughter and her sweet spirit had left Tillie's life. But right now, there was work to be done. She knew little about vampires. They bit people; they drank blood; they were dead, but they weren't. She needed to know more.

There was an untold story that had to be found and wrested from the shut lips of New York City itself.

"It's a Wednesday, Ada. Of course the bookstores are open. I must go."

The next morning, Tillie had only just finished a bit of breakfast and tea when she ordered Ada to call the hansom to the door.

"Send one of the undermaids to fetch it for you," Ada pleaded.

"I want to go myself."

"You're not well."

Ada's hands were everywhere—on her back, pushing her down the hall; fanning her face; straightening the lace around her neck, which felt like a smothering cobweb. Tillie swatted her away.

"Stop, Ada, *stop*. Very well, I shall go upstairs. After I buy the book."

"Oh, Miss."

"What is that?" Down the hallway, she spied another piece of news-print folded in a peculiar way by the front door. "Is that for me?"

"I don't know. I heard someone knock this morning, but Pierre opened the door. Your mother said you're not to have visitors, not until they know you're safe."

Tillie went to it. It was another piece of newsprint; unlike yesterday's article on Lucy's murder, this one was an advertisement for Coca-Cola. *The Ideal Brain Tonic.* On the back, again in pencil—

Miss P,
Did you get my other note? Write me at the World. My legs ache from walking all the way over from the el every day.
—IM

So impertinent. He wrote as if he knew her intimately. Tillie had never received such a note, not even from Lucy. Well, she and Lucy had never needed to write. They'd been too present in each other's lives to ever need the distance of paper and ink.

"I'm shocked that Pierre would allow such a person to leave a card—a note—for you. I'll have to speak to him," Ada said.

"You can speak to him after we get my book."

"Very well. I suppose Dr. Erikkson would allow it, so long as you walk very little. Your mother is at the Fishes' home to discuss hiring a retired watchman to guard the family. If only she'd thought of it before."

Before long, they were headed to Dodd, Mead & Company on Fifth Avenue. But after Ada went inside, she quickly returned to their hansom, shaking her head.

"None there. Why would you want such a book, Miss? There are wholesomer ones to be had."

"Let's try again. Baker and Taylor, on Seventeenth Street."

Once again, there were no copies. Ada's red hair grew more frazzled with each store. "We ought to go home. Send out for it, Miss. The noise from all these omnibuses and carriages is too much."

Ada tried a third store and received the same response. Soon, the hansom was jerking back uptown to Union Square. Saloons, grocers, and dry goods stores passed by like a slow vitascope movie. An Italian organ-grinder stood on the corner with a little brown monkey on his shoulder screeching at the children who clapped around him. Normally Tillie would smile, but her sadness was a nimbus that overhung everything. She was still too full of Lucy and Lucy's absence.

"Wait." Tillie asked the driver to stop beside a bookstore she'd spotted, and she stepped out before Ada could protest. "Let me try."

The store was near closing and rather empty. A single fellow was reading in a corner alone, surrounded by books crammed in every space possible. More were piled up near the cashier. They had already taken their rolling sidewalk racks of books in, and a tall clerk with spectacles waved Tillie away.

"We're closed. I'm sorry. Come back tomorrow."

"Please. I just need one book. This is the fourth store I've been to today."

"We're closing."

"I have a broken bone!" she blurted. The man in the corner looked up from his book, his head barely visible above a stacked table.

"Very well. Which book?"

"*Dracula.* Bram Stoker."

"We only just started selling them. They've done well in London. But I only have one copy left. We're due to get more next week."

"One is as good as a thousand. Where is it?" Tillie said eagerly.

"This one?"

The man in the corner stepped around the stacks. He held a book in his hand, a small one with a brown cloth cover. His hair was a familiar mass of loose dark curls, and Tillie recognized his eyelashes before she recognized his face. He held a cloth cap sandwiched between his arm and side.

"Mr. . . . . Metzger?"

"Well, hello! Didn't you get my notes?"

"I . . ." Tillie shook her head. "I've been busy. I've been . . ." She couldn't finish her thought. Her fists clenched, and she suddenly felt the pain in her broken bone more acutely. Her face soured. "I did receive your notes."

"Is that your keeper?" Ian asked, pointing the book at where Ada's head was poked outside the hansom window, watching Tillie with a frown. "She looks mean."

"I don't have a keeper. That is my maid. And she's not mean."

"She looks like she'd fry me for breakfast." The young man smirked. "You didn't write back," he continued.

"We're closing!" the clerk said, exasperated. He went to the front door and shut it, spinning around quickly. "Please make your purchases, and be on your way. I have to meet my mother-in-law at Herald Square, and if I'm late, she's going to chop me up and throw me in the East River."

"Sounds worse than a river pirate," Ian said solemnly. "But if you prefer to be cooked for breakfast, that lady can help you. I'll bet she could turn you into a bialy without much effort." He jerked his thumb toward Ada, who was now gesturing wildly for Tillie to return to the carriage.

The clerk looked at Ada and shivered. "Shall I wrap that for you?" He pointed at the book in Ian's hand.

"Yes, please," Tillie said. "I need that book."

Ian drew the book to his chest. "So do I."

"Why?"

"To help me figure out why that lady got killed by a vampire. I may sell newspapers, but I've a keen interest in murders. Do you have a better reason?"

Tillie's throat tightened. There was no way to escape the answer. She stared straight at him and tried to speak without crying.

"That lady was my sister."

The clerk and Ian both went quiet.

"Oh. Golly. I . . ." Ian's eyes fell to the book. "I figured you knew her somehow, but I didn't think . . ." He looked up again. "What was her name?"

"Lucy." Tillie's hand spasmed and clenched as she said her name aloud. "Her name was Lucy."

He suddenly looked as if he'd bitten his tongue. "Lucy? There's a Lucy in this book who's a victim of vampire killing. Did you know that?"

"No! I didn't." She clasped her hands together. "But I would know if I owned the book. Please, Mr. Metzger. I'm tired and I'm in pain and I'm in mourning. I've been to three stores already, and my maid—"

"Is apparently voracious and going to eat us both."

"I never said that!" Tillie nearly screeched, exasperated.

"All right, all right. Don't break another bone," Ian said, holding out the book in surrender. "Look. I am sorry for your loss. I really am. How about we share it? You get it for one week, and I'll come pick it up after."

"Share it?"

The clerk whined. "My mother-in-law is going to turn me into a ham sandwich if you two don't finish up here. Twenty cents."

"Fine. Here is my share." Tillie finagled her sacque open with one hand and pulled out a dime. Ian dug into his left pocket, then his right. He fished in the front pocket of his jacket and then his back pocket. He looked like a ringless groom at a wedding. As he patted the outside of his jacket, his eyes lit up. He pulled out a slotted spoon carved with a fernlike design.

"Take this as payment."

"I can't use a spoon!" The clerk looked like he was about to pass out.

"What is that?" Tillie asked.

"Don't you know?"

Tillie wanted to slap him. "Why would I ask, if I knew what it was?"

He held it out toward her. "You cover my half and take this as payment for now, since I used my last pennies on a bowl of oyster soup."

"Ugh, I don't like oysters. I don't eat any animals that don't have eyes. Or an obvious nervous system."

"Oy, I'm more goyish than you are, then," he said, smirking. "So I have eyes, and last I checked, I had a brain too. Would you carve me up?"

Tillie went red in the face. "You would taste terrible." What a nonsensical conversation.

"Anyway. I should have saved my money. Words feed the soul, or so they say. I'll pick the book up in seven days and pay you half then. I promise. On my *bobe*'s good name."

"All right," Tillie said, handing another coin to the clerk. He shuffled them out the door, locked it with a huff, and sprinted westward into the setting sunlight.

Ada, in the hansom, looked like her hair might spontaneously light afire at the sight of her mistress walking with a young man. Tillie ignored her and turned to Ian.

"You know where I live. One week, then."

"Until then." He handed her the spoon. "That'll give you one week to figure out why I'm carrying this around." He tipped his cap and went walking off down the street, whistling a Tin Pan Alley tune.

On the ride home, Ada asked too many questions. Tillie begged to be left alone. She was flustered, and her pain had returned. That newsie had done a marvelous job of frustrating her to the point of forgetting her sorrow. But when it returned, it returned with a vengeance.

She took a few drops of medicine straight from the dropper, and by the time they were back in front of their brownstone, she was asleep. But her fist stayed curled fast around the slotted spoon.

CHAPTER 5

*There is a method in his madness, and the rudimentary idea
in my mind is growing. It will be a whole idea soon, and then,
oh, unconscious celebration!*

—Dr. Seward

Tillie took to her bed for the entire weekend and into the next week, consumed by *Dracula*.

She told everyone that it was her collarbone, that it ached something terrible, and that her despair over her sister's loss had driven her to bed. Too much pain and anguish for Tillie to tolerate being around anyone.

This was only partially true.

She saw ghosts of Lucy everywhere when she was awake. The quotidian activities of the house were warped versions of what they'd been before Lucy had died. She now broke her fast every morning alone, when before, Lucy used to ask Tillie over their breakfast tea, "Give me a word from your dictionary, Tillie. A new one I've never heard of. Astonish me!" When Grandmama would catch them laughing as she walked by (she didn't eat breakfast, as she thought it unwholesome for a woman of her age), she'd snap, "Mathilda!" There was always only one Pembroke lady at fault, and it never seemed to be Lucy. Perhaps now that Lucy had taken the unforgivable step of dying without Grandmama's permission, Tillie was becoming more tolerable in her eyes.

Grandmama hadn't taken away her opium, for example. Not yet.

Tillie asked for copies of the newspaper, but nothing more had been written about Lucy's death. Were the police investigating? She didn't know. Her family and the servants refused to say anything, worried it would hamper her healing and her delicate constitution. And so, between her wretched grief and her foggy hours under the spell of the opium drops, Tillie pulled the copy of *Dracula* from beneath her pillow and read, determined to learn anything that might tell her how Lucy had died.

It was such an awful book. No lady of standing would be caught reading such a story. It was replete with visions that were wholly unchristian. But it had opened a world Tillie didn't know, and that was always heavenly. She wished the mysterious Carpathian Mountains were yet undiscovered and that she could be the first to witness their grandeur. She thought of this monster, this Dracula, and despite her disgust, recognized how elegant and romantic he was. He was in love, and he was lonely.

Tillie read on and off throughout the week. She scribbled down her questions in a tiny notebook she kept under her pillow, attached to a small pencil. Who was this author, this Mr. Stoker? Where did he live? Did any of these stories come from truth, or were they only dark children's fairy tales? At night, she would place a blanket under the crack of her door so no one suspected she was reading by lambent electric light. She banished Ada from waking her up for medicine when she did slumber. In the morning, groggy and underslept, she would force herself to sit up when Ada brought her a supply of sweetened tea and fresh oatcakes speckled with raisins. Then she would quickly shoo Ada from the room after her ablutions were completed.

By the time she had finished reading and rereading the book, her body felt wrung out and weary.

This was only fiction; how could it make her feel this way?

Tillie reread one passage in particular, as if trying to undo a puzzle within herself. It had been written by Jonathan Harker's character after he had become trapped inside Dracula's castle, left to the vices of the count's vampire wives.

> *In the moonlight opposite me were three young women, ladies by their dress and manner . . . All three had brilliant white teeth that shone like pearls against the ruby of their voluptuous lips. There was something about them that made me uneasy, some longing and at the same time some deadly fear . . .*
>
> *"He is young and strong; there are kisses for us all."*
>
> *The girl went on her knees, and bent over me, simply gloating. There was a deliberate voluptuousness which was both thrilling and repulsive, and as she arched her neck she actually licked her lips like an animal, till I could see in the moonlight the moisture shining on the scarlet lips and on the red tongue as it lapped the white sharp teeth. Lower and lower went her head as the lips went below the range of my mouth and chin and seemed about to fasten on my throat.*

Here, Tillie would shut the book and fling it away to the end of her bed, before reaching out and feverishly finding the passage to read it again.

The bite. The bite did not happen in this passage, but it would soon.

At the end of the week, Tillie pulled herself out of the bed and looked about. Her room was in disorder. Empty bottles of opium were scattered on a tray at the foot of her bed, alongside crumbs left over from two cakes she had eaten. Her damask bed linens were bunched on the floor, the matching drapery pulled shut.

In the dim electric light, she looked at herself in the mirror. Her wrinkled nightgown was damp beneath her arms, and her left arm was still bandaged close to her chest. Tillie's dark hair tumbled down over her shoulders in frazzled waves. Purplish shadows haunted the hollows beneath her eyes.

"I look like I belong in the book," she said aloud. Both Lucys—hers and the one in the novel—had succumbed to vampires, but perhaps Tillie herself was more like Mina, Harker's wife. Dracula had fed Mina his own blood to effect her transformation into a vampire. Tillie opened her mouth wide and inspected her teeth. Her sharp canines seemed pitifully small and un-animal-like. How could a person bite someone with these? How could a vampire grow such teeth?

The newspaper said no blood had been found at the scene. Which meant even Lucy's lilac dress must have been spotless. How?

Tillie reached awkwardly across the bed, grabbed her small notebook, and scribbled on a new page.

No blood at scene. How to drink blood without making a mess?

She put the notebook down and went back to her mirror. With her free hand, she yanked at the side of her mouth to gain a better view of her right canine.

"Definitely not sharp enough," she said, saliva pooling under her tongue. Though with her fingers in her mouth, it sounded like "Deffineey nohh sharrfff enoufff."

The door swung open suddenly, and her mother entered the room. Tillie's eyes opened wide, and she quickly pulled her fingers away, a rope of saliva linking her fingertip to her lip.

"Mathilda! What are you . . . doing?" her mother asked.

"Oh. I was . . ." She pointed at her mouth. "My tooth aches."

"Well goodness, if it does, send Ada for some ice to calm it. How are you feeling? You look a fright."

"I'm well. Just going back to sleep," Tillie said, backing closer to the bed so she could slip *Dracula* under her pillow. Mama was particularly sour about ladies reading belles lettres.

"If you're well, then you're well enough to receive guests. You've been in this room too long."

"It's midnight," Tillie protested.

"Mathilda, *it is ten o'clock in the morning. On a Tuesday.*" Shrilly, she called, "Ada, come here this instant." Ada popped into the room as if she had been stored behind the door all along. "Open the shades. Air this room out, and wash the linens. Draw a bath for Mathilda, and have her ready and fed."

Like a pig, Tillie wished to say, but she kept her lips tight.

Her mother picked up an empty bottle of laudanum and sniffed it. She grimaced. "James Cutter and Dorothy Harriman are due to call in one hour."

"I don't want to see them," Tillie said. "I'm not well."

"James is practically a son-in-law, and Dorothy is your dearest friend. You haven't seen them since your accident."

"I saw them at the funeral," she said petulantly. "Mama," she said, remembering one of the questions she'd written down, "whatever happened to Lucy's purse?"

"Oh, I don't know." She waved a hand. "If there is anything to know, Mathilda, I will tell you."

Her mother eyed the empty brown bottles again. "It's time you stop taking this medicine. Grandmama doesn't like it." She put the bottle down and wiped her hands against each other, as if the glass had been covered in ptomaine. "Your temperament is calmer under its influence, no doubt, but a good temperament requires only practice and good breeding. Ada, dispose of these. Mathilda will be fine without them now."

Tillie watched Ada gather up the bottles. There was still half a bottle in her reticule, but she stayed silent about that. She tried to think: When was her last dose? She gently stretched her left shoulder and found the stiffness and pain returned as quickly as a struck match. It must have been six or seven hours ago.

"Well," Tillie said after clearing her throat. She put her hands together demurely and nodded. "I ought to get ready."

Her mother's face lightened, and a rarely seen dimple appeared on her left cheek. Obedience always affected her like a draught might soothe a sore throat.

"Very well." She went to the door. "And put some color on your cheeks. You look ghastly. We don't want James to think you're more ill than you are."

She shut the door, and Tillie eased herself back onto her bed.

"Why on earth does she care what James thinks about my complexion?" she said to Ada, who was picking up discarded clothing from the floor.

Ada said, "Oh, Miss Tillie." It was her substitute for saying, How can you be so ignorant for such a learned girl? Tillie dropped her shoulders too abruptly. The edges of her broken clavicle, slowly knitting themselves together, seemed to catch against each other like silk on sandpaper.

She yelped in pain.

Ada pretended not to hear her. She left the room to run the bath.

After an hour of pain, scrubbing, careful dressing, and Ada tackling her tangled hair, Tillie was presentable. But the black parramatta silk seemed to devour any light nearby. She asked Ada to bring her reticule to her room so she could take a dose of opium, but Ada said she would fetch it while Tillie was having her visit with Mr. Cutter and Miss Harriman.

"But I want it now," Tillie said, irritated.

Her mother's figure appeared down the hallway.

"Mathilda. You're expected in the drawing room. We shall go together."

Mrs. Pembroke was a mountain of inky matte silk. Black lace smothered her up to her neck, and her hands were covered in black net gloves. Jet drops, carved in angles, subtly shone beneath her earlobes. A large pendant with Lucy's braided golden hair around its edge was the only bit of brightness on her person. Even in death, Lucy was a light.

"One moment." Tillie went back into her room. She reached under her pillow for her notebook and pencil, catching sight, as she did so, of the strange slotted spoon casually acting as a bookmark in *Dracula*. Tillie thought of asking her mother if she knew anything about fancy slotted spoons, but her mother might inquire as to where she'd acquired the spoon—a question she wasn't willing to answer. The tiny notebook and pencil were tucked into a fold of her sling, in case she had other thoughts to write down.

Her mother met her at the top of the stairs, and together they descended. Two of her could fit inside her mother, as Tillie hadn't eaten much in the last week. How was it possible, she thought, that vampires could get the energy they needed from blood alone? Humans needed meat and vegetables and desserts. She wondered if any other animals in the world could subsist on blood alone.

Halfway down the stairs, she stopped and pulled her notebook out.

"What are you doing, Mathilda?" her mother hissed.

Tillie leaned the notebook on the banister to scrawl on a fresh page. *How do animals live on blood food alone?* Then she snapped it shut, dropping her pencil in the process. She finally managed to tuck the pencil in the binding, and put the notebook back in her sling.

"Stop that. Please, don't do such a thing during your visit. It would be terribly rude."

"I won't," Tillie promised, without truly promising. "Mama. Have the police said anything about how the vampire—"

"Vampire! Don't be ridiculous, Tillie. Your sister's death was a senseless act. There is nothing else to be done but move forward."

Tillie stopped her descent. "But someone is to blame. Lucy is dead. Forgetting it all would be senseless!"

Her mother grasped her wrist, hard, and pulled her closer. She whispered so no one would hear, but her voice sounded like a tempest, a rising hurricane.

"Forgetting is an act of survival. We are women, Mathilda. We endure to survive. Don't tell your own mother what she is allowed to remember or forget." She let go of Tillie's wrist, but even the release felt like an act of violence. Her mother descended a few steps and turned around, face as sweet as Christmas morning. "Our guests are waiting, dearest."

Tillie followed her. What exactly had her mother so forcefully forgotten that she should feel the need to bury Lucy too? She thought of Lucy Westenra in *Dracula*, after Van Helsing had placed a golden crucifix over her undead mouth, before he and her suitors had staked her heart, beheaded her, and stuffed her mouth with fresh garlic, all in the name of keeping her quiet and dead. Tillie could almost smell the garlic as she followed her mother into the salon.

In the vast room, large palms sprouted from china vases in the corner. An enormous painting of Tillie's grandfather hung above the mantel of the Italian marble fireplace, staring down at everyone with eyebrows that looked like a continuous line of cotton balls and a beard to match. There was no corresponding portrait of Tillie's father, though she treasured an old-fashioned porcelain miniature in her vanity drawer.

The red Utrecht velvet chairs and chaise were brushed just so, and the red carpet was threaded with gold that matched the gilt edging on the furniture and coffered ceiling. James Cutter stood from his chair and nodded. His hair was perfectly styled with brilliantine oil, and his eyes, to her surprise, crinkled in welcome. This was the smile he gave to Lucy when she appeared at the bottom of the stairs.

Sitting on the chaise was Dorothy Harriman, looking so modern in her ivory shirtwaist festooned with a Parisian lace frill along the bust and slim skirt narrowly gored in fine pink cambric. Dorothy was pretty, in a "she's very pretty" sort of way, which was to say that she was tolerable. The Harrimans had few women in their family line, so they employed a lady's companion to keep her happy and entertained. Tillie had heard that the ladies in James's family had companions too. For Dorothy, Hazel Dreyer was compliant, always available—and currently sitting off to the side.

Tillie's mother smiled. "I'll have the servants bring some refreshments." She left with a rustle of silk.

"Mathilda. It's so good to see you. How is your arm?" James asked. He took her good elbow and led her to the chaise next to Dorothy, who smiled benevolently.

"Better and better," Tillie said. Actually, her whole shoulder ached. Two housemaids came to put down silver bowls of dates and silver-colored Jordan almonds.

"And have you heard any further news of what happened to poor Lucy?" Dorothy inquired.

"Goodness, Dorothy. Let's talk about something less upsetting!" James said, somewhat bitingly. He gave Dorothy a severe look, before softening his gaze upon Tillie. He opened up a cigarette case and lit a gold-tipped cigarette, blowing the smoke in the air. Dorothy leaned her head toward him, and he offered and lit one for her.

"I ask out of concern, James," Dorothy said, smoke coiling under her nose.

"You know your father dislikes it when you smoke, Dorothy," Hazel said mildly.

Dorothy waved her away.

"Actually, I'm quite open to hearing news about what happened to my sister," Tillie said. "Also, please stop calling me Mathilda. It's my great-grandmother's name, and I always feel like people are speaking to her instead of me. Call me Tillie."

"Of course, Tillie," James said. He smiled gently. "I've always wished for the permission to do so."

"You have?" Tillie blurted artlessly. She felt her stomach rumble. It sounded like a minor earthquake in her belly.

"Goodness, did you hear that? Tillie, is there a dog in the house?" Dorothy asked.

"No. Not at all." She shifted in her seat. Her insides were far noisier whenever the medicine had dissipated from her body, after the nausea subsided. She had a sudden desire to dash upstairs and suck down a dropperful right now.

"So there is no news, then?" James asked, leaning closer to her. She could smell French milled soap and the scent of lavender-rinsed linen.

"The way the paper wrote about it—a vampire? It makes no sense," Dorothy said.

"It's a deranged killer, and he needs to be found and hanged," James said, unusually vehemently. "Vampires are fiction. The police need to stop thinking of possibilities that aren't real and track down this man."

"Why is it so impossible?" Tillie said, her cheeks warming.

"If vampires were real, then people would have found such a creature. There would be evidence. There are no such things as the undead."

Tillie's mind went to the teeth marks on Lucy's neck. "Of course you're right. It's not like people have found vampires. Real ones."

"They've found them in New England," Hazel said quietly. Tillie had almost forgotten she was there. Hazel had that habit of being forgotten, even though if one looked for more than a second, one would notice her striking green eyes and flaxen hair. Hazel looked like a Parisian doll come to life, with poreless bisque skin and a tiny rosebud mouth. But she dressed in browns and beiges, doing her best to keep in the shadows of her benefactress.

"What do you mean?" Dorothy said. "Are you reading novels again, Hazel?"

"No. It's in the news. I read about some folks in New England, digging up corpses and finding that they hadn't rotted. Their hair had lengthened. Their fingernails had grown after death."

Dorothy now shifted completely to the side to stare at her friend. "When are you reading these papers?"

"I read them every evening after you go to sleep," Hazel said with a smile. "There's a pile of them in the foyer every day that your father purchases, and I'm allowed to read them after everyone in the house is done. I love to read the news."

Everyone stared at Hazel for a moment. James seemed to suppress a smile.

"I never read them," Dorothy said with a shudder, as if news were a disease she could catch. She turned back to James and Tillie. "I'd rather read the *Delineator*. Anyway, enough about all that nonsense. What matters is you, my dear," she said. "Once your arm is out of that sling, we shall go out and get some air together. You've hidden behind dear Lucy all your life. It's your time to shine."

What a horrid idea. "That's not what I—"

"She's right, you know," James said, standing. "I've been remiss in paying attention to Lucy's dear sister, and it's my intention to make sure you aren't forgotten, Tillie. You're a sole heiress now. A beautiful and injured little bird. We must keep the riffraff away from you."

Tillie balked at this description of herself. As if she needed to be kept under a glass cloche, cherished and untouched. But she was more disturbed by James's proximity to her, the way he stood by, his hand on her good elbow. As if she belonged to him, the way Lucy had been his possession before.

"It was lovely to see you. I must be on my way."

"I'll walk you out," Dorothy said. Hazel stiffened. Dorothy acted sometimes as if she were the mistress of every house she stepped into.

Tillie had always allowed it because she didn't care to be in the spotlight, but something nudged her conscience. It was Lucy's voice.

You're the rightful heir in the Pembroke family.

Tillie hesitated. "I . . . I'll show James out. Thanks, Dorrie."

If Dorothy was surprised, she concealed it. Tillie went to the door with James, who turned to her.

"Don't mind Dorothy. She thinks of you as a little sister."

"I should mind more, but . . . I don't like to be in charge of things," Tillie said, flustered. Her hand wrung the fabric of her dress. "I wish Lucy were here still."

"As do I. But you're a lady of the Pembroke family too. And just as exquisite. You oughtn't be forgotten in all this sadness."

He kissed her on the cheek. Tillie's face went bright and hot. "Thank you" was all she could manage to say.

"Perhaps it is time for someone else to take care of you so you don't have to be in charge of things." He met her eye for one long moment, then left. Tillie stood there, mouth agape.

"He fancies you." Dorothy had come up behind her.

Tillie turned around. "No. He's just being kind." But even she didn't believe her words.

"Well. If you prefer to think that, then so be it. And if James is not to your taste, then you should tell him so."

"You think so?"

"Yes. I don't think Lucy was all that happy with the idea of being Mrs. Cutter."

"How do you know?"

"Oh, a woman can tell, just from watching. She never had that fire in her heart for him, you know? But James certainly wants to marry a Pembroke. Why, your estate is enormous, Tillie. James's family was one of Astor's Four Hundred. They have the name, but their finances took a downturn after the Panic of 1893. Your money? His name? It's perfect! There's a dearth of heiresses on this island. All of our

American-dollar princesses are finding royal titles and husbands abroad. Look at Consuelo Vanderbilt, marrying the Duke of Marlborough!"

"I don't think that—"

"Look, Tillie. James had his heart set on the match with Lucy. His parents were so happy they would have burst if not for their waists and corsets. Lucy may be gone, but there is still a Pembroke heiress. The opportunity is far from gone."

James? So handsome that ladies' rose-salved lips dropped open in astonishment when he passed? James Cutter fancied her? There was something alluring about the idea of a match between them, one that would make all the socialites who had ever giggled over her clumsy ways jealous . . .

"Anyway, you're more his fancy," Dorothy continued. "He likes complacent women."

It took her a minute to really hear what Dorothy was saying. The skin on her arms rose in goose bumps, and she felt the full force of her stomach cramps.

"Are you saying that Lucy was not complacent?"

Dorothy's brows rose. "Did you not hear their arguments in the last few weeks? I thought you'd know more than me. They fought like cats and dogs lately."

Hazel had followed them into the foyer. "About what?" Tillie asked.

Dorothy shrugged. "If you don't know, then I don't know who does. Did she not tell you?"

Tillie's face soured. She desperately wanted her reticule. "I don't feel well, Dorothy. I think I must go upstairs."

"Of course," Dorothy said, patting her arm. "I'll come by next week. We should try to get out, take a walk. You look like you need some fresh air and exercise."

Hazel gave a dispassionate "I hope to see you again soon," which was just as lukewarm as it should be, since Dorothy made all the decisions about whom to see and where to go.

As soon as Pierre closed the door, Tillie's shoulders relaxed. Speaking to James had felt like wearing an ill-fitting and itchy coat. She went upstairs. Ada had left her reticule sitting on her bed.

She hastily unscrewed the bottle of medicine and measured out more than her usual dose. Ten brown, bitter drops, right under her tongue. Even as the medicine began to blur her senses, softening her pain and easing her riotous belly, she still felt unsettled.

She withdrew the little notebook from her sleeve. Lucy and James had been fighting.

Why?

CHAPTER 6

Our toil must be in silence, and our efforts all in secret; for in this enlightened age, when men believe not even what they see, the doubting of wise men would be his greatest strength.

—Van Helsing

A voice flitted in and out of her dreams. An insistent voice that nudged and pressed her awake.

"One penny! Whaddya say? Whaddya hear? One penny for the *World*!"

Ian.

"It's been a week!" Tillie said, waking and sitting up suddenly. She winced from the pain, and her back was stiff. She must have slept unmoving for most of the night.

Ada was sitting in the corner, crocheting. "Good day, Miss. Yes, over a week since poor Miss Pembroke left us. And only a few more weeks in this sling of yours. You're to visit Dr. Erikkson again soon."

Tom. The doctor's son. How had she forgotten? He had mentioned something about Lucy being upset the day she disappeared.

"Pape! Get your *World*!" a voice called from the street. For a moment, Tillie thought she was dreaming again, but she heard the sounds of horses clattering on the street, and the warm sun shone through the open curtains. The voice selling papers sounded younger than Ian's. It couldn't be him, but it reminded her. She owed him the book.

"Has anyone left any messages for me? Any cards?"

"Mm," Ada said, eyes on her crocheting. "Yes, but your mother took them."

Oh no. Mama always looked over the calling cards and critiqued them minutely. If Ian had left a message, she had probably incinerated it. How would Tillie know when and where to meet Ian again? After Ada helped her dress, Tillie paused by the door.

"Ada, let me be for a moment. I'll be down soon." With a nod, Ada picked up her crocheting and disappeared.

Quickly, Tillie locked the door. At her vanity, she pulled the drawer open and fished out the brown bottle of laudanum from the back. There were only about two doses left. Once again, she squeezed several drops onto her tongue, her eyes squinting from the burn of alcohol. Five drops this time. Ten put her in a stupor. She needed to be awake today, to only feel normal. Just not in so much discomfort.

She screwed the top back on and hid the bottle. She could smell the pharmaceutical tinge on her breath. Looking around, she found a tin of rose pastilles and chewed three. Mama would be angry if she knew about the medicine.

She sought out the little notebook of hers from under her pillow. Inside, she scribbled:

Tom knew Lucy was upset the day she died. Why was she upset?

As she left her room, she saw Lucy's room down the hallway from hers. The door had been closed ever since she'd gone missing. Opening that door was a reminder of what had been lost. Tillie walked toward it, recalling Dorothy's words from yesterday.

"Did you not hear their arguments in the last few weeks?"

"They fought like cats and dogs lately."

Every time she'd seen James and Lucy together, they had been the duke and duchess at whatever gathering they were presiding over. James, full chested and confident. Lucy, like exquisite starlight that you couldn't quite focus upon. Too perfect to be captured by a mere human eye.

Tillie twisted the porcelain doorknob. Inside, the room smelled like faded roses. And indeed, a vase of wilted roses stood on the bedside table; James had sent them from Henderson's flower shop just before Lucy had died. The room was chillingly unchanged—Lucy's coverlet was perfectly smoothed, the collection of Baccarat paperweights on her vanity grouped together like flowered jewels trapped in dewdrops.

Tillie opened the vanity drawer, finding hairpins and ribbons, nothing of significance. In the bureau, only layers and layers of French chemises and sateen underthings, silk stockings and garters. On top of Lucy's vanity, however, were an inkwell and a pen. A rectangle of dark silk hid the blotter. Lucy wrote here. Tillie hadn't realized that—everyone else in the house used the large escritoire downstairs.

She studied the blotter. It had splotches of ink. Looking in the drawer again, she saw a knife, hidden at the back where she hadn't noticed it. Minute pencil shavings littered the seams of the drawer.

Any letter Lucy had written would have been written in ink. Not in pencil. So where were the other writings? Tillie looked under the pillow, under the mattress. Nothing.

She bit her lip. The bedroom window looked to the back of the house, with its conservatory and small garden. The clouds were a perfect white on turquoise. How rude of the sky to be so blue and pretty when Lucy couldn't admire it. Such a thoughtless sky.

Tillie was turning to leave when she noticed the bedside table. She tried to open the little drawer, but it was locked. No key in sight. Strange. Maybe it had been in Lucy's missing reticule. She wondered if a hairpin would work.

Ada was calling her for luncheon. She would have to consider the locked drawer later. Mama was visiting Mrs. Cutter; she and James's mother were likely consoling each other over fried artichokes and mandarin cake.

Today, Grandmama's red-masked parakeet, Elenora, was perched on a T-shaped bar next to her chair. Usually Elenora lived in the conservatory, where her squawks didn't bother anyone and her droppings wouldn't ruin the carpet, but the conservatory was being cleaned.

"You look tired, after all that sleep," her grandmother scolded as Tillie took her seat. Elenora flapped her wings, and her grandmother murmured, "What a good girl!" before she focused again on her granddaughter.

Tillie knew this stare. It was the daily appraisal. Every day, those beady eyes would settle on Lucy, nod in satisfaction, then move on to Tillie. Eyebrows would rise, followed by a shake of the head. Now that there was no Lucy to dote over, Tillie feared Grandmama would spend twice as much time throwing her critical gaze at Tillie.

"Your dress needs to be taken in. You need a cream rinse in your hair; it looks dry. Sit up straighter. Why do you insist on looking so sleepy?"

"This broken bone still hurts. It's hard to sleep well," Tillie said, mincingly eating the small egg pastry on her plate. The salad of frilly lettuce, summer tomatoes, and nasturtium blossoms was dressed with an acid sauce that she disliked. Her stomach contained acid. It made her think her food was being digested before it touched her lips, and she shivered. "Were there any letters or cards left for me?"

"Why, yes. James inquired after you. He was worried that you seemed out of sorts yesterday. It's rather considerate of him. We will have him over to supper soon."

Tillie flushed. "Anything else?"

Grandmama waved a hand. "Some troublesome stranger who keeps sending you messages as if he knows you. I've told Pierre to refuse any more."

Oh no. Ian. How would she get in touch with him now? Tillie was concentrating on stabbing a bit of buttery pastry crust when Elenora flew off her perch and landed on the chairback. The bird began to play with her hair.

"Aren't you sweet?" her grandmother cooed. "Don't bother Mathilda now. Come, Elenora." She motioned to a maid, who coaxed Elenora onto an arm, then back onto her perch. Grandmama turned to Tillie. With the thick black crape ruffles around her neck, she looked like a fearsome lizard, or at least a very imperious Queen Victoria.

"I do know him," Tillie said. "After I saw Dr. Erikkson last week, I felt ill, and he helped fetch our carriage. I believe it's just neighborly concern."

"He's no neighbor of ours. I saw him on the sidewalk. He looks like a common pushcart vendor, selling all manner of ghastly things. Suspenders and chickens and such."

"Oh, Grandmama. He's no pushcart vendor. He sells papers."

"Not much better," her grandmother said, sniffing.

"Let me write him back," Tillie said. "That will satisfy his curiosity, and I'll ask that he stop writing."

"I absolutely forbid it."

"Otherwise he'll keep visiting, Grandmama! We wouldn't want him bringing more attention to us. Will that do?"

Her grandmother's ruffles seemed to wilt at the idea of a ruffian pacing in front of their doorstep. She raised one gnarled finger in the air, its tip stained slightly yellow from her habit of poking down strands of tobacco into her tiny ivory pipe.

"One letter. *Only one.* And another thing. We've hired a man to guard the house. John O'Toole. He worked in the Twenty-First Ward for over fifteen years. He's guarded banks, other homes. He's to walk the grounds of the house at night."

"Every night?" Tillie asked.

"Of course. From sundown to sunup. It's when most thievery in this area occurs. And you're not allowed out of the house unless it is a sanctioned social activity. Not even for a brief walk outside. No more excursions to the Lenox Library."

Elenora squawked again and flew onto the table this time, her emerald-green feathers brilliant against the ivory linen. She nibbled at Tillie's uneaten crust. The maid once again brought Elenora back to her perch.

"Sweet Elenora!" Grandmama said, smiling benevolently. "So, Mathilda. No more outings. Understand?"

"But Ada already comes with me everywhere."

"To bookstores, or so I've heard."

Tillie dropped her fork, which clattered onto her plate. Elenora chirped with alarm at the noise. She flew to the floor this time and was again brought back to her perch.

"I believe," her grandmother continued, "that is where she left you alone. In a store. With a young man. That shall stop immediately. Isn't that right, Ada?"

Ada curtsied in the corner of the dining room. She looked at her feet guiltily.

"Ada," her grandmother said, "go fetch me some scissors."

"Yes, ma'am." Ada scurried away.

Tillie felt a tangle of anger in her stomach. Their home suddenly seemed so very tiny, despite its enormous space. She was trapped.

"Go and write that letter. If he shows up one more time, we'll call the roundsman and have him arrested. It's time we returned to some normalcy. After Lucy's mourning period, some things will change here. No more visits to the library every day. No more childishness, with your books. I was married with a child on the way before I was twenty-one. Lucy would have been, too, if she had behaved herself."

"Behaved herself?"

"Yes. If she had been proper in all the ways a lady ought, she'd still be alive and readying herself for a marriage."

What on earth did that mean? That Lucy had misbehaved her way into the arms of a murderous vampire? It made no sense. Her grandmother was still talking.

"You need to find a match, Mathilda. And find one you will."

Tillie looked helplessly at Ada, who had returned to place a set of silver shears at her grandmother's elbow.

"Are they sharp?" her grandmother asked.

"Yes, ma'am." Ada shrank into the corner of the room, nearly quaking.

"But what about Lucy?" Tillie asked.

"What about her?" her grandmother asked.

"What is being done to find the vamp—" Grandmama's eyebrows rose so high Tillie thought they might detach and fly to the ceiling. "I mean, to find the attacker?"

"Never mind that. It's out of our hands."

"But . . . if he's not caught, he might hurt someone else. I've been thinking about what happened, and why, and I have so many questions!"

At the increase in her volume, Elenora shook her scarlet face, chirped, and flew off the perch yet again. Her grandmother shot out a hand with a swiftness that belied her sixty years. Tillie watched, stunned, as the bird screeched and pecked at her grandmother, helpless against the gnarled hands that grasped her without flinching. Grandmama flipped the bird over, pulled a wing out onto the table, took the shears, and trimmed a half inch of emerald feathers off. She repeated the process on the left wing with a swift, snicking cut. Finally, the glistening scissors were put down and the bird released. Elenora flopped uselessly, unable to rise into the air. Eventually she waddled to the edge of the table and attempted to fly back to the safety of her perch. She fell with a soft thud onto the dining room carpet.

"Good bird!" her grandmother said, beaming. She turned to her granddaughter. "We'll not speak of this again, Mathilda," she said with a lethal, low quietness. She stood and left the room.

Tillie scrambled across the floor to where Elenora sat like a tiny chicken. She extended a hand, offering to bring the bird back up to the perch, but Elenora bit Tillie's thumb instead, a ratchety, angry crow yelling her protests at all humans in the vicinity.

Tillie didn't blame her at all.

The maids fussed over the parrot while Tillie sat, wondering over her grandmother's words: "We'll not speak of this again."

Did that include Lucy?

Four weeks. Four weeks of mourning, and then she would attend drawing rooms and soirees and theaters and Sunday promenades. Her throat went dry. There would be a wedding. Children. Nurses for the children. Summers in Newport or on the North Shore of Long Island. Planning more balls, soirees, suppers with the best and wealthiest on the island. Dorothy, gossiping with and about her. Some nameless man next to her, retiring to a library with other men to smoke their expensive cigars, drink their crystal tumblers of brandy. At some point, the children would be grown. Her faceless husband would die. She would, black clad, relegate her time to an appropriately benevolent society for helping those less fortunate and worry over the marriages of her children and grandchildren. She would ruthlessly clip the wings of her very own exotic South American parrots.

Tillie rubbed her face as if the action might smear away her thoughts and rose to go to the drawing room. Ada delivered two casually written letters for her, stained with brown blots from who knew what. Sitting at the Queen Anne escritoire, with its tortoiseshell inlay, she read them hungrily.

Dear Miss Pembroke,
Say, how are you? Have the police been by?
It's been a week.
Ian

Dear Miss Pembroke,
That butler of yours looks like a monument to one-way conversation. Why does he sound like a Frenchman and a German had a fight and got stuck in his throat?
Are you done yet? Any news on your sister's murderer?
Dip the quill, if you will. You know where to send it.
Ian

So few words. Such rudeness! And yet, he felt the same burning curiosity she did over the death of her sister. So unlike Dorothy or James or her family. They'd all just accepted it and moved on, but how could Tillie do that?

As improper as the notes were, the ease of his words made her ache for that casual familiarity they had shared at the bookstore. No airs. Just two people without expectations of duty or societal rules of conduct. It had felt at the time like Tillie had been leaning perpetually on a fence and that it had broken in Ian's presence, sending her flying sideways.

She dipped her mother-of-pearl pen into the gold inkwell but paused with the nib over the paper. She'd promised her grandmother she'd get rid of him, but she needed to give the book back. She could mail it to him, but no. She wished to speak to him again. She could not speak to Ada or Dorothy or Hazel or James or her family about vampires.

But how to see him without anyone knowing?

During the day, she could not leave without permission. Perhaps she could ask Ian to plan a chance meeting as she purchased a new hat or gloves. But Ada would tell Mama.

Perhaps she could slip out at night. But how to get about without the carriage? And the new watchman would surely be patrolling their grounds. She would not be able to come or go unseen.

After a moment's more thought, she redipped the quill and began writing.

> *Dear Mr. Metzger,*
> *I am doing better, but the broken bone still hurts.*
> *I am finished with the book and am ready to give it to you, but I am hoping to get another turn in a few weeks. Please meet me in five days on the corner of 5th Avenue and 66th Street at 12:30 in the morning.*
> *Also, my grandmother will have you arrested if you keep coming to the house.*
> *Sincerely,*
> *Miss Tillie Pembroke*

That would give her five nights to figure out how to leave the house without anyone knowing.

If only she had an idea of how to do that. For Lucy's sake, she had to think of something.

Perhaps another letter was in order. She dipped her quill again.

> *Dear Mrs. Seaman (Nellie Bly),*
> *I hope that name works all right for you.*
> *It occurs to me that my first letter may not have made it to you, so I will send a copy of this letter to each of your homes, in the Catskills, in Murray Hill, and your home on the Hudson.*
> *My sister died recently. No—that assumes she left this world under the pretense of accident or illness, which is not the case. She was murdered, you see, and I'm not*

altogether sure if the killer is human or not. As fantastic as this seems, I assure you, this letter is no joke.

Never mind my earlier inquiry regarding elephant odors.

I am not sure what to do anymore. You know how to find out things. I should like some advice, if you please.

Kindly respond.

Yours,

Miss Tillie Pembroke

CHAPTER 7

Water sleeps, and enemy is sleepless.

—Count Dracula

That very afternoon, she met Mr. John O'Toole.

He arrived at the house on Madison looking as he ought. His clothes were neat and clean but not fine enough to be confused with those who lived there. He had a brown beard speckled with gray, neatly trimmed, and nice brown eyes. His eyebrows were permanently in the angry position, squashing the expanse between them into a narrow crease. He appeared in an odd twilight of age, neither young nor old. He lacked that lithe elasticity seen in younger men, but his biceps stretched out his jacket as a fleshy warning to everyone that his punch could fracture a jaw. A pistol was at his hip, and his voice was low, serious. When he introduced himself to Tillie, he did not smile. He only bowed slightly and made no pleasantries about the weather or the trolley strike repercussions in the news that day.

As Ada was perpetually nearby, she was introduced next.

"Ada Clancy," she said primly.

"Miss." John nodded, and his eye twitched. It almost looked like a wink that he had reeled back in at the last moment.

Tillie looked at Ada. To most people, her maid was forgettable, but today Tillie saw her through this gentleman's eyes. A woman in her early twenties, round of waist, with a bosom and hips that were well proportioned—"tidy," as Mama was wont to say when commenting on those whose figures were more generous than she thought entirely proper. Ada's persimmon-toned hair was coiled in a low bun, maid's cap neatly perched on top. She blinked quickly and dropped her eyes to stare at her plain dark shoes. But her cheeks!

Ada was feverishly blushing.

The butler, Pierre, whose real name was Friedrich Fenstermacher, welcomed Mr. O'Toole with his odd accent—"like a Frenchman and a German had a fight and got stuck in his throat," as Ian had put it. French servants were expected in the very best homes on Fifth Avenue, and Friedrich wasn't going to let his heritage impede him.

Pierre showed John about the house, introduced him to the servants, showed him which bathroom to use in the servants' quarters toward the back of the house. Tillie went upstairs, and Ada seemed to drag her feet, clinging to the distant words the men spoke.

That was when Tillie got herself an idea.

"So John is to patrol the grounds every night," Tillie said to Ada.

"Yes. Miss, why are we in Miss Lucy's room?"

"Look. There's Pierre showing him around." She pushed the drapery aside, and together they peered down at the grounds behind the mansion. There was neatly manicured shrubbery; the large conservatory under glass, where hothouse irises and roses were grown; and the plot of the cook's herbs and Grandmama's favorite vegetables. There was no carriage house to look over, as their horses and carriages were kept farther up on Seventy-Third Street with others, where the smells wouldn't disturb the mansions by Millionaire's Row.

John and Pierre walked the perimeter, pointing out the iron fence (fashioned after Cornelius Vanderbilt's, of course), the Fishes' large marble house to their north, the Grants' mansion to the west, and round the side where the Havemeyer family lived. The Pembroke property took up a full third of the block.

"Come! They're going to the front!" Tillie said. Ada fairly ran after her, her cheeks still flushed.

They looked down from Tillie's room to the front of the mansion, where a narrow garden of myrtle bushes flanked the short walk to the door. John looked up at the windows, and Ada and Tillie pulled away quickly, afraid to be seen.

"He's handsome, isn't he, Ada?" Tillie said, nudging her maid's elbow.

"Oh, stop that, Miss Tillie."

They continued to watch John until he had disappeared inside. He was set to meet with her grandmother, who would go over the particulars of the job.

That night, after Grandmama had presumably finished her pipe in her bedroom, and while her mother was bathing her face in buttermilk up at her vanity, the electric lights in the house went dark. Ada had gone to sleep. Tillie went straight to the window. The watchman rounded the house in a regular fashion. He stood on the southeast corner of the property and took a wide look around, up to the windows where thieves might quickly scale the indents of the limestone-and-brick facade, and then he perused the street, searching up and down for anyone coming or going. At this time of night, there was only a distant clip-clopping of horseshoes. Then he would glance amongst the bushes and cherry trees by the street, then head to the northeast corner, where he enacted a similar process. Tillie went first to the north bathroom, then to Lucy's room to watch him make his rounds at the far reaches of their property.

Four minutes, around the house.

Well, perhaps he would grow tired and sleep quietly against the fence somewhere. Perhaps not. The only way to know would be to stay up all night.

So she did.

Tillie walked the triangular path between her room, the bathroom, and Lucy's room to watch the watchman. She found out some interesting things.

1. He took a break approximately every hour, on the hour, to smoke a cigarette, but he stopped only to light the cigarette with a match before he continued his walking.

2. He urinated every two hours in the northwest corner of the property. Tillie was embarrassed but forced herself to watch his habits. It took thirty seconds. His stream landed squarely in the yard of the Havemeyers' property. Good man.

3. He never slept.

4. He never stopped his rounds about the house.

This was a problem.

How could she sneak out with only thirty seconds—perhaps a minute—to get through the gate noiselessly and down the street without being noticed?

There was also another problem. Tillie had run out of opium that night.

The next morning, she could hardly open her eyes. She slept much of the day, until her pain awoke her and her bowels felt like they were careening downhill and her arms were a field of gooseflesh. Avoiding Ada after tea, she went directly to the cook, slipped her fifty cents, and asked her to buy two bottles of whatever opiate drops she could find and leave them under her bed. She added a dollar to pay for her discretion.

"One more thing. Make an extra plate of dessert every night, will you?"

The cook frowned. "Every night?"

"Yes, every night. Keep it aside in the kitchen."

"Yes, Miss Pembroke."

That evening, two brown bottles were found under her bed. Tillie took so much opium she slept fourteen hours, adrift in her very own

Lethe. The next night, she took a more modest dose and executed her plan.

"Ada," she said quietly after dinner. "I cannot finish these butter cookies. They're delicious, but I am absolutely full. Why don't you bring them to John?"

"John?" Ada nearly jumped in place.

"Yes. I was up all night last night from my pain, and I noticed he doesn't take a break. Not one! You ought to bring these cookies to him. It would be a nice gesture from all of us."

"Well," she said, hesitating. "If you wish."

Tillie went to Lucy's window and watched, a little while later, as Ada haltingly entered the back garden. John turned around, his face lighting with surprise. He took the plate of cookies, but Ada did not leave right away. Tillie saw them speak for at least three full minutes before the cookies were gone and Ada took the empty plate from him.

Excellent.

The next evening, she showed Ada the extra custard cup the cook had set aside.

"Ada. This is for John too. Could you bring this to him later? Around midnight?"

"Midnight?"

"Well, we don't want sweets to make him tired so early in the evening. You'll have to wake up to do so."

"Oh. Of course," Ada said.

Tillie noticed that whenever they spoke of John, Ada avoided eye contact. That night, Tillie stayed up to watch Ada deliver the custard. Once again, John seemed surprised but delighted. At one point, he offered Ada a spoonful, and she bashfully opened her mouth and allowed herself to be fed. John reached to wipe a bit of sugary whipped cream from her lower lip. Ada giggled. They spent at least ten minutes quietly chatting over the last morsels of dessert.

The next night, Tillie was ready.

Just before midnight, she took her medicine, then fetched a vial of cooking oil and a feather from the kitchen. She carefully painted the hinges of the front door, then returned upstairs and dressed in the light of the half moon shining through her window. She chose an inconspicuous brown poplin skirt and a simple shirtwaist and looped a scarf around her neck to use as a sling when her shoulder ached. Tillie hesitated before her gilt three-way mirror. She should wear black, for Lucy. Was this not a dishonor to her?

"I'm doing this for you, Lucy," Tillie murmured. Her heart still felt festooned in black crape. Lucy would understand. Her murderer was out there, and he might kill others. Lucy, who'd long volunteered at the Foundling Hospital amongst the orphaned children, had always had a soft heart for those at risk from life's harsh realities.

Tillie doubted she would be out of the house longer than an hour, so she didn't bother to bring any medicine with her. She had noted that she felt her best when she could dose herself every three hours, but surely this meeting would be brief. She checked the time on the tiny brooch watch at her waist, then softly padded to Lucy's room and waited by the window. Soon, Ada came outside, bringing a plate of delicacies to John. This time, they sat down on the stone bench by the back garden fountain.

Tillie did not hesitate. She quickly grabbed her reticule, containing the silver slotted spoon and the vial of oil, plus the copy of *Dracula*. In her sleeve was the little notebook and pencil. She descended the stairs and unlocked the front door, which opened noiselessly. At the front gate, she unstopped the vial of oil and poured a few drops onto the hinges. They opened with only the faintest groan. She lowered the catch as noiselessly as she could and walked south as rapidly as her feet could take her.

She passed Henry Gurdon Marquand's mansion, the one with the reportedly Byzantine chamber, thence westward to the looming darkness of Central Park. As she emerged onto Fifth Avenue, she crossed the darkened street and stood in the shadows of the park, oak and maples rising above her. A block away lurked the enormous French chateau—style mansion of Mrs. Astor. To the north, she could vaguely see the Lenox Library, where she had spent hours and hours perusing the art gallery and rare books.

Tall, T-shaped Edison arc lamps lit the street every 150 feet, dousing a circle of yellow onto the sidewalks.

She had done it. She had left her home in secret to meet a boy in secret, and her heart was full to bursting from the excitement of it all. Tillie looked downtown and saw a figure walking on the park side of the street toward her.

Was it Ian? Of course it must be. But it occurred to her that she was unaccompanied, and the area was deserted. If someone were to attack her, she could easily be dragged into the darkened recesses of the park to be murdered, just like Lucy. What could she bargain for her life? She had not brought any money. All she had was the book, and whose life was worth a silly book?

The figure seemed wide at the shoulders, hunched over as if trying not to be noticed. If it were Ian, he would make himself known. Right now. He would say something. But the stranger was silent.

"I should go home," she murmured and began to walk away as the figure drew closer. She stepped off the curb and started to cross Fifth Avenue. If she ran, she could make her front gates in five minutes. If she shouted, perhaps John would hear her before she reached home.

The figure under the light straightened at her movement and began rapidly walking toward her.

This was a terrible idea. Tillie had started to run when a voice called out to her.

"Wait!"

She stopped and turned. The man stepped under one of the streetlights.

"Ian? Is that you?"

"Yes. Who else did you think it was? One of the Dead Rabbits?"

"One of the Five Points gangs? They don't exist anymore, do they?"

"Probably not. Anyway, this neighborhood is a little too nice for their taste." He joined her in the middle of Fifth Avenue and smiled. "Boy, your streets up here are so clean. Nary a rat in sight. How's your broken arm?"

"Collarbone. It's mending, but it still hurts." Tillie shook away her fright and inhaled some courage. She reached into her reticule and removed the book. "Why do you want to read this?" She shook the copy of *Dracula*. "And why do you keep asking about my sister? Why do you care?"

"Why did you insist I meet you at midnight, when I ought to be getting my beauty sleep? You look sleepy yourself."

She did? Now that she thought of it, she did feel a little foggy. She always did when the medicine first took effect. "Never mind that. Answer my question."

"And talking kind of slowly too. Are you all right?" He squinted, trying to study her face.

"I'm fine, I'm fine. The book. My sister, Lucy. Speak."

Ian put his hands deep in his pockets and rocked on his heels. "It's a good book, I hear. But with the news about a killing, I had to know if there was something real happening, not just the coroner's imagination. It's not every day that you find out a girl died from being bled to death."

Tillie shivered. "Lucy was a real person, not some curio in a cabinet to be examined." She'd been silly to think this boy was someone she could talk to. "Here. Take the book. But after two weeks, I'd like to keep it. You won't need to pay me back. I can't do this again."

"Meeting men you hardly know, in the dead of night? I suspect you kind of enjoy it."

"Oh, stop it, will you? Why do you care about my sister?" she repeated.

Ian lifted his chin and looked at Tillie in a disconcerting way. Like he was studying her so he could draw her portrait from memory later. He shuffled his feet a little sheepishly.

"I had a brother who died when he was a baby. Murdered by the lady who was supposed to be watching him while my mother and I worked during the daytime."

"Oh!" Had she even given any thought to what his life was like? "That's so terrible! What happened?"

"She doped him up because he was crying too much. He was starting to develop the croup, and I kept telling her he was crying for a reason, but she was too annoyed to care." He frowned. "My parents died soon after that."

"I'm so sorry."

He shrugged. "You're lucky to have a family. Even without your sister."

Tillie said nothing to that. He was right, but why didn't she feel lucky? "What were they like? Your parents?" she asked.

"When we lived in the shtetl in Russia, my mother sold bread, and my father taught at the heder. They were both so smart. So tough, you know? When the pogroms started, they fled to the port at Hamburg. For me. To save me. I still remember being crammed into steerage on the ship. And the stench—and the rotten food." His eyes were unfocused. "They found us a room to stay in when we got to New York, and my mother gave birth to my brother. And then one year later, everyone was dead. They made it here, and they died anyway." He wiped his sleeve against his nose.

"I guess they did save you, after all."

Ian allowed a fleeting smile. "I guess they did."

"So . . ." Tillie was wringing her hands around the book. She stopped before she tore the pages. "Here." She handed it to him. "So you want to help."

"I do. I know people."

"Who? Do you work with the police?" she asked.

"No. I sell papers, but I also run errands for the staff, and I help them with their stories sometimes. I have access to the old papers at the *World*, and sometimes at the *Tribune*, so we can look for patterns. And I know someone who works for the coroner. Not very nice, but he knows things that the police don't."

Tillie regarded him. "Really? These people would help?"

"They might." Ian pulled a slightly bent cigarette from his pocket and lit it. The spark illuminated his face, and for a brief moment, he looked almost like a child, with those big eyes of his. "So tell the truth. Why midnight, of all times?" For the first time, she noticed he seemed tired. "In four hours, I have to go buy my papers to sell. That doesn't leave much time for sleeping."

Tillie sighed. "I'm sorry. I had to leave in secret. My family won't let me out after what happened to Lucy. They've hired a watchman to patrol our house. My grandmother won't allow you to visit. And I had to return the book. I promised."

"Princess locked in a castle, eh?" He puffed on his cigarette, and the smoke obscured his eyes. He was still smiling, but it was unlike the smiles she encountered from eligible men when she entered a ballroom. Those were expressions that minutely examined her flaws, quantified her, as if she were a piece of silver to be doled out and hoarded. This smile had the curious effect of making her want to smile, too, though nothing funny had been said. It was as if she'd been wanting such a smile all week long.

"I suppose. After what happened to Lucy, can you blame them for being extra cautious?"

"Of course not." His smile faded. "Look. I would like to help. I know what it's like to lose family. It hurts more than a cannon shot."

Tillie considered the earnestness in his face. He might quiet the questions that had been flooding her mind since Lucy's death. The *why*, and *why her*. Tillie had never truly suffered from want or hunger in her life. But this was a dark, deep hole that begged to be filled with reason and facts.

"All right," she said lightly. "Thank you. And how can I pay you back?"

"Oh, maybe buy me a dinner at Delmonico's. I hear their steak is the best." Ian grinned again—the real thing, no paste jewels. He crushed the stub of his cigarette under his old boot. "So—have you heard anything about who might have done it?"

"No. Mama and Grandmama spoke to the police, and they've learned nothing. Or at least, they don't tell me anything." She lowered her voice. "I think they want to forget it ever happened."

"How could they?" He sounded angry. "You can't forget that. She was slaughtered."

Tillie's throat went dry. That word—*slaughtered*—made her think of abattoirs and blood flowing along gutters after steer met knives and their grisly ends. Against her will, she imagined Lucy fighting some unseen foe. Fighting and failing to save herself.

"You don't have to remind me." Tillie poked at the copy of *Dracula* in Ian's hands. "Which is why I bought this. I've thought about how someone could have done this to her."

"Me too. It seems a strange coincidence that this book comes out this year, and your sister dies just like a vampire victim. Same name too. There must be a connection."

"Oh!" She reached into her bag again. "Here's your spoon." She handed him the silverware with its patterned fenestrations. "Though I still haven't figured out what use it has. Unless it's for embarrassing oneself while eating lemon sorbet."

"It's not for sorbet." He laughed. "You don't know? Well, I'll show you. Do you have to go back home right away?"

Did she? Time seemed to expand for a second, breaching the impossible. Freedom seemed to swell in her chest as she smiled.

"No," Tillie said. "Not right away."

They began walking down Fifth Avenue, from one pool of lamplight to the next. Ian had a habit of rubbing his chin as he was thinking. Tillie kept pace with him, talking.

"My friend Hazel said the papers reported vampire killings in New England."

"Is that so? We should find those articles and see what they say."

"Can you do that? The Lenox Library might have some, but I haven't been able to visit."

"We should go to Newspaper Row, downtown, so we can search the old articles, like I mentioned."

Tillie's face lit up. "I would love that. I need to do something."

"That's a start."

"I've been writing some notes," she said timidly and took out her little notebook. "Just some scribbles."

Ian flipped through the leaflets. "You're asking good questions. Like a reporter! Why would vampires need blood and not flesh? Maybe there's a medical illness that makes people need blood. We may need to speak to a doctor about such things. And the bite. We could talk to that fellow at the morgue too. But there are other questions you're missing."

"What questions?" Tillie asked.

"Well, what happened the day your sister died? Who was she with?"

Tillie handed her pencil to Ian. "Her maid, Betty. But the maid was fired," Tillie said.

Ian nibbled his lip and kept writing and walking. "Has anyone spoken to Betty?"

"I don't know," she admitted.

"There's a place to start," Ian said, brightening.

"Oh, and the doctor's son. He mentioned that he saw her that same day, and she seemed off. I've been meaning to go back and speak with him. And Dr. Erikkson. Luckily, I have an appointment coming up," she said, moving her arm in the sling and wincing.

"Perfect."

"There's another thing." Tillie's face clouded. "Dorothy—she's another friend—she says that Lucy and her fiancé, James, were fighting a lot recently. But I had no idea."

Ian rubbed his chin. "Well, you could ask James, but if he's a suspect, there's no way he'll admit anything was less than a peach between them."

"It's unlikely that James is a vampire—he's always out in the daylight, for one thing." She stood looking southward, where a tall, square building on the corner of Fifty-Ninth Street and Fifth Avenue stuck above the rest like a tooth. "He's been kind to me lately. He never paid attention before."

"Is he sad?"

"Sad?" Tillie stopped walking for a moment. James was like her mother and grandmother—he never displayed much emotion. "Well, I suppose, but . . ."

"No. I mean, if my wife—my fiancée—if she died, I'd be pretty torn up. Love of my life, dead?"

"I don't know if they were the loves of each other's lives." When Ian stared at her, she added, "It was a good match. They were fond of each other."

He snorted. "I'm fond of my fishmonger, but I'm not going to marry him. I guess that's love on Millionaire's Row, eh?"

Tillie went hot in the face. "I loved my sister."

"Sure, and I believe it. But how well did you know her?"

This silenced her. They'd been so close, and yet . . . of late, she'd spent most outings hiding in her hosts' libraries, instead of in the ballrooms where James and Lucy were. It meant that she'd lost opportunities to spend time with her sister. How selfish of her.

"I thought I knew her well," Tillie said faintly. "But . . ." She thought of the locked drawer in Lucy's room. She turned to her midnight companion. "Ian. Can you teach me how to pick a lock?"

"Do I look like a thief?"

Tillie's eyes traveled up and down his impossibly shabby clothes. Ian followed her gaze to his boots, which had holes in the toes.

"Don't answer that," he said. "I'm not a thief, and I don't know the first thing about how to pick a lock. But"—he grinned—"I know someone who does."

CHAPTER 8

Remember, my friend, that knowledge is stronger than memory, and we should not trust the weaker.

—Van Helsing

They walked eastward toward the elevated train on Third Avenue. Tillie was surprised that it still ran so late. Past sunset, she occasionally went to the Grand Opera House with her mother and Lucy, but never anywhere by herself. And always by carriage. She didn't know the first thing about navigating the city under this umbrella of sooty darkness.

"The city is so quiet now," she said as they walked. Most of the homes on either side of Sixty-Third Street were beautifully kept. Some Italianate, some French chateau–style, but all smaller and less grand than the ones on Fifth and Madison. By the time they reached Lexington, a large synagogue had appeared on the southeast corner.

"I used to go to that shul," Ian pointed out.

"Oh," Tillie said. "Why don't you go anymore?"

"I'm busy. And I had some problems with . . . never mind."

"With whom?"

"Not a person. Everything." He gestured to include the darkened sky above them.

"I see." She didn't, but she was embarrassed to ask. Church was for her a duty, similar to dressing as a Pembroke lady ought or dabbing her napkin at the edges of her mouth just so. God was supposedly in charge, but nothing had ever stirred within Tillie that spoke of a grandly written plan laced into her being. The two items indelibly written into her destiny were these: never being quite as wonderful as Lucy and never knowing quite as much as she wished. If anything, he watched her, and occasionally he laughed. But mostly, he provided and thence ignored her. Tillie knew he ignored others with heavier neglect, and this troubled her. Who was to carry the burden, when even Providence fell short of the wretched?

She wondered if that was how her sister had felt, why she'd volunteered at the Foundling Hospital.

Ian fell into silence, perhaps thinking over his apostasy. Or perhaps thinking of food. Tillie was hungry, and heard Ian's own stomach rumble as if they shared kindred organs.

Ahead, they could see the Third Avenue el cutting across the space above the streets. On metal legs, the tracks ran parallel to the ground and formed a dark, looming stripe up above them. They climbed the stairs and paid the fare, waiting for the groan and belching steam hiss that told them the train was nearing the station.

"Nighttime escapes agree with you," Ian said once they'd boarded. "You really perked up."

"I did?"

"Yes. You seemed really sleepy before. You talked too slow."

"Oh." It was probably her medicine wearing off. She hadn't realized she seemed slow. She felt rather normal on it. Strange. She watched the buildings fly past just a few feet away. "Imagine waking up to seeing a train outside your chamber window," Tillie said, peering.

"I don't have to imagine. The last place I lived, I woke up to that every day. I could reach out my window and spit into a train window, if I wanted."

"How did you sleep?"

"Like death," he said.

They said nothing more until they exited on Grand Street and headed down Bowery Street. Unlike sleepy uptown, the Bowery was pulsing with the living. Two parallel elevated trains flanked the street, and storefronts were lit everywhere. Roughs, thieves (probably), women, even children were clustered and scattered here and there amongst the shabby shooting galleries, shops, lottery offices, hotels, saloons, and dance houses crammed on each street.

"Stay close to me," Ian murmured. "Hold your purse in your hand, on my side."

They passed a noisy gambling house, with alternating yelps and peals of laughter pouring forth from the smoke-filled venue. One or two storefronts were hung with red banners containing Chinese writing; inside, on low settees, customers smoked and drank from small cups as they watched the street, eyes heavily lidded. Patrons chatted outside a concert saloon, while inside, music, tinny and distant, accompanied the thumping of feet.

And it stank! The streets here were not clean like those uptown. Piles of refuse obscured and blurred the edge of the sidewalk, and horse manure formed small dark mountains on the cobblestones. The miasma hit her nostrils and nearly made Tillie retch. A few men bumped her as they passed, which jostled her against Ian. She took a sharp inhalation of breath with every jolt.

"Are you all right?"

"My shoulder. It's worse now. I feel like a marble in a fist right now—it's so crowded. My back hurts, too, and my head is pounding."

"Don't you have any medicine?"

Tillie shook her head.

"Here. Stay close to me." He put his arm around her waist and guided her through the crowd on the street. "We're nearly there."

To keep her mind off the pain, Tillie started talking. "The Bowery, that's where we are, right? When the Dutch came here, this area was all thick forest. The little farms were called *bouweries* or something like that. Washington marched through here and lowered the British flag in the Battery in 1783."

"How do you know all that?"

Tillie shrugged her good shoulder. "I like to read things."

"Oh. Here we are."

Ian stopped in front of a darkened grocery store, closed for the evening. A yellow light glowed from the second story. He cupped his hands around his mouth.

"Tobias!" he hollered. "Let us in!"

A man popped his head out of the window. He had curls hanging down along the sides of his cheeks and a thick brown beard.

"Let a man get some sleep!" he yelled back.

"Your light was on. You weren't sleeping."

"I was trying."

"You're awake now."

"That is true. What, do you need to buy something? Who's that lady with you?"

"She's nice, Tobias. Let us in."

Tobias threw both hands down, as if he were done speaking to them. The window closed, and the light went out.

"What do we do now?" Tillie asked. Her stomach was starting to cramp. The pain reached through her belly to her lower back and twisted like a vise. If only she had brought that bottle. Just when she had convinced herself she should turn around and head back to the Grand Street station, a light blinked on inside the grocery, and Tobias—looking like he'd barely had time to put on his trousers—unlocked the door.

"Come in, come in. Before I catch the grippe and die. Come in."

Ian smirked. "Nobody gets the grippe in June, Tobias."

"That would be my luck," he growled.

He relocked the door behind them. In the back of the grocery, a faint light shone. Tobias looked to be several years older than Ian. They had the same nose—straight, with a little bump on the bridge that made them look like statesmen. But Tobias was losing his hair on top and had a spine that hunched and curved slightly to the right, as if he were perpetually turning a corner.

Beyond the crowded shelves of the grocery was a room that held boxes, crates, a small desk, and shelves overflowing with ledgers and papers. Ian leaned against a wall calendar printed with a blonde lady looking over a flowing wheat field, and Tobias indicated a wooden chair where Tillie could sit. He stared at them carefully.

"Are you married?" he asked.

Tillie and Ian both blurted, "No!"

"Too bad. Marriage is wonderful. You should try it sometime."

"*You're* not married." Ian crossed his arms.

"I wasn't talking about *me*. So why are you with this shiksa, Ian?"

"Long story. First, she needs some medicine. Do you have anything?"

"I love you like a cousin, Ian, but I am not handing out free medicine."

Ian snorted. "You *are* my cousin, and we'll buy it. What do you have?"

Tobias sighed and left the office. He came back with a small, oblong paper-wrapped box with a druggist's logo of a tree on the front. "Here you go. Willow extract."

Tillie frowned. "I need laudanum. Opium. See, I broke my collarbone a couple of weeks ago—"

"Did he break it?" Tobias jabbed the bottle toward Ian.

"No!" Ian and Tillie blurted simultaneously again.

"You sure you two aren't married?" Tobias asked, tilting his head.

Ian rubbed his temples. "You're killing me. Slowly but surely."

"What else is family for?" Tobias said, smirking.

"Anyway," Tillie said quickly, "I broke my collarbone, and I forgot to bring my medicine with me. The doctor says I should take it all the time to keep it healing well."

"All right, all right. I don't need the spiel. She knows what she wants." Tobias ducked out and returned with another bottle. "Here you go."

Ian handed him a few coins, and Tillie unwrapped the bottle. Her fingers shook slightly as she measured several drops under her tongue. She used to prefer it mixed with water and sugar, but lately, she enjoyed the burn of it on the tender flesh beneath her tongue. It seemed to work faster this way. She took fewer drops than last time, as she didn't like the way Ian had kept commenting on how sleepy she seemed.

When she put the dropper back in the bottle and sighed luxuriantly, she looked up to see Tobias and Ian were watching her carefully. Ian seemed as if he didn't recognize her.

"What is it?" Tillie asked.

"The girl really enjoys opium, eh?" Tobias said. "So is this why you woke me up? Medicine?"

"No," Ian said, frowning as he turned from Tillie. "I need you to teach Miss Pembroke how to pick a lock."

"What, am I a gonif?" Tobias said, exasperated.

"Of course not! Just . . . teach her. I'll pay you back. Two tickets to the Irving Place Theatre next Saturday. I know someone."

"You always know someone," Tillie murmured.

"Doesn't he, though?" Tobias said, clearly amused. "All right. I'll show her. But you should know, Miss, I know this not because I am a thief but because my good father, Abraham, Ian's uncle, became very forgetful in his last twenty years. He owned a jewelry shop, and all his supplies were locked up, but he would accidentally throw the keys away every week. So I learned to pick the lock from a locksmith, and there you go."

"I see," Tillie said, brightening. This must be the strangest evening she'd ever had, and she was loving it.

"What kind of lock is it that you need to open?"

"A side table drawer."

"Oh. Easy. I'll show you."

Tobias stood and glanced around the cramped office. "Does it look like this?" He pointed to a broken bureau crammed into the far reaches of the office. There was a keyhole in the top drawer.

"Very similar," Tillie said.

"All right. Not too difficult. I can't give you any skeleton key to try, as chances are the shank diameter and bit length will be off. You'll have to figure it out on your own."

Tillie joined him in front of the bureau. Tobias withdrew a skeleton key from one of the drawers. He pointed out the different parts. "This is the shank. This is the bit, the post, and the bow. It's the bit that helps open the lock. This is the part you need to re-create."

Tillie listened with keen ears. Tobias showed her two L-shaped pieces of metal she would need to pick the lock.

"Push this one up until you feel and hear a click. Then use the other to turn, and then it's open."

He demonstrated with the bureau, then handed the metal pieces to Tillie.

She knelt on the dusty floor. She pulled her arm out of her makeshift sling, but her shoulder was terribly stiff and sore. It took at least ten tries before she could unlock the drawer.

Ian whooped. "There! You've done it!"

"Not bad," Tobias said, wheezing a little. He stood up and stretched.

Tillie hesitated. "May I see the inside of the lock?"

"What?" Tobias asked.

Ian looked at her, puzzled. "What for?"

"I want to know why it works. It feels like someone giving me the answer to a puzzle, without figuring it out for myself."

"But—" Ian started, but the look on Tillie's face made his frown disappear. They had time, after all. They had all night. "Tobias? Would you mind?"

"Sure, why not? It's only sleep I'm missing." He grabbed a broken lock that looked like it had once been embedded in a door and started unscrewing the front face. "We're all just walking around half-dead anyway."

"Ah, but it's the half-alive part that makes it all fun," Tillie said, beaming.

"That optimism will be the death of you," Tobias said, wheezing again now that he was cramped over the deconstructed lock. "Okay, Miss Pembroke. This is how a lock works."

They all crowded in to look as Tobias painstakingly went over the mechanism. In the midst of the lesson, Tillie caught her reflection in an old bronze mirror leaning against the wall. What was that expression, that fire in her eyes? Not just curiosity or happiness. Something else.

Ah—she knew.

Incandescence. If a face could be the definition of a word, Tillie had it.

After they left Tobias's grocery store with four different L-shaped metal tools in Tillie's purse, Ian motioned for her to go down the street.

"One last thing I promised," he said. He brought her to a saloon around the corner. It was dimly lit and noisy. Several men stood outside the door, smoking and arguing in Polish. Spotting Ian, two of them smiled. The taller, blonder man, wearing a vest, clapped him on the back.

"Cześć! Czy to twoja żona?"

"Cześć. Nie, nie. Przyjaciel," Ian responded, but his eyes were downcast, and Tillie could swear that he was blushing.

"What were you saying?" Tillie whispered as they went into the saloon.

"They thought you were my wife. Seems a common thought this evening! I said no, but I should have said yes. Now they probably think you're a . . . a . . ."

Tillie blanched. "A what?"

"Well, most unaccompanied women down here can be assumed to be . . . working women." He cleared his throat. "I'll tell them you're my fiancée when we leave so they don't get any ideas."

Now it was Tillie's turn to blush. Luckily, there was so much to look at and absorb. She had never been in such an establishment, and she was taken aback by the noise. People were chatting loudly in every corner, filling tables and standing by the walls. Italian, German, Polish, Russian, Yiddish, all swirling around her. The bar was serving plates of small meat pies, sliced bratwurst, pickles, fried oysters. Ian found a small table for them and hollered to a man behind them wearing a filthy apron.

"Absinthe, for two."

"Absinthe?" Tillie squeaked.

"Yes. If you're going to know why it was found where your sister died, you need to know what it is. Also, it's one of my favorite drinks."

They waved away a bowl of salted pickled herring. Ian wrinkled his nose. "This saloon serves everyone, which means that their food isn't the best. If you want better Russian or Polish fare, I know where to go. Oh, here it is."

The absinthe arrived. There were two small wineglasses, smaller than the ones at Tillie's home. At the bottom was a portion of a faintly green, clear liquid perhaps two fingers high. A bowl with two flat, rectangular sugar cubes sat between them, and two slotted spoons (just like Ian's!) were laid next to the glasses. A carafe of cold water was also placed on the table.

"What do I do with all of this?" Tillie asked, waving her hands. "Why is it green? Is the water for after?" She sniffed the liquor delicately. "It smells like licorice."

"It's the anise and fennel. The wormwood makes it green. They say that it makes you more creative to drink this. They call it 'the green muse.' Didn't you hear that it was a favorite of Lord Byron and all the great artists?"

"I didn't. Fascinating."

"Well, here is what you do. Put the spoon on the top of the glass. And put the sugar cube on the spoon. Then we take the cold water and . . ." Ian began to pour a dribble of icy-cold water over the sugar. It saturated the cube, changing its color from white to slightly translucent before the cube began to disintegrate, and the crystals slipped through the slotted spoon into the drink. As the sweetened ice water hit the absinthe, the clear emerald liquid turned a murky greenish fog.

"That's a good louche," Ian murmured. "Your turn."

Tillie did the same, her eyes wide with fascination. When the sugar was gone and the glass full ("Not too full!" Ian warned, stopping her just in time), they raised their glasses.

"Here's to finding out answers," Ian said.

"For Lucy," Tillie said, her eyes smarting.

She sipped the liquid. It was stronger than she'd expected, even after all the watering down. And it was so strange. Slightly bitter, slightly sweet, with that intense licorice flavor.

"Do you do this often?" Tillie asked between sips.

"Drink absinthe? Sometimes. I think it's delicious. And sometimes it helps me think through problems. It brings a different perspective."

"No, I mean, bring girls to saloons and plan on tracking down murderers."

Ian laughed. "Of course not. You're my first."

Tillie smiled. The drink warmed her stomach and began to send a buzzing sensation through her torso and up to her cheeks. She felt wonderful. Wonderful, but off. Her head felt slightly detached, and she blinked a few times, trying to focus on Ian's brown eyes. She felt like she could fly right now. But somehow, she didn't think she should say so out loud.

"Don't drink it all. It's a little strong, and you had that medicine too."

"Yes, I did," Tillie said, smiling.

"You shouldn't take so much," Ian said, his smile loosening to a look of consternation.

"What? Opium? You sound like my mother."

"Oy, not something I'm usually accused of."

"Tell me about your brother," Tillie said, shaking her head and bringing her focus back.

Ian's gaze was wistful. "He was so cute. Curly brown hair, curlier than mine. And he had these pretty blue eyes, the first blue eyes in the family. If you tickled his ears, he would laugh."

Tillie smiled, but it was the smile of remembering all things precious now gone from the world. Christmas mornings past. The day her father had gifted her her prized dictionary. Lucy, reading out of the very same tome to soothe her.

"You know, that lady who killed him didn't even go to jail. She wasn't even sorry. I hear she eventually left town for Boston, but . . ." He sighed. "I despise opium. You should see people lined up to smoke it on Baxter Street. They look half-alive. It's not right."

Tillie stiffened. "Well, I have a broken bone. My doctor told me to take it."

Ian's face was neutral. "Anyway, I have my sad story. And you have yours." He took some money out and handed it to the waiter. "And now you know what absinthe is, and we need to find out why it was at the scene of your sister's murder."

"Yes," Tillie said faintly. "I don't think Lucy ever drank it. But then again, I can't ask her. Maybe the vampire drinks it. But vampires drink blood, not absinthe, so that makes me think the murderer wasn't a vampire after all."

"That's sound logic. But then again—it might have just been someone's trash, nothing to do with your sister at all."

"That's possible too," Tillie admitted.

Ian walked her to the elevated station, all the way up the stairs, and waited with her for the next train. The slightly cooler air and the walking had cleared her head a bit. The absinthe's effect was melting away.

"You'll read that"—she pointed to the book in Ian's jacket pocket—"and let me know what you think. I have so many questions. You'll find out if we can do some looking into the other vampire claims in the papers?"

"Sure, I can." He yawned. It was three in the morning, and Ian would have to pick up his papers soon. "And you see if you can find something useful in that locked drawer. We can meet again next week."

"Midnight, if that's all right. Where?"

"You really can't go out during the day? You're a vampire yourself." Tillie frowned deeply, and Ian put up a hand. "Sorry. Bad joke. All right then. Midnight. Meet me at Newspaper Row, in front of the World Building. One week from today."

"Very well. Thank you, Mr. Metzger."

"Good golly, just call me Ian."

"And you can call me Tillie."

Ian smiled brightly, but she could see the redness creeping into his eyes. "Oh, and here." He handed her back her little notebook, the one he'd been writing in when they were walking. "Keep writing notes!"

As the train chugged into the station, he offered to buy a ticket to accompany her, but Tillie refused. The train was empty, and she thought he looked rather exhausted.

All the way back, she was the only passenger in her car. Unexpectedly, she enjoyed the solitude. When the train stopped at the Sixty-Seventh

Street station, she walked briskly home, but her pain was returning with every step.

What a night, she thought. She had escaped her house and gone on an adventure in the Bowery, of all places. She'd learned how to pick a lock! And drink absinthe! And spent time with a man, unaccompanied—and nothing untoward had happened.

When Tillie arrived at her house, she watched from a far street corner as John O'Toole rounded the front. The second he turned the corner, Tillie moved as fast as she could. It was difficult to run without being able to swing her one arm. She made it through the gate, up the stairs, and inside just before John wound around the south side of the house to the front.

Her breath came in quick pants. She would have to ask Ada to bring John more food later in the night so she could bookend her comings and goings without fear of getting caught.

Tillie was too tired to try to pick the lock of Lucy's side table. She went instead to her room and, with great difficulty, undressed herself. Her pain was creeping back, as well as that sensation of falling—or was it failing? She was transmuting back into the Tillie that was imperfect, cracked. The timing of this inevitable transformation seemed to coincide with her medicine wearing off. She pulled out the tiny bottle from Tobias's grocery and drew up a full dropperful. She would need to sleep quite a bit, and she had a broken bone, after all.

"I need this. I do," she said, as if convincing an invisible companion in the room.

The medicine pooled under her tongue, burning her mouth in the way that it always did. The alcohol absorbed quickly and warmed her cheeks. As she lay in bed, her heart pounded ever so slightly harder. But it was the opium—the sweet, sickly, bitter opium—that lifted the sad fog, numbed it into submission, turning her body into a soupy morass of contentment.

Opium, she thought vaguely as she drifted away. *And absinthe. I must learn more about these marvelous wonders.*

Something buzzed in her dreams. A bee, maybe.

No, it was a voice.

"Miss Tillie. It's almost three o'clock in the afternoon. You must wake."

"Mmm."

Tillie rolled over in her bed, felt something cold and hard against her cheek.

A bottle. She'd fallen asleep next to her opium.

"I'm up, Ada. I'm up."

She blinked sleepily, noting the slant of afternoon sunlight through her window. Oh, how creaky her bones felt. Like she'd been buried under a glacier for the last ten hours. She pushed herself to her side, then up. Her clavicle felt terribly stiff, her bladder terribly full. She quickly hid the bottle away in her vanity drawer, hoping Ada hadn't seen it. Her notebook was in there. She opened it up, reading Ian's last few penciled notes.

Where was Lucy when she died? What does Betty know?

And then:

What is your favorite sandwich?

Why are gooses geese, but mooses aren't meese?

Tillie giggled and put the notebook away.

Ada helped her get ready but was oddly silent the whole time. Usually she chatted about the cook or the news or, lately, John O'Toole. Today, not so much. Pierre did not greet them with his German-tinged French colloquialisms. The butler looked pale and rather dyspeptic today. Her mother and grandmother were eating a late luncheon in the conservatory, by the small central fountain and the wall of pink and scarlet roses. A tray of steaming tea sat on a rosewood table. Waiting for Tillie was a plate of lobster salad and pea soup. Her mother looked ashen, though her grandmother seemed unperturbed, busy sipping her cup of tea.

Tillie backed up into the hallway and grabbed Ada's sleeve.

"Ada. What is going on?" she whispered. "Everyone looks like Lucy died all over again."

"Oh, Miss Tillie." She went whiter and then motioned for her to come into the kitchen. They went back to the servants' area beyond their library and double salons. The cook and her two assistants were crowded over a page of the *Tribune*. As soon as Tillie entered, they backed away as if the paper were made of acid.

"You'll find out soon enough. Here." Ada pointed to an article at the bottom of the page.

Tillie pulled it close with her free hand and read the small headline.

Second Vampire-like Killing in Central Park

CHAPTER 9

*But he cannot flourish without this diet, he eat not as others
. . . He throws no shadow; he make in the mirror no reflect
. . . he has the strength of many of his hand.*

—Van Helsing

Second Vampire-like Killing in Central Park

June 26, 1899 (Special)—Albert Weber, aged thirteen, was found dead near the southern end of the Museum of Natural History yesterday morning by museum groundkeepers. Like a similar incident on June 8 the body was found with puncture wounds to the neck and seemingly drained of blood. No blood or weapon was found nearby. An emptied bottle of absinthe was again found at the scene.

The boy's mother states that he was in good health, having recovered from a bout of cholera one month ago. Police are collecting information on the boy, as he had been missing since the prior afternoon around

3:00 p.m. Information may be submitted directly to
Det. Herman Porter, Twenty-First Ward Pct.

Tillie read the article with trembling fingers.

"Just like Lucy," she whispered, her throat dry. "Just like Lucy. The absinthe. The wounds on the neck. Oh mercy, I wish I had my *Dracula* book!"

"What happened to your book?" Ada whispered back.

"Oh," Tillie said. She ought to be more careful about her words. "I . . . lost it."

"I'll look for it. I'm sure it's in your room somewhere. In the meantime, your mother and grandmother are waiting." Ada's hands were balled together in front of her apron. "They've been upset all day but won't speak of it."

What must she do? There were too many questions, too many thoughts fighting for precedence in her mind.

Lucy's drawer. She must look there. But first, Mama and Grandmama. And she needed to talk to Tom and Dr. Erikkson again.

She went into the conservatory, the bright light shining down through the open windows of the roof. It was warm, but a breeze made it comfortable. The scent of roses was nearly overpowering, and around their little table, the fountain tinkled merrily despite all the dour faces. Elenora sat on her perch, seeming to know she was confined to her place. Tillie sat across from her mother in silence.

"It's about time you were up." Her grandmother stirred her tea. Ada poured Tillie a steaming cupful, and her mother attempted to not look stricken and overheated at the same time.

"Did you rest well, Mathilda?"

"Not very. My shoulder still aches something awful." She tried to eat the lobster salad, but the creamy dressing made her stomach turn. The pea soup resembled a festering pond. "Mama, may I visit Dr. Erikkson again? To see if there is anything else to be done?"

Her mother sighed but did not seem to possess the strength to fight much of anything today. "Very well."

Tillie drained her teacup, then reached for her toast. "Are you well this afternoon, Grandmama?"

Her grandmother looked up and clawed her Brussels shawl closer over her shoulders. "I would be better if they could close the windows." Grandmama was perpetually cold, even in summer. If she had her way, she'd close all the conservatory windows, and it would be a sweltering rain forest. She frowned. "You've worn that robe de chambre before, Mathilda. We need to order another dozen dresses for her. Victoria, can you not keep up with her wardrobe?"

"But they're all black," Tillie said. "Does it matter?"

"If you're asking that, then your mind is not in the right sphere," Grandmama said severely. "And you must stop waking up so late."

Her mother gave her a defeated look. "I'll send word to the doctor you'll be by today. And Mathilda—do come straight home afterward. Speak to no one. Stay with Ada at all times. Do you understand?"

"Of course. Is something the matter?"

Her mother's face constricted. "You must be safe, Mathilda." She gripped the teacup so hard Tillie feared it might shatter. "Promise me."

Why did they refuse to speak about it? "All right," Tillie said faintly. She abandoned her meal and left to get ready for her visit to the doctor—though she had something else to do first. Before she went upstairs, she caught Ada. "I'm to see Dr. Erikkson today. Ready the carriage in half an hour. Oh, and I do think it would be best to bring John a refreshment in the early hours—around three o'clock in the morning. Mother is so frightened for my safety, and so we must keep John happy as an employee. It must be exhausting for him to patrol all night long. I'll have Cook make more treats for you to bring him."

Ada brightened. "Very well." She curtsied and left.

Tillie wasted no time and scurried up the stairs, first to her room, then to Lucy's. She shut the door, then removed Tobias's metal tools from her pocket, where she had stowed them. She pulled off her shoulder sling and knelt by the locked side table drawer.

She inserted one of the L-shaped pieces into the keyhole and pushed it upward until she felt a click of the locking lever. Then she inserted a smaller tool and turned it as Tobias had showed her.

But the dead bolt would not move. She adjusted the tools, tried again. Her shoulder needled her with pain from the tiny bit of use. The drawer refused to unlock.

A knock at the door jolted Tillie, and she nearly dropped her tools.

"Miss Tillie?" Ada. "Are you in there? The carriage is a-waiting."

"Yes. One moment." Tillie pocketed her instruments, then pulled out a pair of lace gloves from Lucy's armoire. She put her arm back into the sling and opened the door. "I wanted to wear Lucy's gloves. So I could remember her all day today."

Ada raised her eyebrows. "Of course," she said doubtfully.

Within half an hour, they arrived at Dr. Erikkson's small town house. Once again, Mrs. Erikkson opened the door.

"Good afternoon! You are looking a little thin, Miss Pembroke. No doubt from all the melancholy. But I do hope you are eating enough!"

"I am." Tillie tried to smile. "It's the black dress. Anyone with a decent constitution looks consumptive in black."

"So it seems." Her cheeks had a way of being pink and shiny, like an iced cake. "Come. Dr. Erikkson is with my son, but I'll let him know you've arrived."

The small foyer was much dimmer than the sunlit day. An oval silhouette was mounted above a scratched table—it looked just like a little boy.

"Oh. Is that Tom?" Tillie asked.

"Ah, no. That is Tom's elder brother, Edgar. He died of scarlet fever before Tom was born. His poor father did everything he could to revive him, but to no avail. It's a terrible thing to see one's child die young."

Mrs. Erikkson's eyes watered, and she tentatively reached out to pat Tillie's good shoulder. "How your mother must feel. I can understand."

Tillie wanted to say, Mama won't speak of Lucy anymore, and Grandmama hasn't shed a tear. If they did, this might be easier. Come to think of it, Tillie hadn't cried over Lucy either. It was amazing how grief could be so greedy as to take away everything, even tears.

"It must be difficult, having Tom ill as well."

"It is. One day, he's crippled by headaches. Another, his digestion is off. He has rashes, and his balance is terrible. His hands and feet burn like they're in the fire. No matter what we cook, we can't coax his appetite. He's pale as a ghost."

"Oh, poor Tom! Is he well enough for a visit today? I would love to say hello."

"Of course. I'll check to see if he can take a visitor, but he's been quite weak all day." She ushered them into the examination room, ducked out, and closed the door.

Ada took out yarn and a crochet needle from her pocket and busied herself by the window as Tillie perused the enormous bookcase. A thin book caught her eye: *Alcohol, Tobacco, and Opium, and Their Effects on the Human System*, by Thomas R. Baker.

She pulled it off the shelf, placed it on a table, and licked her fingertip to turn the pages.

Opium

> *Opium is the dried juice of a species of poppy which is cultivated in China and India. Morphine is one of its many alkaloids, and laudanum and paregoric are prepared from it. It forms the soothing constituent of various patent medicines, such as soothing syrups, pain killers, liniment, cholera mixtures, etc.*

She scanned the page, her finger landing on opium's effects.

Sleep. Pain relief. The text read, "It is, therefore, a valuable medicine."

"Of course it is," Tillie said.

> *It, however, stimulates the brain, and in large doses induces a dreamy, unnatural condition, in which the judgment is warped and the imagination becomes extremely vivid. Even after the victim becomes able to direct his mind properly he is still under the opium influence, for there has been created in him the desire for more of the drug. The craving must be satisfied even at the expense of all self-control, and thus a habit is acquired, and the person becomes a slave to it.*

Tillie shook her head. "I have a broken bone," she said to nobody, because Ada wasn't listening. On the next page, she perked at the sight of a familiar word.

> *Other Narcotics*
> *Absinthe, a liquid containing (besides alcohol, water, etc.) oil of wormwood, which is obtained from the tops and leaves of a plant called absinthe or wormwood, Indian Hemp, the dried tops of a plant, Haschish, a preparation from Indian Hemp, and Chloral, are narcotics which will produce serious effects upon the system, and should be used only on the advice of a physician.*

Oh. She'd had no idea absinthe was a narcotic. It made sense, given how she'd felt like she was floating after one small glass. Perhaps Lucy had been given too much. She might have been unable to defend herself, nay, even scream, when she was attacked.

The door opened, and Tillie quickly replaced the slim book on the shelf.

"Reading again, are we? You've a curious mind," Dr. Erikkson said. He did not seem charmed by the notion. "Now let's see how that clavicle is doing."

The doctor pulled closed the curtain on the window even farther so that the lit fire provided the only light, and he had her sit down on the chaise. He carefully palpated the bone and tested her range of motion, noting when she winced.

"Excellent, excellent. You can wear the sling for only six hours a day and stretch the shoulder twice a day."

"I think the laudanum really helped to heal it," Tillie said.

"Mm-hmm."

"Mama doesn't think I should use it. She doesn't see how it helps me sleep and keeps the muscles—how did you say? Relaxed, so they let the bone heal better?"

"Yes. It's a fact. But the bone has already come together, so it's doubtful you'll need the medicine much longer."

"I see." Tillie frowned. "But when I take it, I feel better here." She touched her lower belly. "And I'm less nervous and uncomfortable."

"Uncomfortable, where?"

Tillie gestured from her head to her feet. "Everywhere."

"Ah. You likely had a nervous disorder before the bone break. A common affliction in young women. I see no harm in continuing for a little while longer."

"Thank you, Doctor."

As he was writing out instructions for more laudanum, she hesitated. But the question of Lucy's fate begged for answers.

"Dr. Erikkson. If I may. There was another news article about a killing with bites to the neck, just like my poor sister, Lucy."

"Go on." His pen continued to scratch the paper.

Tillie tempered her voice. "Do you think vampires exist?"

Dr. Erikkson rolled his eyes. "You are reading too many novels, Miss Pembroke. Try reading Fordyce's *Sermons to Young Women* instead. They have a steadying effect on delicate constitutions."

"But do you think vampires are real? I know it's an odd question, but you're a man of science. Could it be possible?"

Dr. Erikkson sighed. "Humans need more than just blood to survive. They need a healthful variety of foods. Vegetal, ideally, if you subscribe to Sylvester Graham's theories. Unless . . ."

"Unless what?" Tillie said.

"Well, there are situations where a person would crave certain foods due to a dearth of nutrients in the diet. A lack of salt will cause salt craving. Perhaps a craving might occur, for example, if someone lacked mineral nutrients." He shook his head. "But to this extreme route—it is unlikely. It would be easier to procure a gallon of cow's blood from the slaughterhouses, for free, than stalk and kill a person. And eating a good roast beef would supply hematological nutrients in a more . . . socially acceptable . . . fashion. No," he said, seemingly gathering himself, then heading for the door, "I suspect the killer is not of the human variety, Miss Pembroke. They had better check with the New York Zoological Society. I hear they are gathering all manner of beasts for the park they are building in the Bronx."

"Of course."

Dr. Erikkson opened the door and called for his wife. "Mrs. Eppley is to come by soon for her gout. I need to prepare a poultice. Please see Miss Pembroke out, will you?"

"Of course," Mrs. Erikkson said in clipped, quick words. "And will you be able to check on Tom afterward?"

The doctor stepped out and shut the door. Tillie heard a few angry phrases—"What did I tell you? Never question me; I've told you before"—before the door opened again. Dr. Erikkson was gone, and Mrs. Erikkson looked like a shell of a woman.

"Very well, very well," she said, as if responding to a question that had never come. "Let me see you out. Thank you for coming." She blinked rapidly.

"Oh, Mrs. Erikkson. I forgot—I was going to call on your son. He seemed so kind the last time I was here. May I say hello?"

"What? Tom? Oh. Well, my husband does not approve of visitors—he's afraid Tom will be exhausted from the effort." She glanced over her shoulder and saw the corridor was quiet and empty. "Well. Just for a moment. You must be very quiet. I'm sure it will brighten his entire week to see you!"

Ada stood to accompany them, but Tillie motioned for her to wait.

"Ada, I'll be ready in just a few minutes. Mrs. Erikkson will be with me."

"Very well, Miss."

Tillie followed Mrs. Erikkson down a narrow hallway. A modest kitchen was located near the back of the house, complete with a maid scrubbing a set of pots with sand. When she heard them walking by, she watched them with twitchy, nervous eyes. Off to the right, Mrs. Erikkson opened a door into what might be a parlor but had been made into a bedroom on the main floor.

It smelled musty—not of dust, but of medicines and camphor that stung the nose. The bed was against a wall, the shades were drawn, and a fireplace was crackling. Pans of water of various sizes sat on the floor, and the carpet was stained with brown splotches. Books rose in unsteady piles across a table that held an empty plate and cup and a bowl of uneaten stew. A large wooden tray contained no less than twenty or thirty bottles of medicine in tidy rows.

"Where is he?" Tillie asked timidly.

"Go away." A voice sounded from under a lumpy mess of blankets on the bed.

"Now, Tom. It's a nice lady. The one you met a few weeks ago—Miss Pembroke. She's come to call on you."

"Father won't allow it" came the muffled voice.

"I can leave, if you like," Tillie said.

"Ow! Confound this knife—it bit me again!" came a howl from the kitchen.

"Oh dear. The maid is ruining herself washing the dishes. I'll be back in a moment," Mrs. Erikkson said. She rushed out of the room and down the hall, where she could be heard muttering, "Don't hold the sharp edge when it's soapy, Beatrice. How many times do I have to tell you? I'll get a bandage."

There was a chair near the bed, and Tillie sat down. "Your maid may get rabies from your silverware," she said.

No response.

"I . . . just wanted to say hello."

Still no response.

"May I ask you a question?"

The lump on the bed twitched. "My bowels are twisted up, and I've got headaches and spinal spasms and arthritis in twenty-two joints, and I'm half-blind from fevers. Are you satisfied?"

"I wasn't going to ask you what ailed you," Tillie said haughtily. "It's poor manners. You were so much happier when I last saw you."

"I'm not a performing monkey. I cannot be happy when it's convenient to other people. I'm *ill*."

"I'm sorry you aren't feeling well." Tillie sighed. There was no way she could ask him about Lucy. It was too selfish to expect him to help when he suffered so. "I'll let you be, then. Good afternoon, Mr. Erikkson. I do hope you feel better."

She stood and went to the door. Mrs. Erikkson was now discussing liniments for a burn. That maid was awfully accident prone.

"Wait!" Tom said.

Tillie turned around. Tom had suddenly sat up in bed. He was thin as ever, with those dark-purplish shadows under his eyes. His eyes opened wider with recognition.

"Oh! It *is* you. I thought Mother was playing a trick, trying to get me to wake up." He sat, Turkish-style, with his blankets still piled around him. "Is it about the weather? Please don't speak about the weather. It's dreadfully boring." He coughed a few times.

"No. I came to ask about my sister." Tillie sat back down on the chair. She took a steady breath, steeling herself to speak without trembling. "Lucy. She's the one that died in the park, with the . . ." She touched her neck. "It looked like she had been bitten by a vampire. You said you saw her that day."

"I did. She was with her maid. They had a row."

"About what?" Tillie leaned in.

Tom opened his mouth and paused for a beat before he spoke. "Will you dance with me?"

Tillie furrowed her eyebrows. "They argued about dancing?"

"No. Will you dance with me? And then I'll answer your question."

Tillie blushed. What a forward question, and how utterly inappropriate. He was still in his nightshirt. And his mother was no longer in the room. Ada would come looking for her if she dawdled for long.

"I know it's a terribly strange question, but you see, I'm dying a slow death, though Mother refuses to believe this. I've never been out of my house since I was six years old. I don't want to die without experiencing a few things that other people do."

"Oh."

"It's a mercy dance. For a dying man."

"I don't think that—"

"What would you do? What would you ask for, if you knew you would die soon?" he asked in earnest.

What would she do? Find Lucy's killer. That was first in her mind. And Tom wouldn't give her more information until she danced with him.

But as Tom stared at her expectantly, Tillie thought of her life and what she'd done. And she thought of Lucy and what she would never do.

What would Lucy want? Marriage, children? Her own house and servants to command? Lucy had never spoken of those things with longing. But she'd enjoyed going to help the children at the Foundling Hospital. Bringing baskets of goods, asking for donations for a new water pump or a supply of new frocks for the girls' wing. But that was Lucy, and Lucy had never been given the opportunity to answer Tom's question.

What did Tillie want?

"I would like . . . to know more. About the world," Tillie said. "More than I can learn where I am."

"A college education!" Tom said.

"More than that." A degree wasn't quite enough. "To look beyond what I can see. To know more than what people know. How things work. The truths behind secrets." She clenched a fist, unable to say more. She wanted the world to open up all its treasures, to reveal the whats and whys and hows. And something else. "I'd want to know more about my father."

"What happened to your father?"

Tillie hesitated again. She was so used to being told not to speak of him, but her mother and grandmother were not in the room.

"He died when I was a child. My mother refuses to speak of him."

"Why?" Tom sat up straighter, and his eyes sparkled a bit.

"He was a scholar working to debunk the resurgence in the practice of phrenology. He grew ill one day and died very suddenly. A heart attack, I believe. I was only a child. He adored my mother, and she him, but now she won't speak of him."

"He sounds wonderful."

"He was poor. An unforgivable sin! I believe my mother married him for love. And that was unforgivable, too, perhaps." She covered her mouth. "Oh, I'm so sorry. I've said too much."

"No, indeed. You have your desires, and they are perfectly acceptable. And I would like to have one dance, once in my life, with a lady who wasn't my mother."

"You've danced with your mother?" Tillie asked, smiling.

"She's offered, and I've declined. I've waited for a more suitable partner."

"Very well. For a dying man—though to be honest, you don't look quite there."

Tom grinned as he scrambled from the bed. His face was so thin his eyes looked unusually large in his face, like a boy who'd taken up a man's body but hadn't quite adjusted to his lodgings yet.

"Believe me, I'm not rushing anything." Tom held out his arms. Beneath his nightshirt he wore soft wool trousers, as if he'd been inclined to get up and about but then failed halfway through the effort. His feet were bony and bare.

"There's no music," she noted, as he put his hand on her waist near her bound arm and held her good hand. He smelled strongly of camphor.

"I guess we can pretend there's a waltz playing. That's another thing I'd like to do someday. Hear music that doesn't come from an Edison phonograph."

Soon, they were gently waltzing in a tiny circle within his sickroom, in silence. Tom's hand in hers seemed to tremble, and his steps were staggered and unsure. It didn't take long before he was perspiring and a little short of breath. Tillie stopped dancing.

"I fear you'll exhaust yourself, Mr. Erikkson."

"Oh. Please call me Tom." He let go of her, rather slowly, and returned to his bed. "That was lovely. I can't thank you enough. Sometimes, books are not adequate to keep my imagination going. A person needs to really live to feel alive sometimes."

"Yes, I suppose so."

"Otherwise, we're all just in our little jail cells." He looked at her meaningfully.

Was he insinuating that Tillie wasn't truly living or free? She shook her head. "You've got your name written on my dance card, so to speak. Can you answer my question now?"

"Of course." He untangled his blankets, gently laying them over his legs. "Your sister and her maid were waiting for Father, for he was busy with another patient, you see. Anyway, they were arguing, quite loudly."

"Lucy and Betty? About what, may I ask?"

"Your sister said she wanted to go to the museum alone, and the maid refused. She said something about not sneaking about, like other times.'"

"Other times? What other times?" Tillie asked.

"I don't know. And then your sister said something about stealing, and the maid grew angry again. Mother came in to offer them some tea, and that was the end of it."

Of course. Betty had been stealing, or so the gossip went. Perhaps Lucy had been chiding her for it, and Betty had grown angry, followed her, and killed her. But why kill Lucy in such an odd way?

Tillie stood up. She needed to find Betty. Or take an ax to the side table of Lucy's room, if she couldn't pick the lock after all. Something was hidden in that drawer; she knew it.

"Thank you, Tom. This was very helpful." She paused, then added, "Thank you for listening to me. About my father."

He nodded, and she went to the door. At the edge of the table were no less than three large brown bottles of laudanum and a polished brown box with brass hinges and clasp. She pointed at the bottles. "We share something in common. I take this medicine too."

"As does the worse half of New York," Tom said. "But the morphine injections are better. It works ever so much faster, and the nausea is far less."

"Really? It sounds painful."

"Oh no. Just a tiny prick under the skin. I'm used to it now. Father says it's a gift of the gods. Or at least, Asclepius."

Tillie didn't know who Asclepius was. Perhaps a chemist. Once she'd closed Tom's door behind her, she pulled out her small notebook from her sleeve, leaned it upon her wrist, and wrote, *Asclepius—who is this?*

She left with Ada, but not before Mrs. Erikkson plied her with a baked bun studded with raisins—she looked pale, Mrs. Erikkson said, and the food would do her good. But on the way home, Tillie forgot about the morsel.

There was a second person dead, after all. Something must be done.

Perhaps she should make a visit to Albert Weber's family. She wondered how they might respond to a call just after midnight.

CHAPTER 10

How good and thoughtful he is; the world seems full of good men—even if there are monsters in it.

—Mina Harker

Tillie went straight to her bedroom, dosed herself, and took to her bed. She refused the requests to attend dinner. Her mother visited, murmuring that she hoped this behavior wouldn't become a habit. Tillie waved her off. What she wanted was time to think—and some time to unthink everything.

A passage from *Dracula* played in her mind like a phonograph, over and over again. She whispered passages like a prayer, as the knot of wretched suffering in her body uncoiled like a drunken serpent.

> *The vampire live on, and cannot die by mere passing of the time; he can flourish when that he can fatten on the blood of the living . . .*
>
> *He can even grow younger . . .*
>
> *He throws no shadow; he make in the mirror no reflect . . .*
>
> *He can transform himself to wolf . . . he can be as bat . . .*

He can come in mist . . . on moonlight rays as elemental dust . . .
He can see in the dark . . .
He can do all these things, yet he is not free.

Tillie sighed and turned over in her bed. A vampire was shackled, it seemed, to the lusts and needs of his body. Tillie, too, felt her world as a closed casket, always around her, always constricting her. But unlike Count Dracula, she could enter a house without an invitation (rude as it might be). She could move about during the day, her power not extinguished at the rise of the sun.

She thought about how other people were tethered to their homes. Tom and Dr. Erikkson. And now Tillie.

"Oh," she said faintly, before yawning. "If the murders happen during daylight, then it can't possibly be a vampire. And anyone who cannot stand the sight of a crucifix . . . or a branch of wild rose . . ."

As unconsciousness closed about her, she thought to herself, I ought to start wearing a cross. Just in case.

Tillie woke up around midnight, creaky and aching. It was nearly time for Ada to bring their watchman some delicacies. But she had no reason to leave tonight. She wouldn't meet Ian for several more days. And she had no idea how to find out where Albert Weber's family lived or even where Betty was.

A sudden intake of breath accompanied an idea: Of course.

She put on a linen robe and descended the stairs. The whole house was darkened, but Tillie was growing accustomed to the nighttime. At least at night, she felt freer. But what life was that? One where she had freedom only at night? It was more vampirish than human.

The door near the rear of the house was cracked open; she pushed it open farther. Sure enough, there was Ada sharing a cup of coffee and a plate of biscuits. John's hand went to Ada's waist, pulling her close, as his other hand brushed crumbs off her lips. Ada giggled and pushed him away.

Lately the words of Bram Stoker were constantly on her mind. Van Helsing had championed the virtues of humanity, saying, "We have on our side power of combination—a power denied to the vampire kind; we have resources of science; we are free to act and think; and . . . so far as our powers extend, they are unfettered, and we are free to use them."

Tillie's instinct was to stay hidden, watch, observe. Find the answers on her own. But she needed more than her own limitations could provide. She needed to embrace her power. She needed to act like a Pembroke, not a Tillie.

"Do this for Lucy," she said to herself. She took a breath of encouragement and pushed the door open with a thump. John and Ada jumped apart, and Ada ran to her.

"Miss! Do you need something? I was just . . . I was just bringing John something to eat, like you suggested. And coffee."

Tillie tried to keep her voice low yet strong. "Thank you, Ada. I need to speak to John for a moment."

Ada curtsied, glanced guiltily at John, and skittered inside to the kitchen. Tillie walked over to him.

Pretend you're Grandmama Josephine. Come, Tillie!

"Excuse my appearance, Mr. O'Toole," she said steadily. "My illness usually keeps me confined to the house. May I ask . . . how is your new post? Any difficulties with your duties?"

"None, Miss." He looked straight at Tillie, a flintiness in his eye. He wasn't afraid of much, this one.

"And are you happy working here?"

"Indeed, I am, as I have said to your grandmother."

"Excellent. Well, I will be happy to pretend that you're not taking up the salary we provide so you can break your fasts while on duty."

John said nothing, just stared.

"I require your assistance regarding my sister's attack. I need to find two addresses. My family need not know—they have enough to concern themselves with." She handed him a piece of paper with the names Betty Novak and Albert Weber written neatly. "The other servants say Betty lives near the Brooklyn Bridge, but we don't know where exactly. And Albert Weber was just in the news. Can you find out where they live?"

He scanned the names. "I can try. I still have friends working at my old precinct. I can ask them."

"I'd be grateful if you could."

John took the paper and put it in his pocket. He had a strange look on his face, which made Tillie stop before she went back inside.

"Is something wrong?" she asked.

He took a small step closer. "It must be difficult to endure."

"What must be difficult?"

"Everything." He studied her with such intensity that Tillie wished to shrink away and run. What did he mean? Lucy's death? The pain? Being trapped within this house?

Tillie stepped back. "Well. Thank you again."

She stayed awake much of the night, attempting to unlock Lucy's table. But still it refused to give up its treasures. All the while, she wondered if she'd made a mistake—if John O'Toole would simply confess all to her grandmother. Then she'd lose Ada, too, her only ally in the house. She couldn't chance the wait for him to return to her with the addresses. After all, what if Albert Weber and Lucy were not the only ones to die such a death? What if there were more to come?

She had to get out during the daylight hours and in a way that was sanctioned by her family. After an unrefreshing slumber of several morning hours, she awoke with the solution.

"Oh!" she said, sitting up quickly. It was nearly noon, but not too late. She rang the bell, and Ada came quickly. "I need to get ready."

"For what, Miss?"

"Why, to see James Cutter."

⟞⟝

It turned out Tillie didn't need to ask for James to visit her. He'd been leaving cards for her while she slept and was due to call on her for an outing the next day. He'd even sent a parcel that morning, unasked for: the accompanying note read, *To help speed your healing, a small distraction. A little bird named Ada told me you might enjoy this.*

It was a copy of *Dracula.* Tillie nearly fell off her chaise at the sight of it. Who knew James Cutter, who seemed to do everything properly, who would order a circle to be a more proper square, would gift such a book to Tillie?

That evening, just after midnight, someone knocked on the door. Tillie ignored it. She'd been awake since her afternoon nap and was engrossed in reading *Dracula.* She had taken to reading it aloud, as every sentence felt washed anew when spoken.

"'For life be, after all, only a waitin' for somethin' else than what we're doin'; and death be all that we can rightly depend on. But I'm content, for it's comin' to me, my deary, and comin' quick.'" Tillie licked a finger and turned a page. "Well," she said. "That's outright depressing, if I do say so myself."

The knock came again, and this time Ada cracked the door open.

"Miss Tillie? John has sent you a note." She handed her a folded note, and Tillie read it with eager eyes.

It was an address for Albert Weber.

37 East 9th Street

4th floor

It was in the heart of Kleindeutschland, near Tompkins Square Park. Tillie flipped the paper over.

"Only this note? Nothing more?" Tillie asked.

"No. Did you expect another?"

"I did. Ada, please tell John that I need the other information. His job depends upon it." She smiled. "Could you perhaps convince him to try harder? If it takes more time for you to speak to him, I would understand. Three visits a night, with more refreshments?"

"Oh. Perhaps I could do that," Ada said. "If you wish."

Ada had the utmost difficulty hiding a smile. Lately, Ada had faint dark circles under her eyes from losing sleep, but she also fairly skipped about the house with a tiny mischievous grin. Tillie'd overheard Ada gossiping with the other maids about who danced with whom at the dance halls and who was getting married. Ada seemed afire with having a romance of her own.

The next day at one o'clock, the doorbell rang, and James was ushered inside. By God, he was handsome: broad of shoulder, slim of waist, with those cheekbones that were sharp as creased paper. How had she not noticed for so long? He wore a fine striped suit with a buttoned vest in forest green. Tillie was ready, wearing a dress of dark aubergine (Mother had allowed her to occasionally skip the black dresses in favor of colors that seemed spun out of mist and storms). He was ushered into the salon, where he greeted her mother and grandmother, dutifully asking about their health. Tillie entered the room and smiled, and James's face lit at her entrance. He kissed her cheek.

"You look beautiful. You're starting to get your bloom back," he said.

"I didn't know I had any to begin with," Tillie said.

"You did. Yours is the kind of beauty that has to be searched for, but like any treasure, it's worth the finding." He held out his hand. "Shall we?"

Such a compliment. The attention had its effect of warming Tillie but confusing her as well. He was only just this attentive to Lucy recently. It felt misplaced and wrong. Behind him, her mother and grandmother nodded almost simultaneously with pleasure. Tillie had not received such automatic approval from them both since she had stopped sucking her thumb at age five.

"Where shall we go?" James said as the door shut behind him. He had a rich equipage waiting at the curb. The balmy air was lovely to inhale. Several hansom cabs trotted by, and an electric car drove painfully slowly down the street.

"I've a favor to ask," Tillie said. "It's an odd request, but it will get me a little air and change of scenery."

"Oh? Perhaps out to Long Island?"

"I was thinking more in terms of . . . Tompkins Square Park?"

James paused and cocked his head. "I'm sorry, where?"

"Well, near Tompkins. There's a friend I'd like to call on. If that's all right with you."

"It's not very . . ." James was looking for the right words, and Tillie knew what he was thinking. The area was dense with German immigrants, pushcart vendors, and beer gardens—the kind visited by the working poor of the neighborhood. It was no glossy green avenue of stately oaks. "Are you sure you wouldn't rather go elsewhere? A trip down to the Battery? We might watch the steamships enter the harbor."

"No, thank you. It's nice to see how different parts of the island are evolving, don't you think?"

James nodded tepidly. Tillie had actually never had this thought until she said it, but it was true. Manhattan was developing in ways that struck her with awe—or puzzlement. As a child, she wouldn't have thought that she would see restaurant and theater marquees lit with electric lights all along the Tenderloin district. She had not thought electric cars would hum down the street next to a barouche. Nor had she expected to see the telegraph lines that knifed across the sky being felled with shouts of "Timber!" as the poles were brought down and the lines buried underground, after the horrible blizzard in 1888.

James's driver opened the door, and Tillie was surprised to see that the carriage was not empty.

"Dorrie!" she exclaimed. "Hazel!"

"Good afternoon, Tillie!" Dorothy said, her face lighting with a smile. She was resplendent in a melon-colored poult-de-soie dress. Hazel was wearing a sober gray poplin, but the striking beauty of her large eyes and rosebud mouth could never quite be hidden. "Hazel and I were returning from a trip to the milliners, and James drove by. He offered us a ride home, but when he said he was coming by to see you, we thought we would surprise you!"

"Oh," Tillie said meekly. "Hello."

The carriage seated four. Tillie sat beside Hazel and James beside Dorothy. Tillie wondered if Dorothy had planned the seating as such. Not that Tillie wished to be so close to him. But now that they were seated together, it seemed like Dorothy looped her arm in James's in a certain proprietary way.

"Mathilda would like to see a friend near Tompkins Square Park," James said after they were all inside.

"That far downtown? Really?" Dorothy's eyebrows rose. "Hazel, isn't it just like Tillie to be exploring strange new places?"

"Of course," Hazel said in her benign way. "Tillie likes to learn."

"I suppose we'll drop you off before we go?" Tillie suggested.

"But that's the opposite direction," Dorothy said. She leaned on James. "The more the merrier! And we've missed you so, Tillie."

As they rode on, James chatted with Dorothy, who seemed to monopolize his conversation. Hazel leaned toward Tillie.

"How are you feeling?"

"A little claustrophobic," Tillie replied in honesty.

Hazel smiled. "No, I meant your broken bone."

"Oh. It's all right. It's far from better."

"And how are you otherwise?"

"Otherwise? Oh." She meant after Lucy's death. "I don't know how to be."

"Of course you don't," Hazel said and patted her good arm. "You can read pamphlets on how to properly mourn a person. How many weeks before you can stop wearing black and crape. How to do your hair and when to leave a card. But there is really never a guidebook for your heart, is there?"

Tillie shook her head. "No, there isn't." The significance suddenly crept up on her. "Have you lost someone, Hazel?"

"I have. But not one that I can ever speak of." She faced the window, her hands unconsciously going to her belly. Had she lost a child? Hazel was not married. She spent all her time catering to Dorothy's needs. Such was the position of a lady's companion. She had a roof and good food and good clothing and society, but all for the purpose of keeping Dorothy Harriman content. She was a higher-priced dog with better manners and opposable thumbs.

The scenery changed outside their window as they passed the southern edge of Central Park. Tillie's thoughts went to Ian and their walk beneath the arc lamps. She would meet him again soon. Being in this carriage reminded her how easy it was to speak to him. No frills or furbelows regarding etiquette. In this carriage, she was gently being suffocated.

Dorothy chattered on as they passed the Waldorf-Astoria and, a while later, Madison Square Park. It was green and open, with electric streetcars running down its flanks; what was once swamp and a paupers' graveyard now boasted a bronze statue of William H. Seward. They turned left onto Broadway and continued past Union Square and its lovely oval green.

Down at Ninth Street, the city seemed to have folded closer on itself, and life bloomed with vigor. Groceries were crammed next to churches and dry goods stores, with pushcart vendors hawking tins, apples, and trousers to everyone walking by. Children burst around a corner, chasing an india rubber ball. This was Kleindeutschland, where the sounds of chattering German dialects filled the air.

The Webers' tenement was one of the nicer ones, perhaps only five years old. The sidewalk outside it was populated with pink-cheeked children. One mother, knitting something of gray wool, spoke rushed German to a cluster of sandy-haired toddlers. Two small mottled dogs fought over a scrap of food.

"Here we are," Tillie said as cheerfully as possible.

"Are you going in there?" Dorothy asked, eyes round as saucers.

Tillie was here; this was what she had set out to do. But now James was looking as if he might catch his death just by opening the door, and Hazel was quietly taking in their surroundings. Hazel seemed the least surprised by what she saw—it was the gaze of someone who recognized that their life was one blink away from a different life altogether.

"I'll just be a moment. I have to . . . deliver something," Tillie said. She looked to the driver, who seemed alarmed that he was to let her out here.

"Oh. Are you doing what Lucy used to do? Bringing some castoffs to the poor? Really, Tillie, it would be safer just to drop them off at a church," James said. "This was not what I had in mind when your mother and I agreed to allow you some fresh air."

"I'll be fine," Tillie said. Truth be told, she was terrified. She'd never been in this part of town, never been inside a strange building with strange people. Her hand shook as she readied herself to leave the carriage.

"James! Go with her," Hazel said. "She oughtn't go unaccompanied. Especially—"

Especially after what happened to Lucy, was what she did not say. Dorothy seemed aghast that Hazel had suggested James leave them.

"Very well," James said. He forced a gallant smile.

As they stepped onto the sidewalk, dodging bits of newspaper that came rolling down the sidewalk like printed tumbleweeds, James placed Tillie's good arm about his.

"Stay close. Let's make this brief, shall we? Where is your parcel?"

"Well . . ."

They paused outside the front door of the tenement. The children who had been playing outside, the knitter, all stopped what they were doing to stare at them.

"I thought you said you brought something to drop off." He looked about her. "Mathilda. What is going on?"

"I'm not dropping off a donation. I have to speak to someone here."

"Someone is *expecting* you? *Here?*"

If she told him the truth, he might tell her parents. He might frog-march her back into the carriage and right back home. But there was no other way.

"I've come to ask the family of Albert Weber how he died. He's the lad who was killed the same way Lucy was." James's mouth opened, and she pushed the words out before he could chastise her. "I can't sit still without knowing what happened to her. I have to know. I must."

James closed his mouth. He arched his back to examine the facade of the tenement—brown and dingy, but with windows open and laundry cheerfully waving outside. The children were now racing crickets on strings down the pavement, and the knitting lady had disappeared.

"This is madness, Mathilda. Let the police do their job."

"They haven't done anything. The person who did this to Lucy has taken the life of a child now. I can't stand idly by. I cannot."

James looked at her appraisingly, somewhere between the glance one might give a raw diamond, estimating its worth, and a pile of horse manure on the street, wondering if it could be avoided.

"Very well. I won't stop you," he said at last. "And I won't tell anyone, as long as I can accompany you on these ventures. I'll not lose you like I lost Lucy."

Tillie felt her face untwist into a smile that surely lit the day. James opened the front door of the tenement, and the darkness inside swallowed them. A stench rose from deeper within, and they strode forward, their footsteps moist beneath their soles. The hallway was strewn with discarded newspapers, and black dirt caked the corners and floors. Tobacco spittle stained the once-cream-colored walls.

James held on to her arm tightly as they maneuvered up the stairs. On the fourth floor, they both paused to catch their breath. There were four apartments. Tillie knocked on the first she saw, hoping it was the right one.

A woman answered the door. She was middle aged with light-brown hair combed tightly back from her head. She had the wrung-out look and red-lined eyes of someone who had been crying for days.

Mrs. Weber. It must be.

"Yes?" she asked. A man with brown hair and a beard appeared at her elbow, tall but bowed over, as if he'd spent a lifetime chopping logs.

The man spoke. "Was ist das? Wer sind diese Leute?"

"Mrs. Weber? My name is Tillie Pembroke, and this is James Cutter. May we speak to you? About your son Albert?" Tillie asked.

"No. We already spoke to the police." She had a strong German accent. When Tillie hesitated, she began to shut the door.

Tillie put her hand out. "Please. My sister—she died the same way. I just have a few questions. Please."

The door halted its closing. The lady's eyes still shone, blue and clear as glass in their red rims. James seemed so out of his element that he'd temporarily lost his ability to speak.

The woman opened the door. "After this, no more callers."

Inside was a small room that seemed to act as kitchen, dining room, sewing station, playroom, and bedroom. Or at least, one bedroom. Two doors led to other rooms, and Tillie could hear the sounds of children within them. The walls were papered with a repeating pattern of clocks, an onerous reminder to hurry, hurry, hurry. Smoke stains from the cookstove darkened the paper, which peeled near the ceiling. A whatnot stood in the corner, holding a single framed photo of a fuzzy couple and a few figurines centered with care on embroidered linen circles.

Tillie was overwhelmed by the poverty of the room. She wished she had brought something—food, perhaps, or a blanket, or even sewing thread, the way Lucy would have done. Why, the food we don't finish at our supper could feed this whole family for a day, she thought. And yet, Mrs. Weber had a straightness to her posture that read self-sufficiency. Her clothes were old yet very clean. In a glance, Tillie could see that she was the caretaker of her children, a strong worker, a provider for their bleak and tiny pantry. There was no time to mourn, but she must somehow mourn nevertheless, in the fractions of her day.

"Sit," the woman said as her husband disappeared into another room. "We talk together, and then no more. Too many visitors. I have work to do. Sit." She gestured to a chair.

"Thank you. We won't take much of your time," Tillie said, sitting. James stood behind her, like a human backrest. "Who else has been visiting? The police?"

A tiny explosion of laughter issued from a room behind them. One small child, about four, ran out screaming in glee and hid behind her mother's apron.

Another child followed—a boy, about six, sitting astride a man who ambled in on all fours, the horse to the child's "Giddy! Giddy!" As the man/horse looked up, Tillie jumped out of her seat in surprise.

"Ian!" she exclaimed.

CHAPTER 11

How blessed are some people, whose lives have no fears, no dreads; to whom sleep is a blessing that comes nightly, and brings nothing but sweet dreams.

—Lucy Westenra

"What are you doing here?" Tillie asked, all astonishment.

Ian startled and tapped the leg of the boy on his back. "Das reicht jetzt, Carl," he said. The boy tumbled off and ran after his sister into the corner, where they began playing with a few tin soldiers. Ian slowly got to his feet, not bothering to wipe the dust from his knees and hands.

"What are you doing here?" Ian said.

"That's what I asked you."

"I think we have the same answer," Ian said, smirking.

James cleared his throat.

"Oh," Tillie said, hand to her mouth. "I'm sorry. James Cutter, this is Ian Metzger."

"How do you know Tillie?" Ian asked. There was a slight edge to his voice.

"You mean Miss Pembroke?" James replied icily.

Tillie felt her face grow hot and her heart throb from discomfort. "Ian, James is . . . was . . . Lucy's fiancé. James, Ian is . . . he's . . ."

"I sell papers," Ian said, shaking James's hand. James discreetly wiped his hand on his jacket.

"Sit." Mrs. Weber motioned to everyone. There was only one other chair available, so James and Ian had to content themselves with sitting too close to each other on a decrepit chaise longue by the window. They gave each other wary glances. "Five minutes. Then I must work."

"I didn't know that you and Mr. Metzger were acquainted," Tillie began.

"We weren't until about ten minutes ago, but her kids kept interrupting, so . . ." Ian shrugged. "Let's start from the beginning, shall we?"

Mrs. Weber nodded. "I tell you what I tell police," she began. "Albert is very sick for months, after eating some food brought by his uncle in Germany. His stomach is very bad. My medicine does not work. So I take him to the drugstore, and still the medicines do not work. We try leeches, calomel. Then, *Durchfall*. So much *Durchfall*. We try new medicine, new drink. Smells like . . . what is word? *Lakritze*. Is green color."

"Absinthe?" Tillie asked. Ian caught her eye, and he frowned.

"I don't know the name. People say wormwood is good?" Mrs. Weber shrugged. From another room, Mr. Weber spoke angrily in German, and there was a thump on the wall. "And then Albert, he gets better. He gain weight, he look good. He plays on the street with the other children. A man gives some children some sugar candy, and Albert, he goes away. We look everywhere. And next day, they find him by the reservoir. *Leer. Kein Blut.*"

Ian translated. "Empty. No blood."

"And the police? Do they know who did it?"

"Well, the man who gave the children candy, this is what we think." Mrs. Weber looked at a clock on the wall. It had only an hour hand; it was nearly three o'clock.

"What did the man look like?" James asked.

"The children say, hunched over. Wears an old hat, says not much, only offer candy. But Albert went to him quickly, like he knows this man. We were upstairs when he gone."

"It was daytime?" Tillie asked.

"Yes. Late afternoon."

"And Albert had bites too? On his neck?" Tillie curved her fingers, like fangs about to bite.

"Yes. We think, *der Vampir. Der Blutsauger.* We not think they are here, in America."

"You think they are real?"

"Stories, they always come from somewhere," Mrs. Weber said. She stood up. "And now, I must work. Please." She indicated the door. Tillie, the last to exit the tiny apartment, turned and gripped the door.

"I am sorry—for Albert."

"And I am sorry for your sister," she said. She nodded abruptly, as if that was all the sadness she had time for that day.

Mrs. Weber closed the door. Downstairs, on the sidewalk, James appeared to have woken up from a bad dream, but the dream had kept going. Dorothy was gawking from inside the carriage, and Hazel was holding her arm, trying to keep her from jumping out and joining them.

"What are you doing here?" Tillie asked Ian.

"How do you know this man?" James demanded.

"We met outside of Dr. Erikkson's office," Tillie explained. "He sold me the paper that told how Lucy had been killed."

James raised his eyebrows. "And that constitutes a formal introduction?"

"James. Please. He's trying to help."

"Why?" James asked.

Ian, watching the both of them, seemed more amused than annoyed. "Tillie, I'll see you tonight. We have a lot to talk about," he said, waving casually. He walked down the street, interrupting a game of kick the can by kicking said can far up the sidewalk. The children cheered. Ian turned a corner and was gone.

"Tonight? Are you going to see that person tonight? Alone?"

"No!" Tillie lied. She wasn't seeing him in the way that James thought. So perhaps it wasn't really lying.

"Really, Mathilda. You ought not be speaking with such a person. It's too dangerous. He could be the one who hurt Lucy," James said.

"No, he couldn't have hurt Lucy—or Albert. It's not possible."

"And you know this why? He seems awfully interested. I'd say almost obsessed."

"No, James. I truly think he's only being helpful. He's lost family too." Unconsciously, she had put her hand to her heart.

"A man like that doesn't give without wanting something in return." He leaned in closer. "You forget, sometimes, Mathilda, who you are. You're an heiress. A sole heiress, now."

Tillie was tired of arguing. "I should go home" was all she said. "My shoulder hurts, and I need to rest." Which was only partially true. But she did need her medicine.

James followed her into the carriage. Tillie's insides writhed with a certain hunger and restlessness. She needed to lie down. She needed calm. Her forehead prickled with perspiration.

"She's clean worn out, she is. Visiting the poor. What a dear," Dorothy said, though Tillie couldn't miss the critical undercurrent.

"Do you carry your medicine with you?" Hazel asked softly.

Tillie shook her head. "I only have so much," she admitted. "Grandmama doesn't want me to take it."

"I'll get you whatever you need," James said. "Whenever you need. Your family is not nearly as permissive about modern medicine as others are."

When they arrived at her home, Dorothy and Hazel insisted on helping Tillie inside, shooing Ada away as they began fussing over her in the bedroom. Dorothy nagged Tillie about medicine until she disclosed her hidden stash of opium. Dorothy administered the drops herself. Tillie took them like an infant bird beseeching its mother for a worm. All the while, Hazel watched carefully, as if counting the drops.

Tillie lay back on her bed, ready to embrace the decadent pull toward slumber.

"Sleep, sweet Tillie. Losing sweet Lucy and that broken bone took so much out of you, dearest. We'll make sure you get all the medicine you need."

Tillie blinked slowly, realizing a little too late that Dorothy had probably given her too much medicine. But the effect had left her spellbound, her body feeling absent of gravity, her limbs like butter melting in hot milk.

"Sleep," Dorothy commanded.

Much later, Tillie awoke only minutes before midnight. She still wore her day dress. It appeared that Ada had brought dinner to her room, but Tillie had slept through. A plate of roast beef drowned under a congealed patty of gravy, and buttered bread next to it lay fissured and forgotten.

Tillie had overheard her mother and grandmother whispering in the hallway, when they thought Tillie slept.

"It's the Flint in her. Weak breeding, weak child."

"Hush, Mama."

"If only Lucy hadn't been so headstrong. It was her downfall."

"Was it?"

"If only they'd switched birthrights, it would never have come to this."

What had it meant? Birthrights. Did she mean if Lucy had been the second child, or did she mean something else entirely? Tillie had been too drowsy to understand it, and the comments had receded while she slept.

Tillie readied herself as quickly as she could, drinking her medicine in the small glass of wine from her dinner tray. No sling tonight. Her shoulder was stiff but well enough for a night out without it. She put some money in the pocket of her dress, slipped her notebook in there with a stub of a pencil, and went to the window to see if Ada and John were in the garden.

There was no moon tonight, hidden as it was behind a phalanx of clouds. Tillie peered through the window of Lucy's chamber, searching for them. At first, she saw nothing. The conservatory was dark, and the window was smudged. Tillie rubbed the glass with her sleeve and peered again through the circlet of clarity. A tiny movement caught her eye near the oak tree in the center of the rear property. An ornate iron bench encircled the trunk. Upon it, a mass of murky colors moved strangely, rhythmically, in the dark. Two white logs of newly cut firewood rested on the bench.

Tillie blinked, then looked again. The image instantly changed from a confusing, indecipherable mass into something far more recognizable.

It was Ada, skirts hitched up to her knees, sitting astride John O'Toole's lap. It was Ada's bare calves that shone white, not two sticks of firewood. Her garters had come undone, and her stockings had gathered around her ankles. Ada's lips were parted, her eyes closed and compressing tightly with each union of their bodies.

Tillie pushed away from the window. She wasn't sure what was more mortifying: watching them or enduring the possibility of being caught spying. She gathered her skirts, spun around, and headed down the stairs. She had no worries about John seeing her sneak away tonight.

Tillie hesitated before exiting the house. She went purposefully to the kitchen and gathered half a dozen cinnamon shortbread cakes, knotting them into a napkin. She tied them to her waist with an old silk scarf from the entryway closet and then was out the door in seconds. It might help with her nausea.

This time, everything was familiar. She headed eastward to the Third Avenue train. Studying the paper map in the station, she was happy to see that this line would take her all the way down past Cooper Union and Houston Street and split rightward onto East Broadway.

When she arrived downtown, the moon had exited from behind a wall of clouds, and electric lights lit the corners here and there. She descended the el's stairs with the other scant passengers. Behind her, the shadow of the Brooklyn Bridge rose up, its gothic arches puncturing the space between the tall stone towers. The cables rising up to those towers seemed small and spindly, but last year she had walked the bridge with Lucy and found that those cables were wide as a barrel. Nothing was what it seemed, upon closer examination.

Tillie looked about her. Ahead was a small park, irregular with walkways and trees, hiding half of City Hall, with its three rows of columns and small domed tower, behind it. This was Newspaper Row, though she did not know which building was which.

Where was Ian?

It was so strange to be here alone. A little frightening, but the heady sense of freedom and adventure outshone both sensations. She walked toward the largest building to the right of City Hall. It was more than twice as tall, with an imposing spherical top. The World Building. On the steps was a figure—no, four figures. She hadn't noticed the other three because they were small, unmoving atop the grates on the ground.

"Ian?" she asked as she approached.

Ian had a tweed cap on his head and a sheaf of papers under his arm. He lifted his finger to his lips, turning his head to the slumbering bodies next to him. When Tillie was closer, she realized they were boys. Perhaps nine or ten years old, each asleep with a set of folded hands or a pile of newspapers for a pillow.

"You made it. No escort this time?" he teased her in a whisper.

"Not this time." She sighed. "James is like a brother to me. He almost was, you know." She pointed to the boys. "Why are they sleeping here?"

"Steam grating? Because the weather is good, and it saves the five cents for a bed at the lodging house."

"Where are their parents?"

"Who knows. Lots of the newsies have parents. These are guttersnipes. But they do all right."

Tillie sighed. She wished she had sneaked more food out of their kitchen, perhaps brought a blanket. Lucy would have thought to.

"Well, I have some good news," she said. "You can keep that copy of *Dracula*. James bought me one."

"Isn't that lucky?" He wasn't smiling, though. Tillie's first instinct told her he was jealous, but then her mind reeled in the ridiculous thought. "So let's talk about this book, shall we?"

"Wait. Why did you go to see Albert Weber without telling me?" she asked.

"Hey, ain't ya gonna kiss de lady, Ian?" came a high-pitched voice behind them. Tillie whirled around to see one of the three boys grinning widely, his tousled black hair now propped on a brown hand.

"Tillie Pembroke, this is Piper," Ian began. Two more heads popped up, and one whistled low. The other whistled high. "And Sweetie and Old Man Pops."

"Oh. Hello. Nice to meet you, boys."

"I ain't no boy," said the one named Sweetie. Her brown hair was cut in short curls, her face was smudged with freckles, and if she hadn't said anything, Tillie would never have known. "An' I don't hit like no goil, eidder. Don't you fuhgeddit."

"So, you gonna smack Ian a goodun'?" asked Old Man Pops. He was sitting up now and had aggressively stuck his finger in his ear, digging out who knew what. His hair looked like a bush of yellow weeds, but his eyes had a tired look, like a parent whose children were continually misbehaving.

"No?" Tillie answered.

"You're a muttonhead if you don't know he wants de kisses. All de kisses!" barked Piper.

"Stop," Ian growled.

That made everything worse. Piper and Sweetie whooped and meowed at Ian until he took a step close to Tillie and shook his head.

"I apologize, but this is the only way they're going to shut up." He lifted her hand and kissed it. Tillie had trouble hiding a smile.

The caterwauling got worse.

"Dat ain't a kiss!" Piper yowled.

"Oh, just . . . get it over with," Tillie whispered. She tapped her cheek, and Ian leaned in. He curled his hand around her waist, and for a moment, Tillie felt like she was floating, with only her slippered toes on the ground. When nothing happened, she turned to Ian and said, "I said—"

Ian leaned in quickly. He seemed to be aiming for her cheek but landed on her mouth.

Oh. *Oh.*

She had looked up *kiss* in the dictionary once.

1. To salute with the lips; to smack; to buss.

2. To treat with fondness; to caress.

3. To touch gently, as if fondly, or caressingly.

Fondness? Smacks? Buss? This was not the dry, clinical description from the book. It wasn't just a pressure between mouths. It was an unexpected blossoming of waking nerves and ripples of heat where she didn't know a fever could be had. Just when she thought, I ought to stop this—I ought to breathe, Ian released her from his embrace, and they stepped away from each other, somewhat breathless.

The three newsies were watching with dropped jaws. Even Pops's eyes had grown round. And then they hooted and whistled so loud it was as if Tillie and Ian had performed some feat of magic.

"Well. Usually they really do shut up after that," Ian said, staring at his feet.

"Exactly how many women do they goad you into kissing?" Tillie asked. She was touching her mouth, tenderly.

"Uh. Only one other, I guess. But that was Sweetie's grandma, and she was sixty years old."

Tillie laughed out loud. When she recovered, her hand fell to the package tied to her waist. She lifted it and smiled.

"Instead of yelling at Mr. Metzger"—the newsies laughed at his lofty name—"how about you do some damage to these?" She untied the bundle of shortbread, placing it on Piper's lap. "Share nicely, now."

"Um, this is a treat! I'm stickin' to her like a plaster!" Piper crowed.

Pops was enthusiastically thanking Tillie and shaking her hand, his mouth crammed full of one large square of shortbread. Tillie untied the scarf from her waist and gave it to Sweetie.

"This was a favorite of mine. Take good care of it, or at least trade it for no less than fifty cents."

Sweetie said nothing, her mouth an O of astonishment.

"Stop buying their loyalty," Ian said, pretending to be angry, but not really. The children ravaged the shortbread until nary a crumb was left. Piper took the napkin and tied it around his neck like a kerchief. Ian shook his head and smiled, and he and Tillie began to walk along the darkened street. When they were a block away, three shrill whistles pierced the air. The first sounded like a staccato peep-peep-peep. The second was a trill that climbed an octave. The third was the same trill but in reverse.

"Goodness. Why do they do that?"

"Those three, they whistle like that when they're trying to find each other in the streets. You'd be surprised how loud they can whistle and how far it'll carry."

"Why did they whistle when they're all so close?"

"They're thanking you. You're too far for them to shout."

"So it means 'thank you.'"

"It also means 'You stole my lunch' or 'Good morning' or 'I'm going to smack you if you do that again.' Sometimes it means 'I'm in mortal danger, help me.' But usually it means they need money to buy tobacco."

"Well, how can you tell—"

The three newsies whistled once more, this time a little shriller than before.

Ian looked pointedly embarrassed and started walking faster.

"What did that mean?" Tillie asked.

"You don't want to know," he mumbled.

Tillie turned around to see Piper sticking his pursed lips out, pantomiming a kiss.

Ian hollered, "Go back to sleep!"

Surprisingly, they all lay back down on the grates near the World Building rather quickly. Piper hitched his stockings back up toward his knees and started sucking his thumb. Tillie had seen the state of the dirt on their fingers. That thumb must taste awful, she thought. They each need a good bath and scrubbing. Probably some time in a classroom too. Thank goodness she'd thought to bring that shortbread. Next time she came down here, perhaps she would bring them some new socks.

"I sell papers with them," Ian said. "Some days, they outsell me when I'm doing other work."

"Other work?" Tillie asked as they walked past a small, boxy building with THE SUN imprinted at the top, then past an enormous one with a clock tower on top that read THE TRIBUNE. A marble statue of a seated man stood in one of the entrance archways. The sculpted face seemed to judge Tillie traipsing around at night, unmarried and unaccompanied by a sanctioned person. She pointedly looked away.

"Whatever pays the bills," Ian said absently.

"So you sell the papers of all these publishers?"

"Usually just the *World*. They raised the prices, though. We used to be able to sell back what we couldn't unload, but they changed that. It's a mess."

"That's horribly unfair."

"There's talk of a strike. Haven't you heard about it?"

"No. I've been learning about vampires, instead."

"Oh. Have you heard?" He turned to her. "They dug up another body in upstate New York. Said the corpse was seen attacking children. When they cut open the belly, blood poured out of the stomach. Red blood."

"No," Tillie whispered. "It can't be. It can't. I don't understand what's happening. And then there's Albert Weber." She looked at him sharply. "How did you find out where he lived? Why didn't you tell me you were going to talk to him?"

"I'm not supposed to write to you, remember?"

"Oh. Of course." Tillie felt embarrassed. She couldn't leave her house without an escort, and she couldn't receive letters without them being read through and possibly burned. The limitations on her life were a drawstring pulling tighter and tighter.

"I got the address from the police sergeant. He's fairly talkative if you loosen his jaws with good whiskey. So what did you find in your sister's drawer?"

"I still can't open it," Tillie confessed. "I tried and tried, but I think maybe I need another lesson."

"We can go back to Tobias's grocery store instead of looking for articles about vampires."

"Won't he be angry?"

"Tobias is always angry! But he's tickled by our attention. Makes him feel like he's got a purpose." Ian grinned.

So they did. This time, they walked the distance instead of taking the train. Down by Park Row, it was relatively quiet, but the city gathered a pulse as soon as they crossed Pearl Street. Within fifteen minutes, they'd arrived back at Tobias's grocery store, under the looming shadows of the steel elevated tracks.

"I have a key this time," Ian said and let himself in. The grocery smelled of bread and cloves, of tobacco and a bitter scent of herbal medicine. She eyed several bottles of laudanum on the shelf. She didn't need to buy them now, but an irresistible urge to shoot a hand out and snatch a bottle intruded upon her consciousness. She picked one up and stared at it. Her stomach grumbled like a forlorn dog.

"Don't you already have enough of that?" Ian said abruptly.

"Oh. Yes. Just checking something," she said and replaced it on the shelf. Dorothy said she would bring her more. And surely next week, she would not need to take so much. She disliked the way Ian had looked at her when she'd clutched it in her hand somewhat hungrily.

"Wait here," he said, pausing in the back room. "I'm going to tell Tobias we're here so he doesn't get nervous and shout for the roundsman."

Tillie nodded. Ian disappeared down a corridor, and she heard his footsteps going up stairs above her. She nibbled an errant cuticle, and her stomach rumbled again. Her mending bone ached something terrible, and the discomfort infected and occupied other places in her body. She ravaged her cuticles, trying to ignore the pain elsewhere. Two of her fingers were oozing blood now. She glanced toward the store. Ian was still upstairs. There was time.

Tillie raced back along the grocery aisles, found the nearest bottle of laudanum, and tore it out of its paper packaging. She threw her head back and sucked down a dropperful of pungent brown liquid. Just enough to keep the pain at bay and keep her spirits up. She screwed the cap back on, replaced it in the box, and placed the damaged box behind the others on the shelf. Tobias would perhaps think it was just a mouse that had broken the paper on the package.

She tiptoed back to the office, just as Ian showed up.

"Let's start," he said, beaming, before sniffing the air. "What's that smell?"

She shrugged, keeping her mouth shut. He led her to the bureau in Tobias's office.

"I'm not an expert at lock picking, but I think what you need is a lot of practice. Here you go."

Tillie had brought the tiny, bent iron rods with her. First, she tried the same locked bureau drawer. It took five tries, fewer than her first attempt, before she could open it. Tobias had two other locks to work on: a chunky, rusted padlock and a medium-size wooden chest. Tillie worked at them, under Ian's guidance, until she was able to open them reasonably well.

"I feel better," she said. About the lock picking and about her body, which was now quelled of its discomfort. She realized that she spent most of her unmedicated hours feeling like there was a key stuck in her back, one that had wound and wound her insides into a knot of wretched tightness. The medicine made everything untwist and open. It made her feel normal.

"You're ready to start your felonious career," Ian announced. "Now to find out what that drawer holds. Let's get it now!"

"It's the middle of the night!" Tillie protested.

"And we're already up."

"But what if someone catches you?"

"They won't, not with you showing me around. We can compare notes about what Mrs. Weber said along the way."

"Well, all right," she relented. "I guess I can only unlock things when you're around anyway."

"And we'll bring all of my cousin's tools. And I can return them right away. You'll have better luck," Ian added.

Tillie began to walk back to the elevated station, and Ian trailed behind her. The night was still so very much alive. Even with the backdrop of darkness, she felt like the world was more vivid than a cloudless noon day. The electric lights illuminated the saloons and corner taverns, but much was still very hidden.

"Come on," Ian said. "Let's go unlock some secrets. You and me."

Tillie paused and inhaled the warm city air. The fetid stink of the manure-encrusted sidewalk did not bother her, nor did the sight of a man in a top hat jovially dancing with a woman—clearly a man dressed as a female, with broad shoulders and a touch of chest hair peeking out above the ill-fitting bodice—inside the doorway of a dance hall.

Alive. The world was smelly and dirty. It oozed about her, and yet Tillie felt more alive in it than she had been in her perfumed, waxed, and gilded life. There were safe ways to do things, and then there was this.

She grinned at Ian. "Let's go."

CHAPTER 12

Listen to them—the children of the night. What music they make!

—Count Dracula

Though the quickest way to get home was the elevated train, they decided to walk. Tillie repeatedly fell behind Ian, dawdling to peek inside the speakeasies and saloons of the Lower East Side or to inhale the lemon, mint, and garlic that lingered outside a closed Syrian restaurant. Finally, Ian gave in, stopping to look with her. He showed her his favorite Yiddish theaters and spoke in volumes about Jacob Adler, the king of the Jewish Rialto, who had played a stunning King Lear years ago when Ian was a boy.

"I've never been to the theater down here," Tillie confessed. "I've been to Weber and Fields and the Knickerbocker and of course the Opera House, and to Sherry's afterward for lobster, but not here."

"Oh," Ian said, wincing. "No lobster for me."

"Oh. Because it's forbidden?"

"No," he said, smiling. "I don't follow the rules—haven't for a long time. But some old ways stick. Food is home." He shrugged. "Also, lobsters look like monsters. Have you ever looked a live lobster in the eye?"

"No!" Tillie laughed. They were now at Twenty-Third Street. "But I do know that they're arthropods, which means they're related to millipedes and scorpions. They have three sets of claws, did you know? Not just those two big ones. And they have blue blood! The blood has copper, not iron, which is why those copper roofs over on Fourteenth Street look bluish green, instead of, well, copper colored—"

"How do you know all this?" Ian asked.

"I read," Tillie said simply. "And I read my dictionary a lot. I have *Chandler's Encyclopedia*, but it's not as detailed as I would like."

"You should go to college," Ian said.

"My family would absolutely forbid it. They won't think I need a university or college degree when I'm just going to get married and take care of my house and children and husband."

"Oh."

"Are you going to college?" Tillie asked.

"No. No money. I'm learning by doing."

"Learning how to sell newspapers? How much more schooling do you need to do that?"

"Hey, I learn something new every day. I like helping in the office. And someday, I won't be on the street all the time. So. Do you like eating lobster?"

"Yes. I eat loads of it!"

"Someday I'll take you to my favorite knish shop. The chopped liver one is unbelievable."

Tillie smiled. "Are they open in the middle of the night?"

"Probably not. Maybe you could come some other time."

None of this world was open to her during the day. "Let's keep walking," she said, even though they had never stopped.

They were silent all the way up to the Tenderloin district, with its theaters blazing in electric lights and lobster palaces catering their pricey three-dollar meals to the wealthy. Even though it was past three in the morning, theatergoers were still in the restaurants drinking and carousing loudly. But those weren't the only pleasures here. At Seventy-Second Street, Tillie dragged Ian inside the park to Bethesda Terrace, complete with carved stairs and the beautiful bronze angel statue in the center of the fountain.

Tonight, this statue and this fountain—and all of Central Park—felt like they belonged to her. She stretched her arms wide open, which was not terribly wide, as her arm was so weak and stiff.

"You look like you could fly yourself," Ian said.

Tillie dropped her arms but did not look at him. "In my head, I can fly. Higher than you could ever imagine."

———◆———

Tillie's feet were blistering. She hobbled the last few blocks home and accepted Ian's arm to lean upon. Her ache for more medicine was deepening; even so, it was wonderful to have an excuse to be so close. There was a lot you could learn from just a small amount of physical contact with another person. Ian's arm was steady and wiry; occasionally he would touch her arm with his other hand to make sure she was okay. He never touched her long enough to arouse suspicion that he was taking advantage. And yet, he seemed to lean into her as well. Just the slightest pressure of his shoulder against hers. Perhaps it was an acknowledgment that he, too, enjoyed the closeness.

The Pembroke home was still dark, but the night sky had diluted just a little, a sign that dawn was soon to come. Somewhere on their grounds, John O'Toole patrolled the house. Tillie checked her brooch watch; it was getting close to five o'clock. Ada would have trysted with John two hours ago. They would have to watch him round the house, then run inside before he saw them again. Tillie pulled Ian behind the corner of a brick fence one house away.

"What are we doing?" he whispered.

"We have to slip in so our guard doesn't see us. My grandmother hired John after Lucy died."

"They should get a discount, since he's not watching you."

Tillie pinched Ian, and he wordlessly mouthed, "Ouch!" She grinned.

As expected, John slowly circled the front of the house. He paused at the gate to look up and down the street. Ian and Tillie pulled their faces back just in time. They saw him disappear around the west side of the house.

"Let's go!"

Tillie ground her teeth together to eclipse the pain of her blistered feet, and they galloped to the front gate. They closed it as soundlessly as possible and ran up the stairs to the front door.

It was locked.

"I left this unlocked!" Tillie said, gasping.

"Now what?"

"To the back. We'll follow around, and John won't see us go through the kitchen entrance, by the conservatory."

They spun around to head down the front marble steps, when they froze at the sight of a calm John O'Toole pointing a pistol at them from the bottom of the stairs.

"John!" Tillie squeaked.

John pivoted to point the barrel straight at Ian's chest. Ian raised his hands and took a step sideways away from Tillie. Even in the gloom, she could see John frowning.

"Miss Pembroke! What are you doing out here?" To Ian, he barked, "Who're you?"

"John," Tillie said. "Please put your pistol down. This is Ian Metzger. He's a friend."

At the word *friend*, John raised his eyebrows high. "And what are you doing with 'im, all hours of the night?"

"He's helping me, ah, ah, fix something. Upstairs." Oh, it sounded awful. "It can't take longer than ten minutes." Ian cleared his throat and looked just as guilty. "Please. It's not what you think. You can't tell my mother about this. You cannot."

"I can, and I will. Your grandmother will want to know."

Ian looked at Tillie. He had far less to lose here. All he needed to do was leave, and that would be that. Tillie needed to get that drawer unlocked. It might be the only thing that helped her find out what had happened in Lucy's last hours. It could tell her everything she wanted to know—and everything she didn't.

"One hour. Just let him in for one hour. If you say nothing of this, then I'll promise to say nothing of Ada riding you like a horse in the middle of the night, when I snuck out and you were supposedly watching the house."

John dropped the arm holding the pistol. His jaw clenched. Ian covered his mouth, but he failed to squelch down a tiny "Oho!"

"Look," Tillie said. "If someone else catches Ian in the house, I will take the blame, not you. I'll say it was all my doing. Your job is to keep an eye on strangers, not police me."

John's brown eyes went from Tillie to Ian and back to Tillie. "One hour. Be quick. If I get so much as an inkling that he's hurt you"—he waved his pistol at Ian—"I will crush his skull like a peanut shell, and I will have the law and your grandmother on my side. Understood?"

Tillie and Ian chimed simultaneously, "Understood."

John moved up the stairs to unlock the front door, and inside they went.

This time, it was Ian's turn to drop his jaw. For the first time, Tillie saw her home through his eyes—the tall palm plants rising majestically, the six-foot portrait of her grandmother in the entranceway, the gilt-painted crown moldings and velvet-covered chairs. Chinese vases stood stuffed with peacock feathers and hothouse flowers that would be replenished with fresh roses in a few hours. Statuettes of marble and bronze lurked in every corner, beneath oil paintings by Pietro Perugino, Jacopo Bellini, and Lorenzo Lotto. None of those ridiculous "new" painters found in the Metropolitan, like Manet and Pissarro. The masters were the only ones worth having in one's home.

"Wow" was all that Ian could say. An embossed Bible with gilt-edged paper seemed to judge them from its place on a three-footed table ordered from France, in the style of those found in the salons of Faubourg Saint-Germain. Ian reached out to touch the gilded cover but then withdrew his hand as if in fear. "Wow," he said again. "You really live here."

"I do. It's a beautiful prison," she said.

Ian looked at her, noticing how bitterly she glanced around at the opulence. "Did Lucy feel the same way?"

"I don't know. She was going to get married, and she seemed happy. She would have been the mistress of something like this, all her own."

"Trading one prison for another?" Ian asked.

Tillie sighed. "She never told me she was unhappy."

Now that she thought of it, all Lucy ever did was put her energy into making others feel better. Tillie would slouch at the dinner table under the weight of her grandmother's criticisms, and Lucy would suddenly launch into some gossip about an opulent gazebo being built by someone or other, or a million dollars' worth of jewels being sent from France for a wedding gift. Lucy was brilliant at launching glittering distractions. Later, she would whisper, "I love my smart Tillie. You keep reading. I'll keep Grandmama at bay. Someday, the world will catch up to your brilliance."

"Everyone loves you," Tillie had said once. "Even your sneezes are perfect."

"Never mind my sneezes. And I'm not perfect." Lucy's smile had faltered. What had she meant? But Tillie hadn't asked. She'd never really probed to find what ailed her sister in heart and mind. She'd never consoled Lucy. And now, she was furious at herself. She had been so utterly selfish.

"Tillie?" Ian tapped her on the shoulder. She shook herself out of the cobwebs of her memories. "Come on. Let's go unlock that drawer."

Tillie nodded. Making hardly a noise, they crept up the stairs. At the top, Tillie said, "Wait right here."

She quickly went into her room and, with slightly shaking hands, withdrew a hidden bottle of opium. She took several drops more than usual to help with her blister pain. When she met Ian outside her room, he said lightly, "You all right?"

"Yes."

"Why are you hiding that you take that stuff all the time?" he asked.

"I'm not hiding. The doctor says I must."

Ian's face was neutral, but that certain dark twinkle in his eyes had gone flat. "I know what hiding is."

"It's fine. Everyone takes it."

"That doesn't make it a good thing," he said. "You know, I can tell when you take it. You don't sound the same. You don't act the same. Tonight, it's been subtle. But I can tell."

Tillie opened her mouth, ready to retort, but Ian held up a hand. "I guess it's not my place to say anything. Let's get to work."

As Tillie led him down the hallway to Lucy's room, she tried to tease apart the dark, tight feeling in her belly. She wasn't upset that he had judged her opium habit; it was that he'd declared that he had no stake in caring about it.

She shook off the feeling and opened Lucy's door. Inside, the striped-ivory-and-green taffeta canopies still hung lush and shining, the bed crisply made as if its occupant would be returning soon for a slumber. Tillie knelt before the side table.

"This is the one. No key, and it's the only thing locked in the room. I found a drawer full of pencil shavings, but no paper."

"How do you know she didn't write some letters and send them?"

"Because she wouldn't have written in pencil. I saw her ink blotter too."

"Well, let's give it a go, shall we?" Ian dropped to his knees and pulled out a leather roll tied with a string. He unrolled it and laid out twenty different lockpick tools.

Tillie picked up three tools, one straight and two with curved notches at the end. She started to fit them into the keyhole, pushing the curved piece higher as the longer one felt for the bolt mechanism. "I need another hand. Can you hold this?"

Ian held one of the thin metal instruments, and Tillie pushed the third between them. They were a tangle of arms, and her cheek ended up resting lightly against his bristly one.

"You need to shave," she murmured as she worked.

"If I'd known I'd be doing a locksmith waltz, I would have." She could feel him smile against her, and she took a slow breath, trying to focus.

"Move your hand this way . . . okay, hold it. And we need to turn together." Their hands, perfectly orchestrated, turned counterclockwise. There was a slight click and a weight on the instruments as she began to move the tumbler. One final snick of the lock sounded. Ian raised his eyebrows.

"Oh. We did it," Tillie said.

He leaned back on his arms, after dropping his piece. "I'm a good-luck charm."

"The tools and practice helped too," Tillie said dryly. She pulled the drawer open. Inside were two handkerchiefs of Cluny lace. She lifted them and found a broken pin and scraps of ribbon. She tugged the drawer out farther and reached her hand deep into the recesses. She pulled out a leather-bound diary.

"Eureka!" Ian exclaimed. Tillie shushed him. She flipped to a page in the diary, finding Lucy's beautiful penciled script filling the pages. She touched the back of her hand to her mouth in astonishment.

Here were her sister's words from beyond the grave. Her voice, spoken and yet unspoken. Here she was, and yet Lucy was no longer.

"Lucy!" It was all she could manage to say.

"We don't have to read it," Ian said quietly. He patted her back inexpertly, and Tillie turned to put her face against his shoulder. It was the most natural thing to do: to turn to him for comfort. Lucy had been her shoulder, and Lucy was gone. These last weeks, there had been no one. Her mother never embraced her, and she'd looked on with graveness whenever Tillie's father had been demonstrative. From the Pembroke women, Tillie would receive a kiss on the cheek, an airy one at that, on her birthdays. Even Ada, who attended her every need, kept her distance as society dictated.

It was odd and strange and wonderful when Ian encircled her with his arms and just let her be. After a while, she pulled away.

"It's going to be dawn in less than an hour, and you have to go," she said, wiping her nose.

"I know. But maybe . . . it would be better if you read this while I'm here? I wouldn't want you to be alone."

She snuffled. Ian removed a handkerchief that had been laundered so many times it seemed almost translucent. She took it gratefully. After one last deep breath, she nodded and untied the diary.

Mina Harker had written in a diary too. She had said in *Dracula* that she would write "whenever I feel inclined. I do not suppose there will be much of interest to other people; but it is not intended for them." Just like Lucy had. It felt wrong to read it now. It was not meant for Tillie. But how else could she find out Lucy's thoughts before she died?

The first entry was from a year ago, so they started close to the last few pages, with an entry dated four days before her death.

June 4, 1899

I am scattered and dizzy. There is no respite, no matter where I turn.

Dr. Erikkson says that I am nearly recovered from the typhus and that I must never go back to the Foundling Hospital. It pains me, as I can nearly see it from the upstairs window. But who will go in my stead? I have asked Dorothy, but she is afraid she will catch diphtheria. And after my own illness, her fear is fixed and hard as stone.

Mama and Grandmama refuse to let me go as well. But the children need more clothes, more healthful food, more sunshine. James agrees with my family; he believes a lady should wait until her children are married off before acquiring a habit of philanthropy. He watches me and checks my behavior when the subject comes up, even in the politest society.

The situation with Betty is no better. The other maids have seen Betty taking items from the house. I lied and said I was unconcerned that my garnet and gold breast-pin went missing. I begged them not to tell Mama. They know she took an armful of muslin from the linen closet and charged four pounds of beef loin to our account and never brought it home.

What am I to do? She grows sullen from all the whispers and glances. Betty is dear to me; she knows me and my needs and my despairs better than anyone else. All the others see is a thief.

Tillie stopped reading.

Lucy had been replete with concerns, and Tillie had no idea. She and James always seemed happy together. And Betty had been stealing so much. Why would Lucy have allowed this?

"Let's read more," Ian said. His face was one of quiet consternation; he seemed as troubled by Lucy's writing as Tillie. Tillie turned a few pages farther. It was the last entry, from the very day she'd gone missing.

June 8, 1899

I am to see Dr. Erikkson again. I look forward to the visit. He will say I am all better, and I will challenge Mama and Grandmama about resuming my work.

James has asked to accompany me to the visit, as a husband's right, even though we are not yet married. He smothers me with his attention. I can scarcely breathe when he is in the room. He has been choosing my gowns; he has been angry about my work at the Foundling Hospital. I thought we might reconcile—I suggested I would halt my visits for a time if we could endow a charity that paid the salary of a new teacher and three new nurses.

And he struck me.

I have never been touched by such violence. Even when Papa whipped me with a switch when I was four years old because I broke a crystal decanter by accident, it was done so with remorse. Papa embraced me and cried after, never using that switch again. After James struck me, his face was terrible, all steel and ice. He said, "A wife that does not obey is worse than a dead wife." He removed all the money from my reticule, so I cannot purchase even a penny candy.

I died then. I cannot escape this engagement. Mama and Grandmama refuse my pleas. They side with James and think I am too consumed with charity work. It is a pet preoccupation that was due to stop, they say.

And Betty, my solace, is now suspected of stealing two silver spoons. She will end up in the Tombs, and there will be nothing I can do to stop it. Only I know the entirety of what she has taken from our house. Soon, I will have to confess all her betrayals, and in doing so, all of mine for keeping such secrets.

Tillie could hardly breathe. She touched the last sentence, smudging the word *secrets* ever so slightly. Ian seemed to be staring at the words, too, as if they were pressing themselves into his memory, like thumbprints on clay.

"I didn't know," Tillie said. Her hands shook so; she nearly tore the diary. "He struck her? James? I cannot believe it. How could he?"

"It's not right, but it's common enough," Ian said with disgust. He looked at Tillie seriously. "You'd best be careful around him."

"He's only ever been a gentleman to me."

"Some gentleman he is, smacking around his betrothed. Who would you believe?" Ian asked.

"Dracula was not believed to be a monster when Harker first met him. He seemed sophisticated and learned. Almost royal, the way he's described." Tillie went silent for a long while. "And what about Betty? We need to talk to her. She could have killed Lucy, couldn't she? To prevent her firing?"

"That wouldn't be terribly clever. Lucy was the only reason she was still employed. But Betty seemed to know a lot about Lucy."

More than I did, Tillie thought with a pang. She scoured her memory of those last days. Why hadn't she tried harder to notice that Lucy must not have been happy?

"Perhaps James knew about the thievery. Maybe they fought about it." It made Tillie recoil to think she'd been in such close quarters with James. "Still—if he'd been so angry, why kill her like a vampire?"

"I don't know. He certainly didn't act like a guilty murderer when we visited the Weber family. You know, I'll bet the police haven't done a wink of work since the day after she died. You should bring this diary to them." He stood but seemed distracted, running his hand through his hair. "What was Betty's name again?"

"Betty Novak."

"Right. I should go before the servants wake up."

"Of course," Tillie said. She felt like she was in a dream. They left the room, Tillie clutching the diary to her bosom as she walked him out. When she opened the front door, John was rounding the front of the house. He looked pointedly at them both, but as they seemed more upset than physically rumpled, he simply went on walking.

"I never saw you," he said before rounding the west corner.

"Good thing he's on your payroll," Ian said. He walked out the front door and turned around. "Say. I had a good time tonight. All that walking. Next time, I'm taking you to the Thalia Theatre. It'll be swell."

Tillie bounced on the balls of her toes—the only part of her feet that didn't hurt, though the rest of the pain was dull. "You know what I'd rather see? A vampire. A real one. I'm tired of not finding the answers I want."

"You're reading too much of that *Dracula* book."

"'We learn from failure, not from success,'" Tillie quoted. "Let's not stop now. But what will I do with this diary? If I show it to my mother, she might burn it before it leaves the house. The last thing they'd want to see is all of Lucy's complaints out in the world." She bit her lip. "I could bring it to the police tomorrow night."

"Better yet. Give it to me. I'll bring it to them."

"You will?"

Ian nodded. "They need to do more. There hasn't been a single article about who might be the killer. That's a bad sign. This will get them using those brains again."

"Shall we meet tomorrow night?" Tillie asked, eagerly.

"Oh. No. I have at least a day's worth of newspaper sales to make up for the time I'm going to lose sleeping today. How about two nights? We'll have plenty to talk about by then."

"Okay. Two nights, then. Where?"

"I have an idea. Meet me down the street from here, on Second Avenue. We'll go from there."

As they stood there, not sure how best to say their adieus, John rounded the east corner and hissed at them both. "Are you *trying* to get me fired? Go!"

"I'm going!" Ian hissed back. With that, he opened the gate and ran away into the darkness.

⟐

Tillie was down to her last bottle. She savored every dose, every banishment of her pain and sadness with each burning drop. She kept to her room, sleeping and eating little, avoiding Ada when possible (she couldn't help but remember her and John coupled together). Hazel left a card and promised to call on her, but she refused to see Dorothy or James, feigning illness. She could not bear to speak with them after what she'd read in Lucy's diary.

It wasn't until two mornings later that she felt capable of descending the circular staircase. Even then, she held her stomach, feeling somewhat queasy. She had taken a little too much medicine this morning. She would try to eat some dry toast, then go back to bed. But the effect was that she didn't feel terribly bothered by anything, even the slight nausea.

She had barely stepped into the dining room when the sound of glass shattering reverberated down the hallway. Her mother stood next to the banquette of eggs, toast, steaming ham, jellies, and a mound of golden butter. Broken glass littered the floor by her feet, and her grandmother had her fists balled on the table.

"What's the matter?" Tillie exclaimed, rushing into the room.

Her mother was white as the table linen and looked at Tillie as if she were made of nothing more than fog and ash. Her grandmother had found her voice. She picked up a newspaper from the table and shook it at her.

"Mathilda! How could you speak with such a person? How could you make up such . . . *lies*? Such rubbish?"

"What do you mean?" She walked forward, and Grandmama thrust the paper in her face. Tillie batted it down, shook it out, and laid it on the table.

"Here," her mother said in a wavering voice, pointing at an article at the top of the page.

"Vampire" Victim Lucille Pembroke Feared for Her Life

Servant Lies Uncovered in Diary

Fiancé James Cutter Now Person of Interest

Police Investigation Continues with Renewed Vigor

By Ian Metzger

Tillie reeled back as if bitten.

"Do you know this Ian Metzger?" her grandmother said in a tone so lethal the servants backed out of the dining room promptly.

"What diary is this? There's no such thing. It's lies!" her mother cried out, tears now splashing onto the paper. "There is no such thing!" she repeated, as if convincing herself.

Tillie opened her mouth, but no words would come. Her stomach lurched, and she put her hand to her mouth and rushed out of the room, making it only five feet before she vomited her medicine all over the marble floor.

"Vampire" Victim Lucille Pembroke Feared for Her Life

Servant Lies Uncovered in Diary

Fiancé James Cutter Now Person of Interest

Police Investigation Continues with Renewed Vigor

By Ian Metzger

New details regarding the June 8 murder of Lucille "Lucy" Pembroke—a young heiress set to marry into one of New York's oldest families in an event anticipated as the fin de siècle event on Millionaire's Row—reveal that her death is even more complicated than previously thought. Her fiancé, James Cutter, whose family is one of the oldest and wealthiest of Astor's Four Hundred, is now a prime suspect.

Miss Pembroke went missing on June 8, and her slain body was found one day later by the south wall of the Metropolitan Museum of Art. Information gathered from Miss Pembroke's own sister, Mathilda Pembroke, reveals that the late Miss Pembroke had recently quarreled with her fiancé. The World has in its possession the diary of Lucy Pembroke, verified by the author of this article, who procured it from the bedchamber of Miss Pembroke with the assistance of her sister.

Passages include such damaging phrases as "He has been angry" and "He smothers me" and this particular admission: "He struck me." Perhaps the reader might consider that a husband has a right to strike his wife—or a fiancé, his betrothed. What is most remarkable is the timing of these posthumous words of Miss Pembroke: They were written the same day she was murdered.

Furthermore, details revealed in the diary show that a maid who attended Miss Pembroke had been suspected of lying and stealing. Surely this is a detail that begs more investigation. Could it, too, be related to the angry fiancé? It ought not be dismissed.

The death of Miss Pembroke is particularly confounding to the police of the Twenty-First Ward and of other precincts throughout the city. The recent death of a young boy, Albert Weber, tells us that this murderer has struck at least twice. It is a vicious truth that New York kills its own at a voracious rate, and the morgue and police have difficulty keeping up with the vast number of people who go missing or die under circumstances that are never fully brought to light. However, in the case of Miss Pembroke and Albert Weber, both murdered by exsanguination, both with apparent "vampire bites" to the neck, both brutally robbed of life, we should not be so complacent.

The wealthy may have the privilege that many do not have, but in this case, Lucy Pembroke's death cries out for justice. James Cutter's involvement in the turmoil surrounding the last hours of Lucy Pembroke's life must be investigated further. As this article goes to press, we have been informed that the police will begin an in-depth investigation into Mr. Cutter and his whereabouts at the time of Miss Pembroke's disappearance and murder.

Let us all remember the terrifying vision of a beautiful heiress, much beloved by her family and friends, drained of her blood while wearing her fine lilac silk dress. This innocent maiden was left to rot in the dim shadows of Central Park. Was it the work of a vampire or of a powerful and furious fiancé wishing to make the death appear more macabre than a simple domestic dispute? Answers must be had.

Let us allow Miss Pembroke to speak for herself.

"After James struck me, his face was terrible, all steel and ice. He said, 'A wife that does not obey is worse than a dead wife . . .' I died then. I cannot escape this engagement."

And die she did. But not in vain.

We, the public, will demand the truth.

CHAPTER 13

Therefore, I, on my part, give up here the certainty of eternal rest, and go out into the dark where may be the blackest things that the world or the nether world holds!

—Mina Harker

Tillie wiped her mouth, still coughing. Sick was running down the sateen of her bodice. The nausea roiled worse than before. She had two immediate thoughts.

I just vomited up the medicine. I need to go drink more before I feel even worse. But there is hardly any left. I am loath to bother Dorothy and Hazel about my needs. How shall I get more—and soon?

Her second thought was, Oh, Ian. How could you?

"I need to go upstairs," Tillie muttered, heading for the staircase.

Her grandmother stepped up to Tillie, her foot stepping right through the pool of sick on the marble floor. She grabbed Tillie's wrist, hard.

"You will sit down, Mathilda, and you will tell us why this—this—person—knows about the family. It's written that they have documentation. It says that the *World* has possession of her personal writings. Lucy had no such documents!"

Tillie could feel the bruise forming on her wrist. She was too weak to pull away from her grandmother and dropped down to sit on the bottom stair. Ada and the other maids were rushing to clean up the sick and the mess in the dining room, but her grandmother roared at them.

"*Leave us!*"

Tillie felt the anger of her voice vibrate the air. Once the servants cleared out of view (no doubt they were listening around the nearest corners), her mother groaned and rubbed her temple.

"Is this the same person who was leaving you messages around the time of the funeral?" she hissed.

"Yes," Tillie said miserably.

"Has he been calling here, without our knowledge?"

"No," Tillie said, glad she didn't have to lie.

"Then how on earth does he know so much about our family? About James?"

"There was a diary. It was locked in Lucy's side drawer in her room. I found it."

Grandmama looked at her with her piercing blue eyes. "You mean . . . what is written in this article, about James, about that maid . . . it's true?"

Tillie nodded.

"And how did he get this diary?" Grandmama asked.

If she told them she had been leaving the house, she would never be able to leave again, not unless she was shackled to two chaperones or married off to be someone else's problem. She couldn't suffer being trapped at home again.

"I sent it to him. We've been corresponding," Tillie lied.

Her mother sucked air through her teeth. "Every message you've received from strangers I've burned! And you still did this? How *could* you, Mathilda?"

Tillie could not answer, and the silence coiled around them, ready to whip her whether or not it broke.

"Well. We shall put a stop to that. And we'll demand that he return Lucy's papers immediately. Tell me his address. How to contact him," her mother said. "I'll fix this."

"Like you fixed the last disaster in your life? Oh, come, Victoria! You're about as useful as a drowned cat!" Grandmama pointed a gnarled finger at Tillie. "*This* is the result of your mistakes. *This* is your doing."

"No!" Her mother looked stricken. "She's frail. In the head, as well as the body. It's not her fault—"

"You're right, it's not her fault, Victoria. It's your fault! She's ill bred, and if you'd cleaned up your mistakes the way I said you should, there would be none of this. But no! You had to marry for love!"

Tillie gasped. "Good God. Are you speaking about my father?" Her voice rose to a high pitch. "What mistake, Grandmama? Me? Am I the mistake?"

Her grandmother opened her mouth but paused, realizing that even she had let her emotions run amok. She turned to her daughter. "Fix this." And to Tillie, "You'll not send any messages or letters out anymore." She clapped her hands, and Pierre showed up faster than an electric light switched on. "The servants will bring all cards and letters to me first," Mrs. Pembroke said with finality. "Coming and going. Or they will be fired immediately. No visitors, until I say."

Tillie's fury rose above her reticence. Some other power seemed to push the words out of her body. "You are angry at me and Mama, but why aren't you angry at James? He struck Lucy! They weren't even married!"

"Mathilda—" her mother began.

"Lucy's maid was stealing," she continued. "She was afraid Lucy would tell the truth. James was trying to control Lucy, and she was miserable. And you care only to keep me quiet, trapped under lock and key. What about who killed Lucy? It has been almost three weeks. Three weeks! Do you care that the person who killed Lucy has sucked the marrow out of another child? You are helping that monster kill more people by pretending she never died!"

Her mother threw her hands to her face and began bawling, and her grandmother went apoplectic. She was turning the same color as her dark-burgundy batiste gown.

"And the bite marks!" Tillie went on. "Must I remind you that her blood was drained away? Gone! Like an empty milk bottle! How can you pretend that did not happen? How can you not act? Vampires must be considered. Stoker's book says—"

"Silence!" her grandmother nearly screamed. The chandelier above the stairs shook and tinkled like wineglasses clinking. "Send for the driver. We're going to see Dr. Erikkson. This kind of outburst must be controlled. This hysteria, this behavior—utterly intolerable."

"I am not hysterical!" Tillie hollered. "I know what *hysterical* means! I have read about it in the medical encyclopedias. *My womb is not running about inside, causing mischief!*" She waved her arms in a zigzag and kicked her feet for extra emphasis.

"Mathilda! How dare you speak of such things aloud!" her mother said, hissing. "The servants are listening!"

"Let them hear me! Lucy is dead. And I am not Lucy! I will never be your perfect Lucy! I am a Flint, like my father, and you cannot extinguish that fact no matter how much you try. You cannot silence me into being sold and packaged off to a suitor to make this family presentable again! I'll leave. I'll go to college. I'll work, if that is what it means to be able to speak!"

Her grandmother rose to her full height, two inches taller than Tillie, and came forward with hand raised high. Tillie, still seated, shrank from the coming blow.

For several seconds that twisted like yarn into a thin, everlasting thread, she waited. When she stopped cowering and opened an eye, her grandmother had reeled in her hand and backed away, face white.

"Call for the driver. Victoria, go with her. See that she is treated for this outlandish outburst. I'll go to meet with the Cutters and the sergeant mentioned in the article to quiet down this business."

Her grandmother walked past Tillie into the depths of the library, shutting the double doors with a slam.

"Ada!" her mother barked. Ada peeped a head out from down the hallway, where she was hiding in the butler's pantry. "Miss Pembroke requires a new gown. We're going to see her doctor immediately." Ada scurried closer and began to usher Tillie upstairs.

"We are not done here!" Tillie said, throwing off Ada's arm.

But her mother had already fled. She could hear Pierre ordering the driver to fetch the carriage from the stables.

Tillie could not be calmed. Ada begged her to change out of her sick-stained gown, but Tillie would not sit still. In the end, Ada wiped the worst of it off, and Tillie reeked of bitterness, sour and foul.

All the way to Dr. Erikkson's, her mother and Ada sat on either side of her. They seemed afraid even to look at her. Tillie's hair was in disarray, and in the reflection of the carriage's windowpanes, she saw how wide her eyes were, how encircled with purplish shadows. She was thinner too. She hadn't eaten much in the last few weeks, now that she thought of it. The opium always constipated her so, and it made her belly feel too bloated to eat. As a result, her gowns were fitting loose, and her bosom had deflated to the point where her corset squashed what she had down to a plane of nothing.

All she could think about was the vitriol she would spit at Ian when she met with him tonight. One thing was for sure: she could not let on that she had been escaping the house.

At the doctor's town house, Mrs. Erikkson opened the door. Her matronly cap was perfectly set on her head, her apron clean and white, and she smiled with those apple-ish cheeks, until she saw the sorry expressions on all three women.

"Oh! Mrs. Pembroke, Miss Pembroke." She curtsied briefly. "But you do all look a fright. Please come in. My husband is with Tom, but he can see you shortly."

She showed her mother into an office to speak with Dr. Erikkson in private, and then she shuttled Tillie and Ada into the examination room down the hall. Tillie paced like a wild thing, finding the room's walls cloyingly close. She did not look at the books on the shelves or the brazier by the fire or the few medical curios on the shelves that would normally engross her.

Dr. Erikkson entered. As always, he was tall and spare, with a severe face that lacked adequate real estate for a smile.

"Miss Pembroke. I understand you are feeling unwell today after some distressing news."

"I am not unwell," Tillie snapped. "My arm is much better."

"That's not what we are here to discuss. I can see your arm is better. You move it quite well. Can you tell me, Why is your mother so upset with your behavior today?" He leaned against the edge of the mantel, his arms crossed. Ada just sat in the corner miserably, trying not to be noticed.

Tillie paced the room. "There was a newspaper article written by someone I know. He stole something from Lucy. From me. I made a mistake trusting him. I made a mistake trusting James Cutter! And we still don't know where that maid went—Betty Novak. Who knows if that's her real name? She may have lied about that too! And John never told me where she was."

"And who is this John?"

Tillie opened her mouth wide, before shutting it. She should not have mentioned John O'Toole. They might find out that they had an agreement. She shook her head.

"Is it the man you're corresponding with?"

"Yes. No, it was someone different. A different man. Does it matter?" She waved her arms again. In her current state, her shoulder pain hardly bothered her.

165

"And what did they steal?"

"A diary. Lucy's diary."

"Did the family know about this diary?"

"No! I picked a lock on the drawer of her table—"

"You . . . picked a lock?"

"Yes, I learned . . . I mean, I read some books and . . . why are you asking me these questions? I have questions for you, Dr. Erikkson. What happened when Lucy was here last? Tom said she was distraught. You must have noticed too. What happened to my sister?"

At this, Dr. Erikkson pushed his glasses farther up the bridge of his bony nose. He was so pale, like he himself possessed not a drop of red blood in his veins. Like he bled milk.

"That is not your concern. And in fact, it is not the concern of the police sergeant, either, whom I have already spoken to."

"If someone is biting people to death—" she began, but Dr. Erikkson walked right past her.

"There are no such things as vampires or ghouls or ghosts." He took a key from his pocket and unlocked a glass cabinet. He withdrew a square walnut case not much larger than a cigar box.

"How do you know? There are bite marks. They have all their blood gone!" Tillie turned to Ada. "You know what I'm speaking of, don't you? You heard the news, right, Ada?"

Ada whimpered and shook her head, too terrified to speak. Dr. Erikkson had opened the walnut case and was drawing liquid up into a glass-and-metal syringe. The needle was far thicker than the embroidery needles she used.

"Ada? Is that your name?" he asked the maid. "She'll be needing some new medicine."

"What is that?" Tillie asked, and she took a step away.

"It'll calm you. Your emotions are in a frenzy. Hysteria is not something to be trifled with. Many women have been ruined, utterly ruined, from its effects. This is near to a case of delirium tremens, though without the intoxication."

"I do not have hysteria, Dr. Erikkson," Tillie said. "Or delirium. I made a mistake, trusting that man who wrote the article. And my sister died, and no one has found the killer. And no one has convinced me that vampires are not responsible! And if they aren't, then James Cutter and that maid—they must be questioned."

"Lie down!" Dr. Erikkson growled.

Like he's ordering a dog to obey, Tillie thought. He towered over her, and Ada gently pushed Tillie onto the examination chaise.

"Please, Miss Tillie. Do as he says. You are in a state. Please, Miss."

Tillie exhaled loudly. "I am not hysterical."

"Of course," Ada murmured soothingly, gently pushing until she was lying down. "Show how respectful you can be and how calm." She started to loosen the ebony buttons that kept Tillie's sleeve tight.

"No. Turn her to the side," the doctor ordered. He held the syringe high before him. A drop of liquid glistened at its tip, a quivering seed pearl of medicine.

"What is that?" Tillie asked.

"Morphine," Dr. Erikkson said. "Look toward the wall, please." Tillie was rolled onto her left side. She saw Ada nod to some wordless command from the doctor, and soon her skirts were gathered up, exposing her stockings, garters, and frilly bloomers.

"What are you doing?" Tillie called shrilly.

"Be silent!" Dr. Erikkson commanded. "Draw the curtains. The light is too bright in here."

Ada quickly drew them. Tillie turned her head to stare at the doctor, shock passing through her. Why hadn't she noticed it before? "You never leave here during the day. You're never out in daylight, are you? And it's always so dark in here. Just like vampires. 'I love the shade and the shadow.' Why, Dr. Erikkson?"

"I said silence!" Tillie felt his hand sliding up her stockinged leg. He pushed one lace hem of her bloomers upward to expose her thigh. The air hit her bare skin, and she tensed. "My work hours do not concern you. Now, be calm. Your lady's maid is here as your chaperone. This is simply a medical treatment." There was a pause, and he said, "You'll feel a little pinch. Do not worry."

Tillie clenched her hands around Ada's. At the sudden prick of the needle, she gasped. It felt as if it were making room under her skin where there hadn't been any before. There was pressure, and then she felt the metal slip out from under her skin, leaving her with a lingering soreness.

"There. We are finished for now." Dr. Erikkson returned the syringe to the walnut case, which held several bottles of liquid.

Ada covered her decently, and Tillie sat up.

"Twenty minutes, she should be calm," Dr. Erikkson said. "She'll start regular injections, every three or four hours for the first day, only one-tenth of a grain. Keep up the schedule so she is regularly tranquil." He handed the walnut case to Ada. "Miss Pembroke, rest here. I'll speak to your mother and give further instructions to your maid. It is vitally important you take this to keep your nerves soothed."

Tillie felt nothing, aside from the residual soreness of the injection. While Dr. Erikkson went to speak with her mother in his office, Mrs. Erikkson opened the door. She smiled kindly, though a shadow of pity lingered about her eyebrows.

"May I get anything for you, Miss? Tea?"

"No, thank you," Tillie said. She already sounded more dulcet. Was the medicine working? "How is Tom?"

"Not so well. He's been sick all week. Terrible headache pain."

"I'm sorry to hear that. Please give him my best." She added, "Let him know I'll keep a space on my card for a dance someday, when he's better."

Mrs. Erikkson's eyes flashed with merriment. "Oh! I shall. He'll warm to that, I can tell you. In these dark days, we must hold on for better ones." She looked sadly at the walnut box sitting on Ada's lap. "Oh. You've begun morphine injections, I see."

"Yes," Tillie said. She suppressed a yawn.

"Well. Use it if you must, but promise me—" She looked quickly behind her, as if suddenly afraid. "Promise me you'll stop that as soon as you're better. Morphine is a master like none other, if you take it for too long."

"Doesn't Tom take morphine too?"

"Alas, he does, and I regret the day he received his first dose. It helps the pain, but now he cannot live without it."

A floorboard creaked. Mrs. Erikkson jerked back and turned from the door.

"Mona!" Dr. Erikkson could be heard down the hallway. Mrs. Erikkson sped away without a goodbye. Tillie craned her neck to hear a snatch of words between them.

"What did I tell you about dispensing your advice to my patients? I am the doctor. Nursing Tom and answering the door, overseeing the servants, and paying the bill of groceries—these are your domain. Why can you not endeavor to remember your place?"

More hurried whispers ensued, and a door shut somewhere. Several minutes went by. Tillie's body suddenly felt softer everywhere. The tension around her head and neck melted, and a slow pleasant feeling crept up her arms and legs, as if she were descending into a bath of warmed pudding.

"Oh," she said to no one. So this was morphine. Her stiff shoulder was loosening marvelously. The knots in her stomach untwisted and swirled in a lovely dance of calmness. There was a new wave of nausea and a slight itchiness to her skin, but it was all so tolerable.

Before long, Ada was helping her out of the room; her mother awaited them in the carriage. As they exited, she heard an exclamation. She turned, and down the hallway, Tom had popped his disheveled head out from his sickroom, wearing a blanket like a cloak. Seeing her blink at him sleepily, he grinned and winked. He motioned poking a finger into his thigh and pantomimed his eyes rolling back into his head.

So. It looked like she and Tom were both under the spell of Dr. Erikkson's morphine injections. At least she would not be alone, she thought vaguely.

By the time she was in the carriage, the tide of morphine had washed ashore and drowned her in its treacly stupor, and Tillie did not mind whatsoever.

———※———

Tillie remembered little from the rest of the day. In accordance with Dr. Erikkson's instructions, she received a morphine injection every three hours. She barely remembered being woken to eat some soup and bread.

"What time is it, Ada?" Tillie asked, her tongue thick and slow.

"It's nine o'clock in the evening, Miss. You're to receive another injection now."

Her mind oozed as if it had been dipped in pitch. She glanced around. Her room looked the same. The syringe case was out, and Ada was drawing up the medicine.

"Ada, can you show me how to do that? That way I can give myself the doses, and you can rest tonight."

"Oh, Miss, I don't think so."

"You can check to see if I've taken it all in the morning. You've already done so much. I'm sure Dr. Erikkson is afraid I won't take it, but I promise you I will. I swear it."

"Oh, Miss."

"Please, Ada. I can't have you making mistakes and getting fired like Betty because you're too tired to see straight. You can take over first thing in the morning."

Ada rubbed her exhausted eyes. "Very well. Only once in a while. I'll do tomorrow night, after I've gotten some sleep. John will be missing me tonight, I'm sure."

"I'm sure," Tillie said, trying to hide a grin.

Ada showed her how to draw up the liquid into the glass chamber. She watched Tillie lift her nightdress up and choose a place on her thigh.

"Dr. Erikkson said to inject here"—Ada patted her own rump—"or here, or here." She patted her stomach and upper thighs. "But he said the upper arm was also just fine once I was more confident."

Ada guided Tillie and helped steady her hand. Tillie took aim at her own thigh, a few inches from where the doctor had injected her. She hesitated before the needle tip touched the skin.

Taking laudanum had been so different. No different, it seemed, than drinking tea or wine. But this . . . as Tillie pushed the needle into her flesh, her head grew light and airy, as if stuffed with spun sugar. Her hands went cold, and Ada had to steady the syringe where it trembled. Tillie pushed down on the plunger with her thumb and felt the tight, painful sensation of the morphine pushing into her tissues.

And then, she pulled the needle out, and it was over. Ada took the syringe away and told Tillie how to clean it for its next use, but Tillie was not listening. She stared at the puncture in her thigh, a tiny red berry on snow. She was unwhole now. There was a schism, and Tillie had passed to another place altogether. It had been easy, she thought. Too easy.

"You were very brave," Ada said. "I myself dislike even a pinprick from an embroidery needle!"

Tillie said nothing but laid herself down. As Ada turned the light switch off, Tillie smiled in the dark. She would not go back to sleep. She waited the requisite twenty minutes, feeling the morphine creep deliciously throughout her body. There was a peculiar lifting sensation in her head that felt absolutely delightful, a tranquility like none other.

The dose was lower than at Dr. Erikkson's office, so she did not quite feel as groggy.

She did not want to take the chance that she was going to fall asleep again, so she jumped out of bed. She grabbed her copy of *Dracula*, reading some of her favorite quotes over and over again.

"And oh, my dear, if it is to be that I must meet death at any hand, let it be at the hand of him that loves me best."

How romantic. To trust someone that deeply, to lay her heart upon them, to charge them with such care.

Near midnight, Tillie felt more awake than ever. The last injection of morphine was fading, and this one would have to last all the while she was out of the house. She took the walnut case and carefully drew up a dose for herself that was the same amount Dr. Erikkson had given her. Surely she was well rested enough that it would not affect her too strongly. She lifted up her nightshirt and plunged the needle into the flesh of her outer thigh.

Tillie did her best to dress herself quickly. She wore one of her older dresses, a challis in pink-and-brown paisley, and tied on some soft ankle-high boots. Her blisters had scabbed over. This time, she would not be walking much. She needed her feet to take her only the few blocks to confront Ian.

By the time she opened the front door, euphoria thrummed through her chest. Everything felt possible right now. Though the opiate begged her to succumb to slumber, she shook her head and stepped into the warm night. It was drizzling ever so slightly. The streets were misted with gray.

"Miss Pembroke." John saw her from the corner of the property. He came forward, worry etching his forehead. "I heard what happened. You mustn't go out again. That fellow has nothing good to offer."

"I must. This one last time, at least. Please, promise to say nothing."

He sighed. She knew he was torn between keeping the well-paying job and protecting her. After thinking for a minute, he dug into his pocket and removed a slip of paper. He handed it to her.

"This is the last time I help you. You cannot keep going out, Miss. I'll lose more than my job."

"What's this?" Tillie unfolded the paper.

Betty Novak

Arrested for theft

Awaiting trial in the Tombs

"I had trouble finding her. There was an address, but then some people said she disappeared, and it turns out she was arrested. I think they're questioning her about what was written in the paper."

"I guess it did help to get the word out," Tillie said.

John shrugged, then tipped his hat. "Don't stay out all night again."

She nodded and headed for the gate. There wasn't a single splinter of pain in her body, and aside from the desire to lie down and sleep, she felt wonderful. Even better than when she was on the laudanum. She walked across the avenues as quickly as she could.

A figure stood on the corner of Second Avenue. The sight of Ian doused all of Tillie's warm sentiments. She had prepared a whole host of accusations and demands for explanation. She would ask slowly, carefully, so she could understand why he had lied to her so many times. He would be contrite, no doubt. But when he greeted her with a smile, her composure evaporated instantaneously.

"I have a surprise for you," he said, grinning.

"So do I," she said.

Tillie pulled back her right arm and punched him square in the nose.

CHAPTER 14

Alone with the dead! I dare not go out . . .

—Lucy Westenra

With a painful crunch, Tillie's fist connected with Ian's nose. The swing took her off balance, and she stumbled to the side. Ian immediately covered his face and staggered backward.

"Ow!" Tillie yelped. "Ah, God, that hurt!" She did a jig, shaking the pain out of her knuckles. Now she had pain on both sides of her body. Wonderful.

"Why are you saying ow? I'm the one who got hit!" Ian said, still holding his nose. He sounded muffled and congested. When he took his hands away, blood trickled from a nostril.

"Oh my goodness, you're bleeding!" Tillie said.

"And this is surprising? You just hit me!"

"I've never struck anyone before."

"First time for everything," Ian said, gingerly touching the bridge of his nose.

Tillie rubbed her sore hand and scowled at him. "Aren't you even going to apologize?"

"But *you* hit *me!*"

"I'm talking about that article! For lying to me! You never said you were trying to use me to get your name on a byline. I thought you were interested in helping me find my sister's murderer. I need Lucy's diary back immediately."

"I don't have it!" he said. "I gave it to the police like we planned, remember?"

"There was nothing about writing an article! My family is livid!"

"And so are the police! You know how bad this makes them look?" He held up a hand when she stepped closer. "Just listen to me. I brought the diary to the police. They weren't interested. They said it wouldn't change their investigation because they'd already spoken to James Cutter, and the maid wasn't a person of interest. I figured an article would be the best way to light a fire."

"You should have told me!"

"I tried! I would have written it with you and shared that byline! I sent a message, and it probably got thrown in the fire. Ask your mother. I sent three messages, and I never heard back."

Tillie stared at him. She remembered her mother's words yesterday. "Every message you've received from strangers, I've burned. How could you, Mathilda?" He was right. There'd been no way to contact her.

"I did lie, though. There's an editor at the *World* who told me he'd let me write for them if I had a good enough story. This was the story. I guess I'd hoped something would come out of it, but I always thought—" He dabbed the blood from his nostril. "I thought we could write it together. I didn't want to go behind your back. But this was the goal, wasn't it? To find the killer? Now the police are taking the leads more seriously. You can expect your boyfriend is going to be questioned again, and that maid too. We did good."

Tillie deflated. "You did good. But I'm in trouble. They sent me right off to the . . . never mind." She didn't want to talk about Dr. Erikkson. The morphine was humming under her skin, and the pain in her knuckles had already softened. This stuff was wonderful. "Anyway, they're so angry, and I don't blame them."

"Why is anyone angry? I don't get it. We just found out more information, and the police are asking the right questions. You know, they already have that maid in the Tombs."

"I know. I just found out too." Tillie walked unsteadily over to the edge of the sidewalk and sank down to the curb. Ian sat next to her, still touching his nose.

"Now I'll be so ugly—I should bill you for the loss of my looks."

"That'll be a small bill," Tillie said sourly.

"Ouch. That hurt more than the punch."

Tillie sobered. "I'm sorry. I can't believe I did that. The most violent thing I ever did was eat an entire plum pudding at Christmas before it got sent out to the table."

Ian laughed, but he sobered too. "I never lied and said I wasn't writing an article," he said. "I only said I was helping you, and I was."

"Oh, Ian," Tillie said, sighing. "A half truth is still a whole lie."

Ian chortled. "A halber emes iz a gantser lign."

"What's that?"

"It's Yiddish for what you just said. You're speaking the advice of my grandmothers." He sighed. "You're right, and my grandmothers were right too. I was lying. But you have to forgive me, Tillie, because it's all for the right reasons. Let me tell you a story." He stood and started pacing in front of her, the darkened brownstones a quiet backdrop. In the distance, the Third Avenue train steamed by over its elevated metal legs. "Two years ago, off the pier on East Eleventh Street, some boys found parts of a body floating there. A torso and arms. And then at the Brooklyn Navy Yard and Harlem, the legs washed up. No head. The police investigated, but they couldn't find the killer. They had no leads."

"I remember that story," Tillie said. "They called him 'the Scattered Dutchman,' didn't they?"

"Yes. It turns out Ned Brown—a journalist at the *World*—figured out that his fingers were wrinkled, like a masseuse at the Murray Hill bathhouse. From there, they found that a masseuse named William Guldensuppe had been missing for days, and between Brown at the *World* and George Arnold at the *Journal*, Hearst's and Pulitzer's journalists battled it out to find the killer in only a few days." He paused there and crossed his arms.

Tillie tapped her foot. Her anger still simmered deeply, but she was also curious. She wondered if he knew Nellie Bly and if they'd met. "Well, are you going to tell me who did it?"

"Guldensuppe had a lover named Augusta Nack. But she had another lover, a barber named Thorn. And Thorn was jealous. He and Nack planned the murder, then hacked up the body and threw it into the East River."

Tillie shivered. "So you're trying to be a regular Ned Brown, are you?"

Ian nodded. "Don't you see? The coroners, the police—they're deluged with murders. People die every day, and the world does not give one whit. It just keeps turning. It's up to us to find the answers sometimes. If I knew what I did now, I could have thrown that lady in jail, the one who killed my brother. I'd track her down, but all the leads are gone because it's been ten years. I won't let that happen again. Don't you see? This isn't just about a story people want to read."

"What is it about, Ian?" She crossed her arms.

"It's about light versus darkness. It's the primordial battle . . . good and evil, innocence against rotten hearts. Christ and Satan, if that's your take. That's why the Dracula angle is everything to this story. We all want to destroy the evil."

The clouds had scurried past the moon, and they could see each other like it was twilight. Fairy tales and monsters and dragons. She had a dead sister too. That was no fairy tale. She was suddenly so very tired. "You could have just told me you were on the cusp of writing an article," Tillie said. It sounded like a whine.

"I didn't think it would actually happen, to be honest. I hoped but doubted." He took a huge breath. "I am so sorry, Tillie."

She stayed silent for a long time. Her family was furious with her; that was no surprise, though. But she was glad that the police would do something as a result. Maybe Ian's story would stop another murder.

She sighed. "I know you are."

"I promise I'll make it up to you. I'm in this halfway world between being a newsie—which I've been since I was six—and being a writer, on staff. My editor wants a follow-up article, soon. The *Journal* is already trying to get more information on the maid. They're crawling all over the Tombs right now. That will come out tomorrow. But you and I can get a lead on something else."

"James."

"Yes, and this whole vampire business. It sells papers, Tillie. But I know something that will sell it even better."

He reached out a hand, and Tillie let herself be pulled to her feet. Ian grinned. By God, he was irresistible when he had an idea. "Solving this crime and having your name next to mine on the next byline."

They took the Second Avenue elevated instead of the Third. Ian said where they were going was a surprise, but given that Tillie hadn't said no to anything yet, she followed.

"You'll have to organize your notes and start writing. You need a typewriter—you have one, right? One of those portable index ones?"

Tillie shook her head, but her pulse thrummed. Mina Harker had one like that. She could be like Mina, writing down her notes all the time, organizing her thoughts. She loved the idea. Mina had a Traveller typewriter. Maybe she could get one too.

"Do you read the paper every day?" he asked.

"Lately, yes, if only to remind me what day it is," she said, laughing lightly. Her opium habit did make her forget the days, but she wouldn't say that out loud to Ian. She only scanned the articles, though. She read her dictionary, and she'd gone to the Lenox Library. She'd thought she knew so much. Suddenly her world had spasmed and shrunk. She knew nothing.

"I'm not a journalist," she said.

"I don't know about that. You're always carrying around that little notebook." He touched her arm, and sure enough, the little cardboard-covered notebook dented her shirtsleeve. "You're always asking questions, and you know the most obscure things, like you've been searching for answers your whole life. Surely you write in other ways?"

"Lately I've been writing letters to Nellie Bly," she said, glad that the dim light concealed her blushes.

"Really? Does she write back?"

"Well, no. But maybe Mama has been burning those too. Can I ask if she'll send her responses to you?"

"Of course! What do you write to her about?"

Tillie blushed again and said nothing. It seemed like nonsense in her head.

Ian nodded. "I guess that's between you and Nellie, then."

"But writing letters is not the same as writing newspaper articles. I wouldn't know where to start."

"Not all writers were always writers. Everyone starts somewhere. But you have the nose for finding out information and thinking it through. I think you've been preparing for this your whole life and never knew it."

Tillie thought about this for a long time. When the train arrived at Thirty-Fourth Street, she descended the stairs numbly next to Ian. After feeling groggy from the rumbling sway of the train on the tracks, she roused herself, looking about with curiosity.

"Where are we going?"

"You'll see. I don't want to tell you, or else you might not want to come."

Tillie was intrigued enough to continue walking. But there was one question she couldn't resist any longer.

"Do you . . . know Nellie Bly?"

"Of course. I mean, I've read her. Never met her, though. She hasn't been writing as much since she got hitched to that rich fellow."

"Oh." She tried to hide her disappointment. They walked down First Avenue, and soon, Bellevue Hospital lay before them, with its redbrick buildings and sloping slate tile roofs. A wall enclosed the hospital compound, with an arched gateway on Twenty-Seventh Street. Inside the walls, the hospital's iron balconies were filled with sleeping patients hoping the fresh air would rid them of the consumption that plagued them.

They walked along the compound's wall toward the East River. Tillie could smell the stench of the pier, a mix of garbage and rotting pier stumps and humidity of the river, with the faint scent of the ocean where the briny soup of Long Island Sound and the Atlantic Ocean stirred alongside Manhattan.

A lone grayish-white building, simple and stark, sat apart from the hospital compound, surrounded by its own brick wall and fence—as if banished from being allowed too close to the sick or the living. THE MORGUE was etched in gilt letters above the front door.

"What are we doing here?" Tillie asked, recoiling.

"This is where we'll find out if there have been more victims of vampires, or if the bites even match each other, or if they look made by a . . . well, not a vampire. Nobody has looser tongues than the morgue attendants. They're here all night long."

"No." Tillie stepped back, tripping on the edge of the sidewalk. This was far different than when she had been at the cemetery or on Sundays, where the dead lay just outside the stained glass windows of

Trinity Church. She didn't feel awful knowing that Alexander Hamilton and his wife, Elizabeth, lay only feet away. Here, the dead were not yet buried. They were not at peace. They had been pulled from life, in some cases violently so, and were still lost and unclaimed by their loves—if they had any. "No. I want to go home."

Ian turned to her in surprise. "I thought you wanted this," he said.

"To go to a deadhouse? No."

"I meant, I thought you wanted to learn the truth."

"I do, but . . ." She waved her hand at the white building before her.

Ian's face went from perplexed to awash with understanding. "Oh. You're afraid. They can't hurt you."

She shook her head. "No, it's not that. It's just . . ." She cleared her throat. "They have no voice. Lucy doesn't either. And you're asking me. To be her voice, even as far as writing it in a newspaper. What if I make a complete catastrophe of it all? I'm not Lucy. I'll never be as good as her, and I'll never really know her heart or her voice."

"You don't have to be her," Ian said. He extended her a hand. "You just have to be you. That's hard enough, don't you think? What is Tillie Pembroke capable of?"

Tillie bit her lip. She looked up at the facade. There was a single lopsided window separated from three others, as if the builder had forgotten to place it in the row. It seemed to challenge her. *What are you waiting for? I'll still be here when you are gone forever. But if you're willing to open the door and be swallowed whole, I'll tell you all my secrets.*

Tillie knew what she was capable of. Asking questions and seeking answers. It was all her passions always led to. Why does the cricket make such noises at night? Why do people never shed their skin like cicadas do? Why can't we live forever? Why are we afraid?

She reached her hand out and let Ian slip his beneath hers. "All right. But I'm still furious at you, you know."

"I know," Ian said.

"I'm ready. Let's find some answers."

The gate to the property had been left unlocked. Ian pushed it open, but the front door to the building itself was locked. He walked around the building and past a side area that was supplied with coffins ready to be filled. Tillie wanted to shiver, but she did not. This was the geography of the dead. And she must tread here for a while, with respect and without fear.

A door there was locked, so he went back to the front door and knocked. After several minutes, a young man opened it. He looked hardly older than Tillie herself. He wore a dirty smock, and his boots were filthy from . . . Tillie didn't want to guess. Three of his front teeth were missing, and his hair was bright orange. It reminded her of Ada's hair, but even brighter. In the dim light, he seemed afire.

"What you want?" he said gruffly.

"George. We'd like to look at the book."

"Eh, what for?"

"Looking for someone we lost," Ian said. He took a small bag out of his pocket and shook it softly. "I've one good cigar in there and a pouch of shag."

George's eyes lit up, and he grinned. The absent teeth made a keyhole in his smile.

"Very well, my friend! Come this way."

As they followed him down a dark hallway, Tillie whispered, "That's all it took? Some tobacco and a cigar?"

Ian smiled. "I get the feeling I saved you from spending a few dollars."

"You did." She was impressed. "I should take you with me the next time I go to the hat shop."

"Are we walking, or are we shopping for a new wife?" George shouted. He was several paces ahead of them already. The hallways smelled of sickly sweet rot and a biting chemical scent, as if the floors had been scrubbed with Lysol.

"Why is he shouting?" Tillie asked.

"Because it's dead o' night! Keeps the ghosts away!" George shouted again.

Ian rolled his eyes. It made her less afraid, and she laughed instead of shivering. They reached a darkened room. George hit a switch on the wall, and suddenly electric lights blazed on.

Tillie covered her mouth immediately.

The room was only about twenty square feet. It was divided by a partition of glass and iron so visitors could view the dead on the other side, either as a pastime for the curious or for those trying to claim their lost. Four stone tables sat on iron legs. Bodies lay upon them, covered in sheets. A steady stream of water poured from a spigot, soaking the sheets. The water collected in drains in the floor.

"What is the water for?" Tillie asked.

"Makes 'em rot slower," George said. "This way." He unlocked a door, and they entered the chamber with the bodies. Clothing and accessories hung near each table so viewers could identify the dead using their possessions. Bare feet protruded from beneath the nearest sheet. One foot was pointing down, and one foot pointed up. George hooked a thumb in that general direction.

"That one had his pelvis run over by a train. Nasty way to go. He was talking until they got the train off 'im. And then he bled a gusher and died in seconds. Ah, here's the book."

He flipped through a large ledger. Names, descriptions, and dates were written on page after page. This lady, dead from typhus; another, from consumption. Another, drowned. The list went on forever.

"Wachoo looking for, eh?" George asked.

"How often do you hear of someone coming through here with bites on the neck, drained of blood?"

"Oho, you're on de vampire search, ain't ye? I told de doctor here what I'll tell you, but he wouldn't listen to me." George took the ledger and flipped back what seemed fifty or so pages. "Here. One month ago. The first 'un, a lady, 'bout sixteen. They found her near de reservoir, before dey tore it down. Coroner said it was from de fall, but dem holes in her neck ain't from a fall."

Tillie read the ledger.

> *16 year old female, Caucasian*
> *Multiple contusions on face, arms, back, neck. 1 cm*
> *left temple, 1 cm right cheek, punctures on left neck, 0.25*
> *cm x 2, 4 cm apart. No livor mortis present. Licorice*
> *odor noted. Recent granulomata of lungs, possible healed*
> *consumption.*
> *Time of death, est. two days prior to coroner exam.*
> *Cause of death: suicide via fall.*

A separate note in red ink added a name, Annetta Green, and that the body had been claimed by family.

Tillie took out her notebook and began scribbling quickly. "What does *livor mortis* mean?"

"No purple on de backside," George said. When he received a blank stare, he said, "After a body dies, de blood pools below. Gravity. Turns de backside purple, if dey be on de back. Tells you what position dey died, an' how long ago. This gal, no livor mortis."

"So she was found soon after she died?"

"Naw. Said she was out dere two days before she was found. It was June. She was cookin' a good ways by then. No livor mortis means no blood."

Ian and Tillie glanced at each other.

"She also had consumption, it looked like," Ian said.

"True, but not so much. If she died from consumption, she'd look it. I see dem ones all de time. Look like livin' skeletons, if dey got de galloping consumption. She was lucky, till she wasn't."

Tillie suddenly began flipping the pages again, closer to the current date, looking for something.

"What are you looking for?" Ian asked.

Tillie said nothing, concentrating. Her fingers passed down the lists, one after another. And then she stopped and took a deep breath.

"Here. Albert Weber." They read the coroner's notes, and Tillie's fingertip stopped where the description of the puncture marks was. "Look. Point two five centimeters, two of them, four centimeters apart."

This time, Ian flipped the pages in reverse and found the entry for Lucy Pembroke. "Puncture marks, point two five centimeters, antero-lateral neck. Four centimeters apart."

"Hmm, hmm." George raised his eyebrows in a question. He seemed rather amused and had taken the new cigar out and was sucking on the end, like a baby with a lollipop. "The neck bites. I keep telling dem doctors at Bellevue."

"Why haven't they said anything? Reported it?"

George shrugged. "They dunna got a penny, most of dem dead folks."

"No one pays attention when the poor die," Ian said quietly to Tillie. "Your sister . . . she was lucky enough to be born rich and born beautiful."

Lucky. Yes. She was, and Tillie was lucky enough to be in a position to help, even though she was but a woman. It hadn't stopped Nellie Bly from finding out the truth, had it? Nellie Bly had duped physicians into thinking she was mad and had unearthed atrocities in the insane asylum on Blackwell's Island. She had sped around the world in a mere seventy-two days wearing one plaid traveling outfit and carrying a small bag.

If Nellie Bly could do all that, surely Tillie could find a killer.

Tillie peered back at the book in front of them. "We know that whatever is biting these people, it's the same . . . thing."

"Or person," Ian said. "Someone just stabbing and bleeding, they wouldn't be this exact. They either want it to look like one vampire has been biting them or . . ."

"Or it really is a vampire or animal," Tillie finished. "And the note about the woman said there was a licorice smell. Absinthe again—found with my sister and with Albert Weber."

"Since when do vampires kill absinthe drinkers?" Ian said.

Tillie snorted. "Maybe it's the vampires drinking the absinthe. Either way, we have to work faster. This vampire is going to strike again, and soon, based on these three. We have to find it."

George listened to them, his head toggling back and forth and eyes agog. "If'n dere was a vampire, it'd be in de Wood Museum."

"What's the Wood Museum?" Ian asked.

"Pathologic cabinet. Over in de medical school. If dere was a vampire, de teeth would be in de Wood Museum."

Tillie and Ian looked at each other, before Tillie inclined her head toward George.

"By any chance, would you have the keys to the medical school building?" she asked, sweet as can be.

George smiled broadly, his teeth clamping down on the cigar. It fit perfectly in the hole provided by two missing teeth.

"I surely do not." Tillie frowned deeply, but George wasn't done. "But I know who does. Better yet, I can get de doctor to show you, if you can bring me here half dozen of dese fine cigars."

CHAPTER 15

Ah, it is the fault of our science that it wants to explain all;
and if it explain not, then it says there is nothing to explain.

—Van Helsing

Since Ian and Tillie were out of all tempting tobacco products ("I don't carry cigars in my dress!" she had told Ian, after he asked if she had any up her sleeve, like her notebook), they departed the morgue with no name and no immediate way to get into the Wood Museum. Tillie was home again within an hour.

As she put a hand on the big brass knob of the back door, a voice spoke from the thin darkness.

"This was the last time, right?"

Tillie turned to see John leaning against the house, behind some looming shrubbery.

"You could get hurt," he said.

"I am fine, John."

"I don't know about that."

"I thank you for your discretion. And thank you for the information on Betty."

"Have you spoken to her yet?" He left the shelter of the shadows and walked closer. Though he was there to protect the grounds, and hence the family, she felt an urgent need to get inside immediately and put a locked door between them. The morphine was wearing off, and her anxiousness and discomfort were returning like a wave.

"No," Tillie said. She attempted to turn the knob. "Oh. It's locked."

"Here you go." He ascended the steps and leaned toward her, pulling a key from his pocket. Tillie caught a scent that was like lemon polish—like Ada. And something else too. A salty, musky scent, like the ocean. "If I wasn't stuck patrolling this house, I'd be happy to watch you too."

"Thank you, John," Tillie said, slipping inside and feeling thoroughly unclean.

As soon as she went upstairs, she felt ready for sleep. Her mother wouldn't expect her until midday, which still gave her seven hours to slumber. Long enough for her to dissolve into another realm altogether. She went to the walnut box on her dresser, filled the glass syringe, and plunged the medicine into her thigh.

But her mind was not quiet as she slept. There was a jumble of images and voices in her head—the smell of the morgue, the smell of John O'Toole, images of puncture holes in necks, Ian's words of apology to her for the article, and the excitement and fear of writing one herself.

And John's voice, a purr with a sliver of menace within it.

"I'd be happy to watch you too."

⋅——⋅

Her family's anger remained warm and simmering when she awoke for luncheon. But Tillie had dosed herself just before heading down. With the opiate in her, everything felt proper and correct again.

It had been a while since she'd felt severe pain in her collarbone, but perhaps Dr. Erikkson was right, and she did need the quieting normalcy of the morphine. Not so much for an irksome womb but for a mind that desired far more activity—nay, demanded it. And now, when she was forbidden from her opinions, the deprivation caused intolerable suffering.

Her mother and grandmother hardly spoke to her over the delicate salad and beef aspic. But Tillie, content and quiet, must have passed some test, because in the midafternoon as she was drowsing on a chaise in the salon, her mother came and touched her elbow.

"Tillie," she began.

"Mmm."

"Is the food all right?"

"Mmm." It was tolerable, but she was craving paprika *hendl*, the chicken dish that Jonathan Harker ate in *Dracula*. It sounded delicious.

"Are you feeling well?"

She opened one sticky eyelid. "Delightful, actually. Dr. Erikkson's treatments are quite soothing."

"Well. I don't wish for you to use them too much. Temperance . . ."

"I'm not drinking whiskey. It's medicine. You sent me to the doctor, and he said it was necessary."

Her mother sighed. "Well, you do seem so much better." She furtively glanced toward the other end of the salon, where Grandmama was pretending to read but snoozed with her bottom lip sagging low. "In fact, I have an invitation. Bradley Martin is having a small soiree."

Tillie opened her other eyelid and raised an eyebrow. "Small? Bradley's last soiree was seven hundred people and twenty-eight courses at the Waldorf. We all dressed as kings and queens. He doesn't do small very well."

"No, it won't be quite so big. Probably seventy or eighty guests. I asked, as I knew something grander would be too much for you. And after our mourning period, it's not appropriate to revel in such gay festivities. I have a new dress laid out for you, in a dark-purple silk. Quite suitable. Dorothy promised she would be at your side all night."

"No cotillion?" Tillie asked.

"No, no dancing."

"Very well," Tillie said with satisfaction. "So long as James isn't there. I couldn't bear to see him."

"James Cutter? Why?" Her grandmother had woken up and was listening intently.

Wasn't it obvious? "He hit Lucy," Tillie said, incredulous. "He's a suspect in her death! I can't ever see him again."

Her grandmother stood from her chair and ambled over. "Victoria, leave us. Bring the servants with you."

Tillie's mother hesitated, her focus traveling from mother to child, but it lasted only a moment. She left the salon, followed by the two servants. Tillie was alone with her grandmother.

"Grandmama, I can't," Tillie implored. "Not after he treated Lucy that way."

"Listen to me, Mathilda." She sat down next to Tillie on the chaise. Tillie tried not to flinch, remembering how her grandmother had nearly struck her. But she only petted Tillie's head gently. She even tried to smile a little. "It's a lie. I've spoken to James myself. He never so much as touched her in such a way. Lucy lied, and that is the end of the matter."

"No, she didn't. She was writing in a diary. She had no idea anyone would read it. There was no reason to lie to a diary!"

"Mathilda, you must try to speak to James. Kindly, as if the article was never written. It's the best thing to do."

"No. I won't." She looked up at her grandmother, all her sullen anger suffusing her body. The hand that was petting her head swiftly slipped into Tillie's knot of hair and yanked her head painfully back.

Tillie screamed. Her grandmother twisted the knot harder. The pain of her hairs being torn out was like a searing fire all over her head. She screamed again.

"Hush, child. Hush," her grandmother crooned.

Tillie shut her mouth, letting her protest decrescendo into a whimper.

"Better. You will see James Cutter, and you will receive his attentions," she said, as calmly as if she were speaking of the weather. "Your sister may have ruined her prospects, but you will not. Do you think your life is your own?" She pulled again, and Tillie gagged on the phlegm gathering in her throat. "All of our fortunes, all of our reputations, are one and the same. James did nothing that your sister didn't deserve. But he says he is not responsible for her death, and I believe him. More than your sister, who lied relentlessly about that thief of a maid."

Suddenly, the fingers released her hair. Tillie's head came forward, and she choked into her hands, gasping for breath.

"Clean yourself up. You and your mother are to leave in a few hours. You'll be on your best behavior, and you will give James the attention he deserves. Do you understand?"

Tillie nodded.

"Answer me like a proper lady."

"Yes, Grand . . . ma . . . mama," she hiccupped, unable to control her voice. "Y-y-yes, ma'am."

Her grandmother leaned in, and Tillie recoiled reflexively. Grandmama kissed the top of her head. "You are a sweet girl, but we have grossly neglected you, and for that I am truly sorry. It's time you received the attention you deserve, no matter what your father was. You're a Pembroke, not a Flint. Never forget that."

She didn't know her grandmother had left the room until Ada was at her side, smoothing her hair and rubbing her back.

"Oh, Miss Tillie. Come upstairs. Let's get you cleaned up. Come now. Everything will be all right."

She let Ada pull her off the chaise, guide her upstairs, where Ada carefully brushed her hair and finger combed all the loose strands that had been torn out. Without asking, Ada gave Tillie a large injection of morphine, and the throbbing of her scalp subsided. All the while, Ada plied her mistress with the same words: "It's going to be all right. You'll see. It'll be all right."

The words weren't a balm, though. As Ada put her into a shimmering aubergine gown, lustrous with gold embroidery at the bodice, Tillie watched Ada and thought to herself, Oh. My maid is a liar too. Because it's not going to be all right. It never will.

By six o'clock, Tillie was deadened to the coming event. Whether it was due to the medicine or her bruised and numbed heart, she wasn't sure. Ada had dusted fragrant powder over the bump of her broken collarbone, décolletage, and shoulders. Her skin shone satiny under the electric lights of her vanity. Long kid gloves went up to her elbows, and a tasteful amethyst-and-gold collar went on. It would be a suitable follow-up to her sober jet jewelry of mourning. No brilliants tonight.

Her mother said little on the carriage ride. Had she heard what had happened? Watched from a distance? All Tillie knew was that she'd allowed it to happen. Tillie promised herself, as fiercely as she could under the softening influence of the morphine, If I ever have a child, I shall never let anyone hurt them.

They traveled only a few blocks down Fifth Avenue, not far from Cornelius Vanderbilt II's enormous abode and William K. Vanderbilt's Petit Chateau. The Martins' mansion was smaller than its neighboring behemoths but still grand enough to comfortably hold two hundred guests in the main ballroom. A carpet led from the street to a temporary awning over the entrance, complete with policemen and countless drivers and footmen attending to their passengers.

Tillie entered the foyer, ablaze with electric lights and the squawking of no less than three macaws—green, scarlet, and gold and yellow—and dipped a bow to Mr. Martin. He appeared a bit worn out. Even his enormous handlebar mustache drooped. Perhaps the bad press after his ball two years ago still made him melancholy. He'd transformed the Waldorf-Astoria into Versailles (including five thousand roses and three thousand orchids, a decadent twenty-eight-course menu, and guests dressed as Egyptian princesses and Pocahontas), but the extravagance had been sharply criticized. Tonight's event was a shadow of the prior, though wealth still spoke in the splendorous decor.

"Tillie! There's a dear!"

Tillie saw Dorothy and Hazel through the crowd. Dorothy's bloom was on full display in a deep-pink dress with white floral accents. Hazel wore a pearl-gray dress, muted but elegant.

"We've missed you!" Dorothy said, grabbing her arm. Her bad arm. Tillie winced but bore it, as one must bear many things around Dorothy. They accompanied her to the quietest corner, where a servant in white gloves and a black swallowtail coat brought wine, and Tillie could sit on a pouf and exhale for the first time since she'd entered the mansion.

"How have you been since that scandalous article came out?" Dorothy asked. Hazel touched Dorothy's arm, shaking her head. "What? Can I not ask my best friend how she fares?" She turned to Tillie, eyes wide. "I hear he stole a diary of Lucy's from you and lied all about it! What a terrible man!"

"He's not terrible, Dorrie. He's trying to help."

"But insinuating that James had anything to do with it? Ridiculous. James, kill his own fiancée? The perfect Lucy Pembroke? Why would he do such a thing?"

"Perhaps because she wasn't as docile as he liked," Tillie said, sipping her wine. The wine warmed her stomach and relaxed her. Her head felt slightly detached from her body. An odd sensation and not terrible. "You said it yourself."

"I was with him that day, you know," Dorothy said. Again, Hazel touched her friend's arm in warning. Dorothy suddenly began waving at someone past Tillie's view, and she stood up. "It's Charles Potter. We danced a few quadrilles in Newport last summer. I'll be right back."

Hazel smiled wanly at Tillie, both of them used to being left behind in Dorothy's wake. Apparently, Hazel's mother had also been a lady's companion to Dorothy's mother.

"Are you quite all right, Tillie?" she said solicitously. "You seem out of sorts."

"I'm fine." She frowned at Hazel. "Dorrie was with James that day? Why?"

"Not alone. We all saw each other in Union Square, is all. Just a passing hello." She glanced out at the ballroom and then back. "I apologize for Dorrie's behavior. Running off like that. She's getting anxious these days."

"About her safety? I can imagine, after Lucy—"

"Oh no. Not about that." She lowered her voice in a conspiratorial whisper. "She's twenty-eight."

Tillie looked over at Dorothy, who was shamelessly flirting with Charles Potter. Charles seemed more taken with another woman nearby, Margaret something or other, who appeared barely sixteen.

"Twenty-eight," Tillie said.

"You have a decade of good years to find a match," Hazel said. "Dorothy, not so much." She frowned, and then her face lit up. "Oh. I have something for you. I've been meaning to deliver it, but Dorothy has kept me so busy . . ." She pulled two very small bottles out of her reticule. "Opium tinctures. A stronger concoction than you were taking before, so you can carry it with you."

"Oh! The doctor ordered injections, so I may not need it, but thank you."

"It's always good to be prepared. You'll never believe how many things I carry for Dorothy. Lip salve, aspirins, smelling salts, peppermints."

"You're a regular walking pharmacy," Tillie said, smiling.

"I have so many pockets in my dress—it's practically a closet." They laughed together. The wine was dancing with the morphine in Tillie's blood, and she felt wonderful. Absolutely wonderful, except for a nagging drowsiness in her core that said, *If you quiet down for a second, I'll bury you. Just give me one minute of your time.*

Not now, not yet, Tillie thought. "Can I borrow your smelling salts? If I get drowsy, I might need them."

Hazel nodded and handed a tiny vial over. "Oh. There's James," Hazel said. "Put all this away before someone sees it." Tillie dropped the vials into the pearl-beaded reticule hanging from her wrist. As soon as she looked up, there was James, parting from his crowd and coming toward her. Everyone seemed to be watching.

"Darling. You must be so tired from all the fuss. Are you well?" he said in earnest. He looked so contrite, so concerned. "If I had known that gentleman was to treat you and the memory of Lucy so ill, I would have called the watchman on him directly. Shameless, these yellow journalists."

Tillie's usual desire to disappear in the shadows was eclipsed by anger.

He had hit her sister. She could not ignore that truth.

"Yellow or not, Ian seeks the truth," Tillie said crisply. "As do I. Lucy was unhappy before she died. Unhappy with you, James."

James recoiled but recovered quickly. "She was. Lucy wanted so much to work with those poor orphans, but it nearly killed her. She caught typhus, for goodness' sake! I tried to tell her to stop the work and help them in a way that would preserve her health, but she wouldn't listen."

Tillie stood up, and Hazel, wisely, moved away to give them privacy. Her pulse raced, making her slightly dizzy. "Lucy said—she wrote that you hit her, James. What have you to say about that?"

James's face contorted and settled into a pained expression. He looked utterly deflated, a strange mien for such a man. He actually looked sad. "But it's untrue. You must believe me. We did have a few disagreements, but by God, I would never strike a woman. Never."

He extended his hand. "Please, I owe you an explanation. And I have something to show you, which I think you would appreciate. But you can't see it if you're sulking and angry in this corner."

"I'm not sulking!" Tillie said, a little too loudly. At the sudden turn of heads in her direction, she cowered.

"Please," James said. "I wouldn't wish ill between us. You and I have had a loss in our lives we shall never forget. We should not be enemies. So let me explain, since Lucy has already had her word in the matter. I was perhaps not a perfect fiancé, though I'm sure you were a perfect sister."

Again, that contrite expression. James looked younger than his thirty years—almost Tillie's age, for a moment. And for a moment, she felt sorry for him. Especially given that Tillie had been anything but a perfect sister. She'd been too ensconced in her books and dictionary and library to pay much attention to her sister, who swam in attention ever since her engagement. It wasn't fair to imagine that everyone else was perfect.

From afar, Dorothy and Hazel whispered to each other. Dorothy caught Tillie's eye, and she waved her hand a little bit, as if to say, What are you waiting for? Go with him! Shoo!

Tillie hesitated. James leaned forward and whispered near her cheek.

"And I do have a surprise to show you. Consider it a little gift." He paused expectantly. "It has to do with fangs."

Tillie's eyes widened. "What? Fangs? Tell me!" She nearly jumped in place from excitement. She wouldn't take his hand but matched him step for step through the ballroom. The electric lights made the parure sets on the women sparkle as if stars had come to earth to rest on their necks, earlobes, and fingers. Tillie's mother was speaking in earnest to James's parents near the door, and they looked with cool approval when she and James passed them. "Are these the fangs?" Tillie asked. "This society has plenty of teeth between them."

196

"Don't be silly, Mathilda. We all have the capacity to bite. It's only our good breeding that prevents us from being the animals that much of humanity is."

"Good breeding?" Tillie spoke louder than she realized; several people stared. "If most of these people were at risk of losing their fortunes, they would become rather savage, I believe. They'd bite down and never let go."

James didn't chide her or shush her, as she expected. Instead he said affectionately, "You have more cleverness than anyone gives you credit for. You know, I loved your dear sister so very much, but I always was entranced by your spirit, Mathilda."

Tillie blushed. She wobbled a little, and James steadied her. He put her arm over his, and she allowed it.

Down a dark hallway, away from other ears, James paused and turned toward her.

"Now, hear me out. It is true that Lucy and I disagreed. And the day before she disappeared, we had the biggest disagreement we'd ever had." He closed his eyes and swelled his already broad chest. "I'm sorry to say—Lucy struck *me*. It wasn't the other way around. When she tried to hit me a second time, I held out my arm to block her, and my hand hit hers away. I'm sure it hurt, the way she was thrashing against me. But I did not strike her first. I absolutely promise you this. Surely, you could imagine in the fury of a moment, she might see it differently. Have you ever been in such a state that your memory wasn't accurate?" Tillie considered this. She must have still looked unconvinced, because James added, "Do you remember everything from your fall, when you broke your bone? What I said to you when you fell?"

Tillie thought. She could remember James's face but could not remember a single word. "No. I don't remember."

James looked contrite. "I said that your sister would be furious with me for not looking after you. I was angry, mostly at myself. Do you recall now?"

She shook her head, and her shoulders sagged. "I suppose it's possible Lucy remembered things differently."

"Then please let my behavior now speak for itself. For example—" He strode forward, pulling her along, then pushed aside a curtain to a narrow hallway. "Ah. Here we are." The walls were covered in paintings of wild animals. Cheetahs, lions, lush pink flamingos. Several racks of antlers hung above eye level.

She loved the offering and could not hide it.

"Musk ox, water buffalo, kudu, oryx," Tillie said, naming them one by one. "The paintings are wonderful," she admitted.

"But that's not what I wanted to show you." The hall was dimly lit, and at the end was a set of french doors. He opened them, and Tillie gasped.

It was a menagerie. Somewhere in the back of the mansion was this room—an octagonal space with a glass ceiling. The night sky beyond was impeccably clear, the half moon shining through the northern panes. A large aviary contained tiny multicolored birds fluttering here and there. Without the light on, it gave the impression that Bradley Martin had been in the habit of imprisoning beating hearts.

James searched for a light switch, and the wall sconces came alive with a snap and a slight sizzle. Stuffed beasts and their valued parts were everywhere—on the floor, on mounted shelves that filled the walls. There were orangutans, elephant tusks, a fierce baboon with fangs nearly five inches long.

It was marvelous. Tillie turned around, eyes adjusting to the light. "Oh!" she said. There was a lady seated in a chair by the aviary, staring at her with piercing eyes.

James turned in surprise, too, then exhaled in relief. "Lady Remington. Why, whatever are you doing in this dark room?"

"What does it matter? You've shocked the fruit bats into submission, you have. Congratulations." She spoke with a decidedly British accent.

"You're welcome," James said grandly. Lady Remington snorted and rolled her eyes.

"What are you doing hidden back here in the menagerie?" Tillie asked.

"Like most of God's creatures, I dislike stuffy gatherings where one's purpose is to show off, especially when one is no longer a breeding candidate. And it is always breeding season in New York." She was a stout woman nearing her seventies, with white hair in a neat knot atop her head. Her dress was a simple black satin, with an enormous pearl the size of a robin's egg hanging from a golden bar pin at her throat. Her left dress sleeve and skirt looked smudged with dirt, as if she'd been lying on the ground recently.

"Mathilda Pembroke, this is Lady Jeremina Remington. She's been helping to gather specimens for the new Bronx Zoological Exhibit."

Tillie curtsied. Lady Remington took out a cigarette. She waved James away with irritation when he offered to light it; she lit it herself from a taper near the fire.

James had promised fangs, and here they were. Tillie turned in a circle.

Now she could see there were live animals, too, not just the variety of canaries. A cage hung with several dark lumps housed the irritated and shy fruit bats. A large glass box held a python nearly as thick as Tillie's thigh, coiled and staring unblinkingly at all of them. A bird of paradise, with gold-and-brown feathers and an emerald throat, bobbed up and down in a separate cage. A large cat that appeared to be a smaller version of a leopard—an ocelot—paced an iron enclosure behind them, next to a fossilized skull of a saber-toothed cat. Tillie touched the long fang of the fossil and then the teeth of the lower jaw, then twisted her head to investigate the very tips of the fangs.

"A curious one, I see," Lady Remington observed.

"She has a particular interest in biting animals," James said.

"Biting animals? Or being bitten by them?" Lady Remington said.

"How they bite. How they eat," Tillie murmured, still investigating the skull. "And in particular, animals that feed on blood."

"Ah." Lady Remington exhaled a cloud of smoke. "Hematophagy," she said.

"What's that?" James said.

Lady Remington ignored him. Tillie had stooped down, the aubergine silk pooling about her. The ocelot saw the lace on the edge of her hem nearing the cage, and he softly approached and sniffed it.

"Eating blood," Tillie explained to James, who stiffened at the definition. Tillie fished about in her silk sacque and pulled out the smelling salts. She uncorked it near the cage, and the ocelot sniffed it, before grimacing over and over again, the volatile ammonia salts irritating his senses.

"Look at that. His canines, the way they fit perfectly with the lower jaw. And the lower canines are large too. Not as big as the upper set." She pulled the tiny notebook out from her sleeve and began scribbling.

"And what is the significance of that?" Lady Remington noted. "Most canids have smaller canines on the mandible."

"Lower fangs would leave a mark during a bite, don't you think?"

"They would, unless it were a viper. Why this peculiar line of questioning, my dear?"

"Well, if . . . in theory . . . an animal bit a person, would there not be marks from both sets of teeth?"

"There ought to be, yes. But it might be too bloody a mess to notice. Canines are built not just to puncture but tear. Here." Lady Remington pointed to the soft area under her jawline. "And here." She pointed to her belly.

"But some bite with poison. The fangs of this animal are hollow, are they not?" Tillie walked over to where the python sat next to a skeleton of a viper. The taxidermist had set up the skeleton so it looked as if it were about to strike.

"The python is not poisonous," Lady Remington said, annoyed.

"Oh. I know. I was speaking about the viper. It doesn't bite to exsanguinate. It bites with poison. How would an animal bite, with the purpose of drinking blood?"

"Well, for that you would want to observe the vampire bat."

James leaned quietly against the wall in the shadows. He watched them parry, lighting a cigarette and seeming rather entertained. They discussed how the bats would bite small wounds on cattle, then lap up the blood. How the venom of certain snakes would make the blood of humans pop—exciting Tillie, as she thought that perhaps the human victims had been poisoned, until she realized that hemolysis, or the bursting of the red blood cells, would not have rendered them bloodless. Just dead. And then there were bloodsucking butterflies, the ones that would search for liquid and minerals in any place, such as a mud puddle or a patch of sweat or a bloodied limb. Tillie crammed her notebook with details, but she was still left with several lingering questions.

Animals, and theoretically vampires, bit their victims to kill, but most fangs were not made for neat puncture wounds and clean drinking afterward. And hollow fangs were never for sucking blood but for delivering venom. But perhaps a vampire was unlike any normal creature in the natural world? One thing was for sure. She needed to learn if any humans existed with the length of canine needed to puncture a neck, yet not leave a bite mark from below.

"This was altogether so very enlightening. Thank you, Lady Remington."

"You're very welcome, my dear. I say, when our zoological park opens, please do visit. In the meantime, I believe you would make an excellent graduate student in the program up at Oxford. Have you considered it?"

"I haven't gone to college," Tillie said, lowering her head.

"One thing all of us so-called civilized creatures have in common with the most basic leech: opportunity. If you chance upon it, don't let it go."

"I don't think my grandmother would allow it," Tillie said.

"That is a shame," James said, finally speaking. Tillie had almost forgotten he was there. "I think everyone needs an occupation."

She stared. Was this the same James whom Lucy had complained about in her diary? The one who was angry that she seemed preoccupied by helping others?

As they left the room, Lady Remington fished out a card from her person and said, "Contact me if you wish to discuss your education. A woman's mind is ever in need of being uncaged."

Tillie curtsied and departed the menagerie—reluctantly so; she would have wished to watch the animals, investigate the drawers of specimens that Bradley Martin had acquired over the years, and to discuss it all with Lady Remington, but they had already been gone too long. She dreaded the looks and whispers directed toward her when she returned, the snickers over Tillie's inevitable gaucherie. Oh, how she wished Lucy were here!

Tillie took to the lady's retiring room to freshen up and relieve herself. Behind a silk screen, she removed one of the vials of opium that Hazel had given her and studied it. Two to three drops was the normal dosage. She decided on eight and plopped the bitter liquid under her tongue. The bitterness meant potency. Good.

She returned to the ballroom, surprised to find that no one teased her about her absence. It was as though James's approval inculcated her from the gossip of others. Perhaps her grandmother was right. Maybe it was time to settle down. Maybe marrying would allow her freedom in a way she hadn't fully realized. But marrying James would be an unforgivable betrayal of Lucy.

For the first time, she regretted taking such a heavy dosage. The remainder of the evening passed in a blur, and she suddenly found herself already in bed, annoyed by the yellow moonlight entering her room, and stumbled to close the curtains. When she looked down from the window, she saw John O'Toole staring up at her.

That night, she dreamt of John and Lucy having tea together as Lucy delicately touched the gaping holes in her neck. Dr. Erikkson, of all people, was pouring the tea.

"Only a little while longer," Lucy said in the dream. For some reason, the teacup had fangs that hung over Lucy's fingers.

"Until what?" John asked. He stared at Tillie in her dream, not Lucy. Unblinking, like a taxidermied viper. Dr. Erikkson was placing lump after lump of sugar into their teacups. No one seemed to care or notice.

"Why, until another murder." Lucy drank her tea, and the amber liquid dripped from the cuts in her neck, staining the lace of her white dress. "And then, I shan't be so alone."

She stared at Tillie then, still oozing. Unblinking, like John. Dr. Erikkson paused his tea service to stare as well.

"Hurry, Tillie." She sipped languidly. *"Hurry."*

July 2, 1899

Dear Journalist Bly,
That title is terribly unpoetic. My apologies. I am now send-
ing the letters in quadruplicate (I was so happy to see that
this is a real word. I checked the dictionary to be sure) to
your house in the Catskills, the brownstone in Murray Hill,
your home on the Hudson, and your editor at the World.

I have looked into my sister's death, and I still wonder
if vampires are real. It would be easier to blame my dear
Lucy's murder on vampires, because somehow it is ever so
much harder to know that God's own children are such
terrible creatures.

Do you have any tips on finding undead creatures?
I do promise I am completely serious about this question.

Kindly respond to Ian Metzger, at the World. My
mother of late is confiscating my letters.

Also, I know I said I didn't care to know about what
an elephant smells like, but if you know, I suppose it
would be nice to know after all.

Yours, Tillie

CHAPTER 16

You might as well ask a man to eat molecules with a pair of chopsticks, as to try to interest me about the lesser carnivora, when I know of what is before me.

—R. M. Renfield

Tillie woke to the sensation that someone was watching her. When she saw a figure sitting by her bed, she sat upright in a panic.

"Who? Who died?" she croaked.

"For goodness' sake, be quiet!" Her mother was at her bedside, wearing a navy-blue faille dress. "No one has died. I'll be out with the Temperance Society all day today, and I wanted to speak to you."

"Oh." Tillie lay back down. Her head pounded, and her eyelids puckered closed.

"Really, Tillie. Last night's behavior . . . you were positively intoxicated."

"Was I? I suppose the wine was stronger than I expected," Tillie said, shielding her face from the morning sun. "I dreamt I woke up and . . ." She had written a letter to Nellie Bly, hadn't she? Hopefully it wasn't altogether ridiculous. But she said nothing, not wanting her mother to stop the letter from being mailed with the other household correspondences. Oh, but she was tired! She needed at least three more hours of sleep. And an aspirin. And some Bromo-Seltzer. And medicine. She eyed the walnut syringe kit on her armoire, and her mother followed her gaze.

"You only need that for your bad states, not every day." She went to the box and removed all but one of the vials.

"You don't have to take that away," Tillie said. "I won't use it once today, and you'll see."

Her mother brightened. "Very well. Now, if you should like to go out today, Dorothy said she would be happy to take you to buy more frocks. We spent so much time on Lucy's wedding clothes that we have neglected your wardrobe. You'll be out of your mourning clothing soon, and you'll need some brighter frocks."

Shopping. How she disliked it. Especially now, when she needed to find out more about the vampire—and quickly, before another victim showed up. There was so much to do if she wanted to write the article she and Ian had discussed. Last night's encounter with Lady Remington had inspired her.

She suddenly had a thought. Clothing would be billed to their account, but Tillie needed money for other reasons. For the elevated, and her forays with Ian, and perhaps to purchase more medicine. She liked the opium that Hazel had brought her.

"Shopping. Very well. Oh, I need more pocket money, Mama. Dorrie and I like to go to that sweetshop on Madison, and we may go for tea too."

"Of course. So long as you're with Dorothy."

An hour later, Dorothy appeared, and in a bright mood. She chattered on to Tillie and Hazel about the new brocades that she had seen last night and which store was showing the newest Paris fashion for kid slippers with the more pronounced heel. B. Altman, W. & J. Sloane, and Lord & Taylor were Dorothy's favorites, spanning Broadway, Fifth Avenue, and Sixth Avenue below Twenty-Fourth Street. Dorothy often said, "When I die, my heaven will be a circulating, never-ending excursion to Ladies' Mile, my dears."

Tillie had another idea of heaven.

"What about you, Hazel? Do you need to go anywhere?" Tillie asked. Because no one ever asked Hazel.

"Oh, I'm quite satisfied with my wardrobe." She smiled gratefully at Tillie. "Dorothy, how about B. Altman first? I'm sure they have some of those new chiffons."

"Perfect!" Tillie said. "You can drop me off at the Astor Library on Lafayette."

Dorothy looked at her with concern. "You want to go to the library and not to Ladies' Mile? Have you lost your senses?"

Tillie grabbed her hands. "Oh, Dorrie. You have better taste than I do. You can shop for the both of us—"

"Well," Hazel cut in, "Dorothy won't be shopping. We're only here for you." Dorothy seemed to deflate, as if Hazel had just jabbed her spirits with a hatpin. Was she not allowed to spend money? Tillie looked at her, really looked at her, and noticed that Dorothy was wearing the same hat she had worn last week. And the same dress. Usually, she was rarely seen duplicating her dresses.

Tillie shook it off. "Dorrie, just pick out what you think is best and have it charged to my account. And then you can pick me up, and we'll have a splendid tea together. They have my measurements from my last fittings."

"I don't think that's what your mother had in mind, Tillie dear." She paused. "However, you do need some air, and a library is harmless." She clasped her hands together. "And then I can have my way with your wardrobe! What a doll you'll be!"

Tillie hid a grimace, thinking of the styles she would pick out—too many frills, too much décolletage showing, flounces and tucks enough to drown her. But a day at Astor Library to research her article! It would be marvelous. She had her notebook in her sleeve, ready to fill more pages.

By the time the carriage stopped outside the library, Tillie's ears were ringing from Dorothy's incessant chatter, and Hazel had done nothing but encourage the twittering. Tillie was regretting her promise to her mother to forgo the morphine today.

There was talk of the Astor's collection being combined with the Lenox Library's volumes and the whole lot being rehoused at the new library being built over the Croton Reservoir. But for now, there was this lovely establishment. The trees waved merrily as Tillie said goodbye to Dorothy and Hazel and crossed the street, looking up at the simple facade of brick and brownstone, with its Romanesque arches of the Rundbogenstil. A birdlike whistle sounded nearby, a staccato burst of peeps that sounded familiar. She turned to see a newsie at the corner shielding her eyes from the sun. Tillie did her best and whistled several short notes, and the newsie jumped up, grabbed her pile of papers, and jogged down the street.

"Sweetie!" Tillie said. "I thought that was you. I'll take three," she said, holding out a small handful of coins.

"Thank you, Miss Tillie!" Sweetie looked at Tillie critically, then sideways, before adding, "You look like a stick."

"I'm very well," Tillie lied. She was feeling oddly anxious and cold in the summer sun.

"You need to eat a good pork pie an' some jam."

"Well, I'll try to do that. Thank you, Doctor!" She paused. The dream about the peculiar tea party reentered her mind. "Hey, Sweetie. Can I ask you to do something for me?"

"Whassat?"

"Can you . . . sell papers on a particular street and tell me if a certain gentleman ever leaves during the daytime?"

"Sure."

Tillie gave her the address of Dr. Erikkson's home and a description of the doctor. "You can switch off with the others. If you do, I'll promise to bring you a big feast one of these nights."

"We'll do it! Well, g'bye!" Sweetie ran away with her papers, whistling and hollering. "Papes!" Peep-peep-peep. "Pape! Get your *World* here!" Peep-peep-peep.

Tillie smiled, then rubbed her stomach, which clenched and unclenched for a moment. She stepped inside the library, soothed by the dim illumination from the overhead skylights. Huge arches lined the cavernous space, marking the colonnades around the upper floors. Tillie signed in and merely stood in the atrium sighing in pleasure. To be surrounded by books, by thoughts, by places and people and things that she had not yet met—it was a haven unlike any other. She took out her little notebook and went to work.

The three hours passed quickly. She found the origins of the word *vampire*, or *vampir*, in an eighteenth-century travelogue from Germany. The French had spoken of the *vampyre* in works from that time too. In Austria, after the Treaty of Passarowitz, exhuming of bodies and killing of possible vampires had occurred. Fears abounded that vampires were revenants, or animated corpses, or were spirits of those who had died from suicide or were witches or were evil spirits possessing a corpse.

Tillie's notebook was full, and she had to scribble on the papers bought from Sweetie to continue her work. The history, the word origins, the myths, and the stories that swirled around vampires were put to paper, organized, numbered, crossed out, and rewritten. She made notations on how to protect oneself from the creatures (hawthorn and wild rose, in addition to garlic) and how to kill them soundly with staking or decapitation or by placing bits of steel in their mouths. Or even a lemon! Their vulnerability to sunlight and the inability of a vampire to cross running water. Tillie nearly laughed at the advice on how to identify a vampire's coffin: a virgin boy, riding a black virgin horse over a cemetery, would balk at the proper grave.

She was particularly intrigued by what vampires looked like. Bloated; reddish or purplish; blood seeping from the eyes, nose, or mouth when it was resting in its coffin; some were living beings, and some were the dead come alive. Fangs, however, were not always mentioned and were scant in the earlier literature.

"If there were no fangs two centuries ago, then why now?" Tillie whispered. Lord Byron had written of a "living corpse" that sucked blood from people. More recently, *Dracula* had made quite a scene in the literary world. The vampire of that story was taken from folklore, it seemed, polished up and made even more real by a talented author.

She studied animals, which ones drank blood, and how. She read about mosquitos, ticks, leeches, flies, worms, lampreys, even birds that pecked animals to drink their blood. She read of certain cultures where animal blood was drunk and cubes of cooked blood eaten in soups. Transubstantiation was the metaphorical drinking of blood. She thought of the last time she had taken Communion. She wondered if Ian's family had known any myths about vampires. She thought of her own family, whose inherited wealth invested in businesses that paid their workers a mere fraction of the money that came back to their coffers. Money that paid for the lavish surroundings that had made Ian gawk.

"We are all vampires," she said quietly, and she folded up her notes and stuffed them up her sleeve. All her studying had made her incredibly tired; her body felt chilled, and she needed to use the toilet. An ache rose from her gut, wound around her joints, and made her clench her teeth. When Dorothy and Hazel's carriage stopped outside the library, she had to lean heavily on the driver's hand to step inside. A pile of wrapped packages sat on the seat across from her.

"You should see all the dresses I've ordered!" Dorothy exclaimed. "They'll make them right away. We found a glorious peach silk and a cream chiffon and—Tillie? Why, you're white as snow!"

Tillie held her stomach and leaned her perspiring head against the carriage window. "I feel awful."

Dorothy barked an order to her driver to take them back home, but Tillie raised a limp hand.

"No. I need to see Dr. Erikkson." She didn't want her mother to see her like this. Then she would never get those other vials of morphine back.

"Of course."

As the carriage drove uptown toward Dr. Erikkson's town house, Hazel dabbed her linen handkerchief on Tillie's brow and fed her a peppermint.

"Where is the opium I gave you?" Hazel murmured.

"I left it at home," Tillie said, wincing at the cramps coming in waves in her belly. "We left so quickly I forgot to bring it with me. Have you any more?"

"No, but I'll get some for our next trip," Hazel said. She rubbed Tillie's back, and Tillie folded herself over and struggled to keep the bile from rising up her throat.

By the time they were at Dr. Erikkson's, she needed her friends' help to walk even a step. They knocked, and Mrs. Erikkson opened the door, her eyes all astonishment.

"Goodness! Miss Pembroke! What happened?" She opened the door wider, and Tillie's friends brought her inside. "No, not the examination room. Take her to my bed. Dr. Erikkson was up all night attending to Tom, and he's taken the day off to sleep."

They put Tillie in a plainly furnished bedroom down the hallway, with a single narrow bed, Quakerish wooden furniture, and no decorations at all. Tillie curled into a ball. Dorothy stood back while Hazel spoke with Mrs. Erikkson.

"She's been taking opium, on a daily basis. But I believe she said she started injections recently. No doubt, she missed her dose while we were out. She forgot to bring her medicine with her."

Mrs. Erikkson felt Tillie's forehead, which was cold but damp. She had soaked through the cambric of her chemise.

"Toilet," Tillie gasped, holding her cramping belly. Mrs. Erikkson helped her to the water closet, and when Tillie returned, she felt hollow as a reed. Mrs. Erikkson helped lay her down in the bed and brought a cool compress for her head.

"She needs morphine. It's the only thing that will make things right, quickly." Mrs. Erikkson bit her lip and shook her head. "I knew it was a terrible idea. The city is overrun with young ladies becoming morphinomaniacs."

"Morphinomaniac? Has it really gotten so far? I thought she only took laudanum," Dorothy said.

"She is, and it has gone too far." Mrs. Erikkson went to another room and returned quickly with a wooden case. "She'll need treatment to wean herself from the medicine, and a slow tapering of her doses, or she'll be quite sick all the time."

"I'll tell her mama directly," Dorothy said as she backed slowly toward the bedroom door. She'd put her handkerchief to her mouth, as if suddenly afraid to inhale the miasma in the room.

"No!" Tillie reached a trembling hand toward Dorothy. "Please, don't tell her. I'll be well. Just give me an hour or two."

"But—"

"I beg you. Don't tell her. She'll be so angry with me! And then I'll never be let out of the house, not with you or with anyone."

"Very well," Dorothy said. She looked at Hazel, who did not seem overly concerned. It was as if she were used to seeing morphinomaniacs every day of her life. Or perhaps this was Hazel's job, as a lady's companion—to allow her mistress the full spectrum of emotion while she calmly stood by, awaiting her next order. "We shall be back in due time. Let Mrs. Erikkson do her work. Come, Hazel." And they were gone.

Mrs. Erikkson looked at the vials of morphine in the box, checking the dosage. "A full syringe should make you feel quite better. I'll go get Tom."

Tillie sat nearly upright, which made her whole body jolt with pain. "Tom! Your son? Why do you need to call him?"

"My husband is asleep, and I shan't wake him. Someone must administer the medicine." She reddened with embarrassment. "I should have liked to have been a doctor or a nurse myself, but I cannot bear being so close to needles. I faint at the sight of them. Tom administers his own injections, and he shall do yours as well as any doctor. He's quite good, with a steady hand." Mrs. Erikkson held hers up, and they were already trembling. "You see, even thinking about needles, I'm useless."

"I can do it," Tillie said. She stretched out her fingers to show their steadiness, but she was shaking so badly she could hardly focus on them. Mrs. Erikkson raised her eyebrows, and Tillie dropped her hands in surrender.

"I'll get Tom," Mrs. Erikkson said, leaving. After a few minutes, Tom entered. He was wearing a gray plaid robe, old soft trousers, and a nightshirt. As usual, he seemed too tall for his person, hunching over slightly. A hand nervously swept his curls away from his temple.

"Mother said you needed some morphine. I hope you don't mind. I've done this so many times I could probably perform the procedure in my sleep."

Tillie's cramps were coming in waves again. All she could do was wave her hand and gasp.

"Do it," she said.

She lay back on the bed, and Tom carefully unbuttoned her sleeve and exposed her upper arm. Tillie looked away. She felt a sharp point rest against her flesh, then the prick and pain. She sighed, her other hand clenching the sheet beneath her.

"There you go. And now, my turn."

Tillie turned over and watched Tom reload the syringe. He undid the tie to his robe, lifted his nightshirt. Tillie looked away, looked back. His stomach was firm and taut, with tiny mottles of bruises here and there. When he was done, he put the syringe back into the box.

"I'll clean it later. Mother can't stand to even look at the kit." He closed the lid before staggering a slight bit. "Poor thing. She likes to be my nurse and spends all her days in the sickroom with me when Father can't. And yet the sickroom makes her sick!" He stepped toward the door but staggered again and gripped the bedstead.

"What's the matter?" Tillie asked.

Tom steadied himself on the bed. "Dizzy. Again."

"It's not the morphine?"

Tom laughed ruefully. "No, of all the problems I have, morphine is the least of them." Tillie patted the edge of the mattress.

"Sit down, Tom, before you faint. Sit."

Tom sank down gratefully, leaning forward and resting his head in his hands. He took shallow breaths, as if trying to make the sensation pass.

"Your mother can bring you to your room when she's able. Rest a bit." Tillie moved over and covered herself decently with the bed linens. Already, she could feel the opiate spreading in her blood. A calm had begun to wash over her. The gooseflesh was retreating, and the sweating had begun to abate. Soon, her knotted belly would untwist and relax. She sank deeper into the feather bed.

Tom lay next to her, with one leg draped over the frame of the bed, as if a foot on the floor prevented the situation from being entirely improper.

Tillie realized she had fallen asleep only when she awoke. Mrs. Erikkson occupied a rocking chair in the corner and was busily crocheting a blanket out of gray wool. When she saw Tillie blink, she smiled.

"I'm glad you're better. Your friend will be here momentarily to take you home."

"How long have I been asleep?" Tillie asked, her voice creaky.

"Naught but an hour."

Tillie raised her head and saw Tom slumbering next to her beneath a gray blanket. She went crimson with embarrassment.

Mrs. Erikkson looked apologetic. "I would have moved Tom, but he's twice my size, and once he's taken the morphine, I can't even move his leg. But I've been watching you both, and nothing improper occurred—I promise." She got up from her chair and put aside her woolwork. "Come, I'll help you get yourself ready to go." She went to Tillie's side of the bed and gently helped her to sit. "Drink this. It's water, with a little sugar and salt, to keep you from swooning. There you go. Now, stand slowly."

Tillie did as she was told, and Mrs. Erikkson busied herself with brushing her dress to smooth the wrinkles and carefully tucking wayward wisps of hair back into her knot. She brought Tillie to the rocking chair and sat her down. "I'll get your things. I'll give you a supply of morphine for the time being. You shouldn't have stopped taking it so abruptly. You should wean yourself down, slowly, until you don't need the injections anymore."

Tillie nodded. She would stop, once all this business with Lucy was over. But there was too much fraying of her nerves right now.

Mrs. Erikkson left the room, and a drowsy voice came from the bed. "Are you better?" Tom rose to lean on his elbows, blinking sleepily.

"Are you?" Tillie asked.

Neither answered the question. Perhaps neither wanted to speak the truth.

"You're lucky," Tillie said. "Having your mother be your nursemaid and a doctor at your beck and call."

"Mother, yes. She's an angel in darned wool." He smiled before he sank back to the bed and closed his eyes. "My father is another beast altogether."

"I thought he was very concerned for you."

"Oh, he's concerned. Plying me with this medicine and that one, some new poison from the West Indies and another from France and another from Belgium. And all his odd ways."

"What odd ways?" Tillie asked, before she realized she probably should not ask. It was rude.

He gave her a sheepish look. "He refuses to eat in front of any other person."

"He won't eat in front of anyone? Not even his family?"

Unbidden, a passage came to her from *Dracula*.

"He cannot flourish without this diet; he eat not as others. Even friend Jonathan, who lived with him for weeks, did never see him to eat, never!"

"No, he doesn't even eat with us." Tom fidgeted a bit, as if the details he kept to himself had been waiting for the right person, the right moment, to seep out. He glanced at her in shame, then looked down at his lap. "You know my father never bathes? He believes humans were not made to be soaked in water, because we're land mammals. He only cleanses his skin by rubbing it with sand or a hard brush." He dropped his voice. "I once saw him having relations with my mother, and he refused to take his clothing off—"

"Tom!" Mrs. Erikkson had stepped into the room. Tillie's face flushed crimson, and so had Mrs. Erikkson's. But Tom seemed rather delighted at how uncomfortable everyone had suddenly become.

"Well! It's time for my bath. Goodbye, Miss Pembroke. I am so glad you are better." He shuffled out of the room, and Mrs. Erikkson shook her head.

"You must forgive my son. It is our fault he hasn't been in the company of proper society. He has quite an imagination—" She waved her hand hastily, but her cheeks were still ruddy. "He ought not say such things, and to such a lady as yourself. My deepest apologies."

"Oh. It's quite all right. He's not well, and he's to be given some liberties, surely." Tillie gently stood from the chair. "I ought to go."

Mrs. Erikkson stood aside so she could pass, but Tillie paused.

"I can't thank you enough for your care, Mrs. Erikkson."

She smiled. "It's my pleasure. There are women doctors today, you know. If I could have had an education—a real education, beyond the schoolhouse, as a child . . . but"—she sighed—"I chose love, and I chose family." She clasped her hands together. Her passion seemed to blaze bright for a moment, sparking and snapping in her eyes. "We are on the cusp of a new century. Who knows what women will do in the next years? Promise me you'll think of me, when you decide what you shall do with the time you have before you."

Tillie didn't quite know what to say. Did she have a choice about her future? Did she?

Mrs. Erikkson handed her a small brown parcel of medicine, repeating the advice that she stop the injections as soon as she could, and Tillie was released into the company of Dorothy and Hazel. Soon, she was home to tell her mother about dresses she had bought but not seen and the silks she had raved over but not touched. She was late, she explained, because Dorothy insisted on seeing two newly opened stores on Sixth Avenue.

At dinner, there was roasted duck with creamed peas. Her mother commented endlessly over the minutes of the Temperance Society, while her grandmama fed Elenora bits of strawberry from her silver fork. Meanwhile, all Tillie could think about were her notes from the library and Mrs. Erikkson's words.

Nellie Bly had found fame exposing the realities of Blackwell's Island Asylum. She'd traveled the world. But Nellie Bly had never exposed a vampiric murderer who had slain her own flesh and blood.

The brass ring was seemingly out of reach, but Tillie would capture it. No matter what the cost.

CHAPTER 17

May I cut off the head of dead Miss Lucy?

—Van Helsing

So long as Tillie's behavior remained appropriate, her mother's direct gaze upon her became intermittent and unfocused. When her dresses arrived later in the week, Mama praised her taste. Secretly, Tillie fumed at the candy-bright colors that Dorothy had chosen for her. Iced pink satin? Peach, with green silk trim? She must think that Tillie was a petit four instead of an actual person.

Tillie had begun reading the papers every day—scouring them for any details of fresh murders, yes, but also studying the articles. There was a rhythm to how they exclaimed out their news and how tidy the opening paragraphs were in condensing the information and drawing the reader to the rest of the story. A flow and ebb that was becoming audible music to her.

James's words came back to her—"I think everyone needs an occupation." Had he meant it?

That night, Tillie waited for Ada and John to occupy themselves, then crept out the front door. By the end of the hour, she was at Newspaper Row. Ian met her on the front step of the World Building, smiling grandly at her.

"I have something to show you."

"More secrets?" Tillie asked, smirking.

"I deserved that." But instead of saying anything more, he took her hand and pulled her along Nassau Street, then turned onto Spruce Street. A churning, chugging sound grew louder and louder as they passed by the few brick buildings, before Ian knocked on a nondescript front door. A man in a dirty white smock opened the door and nodded at them.

"Just five minutes. Don't touch anything, and don't leave a smudge!"

"Thanks, Peter."

Down a hallway and through a door, Tillie and Ian descended to a basement. The churning noise grew louder and louder. They entered a vast room, and Tillie gasped.

Two enormous engines were situated in the space. The large one seemed to be quiet, but the smaller one had a massive flywheel turning at a rapid pace. Metal shafts thicker than her leg were spinning out of it, and black belts were turning and twisting out of the great machine into the walls and disappearing thence. Not a single smudge lay anywhere on the walls or floors.

"The big one is one hundred and fifty horsepower; the smaller one is seventy-five, and it's running one hundred and fifty different presses nearby."

"Right now?" Tillie asked, watching the machine. "At all the different houses? The *Tribune*? And the *Sun*?"

"The biggest ones, like the *Herald* and the *World*, have their own in the basement."

They left, with Ian palming some coins into Peter's hand, before they went back around the corner toward the World Building. The structure was beautiful—a dome-topped skyscraper with an arched opening that made Tillie shrink in consequence.

"Pulitzer's office is in the dome. He likes to look down at the street and the other printing houses." Ian waved at a guard inside, who opened the front doors to the marble lobby.

To the right, sectioned off with glass plate panels, a main public office was paved with tile and filled with solid walnut desks. They went into the wood-paneled elevator, and Ian showed her the editorial room upstairs, where the men decided upon which stories would be written and published, and in which edition, the morning or evening. There were speaking tubes and a telegraph office and a dumbwaiter that delivered messages to the pressroom, filled with tiny desks and typewriters. Another floor had a library of newspapers bound into gigantic books.

"Here you go. I can't get into any other building yet, so we'll have to make do with this for now."

Tillie touched the leather-bound archives on the shelves around her. "Is there an index?"

"Not a good one."

She looked through one handwritten index, which had yet to be typed into a formal one like the other volumes. Ian, meanwhile, took off his jacket, bunched it into a pillow, and lay down on the bare floor. He shut his eyes immediately.

"What are you doing?" Tillie asked, hands on her hips.

"You're going to research. I'm going to sleep. Until they promise to print my next article, I'm depending on my paper sales to pay my rent."

"Oh." Tillie felt awkward. She didn't have to worry about her housing or food. Now that Ian was motionless on the floor—apparently, snatching rest where he could was a honed skill—she noticed how his elbow patches had been darned multiple times and how the holes in the toes of his boots had gotten larger. A good rain, and his feet would be soaked and at risk for winter chilblains and summer infections.

All these days . . . where did he eat? What did he eat? Why did he care so much to write these—

"Tillie, can you stop staring?" Ian said, eyes still shut. "I can't sleep with an eyeball trained on me."

Tillie spun around and marched deeper into the archives, her face stovepipe-hot from shame. She spent the next three hours refusing to even glance at Ian, while she pulled tome after tome filled with the thin pages of the *World*. It didn't take long before she was ensconced in stories of blood and death and the undead themselves.

There was an article in 1882 about Mercy Lena Brown, a young woman dug up from her grave in Exeter, Rhode Island, in order to prevent her from sucking the lifeblood out of her brother Edwin, who was dying from galloping consumption. She looked well preserved after being dead for months. Her heart and liver were burned and her brother made to eat the ashes.

"Not . . . tasty," Tillie murmured to herself as she wrote notes.

Edwin died soon after, nevertheless.

In 1854, corpses in Griswold, Connecticut, were apparently rising from the dead to feast on the living. They, too, were exhumed and burned so that their "essence" could be consumed by the living to save them.

There was another young man, a Portuguese sailor. He had already killed a fellow sailor when he was found sucking the blood of another and sentenced to death by hanging. Clearly, if they had been able to read *Dracula*, they would have known that hanging was not the most permanent way to kill a vampire.

Beheading was ideal. Tillie bit her lip and thought of Lucy; she shivered and read on.

At the end of three hours, Ian awoke to walk her out of the building, and they said their goodbyes.

But one night would not be enough.

Tillie escaped from her house five nights that week. Ian even opened up the pressroom on the upper floor, where Tillie learned how to use a typewriter, haltingly at first and with slightly more confidence as the hours went on. After an hour or two of reading papers and scribbling notes, she'd go to one of the Remington typewriters and type her notes in a more orderly fashion. She felt like Mina Harker, type-type-typing away. Mina, helping to save her best friend, Lucy, from the dark and unholy nether life. Tillie, helping to solve the violent murder of her sister, Lucy. Mina Harker and Tillie Pembroke, together, every time her fingers touched those typewriter keys. All for Lucy.

At the end of the night, Ian took her notes home with him so there was nothing to be accidentally discovered by her mother. Maybe it was stupid to trust him so. But Tillie was so desperate for this article to be written that she was willing to risk it. If he asked her to swim in the East River alongside rats and flotsam for the sake of research, she would.

Every day, Tillie roused herself from her late-morning sleep and morphine stupor to eat luncheon with her mother and grandmother. All the while, she would secretly practice typing on her lap so she could get more efficient. Her mother would notice her arms moving slightly with her hands beneath the table, in between her salad and soup course.

"What are you doing, Mathilda?"

"I have an itch," Tillie would explain and go back to her exercises.

C-A-T-C-A-T-C-A-T

D-O-G-D-O-G

And of course:

V-A-M-P-I-R-E-V-A-M-P-I-R-E-V-A-M-P-I-R-E

B-L-O-O-D-B-L-O-O-D-B-L-O-O-D

But some other combinations kept creeping into her exercises.

I-A-N-I-A-N-I-A-N

T-O-M-T-O-M-T-O-M

On the fourth night—Ian had managed to get her into the archives of the *Tribune* and the *Herald*, for the exorbitant cost of a two-dollar bribe each time—she was finishing up her work at the *Tribune* and enjoying the use of a fine Munson typewriter, for a change. Ian yawned and asked if she was done.

"I am, just about. But I feel terrible that you should sleep on these horribly hard floors."

"It's better than work."

She smiled. Ian looked exhausted, and it took her smile away. "How are the paper sales going?"

"Not well. Pulitzer and Hearst have made us pay ten cents more a bundle for months now. I'm barely making what I need just to buy the papers in the first place."

"That's ridiculous!" Tillie exclaimed.

"It is. We've been trying to talk to them, but nothing."

"How are Piper? And Sweetie and Pops?"

"They're up late, trying to sell every paper since the *World* won't buy the unsold ones back anymore. Oh." He winked at her. "And they've been watching your Dr. Erikkson. Never leaves the house. They've even watched to see if he leaves from a back door. He's as afraid of the sun as our Count Dracula."

"Really!" Tillie said, astonished. "He doesn't eat in front of people, too, you know. And he doesn't bathe using water. There's something quite wrong with him." She couldn't bear to bring up how he had his relations with his wife.

"I'll say. He's an odd duck. I hate eating alone!"

"Speaking of. Are Piper, Sweetie, and Pops getting enough to eat?"

"They go to the lodging house, and sometimes the nuns give them a free meal. Old, hard bread and coffee barely fit to drink. They donate the best they can."

"I should like to feed you all," Tillie said and bit her lip. "I promised those scamps I would. Mama doesn't give me much walking-around money. She says that if I'm to buy clothing to just charge it to our account." Which also meant when she ran out of morphine in two days, she would not have the money to buy it. She still had Hazel's tincture, but perhaps Dorothy could buy more, for her. "How about I bring a basket tomorrow? I'll find a way."

"Sounds good. But we can't have a picnic here. I tell you what. Since you're so sore about me sleeping on these hard floors, how about we go to my place? It's a luxurious lookout, let me tell you."

"All right." With the children, surely there would be nothing to worry about. "Tell me where, and I'll see you after midnight. Though I hate the idea of waking up those children, wherever they are."

"Aw, don't worry about that. I'll have them come stay with me."

The next night, after Ada had already met John in the back of the house, Tillie crept about the kitchen, careful not to bump any hanging pots. The pantry was enormous, well laden with potatoes, onions, carrots in the root baskets, and barrels full near to the brim with flour and sugar. Spices sat in jars beside strings of garlic and wreaths of dried thyme and rosemary. There was a large icebox for holding cream, milk, meat, and fish, but also a large old cellar beneath the pantry for extra goods.

Tillie found a clean, empty flour sack and filled it with two loaves of bread, half a dozen sausages, dried fruit, and an enormous wedge of cheese. She added several cookies, then scurried to her grandmother's office to take a small bottle of port off the liquor trolley. She slung the booty over her good shoulder and took a quick peek out the window by the kitchen.

The moon was only a sliver, and it took her a moment to see within the darkness. Movement caught her eye by the iron fence abutting the Havemeyers' lot next door. John was leaning against the fence, Ada's back pressed up against him, her eyes closed as if dreaming. John had his hands around her waist and seemed to be whispering in her ear. Tillie was about to draw away from the window, when John's eyes flicked upward and caught hers. Or did they? He glanced down, smiling ever so slightly, as if he had an audience. His hands slid around the small of Ada's back to her belly, then upward as he cupped her bosom over the bodice of her dress. Ada's mouth opened in pleasure. John's smile grew wider. His eyes flicked back up to the house, and Tillie fled.

Ian met her at the station on Grand Street. This time, they went a few blocks farther east to Forsyth Street, where he stopped outside a rather shabby tenement, a duplicate of at least three others on the block.

"Here we are. My castle." He seemed oddly nervous. Ian was never nervous.

"Well. Let's go up."

"Okay. The scamps are already upstairs and waiting." He gestured to the sack on her back and said, "Are you playing Santa Claus? In July?"

"I guess I am."

"Can I carry that for you?"

"No. I'm just fine."

Ian led her up several flights of stairs. The building was dark and dank, as if air never passed through to cleanse the hallways. On the fifth floor, she looked about her.

"Well? Which one is yours?" There were two doors, one near and one down the hallway. She pretended not to see a mouse scurry along the edge of the wall.

"This one. But we're not going in."

"Why on earth not?" Tillie asked. "Where are the children?"

Ian shuffled his feet a little. "Well, see. I stay with a family. Mrs. Salzberger and her four kids and her sister and her sister's two kids."

"Too late to intrude, then?"

"Well, no. I can come and go as I please. I have a cot in one of the bedrooms, with their boys. But in the summer, it's a veritable oven. An oven baking week-old pickles instead of dough. So I stay up on this tar beach at night." He opened the other door to an extremely narrow set of stairs. At the top, he opened another door, and a puff of warm night air hit Tillie. It smelled like a summer breeze, instead of the warmed-over gutter stink from the street. The roof was covered in wooden slats, and an iron pole across one side held two shirts hanging in the wind. An oil lamp sat nearby, illuminating a pallet with blankets in the corner. On it, three indistinct lumps lay.

Tillie spied one curly head, one with bushy blond hair, and another dark head. Pops was sleeping on his back, mouth sagging open. Piper had been sucking his thumb but had released it so it lay temptingly an inch from his drooling mouth. Sweetie was curled up so tight she looked like a pill bug. Ian leaned over to wake them, but Tillie pulled his arm back.

"Don't," she whispered. "When they wake up, we'll give them something to eat."

"All right." Ian pulled a satchel off his shoulder and took out a sheaf of papers. "Here are your notes. And two pencils and a copy of that issue from the *Brooklyn Daily Eagle* about the sailor vampire."

"Thank you. This is wonderful. There's just enough light that I can work." She looked around. "You really sleep up here in the summer?"

"I do. I have the whole sky as my room. What's not to like?" He smiled, but it was crooked. The smile that meant he was slightly embarrassed but trying very hard not to be.

"I guess you have some privacy," Tillie thought aloud.

"I do, but some days when I sleep in, there's a nurse walking across the rooftops visiting families in the tenements here. One of them almost stepped on my face."

"Still, you have your freedom. Nobody watching you, nobody always checking on you."

"Well, that goes both ways. I have no parents, so there are days when I wish someone was checking on me. Mrs. Salzberger doesn't count—she just wants to make sure I'll pay her my ten dollars every month. At least you have a roof over your head, no matter what."

"I would trade that for this roof, any day," Tillie said. "So long as no one steps on my face," she added. They both laughed softly. Tillie looked around. "Where should I sit?"

Ian procured a blanket and spread it over the roof halfway across from where the children slept. The clouds dimmed the rictus moon in the sky. A small oil lamp provided a tiny warm glow.

"No typewriter here, but you should be able to work well enough."

"How will we divide the writing?"

"How about you write what you can, and I'll edit it and add what's missing, and we'll go from there?"

"Ian. I've never written anything in my life, aside from letters and a few things my teachers asked of me, and that was when I was thirteen. What if it's terrible?"

"Don't give up before you try. Defeat is particularly lethal early on in any journey; don't let it be your compass." He settled in nearby and folded his hands behind his head for a pillow. "My mother and father, if they knew how tough it would be here, they never would have left the shtetl. But they did. They did the impossible."

"And what about you? What are you using as your compass?"

He looked at her seriously, then tapped his chest. "Here. I hear my mother's words all the time. Di liebe is zees, nor zi iz gut mit broyt. And my father's. He'd tell me not to take anything too seriously. And my brother—and his giggles. They're with me, though they're not. And I know what they want me to do. I just have to do what's right in my heart too. There's room enough for all the right choices."

He closed his eyes, and Tillie wasn't sure if he was feigning sleep or exhausted. Everyone had their own north, and Tillie's right now was on her lap. If writing this article helped find Lucy's killer, then it was all worth it.

She went to work organizing her notes. After an hour or so, she stood to stretch and walked to the edge of the roof. Laundry hung between the buildings, flapping like tiny flags in the darkness. There was the pointed spire of Trinity Church to the south and the towers of Brooklyn Bridge to the southeast. A chill iced her insides. She shivered, but it did not go away.

"Hey. You okay?" Ian had woken and lay propped up on his elbows.

"Yes. I was just thinking. Somewhere out there, asleep or awake, is that monster who killed Lucy. And Albert and Annetta. Probably more." She frowned. "He's probably already drawn a bead on the next one. It makes me want to scream and do something useful. I don't know if writing a silly article about vampires is going to catch anyone."

"It's what we have. Our sword is the word. You and I aren't the other kind of soldier." He walked up behind her and put a hand on her shoulder. She was tempted to grasp that hand with both of hers and squeeze it hard enough to bruise his skin. "Come away from the edge of the roof. You're making me nervous."

They sat again on their blanket. "You know, we still don't know anything about Betty. Lucy's maid. Last I heard, she was in the Tombs for thievery. I wish we could speak to her."

"I wish we knew someone there who could get us some information."

Tillie hesitated. John O'Toole had friends there, but she was loath to ask him for any more favors. But Betty would know Lucy's exact movements the day she'd died. She'd been found near the museum, but had she gone straight there? Lucy had written in her diary about being eager to return to the Foundling Hospital once Dr. Erikkson fully cleared her.

"Ian. The three victims—they were all sick before they died. I mean, they were sick, but then they got better. It's so odd."

He frowned. "I don't understand the connection."

"Lucy had typhus. The boy had cholera, it sounded like. And that woman, she had consumption. What if they were killed because of their diseases?"

"You've been sick. With your broken bone and all. Nothing's tried to attack you."

She deflated for a moment, then perked up. "But the others were infections, not a simple broken bone. It's different."

He shrugged. "I still don't see why a vampire would target sick people. Drink the blood of someone with the plague or leprosy? No thank you." Ian's stomach yowled plaintively, and they both laughed. "Speaking of food, though, I'm hungry."

"Me too," Tillie said. She gathered her bag and showed him the bounty.

"Jiminy Crickets! Did you empty out your whole larder?"

"No," she said. "We have plenty, though I'll have to explain to the maids that I was very hungry last night."

Ian had already broken off a piece of bread and was munching it with some dried apricots. He cut off an edge of the cheese, then alternated bites from each fistful of food. He was hungry. Very much so. It made her mournful. How often did Ian ignore his physical discomfort because he lacked funds to appease it? A shuffling noise came from behind her.

Sweetie appeared, groggy eyed. Her brown hair was matted against one side of her head. Pops was rubbing his eyes, and Piper suddenly rolled over and farted rather loudly.

"Weren't you going to invite us?" Pops asked.

"Of course! Sit down and eat!"

The three children quickly shook off their tiredness and began eating with zeal. They oohed and aahed over the food. Ian went downstairs and returned with a jug of water that they passed around.

"Next time, I'll bring some good milk," Tillie said.

"Next time, bring more cookies!" Piper said.

Sweetie added, "Cake! I like cake!" Her words were puffy from having a jaw full of bread.

"Be polite, will yeh," Pops said. He was probably younger than the other two, making this parental comment particularly odd. "Hey, Tillie. We've been takin' turns watching that odd doctor."

"Oh! Ian said he really does stay home all the time?"

"Almost always," Piper chimed in, his face smeared with crumbs.

"Almost?" Tillie asked.

"I followed him one evening, almost sunset. He went into one of those saloons. With the ladies!" Sweetie wiggled her eyebrows, and everyone knew what kind of saloon they were speaking of.

"But if he left before the sun set, that's not so vampiric, is it?" She looked at Ian, who shrugged.

"Perhaps he's not a vampire. Doesn't mean he's not a killer."

"I just can't see it," Tillie said.

"Neither can I. But perhaps that's the point. A murderer doesn't want to wear a sign around his neck that says he's a killer."

"True."

While they chatted on and ate, Tillie portioned out the food so they could each take some along for later. The sausages would need to be cooked, but there was still at least a bundle of dried fruit, a small wedge of cheese, and half a loaf of bread for each of them to take with them. Glutted, they took their bundles thankfully and went back to their pallet in the corner of the roof and fell instantly back asleep.

Tillie and Ian passed back and forth the small bottle of port. It was deliciously sweet and strong, and Tillie's spine felt relaxed and watery. The tincture she took while the others were busy eating helped ease the growing discomfort.

"I've been thinking about Mrs. Erikkson," Tillie said. She stood up and swayed in the breeze. "She said she wished I went to school." Lady Remington had suggested something similar. She turned to Ian. "Do you think I should go to college?"

"What do you want?" Ian asked. He stood too. When Tillie got too close to the edge of the roof, he gently took her hand and pulled her back toward him. "Hey. You keep going too close to the edge. Stop that."

"I like it. It makes me feel like the horizon is closer. Which it can never be, given that we are on a planetary sphere. No matter how much I run or walk, it never gets closer." Tillie stumbled, feeling the effects of the port wine and the laudanum mixing in her veins. Her limbs were loose and rubbery. A melting sensation had spread throughout her body. God, it felt delicious.

"It's our lot in life, like moths to flame. We keep heading that way, or else we might as well die."

"Are you a moth?" Tillie asked. She spun around to him, and their bellies touched. Ian steadied her by holding her arms.

"Hey. Are you all right?" he asked.

"Why don't you ever answer my questions?" Tillie asked seriously. Ian was swaying now too. No; that was just her own body, shifting them both left and right and left.

"I think you might be drunk," he said.

"I think I might be too." She looked up at him. That curly hair. Those brown eyes. She reached up and wound her fingers around the back of his neck. Ian closed his eyes halfway and inhaled sharply as she put her other hand around his waist. "Your eyelashes are entirely too long for a boy," she said. And then she leaned in to kiss him.

For a short moment, their lips moved beneath each other's. Ian tasted of port and cinnamon cookies. She leaned against his chest, feeling the warmth of him seeping toward her. And then he gently pushed her away.

"You're drunk," he said again and wiped his mouth.

"I am fine."

"Drink some water and sober up." He seemed disappointed and angry and sad, all at once.

With this kiss, there had been no Piper, Sweetie, and Pops watching. No dare to be had. And it had ended far too quickly. Tillie had felt like she were flying and falling at the same time, before she crashed.

"I thought all the boys wanted to kiss a girl," she said, before plopping back down on the blanket. Her head was spinning.

"Not like this." He sat back down and looked through her papers. "Come on. Drunk or no, we have work to do."

Tillie did sober up in measures over the next two hours. By the time her head was clear, they were organizing paragraphs, and she was ready to start writing. The newsies had woken up at the faintest lightening of sky on the eastern horizon.

"Time to buy the papers," Pops said, yawning. "Thank you for the food, Miss Tillie." His small hand touched his cap. They scrambled down the stairs from the roof, and in a few minutes, she could hear their feet thrumming on the street as they ran downtown toward Newspaper Row. Tillie carefully peered over the edge of the building. They looked so very tiny in the distance. It would be too easy to pinch them into nonexistence. Something caught in her chest, and she looked away so she wouldn't see them completely disappear down Bowery Street.

Ian was strangely formal and stiff when they readied to leave. Tillie carefully gathered all the papers. For once, she had to bring them with her so she could complete her work at home.

"Ian, turn away for a minute."

"Why?" he asked, staring.

"Just . . . turn away. I have to hide these notes."

"Oh. Oh!" He turned around quickly. She folded the papers once, then carefully bent over to sandwich them between her bosom and her corset. Lately, her corset had been fitting loosely. How convenient.

"All right. I'm done."

Ian turned around. "Where did they go?"

"A gentleman would never ask such a question," Tillie said, smirking.

"And a lady would never hide secret documents in her undergarments," he retorted.

"Oh mercy. Can we please stop talking now?" Tillie covered her face.

Ian changed the topic to discuss when she would bring him a rough draft. That would be the last of her work. For now.

"We still need to go to the pathologic cabinet," she said.

"We have enough information for now. We can add that at a later time."

"Shall we meet here or at Newspaper Row again?"

"How about you just mail me your article? I don't want you to get into trouble, sneaking out all the time." He thrust his hands in his pockets and smiled. "Good luck on your writing."

Tillie nodded at his friendly goodbye, waiting for something. What, exactly? Now that her head was clear, she wasn't sure. She descended the dark tenement stairs and headed back to the elevated train. It was about four blocks away, and Ian had left to go south to Newspaper Row. As she approached the station in the soft darkness that was already loosening with the coming dawn, she saw a figure standing by the metal stairs heading up to the station.

Tillie felt exposed and vulnerable. The first time she'd met Ian in the darkness of Fifth Avenue, she was frightened too. But since she knew this couldn't be him, her fear swelled. She hugged her chest, feeling her papers crinkle against her skin. Perhaps she could walk to another elevated—but then she might arrive home too late. She couldn't afford to enter the house after dawn. She decided she would just walk past him, and if she needed help, the stationmaster was just up the stairs collecting fares.

As she approached, the man pushed off from where he was leaning and began to walk toward her. She had a foreboding sensation, a familiar one. A pair of unwelcome eyes had been on her of late. She raised her hand in protest, ready to tell John O'Toole that he had no business following her but terrified that her transgressions would finally be reported to her mother and, worse, her grandmother.

When it came down to it, she had no idea what to say to him. In the shadows, he spoke first.

"Mathilda Pembroke. What do you think you're doing?"

And that was when she realized it wasn't John O'Toole.

It was James Cutter.

CHAPTER 18

I have tried to keep an open mind; and it is not the ordinary things of life that could close it, but the strange things, the extraordinary things, the things that make one doubt if they be mad or sane.

—Van Helsing

"James!" Tillie put a protective hand to her bosom and the papers. "What on earth are you doing here?"

"The more important question is, What are you doing here, Mathilda?" James walked to her. She'd expected him to look angry, but his face was all worry. "You could have gotten hurt." He nodded to a carriage nearby, the only carriage on the street. The driver stepped down and opened the door. James offered his hand. "Please."

"I can take the elevated," she said.

The worry on his face transformed to confusion. "You took the train down here?"

"Yes."

"By yourself?"

"Yes."

"What were you doing?"

"It's not your concern, James." She didn't say this meanly, just plainly. "I'm fine."

"Well, now that I'm here, I insist on taking you back safely." He held his arm out toward the carriage. Still, Tillie didn't move.

"I don't need a governess to watch over me," Tillie said quietly.

"No, you need an escort."

Still, Tillie didn't move.

James took a small brown bottle from his pocket. "I suspect you'll be needing this soon. The carriage will be faster. You'll be home well before your family learns that you were gone."

"How did you know I was here?"

"John O'Toole followed you, and he contacted me. I recently started paying him to keep an extra eye on you, for my sake. I didn't realize I'd be alerted so soon."

Now all her secrets were no longer hers.

"Come now. The last thing I want is for you to be hurt, like your sister."

Tillie looked at the bottle. Her hands curled into fists. James had come closer and gently put his hand on the small of her back. She walked forward, afraid the pressure of his hand might crackle the paperwork in her bodice. Even so, the lure worked well. Tillie had her own medicine bottle in her pocket, but procuring more was always an issue. The port and opium she'd taken before seemed to have evaporated clean away.

"Very well." Tillie took James's hand and allowed herself to be helped into the carriage. The velvet cushions were plush and sleek, compared to the elevated train seats. Then again, she'd grown accustomed to the jarring rides on the train. She liked them.

"Here," James said once the carriage pulled forward.

She felt ashamed at her need, but she couldn't resist the shiny new bottle. She unscrewed the top and dropped a comfortable dose under her tongue. She screwed the top back on and put it into her pocket.

"Thank you." The opium dissolved right into her mouth and throat. Ian seemed to always be judging her for her need, but James never did.

"So Mat—Tillie." He smiled. "Habit. I do like the name Mathilda, you know."

Tillie leaned her head against the cushioned back. "Mathilda is my great-grandmother's name, on my mother's side. My middle name is Cora, after my father's mother. I'd rather be called Cora, but Mama doesn't like it."

"Why? Cora is a perfectly nice name."

"Oh, they weren't terribly wealthy. Papa's parents lived in Philadelphia. When they died, he had very little money, but he was clever and learned. As was Cora." She shook her head, a hazy fog trying to pull her into thoughtlessness. She smiled sadly. "That's all I really know about them. Is it possible to miss someone you've never met?"

James looked at her fondly. "I've never considered the notion. You ask the most penetrating questions, Tillie."

"Oh! I quite forgot. You and I are very distant cousins, James. Did you know? Apparently my great-grandmother on his side was a Cutter."

"I had no idea!" James said. The carriage hit a divot in the street, and James put his arm around her to steady her. It felt nice to let her head rest against his shoulder. She yawned and closed her eyes.

"I need to sleep."

"I can imagine. When you get home, you must promise me one thing. You mustn't go out at night again like this. It's too dangerous."

"I'm in no danger of being killed by a vampire," Tillie said, yawning again. "I'm too healthy. There's always a pattern. I have to be sick first from some sort of infection and then recover. I wonder if . . ." But she let the thought trickle away. Her eyes closed involuntarily.

She dreamt about rooftops that went on for miles, each with their own miniature lakes and forests. She heard children laughing, jumping at loaves of bread growing off trees. They passed around newspapers that Tillie bit into, and the newsprint dissolved like sugar wafers on her tongue. And then the carriage stopped, and James was gently waking her.

"You're home. Go in quickly."

"Thank you, James." She turned to the open carriage door, but James grabbed her hand.

"Tillie. Promise me you'll stop seeing that street boy. That newsie. He's below you. You cannot trust him. He has already publicly taken advantage of your family for his own benefit."

Tillie opened her mouth to protest, but James was fumbling with her hand. Something warm and smooth slid up her finger.

"Just promise me you won't, and you can keep this. Forever."

Tillie took her hand away. On her finger was a gold ring with a rosette of diamonds around a pink center stone. It was beautiful. It was . . . it was . . .

"Is this an engagement ring?" Tillie asked shrilly.

"Shhh! Be quiet!" He leaned closer and looked at her seriously. "Keep it. Think of me. And if you accept it, well then, perhaps you and I can be going on secret trips at night, instead of you risking your life."

"Oh, James. I don't . . . I can't . . ."

"Just think about it." He shook his head. "Listen to me. I was matched with your sister because she was the eldest, and I am the eldest, and it seemed right. But there was no true affection there. Surely, you saw that too. I had always had my eye on you."

"You never even looked my way," Tillie said, unbelieving.

"Because I couldn't. I had no choice. Being with Lucy, it was your family's and my parents' wish. I had to obey. But now Providence says I have another chance. Your mother and grandmother approve. They've told me as much."

"But Lucy," Tillie said. Had Lucy been in love with James before things had soured between them? She no longer had Lucy's diary in order to know. Still, it seemed wrong. So wrong. They were just barely out of the mourning period. Her sister's attacker was still out there.

Tillie touched the ring. Even in the low light, the stones glittered, as if gathering all the ambient light around them and shining it outward like tiny, glistening beacons.

She curled her bejeweled hand into a fist and held it to her breast. "James, I need time. To think."

"Of course."

"And I want . . ." She wrung her hands together; the ring kept catching her other palm.

"Yes? Anything, dearest. I'll give it to you."

"I would like to visit the pathologic cabinet at the medical school downtown." She raised a finger in the air, remembering. "And a typewriter."

When Tillie awoke, she felt puffy from all the port she had imbibed the night before. The need to take medicine filled her waking moments, before she noticed something uncomfortable squeezing her finger. She lifted her hand before her face.

The ring.

"Oh no, no, no." She covered her face, her mind a film reel that wound backward through the evening before.

James loved her. More than he'd loved Lucy. How could this be? He had hit her, according to Lucy's words. Was it possible to hurt someone you'd planned your whole life with?

Now that she thought of it, yes. It would be possible.

But then there were the memories of her time on Ian's roof, with Piper, Pops, Sweetie, and Ian. The small feast they'd had in the light of that lone oil lamp and the comfort of feeling like she was exactly where she belonged.

And there'd been a kiss.

Or had there? Had she dreamt that she'd kissed Ian? She wasn't quite sure. Even so, it was a delicious dream, but one that would be nothing short of a disaster from the perspective of her family. Speaking of which, there was a bustle of voices and movement outside her door. Ada entered, looking flustered.

"You must get ready, Miss. Your mother is in a state. Come, she's been waiting an extra hour for luncheon, and the beef is already cold."

"The beef is cold? And that's why she's in a state?"

Ada flapped her hands in the air. Her freckles looked brighter than usual. "Oh. Just get ready. I'm not to say anything!"

She helped dress Tillie quickly, and as usual Tillie banished Ada from her room to give herself a dose of morphine. She had hidden the extra supply in an empty perfume flask. Last night, she had taken some thumbtacks and pushed them into the wood frame beneath her bed, strung some darning yarn between them to make a sling, and stored her papers and notebook there. She checked to make sure all was secure.

Just before stepping outside, she remembered the ring. But her flesh had swelled overnight from all the drinking; when she tried to pull it off, it wouldn't budge. Not a mite. Finally, desperate, she twisted the ring so the gems were hidden on the palm side of her hand.

Decked in a new day dress of cerulean (too bright—one of Dorothy's purchases for her), she joined her mother, the cook, Ada, and three other servants gathered around the dining room table.

"I guess the roast beef must be very cold, indeed," Tillie said cheerfully as she entered the room.

"Mathilda!" Her mother spun around, and the others scattered. "What is the meaning of this? It arrived just after breakfast."

Tillie stepped forward. On the table was a brand-new Remington 7 typewriter, still in its carrying case. Her mouth opened to a perfect oval of wonder. She touched the handle on the top and undid the latches at its base. Her mother was saying something to her, but she couldn't hear a word. She lifted the case to reveal the glossy black typewriter with its gleaming round keys staggered and rising like a group of choirboys at church, waiting to be told which hymn to sing. A single piece of paper was in the carriage, trapped under the paper bail.

Dearest Tillie,
Please accept this gift as one of many to come in our
future together.
   Write to me.
   Yours,
   James

Tillie could not prevent her mother from leaning over and reading the note. Her face went from slightly greenish to peony pink in a matter of seconds.

"This is a gift? From James Cutter?" Mama's hand went to her breast. And then her eyes dropped, scanning Tillie's hands where they skimmed the shiny keyboard. The tiny circlet of gold shone on her finger, and her mother quickly grabbed her hand and flipped it over. The diamonds were even brighter in the daylight.

Mama nearly hollered and clapped her hands together. "You're *engaged?*"

"No! Not yet. I mean, no! I don't know! I said I would think about it!"

"We had hoped, Grandmama and I, but . . . goodness! We spoke to his parents only days ago . . . when did he give this ring to you?"

Tillie said nothing. She could not tell her it had been last night. It would lead to all sorts of questions that she refused to answer.

"Oh, a few days ago. I haven't given him an answer," Tillie said, still flustered. "It's too soon after Lucy. I don't know how I feel right now. I would have taken the ring off, but it's stuck."

"A little butter will take care of that," the cook said.

"Yes. True. It would be untoward to announce such a thing, only a month after Lucy has departed us. But another engagement! And with James Cutter. Such a match! Such a—" Her mother halted, seeing Tillie's frown. "Are you not happy, my dear?"

Her mother's incandescent joy had been fettered quickly by Tillie's tepid response. She did not love James, but it was impossible not to love the idea of him. A name to be proud of, approving glances from everyone when they walked into a ball together, a future with money and houses, and to be her own mistress instead of being locked away and skittering about at night. Perhaps they could put off a honeymoon so she could attend college. She might teach! She might become an expert in something—birds of paradise or gems of South America—go on tours of Europe to research anything and everything, meet people and see places and spend her days endlessly answering the questions that always filled her mind.

Grandmama entered the room then. Her imperious eyes, keen as a hawk's, saw her daughter's astonishment, the new typewriter, and Tillie's bejeweled hand in her mother's. She snatched the girl's wrist and held her hand aloft. The gems glittered against Tillie's palm.

"James Cutter" was all her mother said, and Grandmama nodded in satisfaction.

"Finally, you'll do something right in this family," she said. "Unlike your disaster of a sister."

"What did you say?" Tillie asked her.

Her grandmother pointedly ignored her. She barked at Ada, who was watching wide eyed from the corner. "Tea!"

Tillie opened her mouth to argue, but the richly toned doorbell rang, and their heads turned in unison. There was a murmur of male voices in the hallway. One of the older maids stepped into the dining room.

"Mr. James Cutter here to see you, Miss Pembroke."

Tillie's mother gripped the back of the chair, as if about to swoon. Her grandmother's expression was one of utter contentment, as if the world were back to obeying her every wish. Tillie wondered exactly who was being courted.

"Tell him I'll be there shortly. I have to eat something," she said. The truth was she wanted to play with her typewriter first. But most of all, she wasn't ready to speak to James so soon after last night. What had she said, exactly? Had there been an assent or an implied yes? She wasn't sure.

"Invite him in for luncheon," Mrs. Pembroke said. Tillie started to protest but stopped when she saw how ecstatic her mother was. She hadn't seen her like this since before Lucy had died. "I'll let you two have the dining room." She clapped her hands and told the servants to ready two place settings.

While the servants set the sideboard with dishes of roast beef (not cold, after all), creamed potatoes, and sugared peas, James took Tillie aside. He looked slightly tired. No surprise, as he had been awake at four in the morning and had somehow procured a typewriter and had it delivered, all by breakfast time.

"I've spoken to a friend already this morning. I have a surprise for you this afternoon."

Tillie clapped her hands. "The pathologic cabinet?"

"Yes." He smiled. "The Wood Museum, at Bellevue. Dr. Hermann Biggs, a pathologist, is a friend of Father's. I've never known a woman to be so happy to see an anatomical museum." They sat, and James bit into a piece of toast, sleek with butter. How he managed not to get a single crumb or smear anywhere was magic. "They don't let ladies visit Kahn's museum downtown, even with a male escort."

The doorbell rang again. Who could that be? A few moments later, Dorothy and Hazel walked into the dining room.

"Well! I did not expect to see that the festivities had begun without us." Dorothy laughed and sat down. "Tea, please. No sugar. I'm watching my figure."

James looked up briefly. Hazel seemed to catch his glance, then look away abruptly. What was that about? Tillie wondered.

"What brings you here?" Tillie asked. Under the cover of the table, she yanked at the ring again, twisting and turning it, but it still would not budge.

"Your dresses! This one looks delicious on you. Don't you think, James?" Dorothy wasn't smiling—it was almost like she was daring him to respond positively.

"I'm not one to notice things like laces and trims and whatnot." He was drinking strong coffee now, and he took a deep pull from his china cup. "But I do notice, Tillie, you're not eating much. You ought to have more beef. You need more strength."

Dorothy looked at Tillie, who blushed and cut some more roast beef just to get James to stop talking about such things. And then Dorothy looked at James, who was glancing over at Tillie with an unabashed degree of public fondness that had not been noted on any Cutter face in the history of the Cutters. Even when they were speaking of the banking industry.

"Well. Hazel wished to know how you were feeling. Didn't you, Hazel?"

"Yes. I was worried about you too. You must take better care of yourself, Tillie. James isn't the only person to note that your bloom is not what it was since poor Lucy died."

At the mention of Lucy's name, James straightened in his chair and leaned slightly away from Tillie.

"What's that monstrosity doing here?" Dorothy pointed her chin at the typewriter, which was still living happily on the end of the oblong dining table.

"It's my new typewriter. So I can write notes instead of using a pen." Tillie added, "I suppose it's easier on my arm."

"How very modern of you! Do write me a letter so I can see. It'll be like reading a book. Let's see you try."

Tillie flushed pink. She didn't want everyone's eyes on her hands and that ring. Not now. She remembered what the cook had said about butter.

"Oh, perhaps later." She reached over to her toast, buttered it lavishly, and made sure to get a glob on her finger. Under the table, she buttered her finger and the band of the ring, and twisted. The butter worked too well; the ring slipped over her knuckle and flew out of her oily fingers. There was an audible clink as it hit the table leg and bounced on the floor.

A servant retrieved it immediately. The shining diamond ring, cloudy with its film of butter, was put next to Tillie's plate. "Your ring, Miss."

Dorothy stared. Hazel did, too, though not with quite the acid expression on Dorothy's face, which magnificently transformed into elation.

"Oh! Is that . . . an engagement ring? Tillie? James! Are you—"

"Goodness. It's nothing but a token. There is no announcement, Dorrie," Tillie said hastily. This time, it was James's turn to look dyspeptic.

"Well. Tillie, it's time we go. Shall we?" He rose, and Tillie blotted her lips. Not knowing what to do with the ring, she put it back on. She wanted to leave so that Dorothy would stop staring agog between her and James.

Before they left, Dorothy secured a promise from Tillie to have tea and, as she whispered, "discuss *everything*." Hazel grasped Tillie's hands in a goodbye.

"Just in case. I know how hard it can be to come by money when everyone is watching you," she said quietly. "And I know what it feels like to have pain that must be concealed."

Tillie took her hands away and saw three vials of morphine tied together with a chartreuse ribbon.

"Oh. Do you use opium, too, Hazel?"

Hazel shook her head. "No, I don't. But if I did, I might never stop."

CHAPTER 19

What manner of man is this, or what manner of creature is it in the semblance of man?

—Jonathan Harker

James waited by the carriage as Tillie freshened herself and hid her extra vials of morphine upstairs.

In the carriage, he said nothing for a long while. Tillie was grateful for the quiet and actually sighed aloud.

"What is it?" James asked.

"The silence. It's nice, sometimes."

James laughed. "I like it too. Sometimes Dorothy's chatter is welcome and other times . . ." He shrugged, too much of a gentleman to say more. "I feel sorry for her, though."

"You do? Why?"

"She's rather desperate to get married." He looked out the window, where the sun shone on the carriages passing by. They drove past the Hotel Netherland and the Savoy. The park in front of the Plaza was resplendent with green and perfectly round trees, and Central Park disappeared behind them. "Hazel is desperate too."

"Hazel? I had no idea she was shopping for a beau."

"Not for her—for Dorothy. They lost a lot of money, the Harrimans, in the stock market a few years ago. I heard Dorothy's father speaking about it to my father. They may have to let Hazel go if Dorothy's prospects don't improve." He raised his eyebrows. "And what kind of job Hazel would get, I can't imagine. Being a lady's companion, even to someone like Dorothy, can't possibly be as difficult as scrubbing floors or sewing. For not nearly as good pay."

"Dorothy probably wants to marry you," Tillie said artlessly.

"Dorothy is a sweet girl," James murmured, turning to Tillie and smiling. "But she's not you. She's not a Pembroke."

Tillie's back prickled. She felt like a brand of bestselling bromide on the shelf.

They passed Bryant Park, where the Croton Reservoir was now completely gone and heaps of dust and rubble lay as they began building the foundation to the library. Tillie sighed in pure pleasure.

"Does the sight of rubble make you happy?" James teased.

"A library. An enormous library, bigger than the Lenox Library and the Astor Library combined. It's wonderful."

"I'd build you a library to rival that, if I could. A library with every story in it, every book you could imagine. Worlds within worlds."

"Golly! Wouldn't that be a dream!" She laughed. "But you've already given me a typewriter."

"And I anxiously await your first communication," he said, taking her hand in his.

He kept up conversation for the rest of the trip, but Tillie had some difficulty trying to stay lighthearted. She could think only of Lucy. Would she warn her about James or think, What a perfect match? A man who will buy you a typewriter, a whole library! She still had unresolved questions about whether James was as innocent as he claimed to be. She twisted the ring on her finger. It didn't seem as foreign as it had yesterday, but it still felt conspicuous and heavy.

They finally rounded Twenty-Sixth Street, past Matthew's Soda Factory, and turned onto First Avenue, where Bellevue Medical College stood. It looked so different in the daylight, compared to when she'd passed by with Ian. James helped her out of the carriage, and they entered the building; a wooden staircase in front of them led upstairs.

"James! Good to see you."

They saw a severe-looking gentleman with a white coat, brass spectacles, and a dark mustache. A younger man in a dapper twill suit stood beside him.

"Dr. Biggs. And Andrew! Good to see you. Miss Pembroke, Andrew is an old schoolmate, the nephew of Dr. Biggs."

"Thank you for taking the time, Dr. Biggs," Tillie said, curtsying. She nodded at his nephew and dipped a curtsy again.

"Shall we begin the tour?" Dr. Biggs held out his hand, and Tillie took it.

"Uncle, may I speak to James for a moment? We have some catching up to do. I don't believe he has the stomach for such a museum, as I recall from our university days."

James winked. "Indeed, he remembers well. I believe the sight of a dead cat nearly did me in once."

"Pooh!" Dr. Biggs waved his hand. "It's those other atrocious venues, like Dr. Kahn's Museum of Anatomy in the Bowery—that are filled with only titillating exhibits. Pure trash. Here, we strive for education, not for spectacle."

"Still, I think I'd be unwise to risk it. I'll be here, Tillie, if you need me," James said.

Tillie nodded, and together, she and Dr. Biggs ascended the stairs.

"The museum was begun by Dr. Wood just around 1850. He amassed quite a collection, and our pathologists have been adding to it ever since. We've over two thousand specimens, in comparable anatomy, normal anatomy, embryology, and pathologic specimens."

"Do you have . . . any vampires? Or vampire victims?" Tillie asked when they approached the top landing.

Dr. Biggs let go of her arm and turned to her, his eyebrows furrowing so deeply she could only see half his eyes.

"Are you in jest?" he asked, nearly a growl.

Tillie attempted to hold on to her bravery. "Absolutely not, sir."

"I thought interest in vampires had left after those horrible penny dreadfuls stopped being read all the time. What was that one? *Varney the Vampire*, wasn't it called? An absolute joke!"

"It's not a joke. Have you read the papers?" Tillie threaded her fingers together. "A girl—my very own sister—was killed by a bite to the neck and all the blood drained from her. There are stories and tales that are all imaginary, for sure, but a pattern of deaths like hers requires investigation, even if it means entertaining the fantastic. Even germs were once considered fantasy, in the eyes of the most preeminent surgeons. Now we have Lysol and carbolic acid to fight them." She swelled her breath. "I need to know if such a human creature, if it may be called human, could possibly exist."

"Nonsense. No such creature exists."

"But how do you know?"

"There are legends, and there is truth."

"Then show me the truth so that I may be soothed by what is real and what is not," Tillie implored. They were standing in front of the Wood Museum now, but the doors were locked. Dr. Biggs had a key in hand but hadn't yet opened it. "I refuse to accept an answer that does not include evidence and thought, instead of speculation."

Dr. Biggs saw that she was not laughing or smirking but perfectly serious. He sighed heavily. "Very well, my dear. Very well."

He unlocked the door, swinging it open and stepping aside. Tillie entered. The room was large and yet somehow small at the same time. There were columns in the center and cabinets in rows on either side.

It was like a small library, except instead of books, the cabinets held specimen after specimen of health and disease.

Tillie walked to the first cabinet, seeing an entire row of glass jars. These were embryology examples, tiny fetuses curled like the ends of violins or young ferns, never to grow and unfurl themselves upon the world. Many were normal examples of development, and Tillie shuddered to think why they'd ended up in jars of beige preservative instead of walking the streets of the city, playing rounders and kick the can. Other jars held examples of the unborn never destined to survive—ones with heads too small, internal organs twisted upside down or never formed at all. Tillie bowed her head slightly as she passed them. She was glad they were not on display in a gaudy showroom downtown.

Dr. Biggs stood back and let her explore the aisles. "I'd heard a passing comment about your sister's case. I thought it was another example of the *World* getting overenthusiastic with their imagination, all to sell more papers."

"I saw my sister's wounds. It's very real. What I don't know is the nature of the killer. If he is what everyone thinks he is. Here." Tillie stopped to point to a case holding preserved skulls. Beneath them was a label.

MALFORMATIONS OF THE SKULL

1. CALVARIUM TUMOR 2. SEVERE MALOCCLUSION 3. MICROCEPHALY 4. SUPERNUMERARY TEETH

She peered closer at the skull with the supernumerary teeth. It had been displayed with the jaw opened. A second set of teeth pushed against the row of normal teeth, but they crowded in such a jumble that they appeared to be a weedy garden of tooth points.

"Is it possible that someone could grow teeth sharp enough to puncture skin?"

"Well, of course. We all have teeth that can puncture. It's what you do when you bite into a roast beef. We are simply too civilized to bite living persons. Unless you are a misbehaving child, I suppose, or rabid."

Tillie straightened, prodding the pointed canine teeth in her own mouth with her tongue. She turned to Dr. Biggs. "But two clean holes? Is there any condition that could cause a person's teeth to become sharp and large as, say, a wolf's or big cat's?"

Dr. Biggs shook his head. "None in the literature."

"Which means such a person cannot exist."

"No, it means that if such a person exists, no one has been able to reliably document them. Medicine and science rely upon observation, repeated observation, and repeated analysis. Without any word of such an existence, it is hard to fathom that a huge-fanged human exists, unless they are incredibly good at hiding. But then again, any such creature cannot live in a vacuum undetected forever. Even bacteria, even germs, were the ghosts of the medical world until we found them through analysis and microscopes. As you so eloquently noted before."

Tillie walked to another aisle. Here were more specimens, pickled in formaldehyde or created through waxworks and plaster casting. She found one wax model of a woman's head and neck, the neck splayed open and diagrammed with different-colored paints to explicate the anatomy of the neck. The woman's face was beautiful, with dark hair and half-closed lids over deep brown eyes. She looked a bit like Tillie herself, if she thought of it. Shivering, she looked at the tiny inscription, which read,

ARTIST: ALEXANDER TRICE, 1849

Dr. Biggs looked at it as well and shook his head. "We will likely remove the wax sculptures; they were initially created to bring in the crowds for entertainment, rather than academic study." He pointed at the neck. "You said there had been . . . bites? Can you show me where?"

"Here. And here." She pointed to where the carotid artery was painted cherry red next to the thick blue jugular vein.

"The neck tissues must have been torn terribly," he remarked.

"Not at all. It was so clean, just two puncture holes."

"Not even behind the neck?" He pointed to himself, above his starched collar. "Anything that bit down hard enough to exsanguinate would leave bite marks in the back. And it would not be two simple, clean punctures. I tended to a child once with bites from a fighting dog. The skin tore, and where there were punctures, there were matching ones to counteract the force of the top jaw."

"I've considered that too. I don't recall seeing cuts on the other side, but then again, I didn't lift her head to look."

"Also, consider—to bleed out through a bite, there must be the bite first and then a sucking action. Surely, it would also leave a bruise, circular, where the mouth applied suction. A creature would bite and lick or suck, but even so, to drain such a quantity of blood from the large veins . . . and if the arteries were bitten, why, no animal could consume so much blood quickly or so cleanly. An artery would bleed like a fire hose. In either situation, consuming blood and leaving either no suction marks or a bloodless scene would be impossible."

Tillie's pulse raced. "Are you saying that a creature—let's not name what it is—could not have done such a thing?"

"I am a pathologist, Miss Pembroke. I have seen all manner of disease and all manner of death by the hand of fellow humans. My opinion? Someone is killing these people. A human, a person, not an imagined vampire. But they would like it to resemble the work of a vampire."

"Why?" Tillie asked. "Why go through the pains to make it look so macabre? So fantastical?"

They had walked all the way through the museum and now were back where they had begun at the top of the stairs.

"Why would any murderer try to hide themselves?" Dr. Biggs asked. "Why, they wish to avoid discovery. What you need to find out, Miss, is, Why blood? The victims likely died within minutes of the bleeding, but you said that most of their blood was removed. That is an unnecessary step if death were the only purpose."

"Perhaps death was not the purpose," Tillie said. "Perhaps it was an unintended consequence of gathering the blood."

"For what use?"

"I don't know," Tillie admitted. "I have no idea."

Dr. Biggs locked the museum doors behind them. Downstairs, James was shaking Andrew's hand. Dr. Biggs halted on the stairs and leaned in close to Tillie. He almost seemed afraid that his words would reach James.

"Miss Pembroke," he said quietly. "Keep in mind that someone who wishes to kill innocents and blame it on a pretend vampire also has another motive. They wish to *continue* to kill. If there is one thing that a murderer despises more than being caught, it's the person who discovers them. Do take care of yourself."

"I shall. Thank you so much."

Dr. Biggs accompanied them out of the building and to the carriage. He waved goodbye cheerfully, but as the carriage pulled away, he continued staring at them until they rounded Twenty-Fifth Street.

Tillie could not shake the feeling that Dr. Biggs was afraid to leave her in the company of James, alone.

——◆——

At home, Tillie first wrote down everything she could from her meeting at the museum, then dosed herself heavily with morphine and collapsed in her bed. When she awoke, she took a small supper by herself. Her mother was reading by the fireplace, but her paper had fallen onto her lap, and she was snoozing ever so gently. Her grandmother was already in bed.

Tillie went to the other end of the table, where the typewriter sat. She took the cover off and saw that the message from James was still there. She pulled it out, and the register spun with a zipping noise. In their escritoire, she found sheets of creamy paper. She fed a piece into the back of the cylinder, rolled it up the front of the register, and sat down.

All she needed to do was start typing the story.

She had no idea where to begin. When she closed her eyes, the story was done in her head, polished and perfect, drawing the reader in and releasing bits of information like crumbs off a loaf of bread, luring in whoever was hungry for more. Before her, there was this grand typewriter, and there was a blank page.

She longed to see Ian again. His encouragement from before had dissipated. She wished to discuss her notes and go over her theories again. But he was awaiting a copy of a draft by mail.

I have to start somewhere, she thought. Why not start with her name?

So she typed *T*.

The key hitting the paper sounded like a tiny gunshot. Down the hallway, there was a sudden squeal and a "What in heaven's name!" Footfalls thumped the floor, and her mother appeared, red eyed and confused.

"What are you doing, Mathilda?"

"Typing."

"I can see that. But it is nearly eleven o'clock. You ought to be in bed. You may write to James tomorrow."

Tillie stood up and smiled. "Of course. You're right. Good night, Mama." She kissed her cheek and skittered up the stairs.

Tillie waited until her own witching hour, near midnight. Then, the whole house would be slumbering, and John would be touring the grounds, and Ada would visit him with gifts of bakery sweets and of herself. Sometimes both, but never simultaneously, which would be a carnal catastrophe of crumbs, now that she considered it.

Carnal Catastrophe of Crumbs.

It sounded like an excellent title to something that Tillie best not write.

Wearing her nightdress and a wrapper of pale-blue sateen, she gathered her precious papers to her chest. The main floor was quiet and perfectly empty. She would have to find somewhere the sound wouldn't carry.

Outside? She didn't want to be near John. Anyway, the sounds of the typewriter might still wake someone up. The attic? She hadn't been up there in ages, but as a child she clearly remembered hearing the servants calling for her straight through the floorboards while she explored old trunks and treasures. No, that would not do.

There was only one place in the house that was nearly soundless.

Tillie latched the cover onto the typewriter and hauled it out of the dining room with her good arm. She staggered into the kitchen, past the massive cookstove, and thence to the pantry and its trapdoor floor. She pulled it open and turned on a switch, and a single light bulb illuminated the tiny cave-like space populated with ropes of onions, dried herbs, and tubs of butter.

She carefully descended the steps, found an empty crate, and flipped it over to set the typewriter down. A cask of wine was her chair. Soon, she had paper nearby, her dim light, her brooch watch to keep track of the time, a wedge of cheese and a hunk of bread to keep her hunger at bay, and finally—a trip back upstairs to her room for a dose of morphine to keep her going. She remembered the euphoria she'd felt on the rooftop with Ian and, wishing to feel unlocked, poured herself a generous glass of wine from the cask beneath her.

Tillie threaded a paper into the typewriter and began.

July 11, 1899

Dear Mrs. Seaman-Bly-Cochrane,
I know for sure that I am getting your name wrong now.
  I am thinking I am no closer to finding my sister's killer. What's worse, I find that I am being watched by my family's hired help, and worse, by the gentleman wooing me. On another note, I have done something rather brash and unthinkable.
  I have written an article. In fact, I have just stayed up all night typing it.
  I do not know if it will be published, but the process brought clarity to my understanding of the undead.
  Clarity is a wonderful thing. Sometimes, obfuscation is too, but I digress.
  I have written an article! I had to write that twice, because I had never written it before and I wanted to celebrate twice in one letter. We are more similar than I realized! Although I confess, I am very good at responding to letters.

I apologize for asking about the elephant before. It occurs to me that it is a very rude thing to ask, but I am always doing things wrong, and sometimes I don't know any better.

I still don't know what they smell like, though.

Kindly respond.

Yours,

Tillie

CHAPTER 20

*I asked Dr. Seward to give me a little opiate of some kind . . .
I hope I have not done wrong, for as sleep begins to flirt with
me, a new fear comes . . . Here comes sleep. Good-night.*

—Mina Harker

Tillie woke up just after noon. As soon as her eyes opened, a thrill ran through her body.

She had done it.

The article was written. Perhaps it would be published, perhaps not, but either way—the accomplishment was like a firecracker in her belly. She squashed an urge to open the window of her chamber and shout out her glee.

Under her pillow, an envelope with four typewritten pages lay sealed, Ian's name and the address of the *World* typed on the front. Stacked below it were the four copies of her letter to Nellie Bly. She would post them today herself, somehow. She did not trust Ada or anyone else in the household to handle it. It was far too precious.

Oh, but she wished Ian could read her draft now! She wished she could tell someone. Anyone. Who knew if Nellie Bly was receiving any of her letters?

Once she went downstairs, her mother prattled on about how Tillie really needed to get back to a normal schedule.

"You'll have far too many things to do to sleep in so late. And you're so much better, now that you don't take that terrible medicine anymore."

Tillie said nothing, only drank her soup as soundlessly and slurplessly as she ought. But her mind went back to what she'd seen in the museum—particularly the wax figurine of the lovely woman whose neck was flayed open. She had looked vaguely like Tillie, which made her think of her father.

"I miss Papa," she murmured.

"Don't speak of the past."

"He was my father. He's not something to be erased." She put her spoon down. "Are you so ashamed that he was part of our family?"

"Ashamed? I married him, did I not?" She had lowered her voice and tilted her head, as if worried that her own mother might hear. It occurred to Tillie that she hadn't exactly answered the question. "But goodness! His family, poor as paupers. I always promised that you would never have to suffer as they did. Or as your father did."

"Was he not happy?"

"Happy, yes. Secure, no. Marrying for love is a dangerous proposition. Your grandmother did not remarry after she became a widow, to keep control of our estate. If not for that, you and I might be penniless." She looked severely at Tillie. "Not every lady could be so lucky, and luck only lasts so long. I was lucky that your father would have me, in my condition."

Condition? "Mama, what do you mean?"

As if realizing that she had spoken carelessly, Mama laughed. "Oh, I just meant I was a spoiled miss then."

But the way Grandmama spoke of Tillie's father, it certainly seemed like the union had been shameful. Why, the only reason a lady might feel lucky to be married to someone of such stature was if she were somehow a poor choice for Papa . . .

Tillie's breath caught—was there a chance that her mother had been pregnant with Lucy before she married? Could it be? It would explain where Lucy's flaxen hair came from, given that Tillie, her mother, and her father all sported dark chestnut hair. It would explain Grandmama's comment the other day. Something about Lucy being a disaster.

"Mama? Is there something you want to tell me about Lucy? About her father?"

Mrs. Pembroke's startled face said all Tillie needed to know. "No," she said hastily. "Her father . . . your father . . . there's nothing to tell." She laughed again, the airy laugh that meant she was entirely uncomfortable.

"But—"

"But nothing. There is nothing more to say." She smiled, this time tenderly. "I know Grandmama can be a bear sometimes. She was with me too. But it's because she wants the best for you. I do too. You do as you're told, and you'll never suffer."

Mama seemed to think that they had spoken enough and stood. Just then, the doorbell rang. Pierre ushered Hazel Dreyer into their midst. Mama looked at her benevolently, as a lioness might gaze upon a rat that wasn't worth a swat.

"Good afternoon," Hazel said. "I was passing by, and thought I could deliver a message directly. Dorothy wishes you to come with her to the New York Theatre on Saturday. There's a marvelous show, *The Man in the Moon*, and her parents are unable to attend."

"I'm sure Mathilda would love to go."

"Of course!" Tillie said. Any excuse to leave the house was a good excuse. "Where is Dorothy?"

"Oh. Dorrie has a terrible headache today." Hazel's quiet nod meant Dorothy was likely in the midst of her monthlies, probably lying in bed with a hot water bottle on her stomach and taking aspirin for the pain.

"And what are you up to today? Do you need any company?" She'd spied her opportunity to get out of the house and mail the letters.

Hazel brightened. "I would love some company. Is that quite all right, Mrs. Pembroke? I have to buy some lavender salts and a few yards of muslin for a dress that needs mending. We'll be close by."

Tillie's mother assented, and Tillie went upstairs. She folded the letters and placed them in her reticule alongside her bottle of opium, hugging it to her body as they stepped outside onto Madison Avenue.

It was cloudy out, a relief from the heat lately. As soon as they reached the first store, Hazel hooked Tillie's arm. Tillie hummed and smiled, sniffing through different eaux de toilette in the scent shop.

"Tillie, you are really in a state. If a person could be a set of fireworks, that would be you. Why are you so happy today?"

"Oh, nothing," she said, humming.

A smile dawned on Hazel's face. "It's your engagement, isn't it?"

"Oh!" Tillie's smile disappeared. She had not worn the ring since she had buttered it off a second time and stowed it in her dresser drawer. "We're not really engaged. And no, that's not why I'm happy."

"You won't tell a friend?" Hazel looked crestfallen.

Tillie bit her lip. Come to think of it, she'd shared more intimate feelings with Hazel lately than with Dorothy. But no one ever asked Hazel how she felt. If she felt. "I'll tell you what. I'll tell you a secret if you tell me one."

"All right," Hazel said, brightening. It might be the widest smile that Tillie had ever seen on the girl. "Because I have a secret too. But you first!"

"Very well." Tillie took a deep breath and looked to make sure no one was listening. "I am on the cusp of submitting an article to the *World*."

Hazel nearly tripped. Her eyes went wide, her mouth, wider. "Oh! Tillie! That is absolutely wonderful! Why, you'll be just like Nellie Bly! You'll be famous!"

"I don't know if it will be accepted. But I did write it and research it. I'm terrifically proud, Hazel. And no one knows but you and . . . my contact at the *World*." She didn't want to mention Ian's name. Not yet. "And you? What's your secret?"

"I . . . I'm going to get married," she said grandly. "Dorothy is furious with me. She thinks she'll lose me and never see me again. But my fiancé is traveling most days of the year, and his salary is meager. I can spend all the time in the world with Dorothy, as if nothing has changed."

"But things have changed. You're in love!" Tillie gently pinched Hazel on the arm, and she blushed. "Won't you want your own home?"

"No. The expense would be too much. This is better. I enjoy Dorothy's company, and the position suits me. And if Dorothy ever marries, it would be best for me to be married too. She couldn't have an unmarried woman living with her husband under the same roof. It wouldn't be proper."

"Of course." She remembered James's words from the other day. Without her mistress's wealth, Hazel would be working somewhere, living a life that would not have the luxuries of the constant carriages, sweets and food at her fingertips, balls and gossip.

"Plus, Herbert is a dear. I'm lucky. We're to be married at City Hall, with a small reception afterward." Ah. No fancy Grace Church wedding, and likely only one clergyman, instead of two (the latter always made for easier society divorces—an arguing couple could annul a marriage with ease over the dual clergy present). "You'll come, of course?"

"Of course!" As Tillie hugged Hazel, she remembered that moment in the carriage when Hazel had put her hand on her belly.

Without thinking, Tillie blurted, "Hazel, have you ever had your heart broken?"

Hazel smiled. "Every day." She winked at Tillie and laughed. Tillie joined in. But she wasn't sure that Hazel was joking at all.

Together, they went on to the post office. The street was filled with US mail wagons, some immense with six horses, and others with a single horse for intercity delivery. Inside, lines of customers snaked through the room. The incessant pounding of clerks rubber-stamping dates and origins reverberated against the walls. Tillie paid her two cents, and the clerk glued stamps onto her envelopes and thumped an ink print on the front. It was done—off to meet Ian downtown, hopefully within the day.

But soon after she mailed the article, her happiness over it vanished. All sorts of worry had replaced the good feeling. What if the writing was terrible? What if Ian or his editor laughed aloud at the contents? What if all her efforts were for nothing, and it wouldn't be published? When they passed by only one block from Dr. Erikkson's office on the way to their next destination, Tillie paused.

"Hazel, would you mind if I dropped by to say hello to the Erikksons?"

"Do you need more medicine?"

"Oh no, it's not that. I just wish to say hello." The truth was, her medicine was wearing off, and the telltale sinkhole of hopelessness and achy unhappiness was enlarging, threatening to eclipse every sense of well-being. Perhaps Tom would offer a dose, in private. It would be far more satisfying and potent than the tincture in her purse.

"Of course. I'll head on to the dry goods store, then meet you back here in fifteen minutes. Only that! You can't be out of my sight for longer. Would that do?"

"Perfect."

Tillie relished escaping the steady gazes always upon her. She could buy an ice cream or sit in one of the little restaurants on Third Avenue and enjoy a lemonade. She could read the newspaper under the shade of a tree in Central Park. But she had too little time, so she walked quickly to the Erikksons' town house. Her body felt jittery and eager.

Mrs. Erikkson answered the door as usual.

"Oh! Miss Pembroke! What brings you? Are you ill?"

"I just wanted to say hello. How is Tom?"

Mrs. Erikkson let her inside. "See for yourself. He is out of bed and reading, for a change. I think he is doing better this week. Your visit will do him even more good."

They went down the hallway to the camphor-scented room. Tom was sitting in a chair before a small fire, making the room even warmer than usual. He looked up. The circles under his eyes weren't as dark as usual.

"You do look well," Tillie said, smiling. "Truly well." She eyed the syringe kit near his bed and the bottle of clear liquid morphine next to it. She kept her hands folded atop each other, trying to stanch an impulse to grab the whole bottle.

"Father started a new treatment for me. I think it's working. I feel stronger." He glanced at her face, and then at his mother, and then at Tillie again. "Are you all right?"

"I'm well," Tillie said. She couldn't help but grin. "I'm very well. I may hear some good news soon."

"An engagement!" Mrs. Erikkson clapped her hands together and looked exultant.

"Oh no. Not really that. Something else." She cleared her throat. "An occupation."

"Even better," Mrs. Erikkson said. She glanced over her shoulder. "I should like to hear all about it, but Dr. Erikkson is due to visit Mrs. Stevenson, and he always requires my aid with her dressings."

"Dr. Erikkson is actually going outside?"

"Well, yes." She laughed. "Don't tell your mother! She'll be livid to know he makes the rare house call, Miss Pembroke."

"Oh, please just call me Tillie."

"Very well. Our maid, Beatrice, is in the kitchen. Call for her if you need anything." Before she left, she wagged a finger at Tom. "And do behave, Tom. Tillie, you must be sure he doesn't tease Beatrice."

"I don't tease the maid! I can't help it if she keeps trying to break my leg every time we pass in the hallway." Tom smiled at Tillie as his mother left. "It's ridiculous. I've gathered at least ten bruises by just being in Beatrice's vicinity. Sometimes I trip over her mop; sometimes she polishes the floor, and I've nearly crushed her beneath me."

"Housework can be deadly," Tillie said. She settled in a chair, still eyeing the morphine every few seconds.

"Apparently so. Now, will you tell me more about your new occupation?"

"I shouldn't. I don't know if anything will come of it."

"Does your family know?" He reached for the syringe kit and began preparing a dose for himself.

Tillie licked her lips. "No." She paused. "Do you need help with that?"

"Oh no, thank you. I'm quite used to doing it myself."

"Doesn't your mother scold you for using so much?"

"She does, but Father feels differently. He believes that just as some people need certain foods more than others to stay well, some people must lean on the effects of morphine to function well. There's no shame in it."

"I confess I've been using more and more lately. I feel so much better under its effect."

Tom looked at her seriously. "Are you due for a dose?"

"I may be, perhaps." Tillie's hands were shaking.

Tom held up the filled syringe. "You can use this. I'll do mine afterward."

"Are you sure?"

"Yes."

"Is it the right amount?" Tillie had inched so far forward she risked falling off her chair.

"It's probably a little more than you're used to. Maybe half a grain. There are different doses I use for different reasons. Ones for pain." He drew up extra liquid as he spoke. "Ones for when I'm well, ones just to feel normal, and . . ." He pulled harder on the syringe. There must be three times her usual amount. "And ones for celebrating."

Tillie felt like celebrating, like forcing happiness to smother the pall that had descended after she'd sent the letter. Everything in her life was about to change. Even if this article didn't get published, it wouldn't prevent her from trying to write others. Perhaps for the smaller weeklies or the lesser-known papers. She would try again, and again, and again. Nothing would stop her, just as nothing would stop her from finding Lucy's killer.

Tom handed her the syringe. "Cheers to you."

Tillie took the syringe, and Tom turned away. She could use her arm, but unbuttoning the ten pearl buttons of her sleeve was too difficult with a single hand. Instead, she pulled her petticoats and silk skirt up her thigh, not caring that she was an unmarried woman in the presence of an unmarried man. Against her pale skin, there were tiny bruises everywhere, like a field of ill-looking poppies.

Tillie found a new spot, slipped the needle beneath her skin, and pushed the medicine in.

She sighed and handed the syringe back to Tom, who drew up a dose for himself.

"Would you like something to drink while you wait? We have some wine. And other spirits," he said. "That green smelly stuff that everyone likes."

"What?" Tillie wasn't listening. She was concentrating on the tiny soreness from the pinprick, knowing that when it disappeared, that meant the morphine was working. Tom kept her chatting for a while, but they spoke of nothing important, as if they both knew that the primary purpose of speaking was to pass the time until the opiate took effect.

And take effect it did. Tillie had never used such a high dose before, and it swept her into a euphoria so strong she laughed out loud when it heralded its arrival. She turned to Tom, her eyelids feeling like they were weighted down with pond stones. Vaguely, she remembered—shouldn't she be meeting Hazel again? When was she expected, and where?

A voice spoke from miles away.

"I told you it was time to celebrate."

Tom gently pulled Tillie from her chair, and he twirled her waist in his thin hands. Dizzy and laughing, she gently fell onto the bed. She blinked luxuriously, working her hands open and closed to examine how everything felt different—good and also bad. There was no question there was always a bad feeling too—like taking a bite of a poisoned cake that was so delectable you didn't mind if it killed you in the process. Tillie felt a hand brush the hair at her temples.

"By God, you're beautiful when you're like this."

There was laughter. Countless, echoing laughs, like a Coliseum's worth of people were all jubilant and enraptured along with her. She heard a door open, shut, open again, and shut forever. There were voices far away, murmurings that were silk against velvet, and a goodbye.

And then there was darkness. It dragged Tillie into its thick, syrupy blackness. She let it take her, oh so willingly.

The dream was a terrible one.

She was fighting a thick, swampy mire that had somehow trapped her arms and legs. No, they were ensnared beneath a tree. Or tree roots. Or vines. They were stuck fast, and there was no escaping.

A boulder-size weight had fallen on her chest, limiting her breaths to shallow rasps.

And then there were the teeth. She always thought that being bitten would be a cold affair, but the fangs were warm against her neck, just as the lips were. She could feel the throbbing of her pulse, those teeth that grazed her skin without cutting.

It would take only one bite, and she would bleed. One bite, and she would bleed every blessed drop of herself away.

Tillie's eyes opened.

She was in a darkened room, one that stank of camphor and illness, like the dust of a thousand old memories all within one single, stifling room. She couldn't move—something was on top of her.

Not something—someone.

It was Tom.

Tom had pinned her to his bed, and despite being thin and apparently sickly, he was remarkably strong. Tillie had lost her strength from not eating in the past weeks, and her limbs were already tired without having done much to fight back. Her legs and hips were trapped under his, and her good right arm was locked above her head by his strong grip on her wrist. His head obscured her vision.

His mouth was on her neck, kissing and suckling the skin there. She could feel his teeth scrape against the tender area beneath her jaw.

Tillie opened her mouth and screamed.

"Shhh. Be quiet. You'll be fine in a few minutes," Tom murmured in her ear. "Let me get some more morphine."

"No, no more. Stop. Let me go," she yelled. But her voice was hoarse, and it hardly came out louder than a whisper. "Hazel—Hazel is coming back for me."

"I told her you already went home."

"No. Your mother—"

"She's still out seeing patients with Father. It's all right." He kissed the other side of her neck as she flipped her head, refusing to face him. "I'll tell anyone who asks that you wanted to be here. That you lay with me, and what will happen to your reputation? Who will believe that

267

someone as sick as me could overpower you? You'll be ruined. So this is what we'll do. You'll come visit me every so often, and I'll send Mother away. And we'll have our little time together, with the morphine. You'll hardly feel anything. You won't even mind it."

Tillie began to hyperventilate. Her bad arm could hardly push him away. With his free arm, he reached for the syringe at his bedside. In one swift movement, he stabbed the needle into her thigh, right through the silk and cotton of her skirt. It hurt so much more done callously, and she shrieked when it pierced her flesh. She felt the morphine expanding under her skin. How much longer would she be able to fight him off before the medicine subdued her to complete senselessness? She kicked, but her movement only drew her legs apart, and Tom's hips slipped between her knees. She felt his hand scrabbling between them—on her bodice, reaching lower for the hem of her dress.

"Please, Tom. Please stop," she gasped. She kicked harder this time and loosened her good arm from his grip. "Stop!" Her voice was angrier, louder.

Tom's teeth sank into her neck.

The door burst open. John O'Toole paused for a second, seeing everything at once. Tom scrambled off Tillie, sheer surprise on his face. Tillie looked down and saw what John must. Her rumpled clothing. A bloodstain on her bare thigh from the injection. She could already feel the bruise forming on her neck from the bite. Her terror mutated to shame and relief.

John swept in, shoving Tom so hard that he landed with a thump against the table. The bottles toppled in a tinkle of broken glass. John scooped up Tillie into his arms like she weighed no more than a child. She hid her face in his shoulder as he strode out of the house, banging through the front door and leaving it agape as he went to the carriage waiting outside. Her carriage.

He placed her gently inside, climbed in, and slapped the front of the carriage wall. It jolted forward.

"How . . . how did you find me here?"

"Your friend Hazel came to us. She said that you had left the doctor's house to go home alone, and as that is exactly what befell your sister before she died, your mother panicked and called for me to find you. We looked through the streets between there and home and in the park as well. And then it occurred to me that perhaps you'd never left the doctor's house. When no one answered, I thought it odd because I could hear a voice inside. A woman's voice, in distress."

"I don't know how—I know, but I didn't think—I'm so sorry! I'm an absolute fool." Her hands clasped her arms as she sobbed. "I . . . I can't believe Tom . . . what will Mama think?"

"You can't even breathe. Here, drink this." John handed her a small green bottle of spirits, and she drank it. It was bitter and strong and reeked of licorice.

"Oh God. What is this?" She held the bottle away to read the label. "Absinthe? Why on earth do you have this?"

John didn't answer. "Drink it," he said.

"Why do you have absinthe with you?" Tillie shrieked.

"You don't want to know." He looked out the window. "Drink it, and you'll feel better. It would be best if I didn't return you to your mother in absolute hysterics."

When she protested, John put a hand on her neck, and the gesture was both repelling and terrifying. His fingertips were over the most tender areas of her neck. Press but a little, and she would lose consciousness.

"Drink it, Mathilda." He spoke in such a commanding tone that she took one more mouthful of the bitter spirit, forcing it down. She was already so drowsy she could barely open her eyes. The last injection of morphine that Tom had given her might have been big enough to fell a bear.

Unconsciousness was coming quickly. For all she knew, John could be delivering her straight to a fresh grave at Woodlawn Cemetery.

Right next to Lucy's.

CHAPTER 21

We seem to be drifting into unknown places and unknown ways.

—Jonathan Harker

There was a terrible smell.

A combination of old rose perfume rotting together with a faint scent of stomach acid. Someone had vomited recently and covered it up with scent.

It took a monumental effort for Tillie to open her eyes. Every sinew of her body felt like the foundations of a building—unmovable, perhaps, for centuries. She forced herself up on her elbows and looked around her room.

It wasn't her room.

She was lying on a narrow bed, neatly made with brown blankets and a slightly musty pillow. The room was tiny and wallpapered with faded yellow flowers. A trunk had been placed near the door. She recognized a dress of hers folded neatly on the top. A window near the bed had its curtain drawn. Tillie shuffled to it, pushed the fabric aside, and looked outside.

It was midday, wherever she was. On the small street outside, birds chirped merrily on a cherry tree. Across the street was a beautiful home, three levels with a pretty veranda skirting its main floor. A line of men waited to enter its front door. Some were barely twenty years old, others nearing seventy. Some were wealthy, some shabbily dressed. One of them was staggering away, and several others reeled him back to the queue. A couple walking down the street made a wide berth to pass the house. A group of schoolchildren laughed on the veranda, on tiptoes peeping through the windows to watch whatever spectacle occurred within. One girl grinned and pointed at her friend.

"Take your dope! Or you'll get the shot!" The friend screeched in mock fear, and they chased each other around the back of the house.

"Where am I?" Tillie croaked. She was still wearing the dress she had worn when she had been found in Tom's room.

Tom's room. Tom. Her stomach lurched with nausea. John O'Toole had rescued her and then plied her with absinthe. Where was John now? He needed to explain why he'd forced her to drink that awful stuff. Where had he taken her? She put her hands to her face.

What had happened? Why was she here?

There was a gentle knock on the door. It opened to reveal an older lady with gray-and-brown hair. She closed the door; in her hand she held a glass bottle filled with a brownish liquid. A spoon appeared from the depths of her apron pocket.

"Well! Good day to you, Miss Pembroke. I am Mrs. Ricker, the manager of the boardinghouse for women."

"Mrs. Ricker?" Tillie shivered, and her stomach lurched again. She sat unsteadily back down onto the edge of the bed. "Where am I?"

"Why, you are in White Plains, New York. At the Keeley Institute. We are here to rid you of your dreaded morphine habit, my dear."

"But how did I . . . how long must I be here?"

"Four weeks."

"According to whom?" Tillie said, her voice rising.

"Your good family has paid one hundred dollars in advance for your four-week treatment. You will get good, plain food. Plenty of

271

rest. You must drink Keeley's Tonic every two hours while awake, and Dr. Millspaugh will be here to administer your shot four times a day." She smiled merrily. "You needn't wait in line with the men. With our ladies, we are far more discreet to protect you and your privacy."

Mrs. Ricker unstoppered the bottle, poured out a teaspoon, and mixed it in a glass of water from a pitcher on a very plain bureau. She offered the pale-amber liquid to Tillie. "Drink this."

"No."

"You won't get better if you do not. And your belly will gripe until you do."

Tillie's shoulders sank. She reached for the glass and sniffed it. It smelled like herbs and a touch of alcohol. It was bitter, and she drank it all down.

"Very good. Dr. Millspaugh will be here shortly for your injection."

"What injection?"

"Why, our Gold Cure, of course! Bichloride of gold. It'll make you forget all about that morphine." She stood and took the bottle with her. "Are you also a slave to the drink, dear?"

"Good God, no," Tillie said.

"Well, if you are and you aren't being truthful, we have whiskey available if you are feeling particularly wretched." She smiled again. "Your family didn't provide a maid, so you'll have to attend to yourself and come downstairs for your meal. I shall see you soon."

She shut the door and was gone. Tillie dressed in fresh clothing, but her body felt sore everywhere. Inside the little trunk was nothing to write upon, no jewelry, no perfume, which meant, of course, no morphine bottle. What had happened to the article she had written? Had Ian received her letter?

She was so angry at herself. If she had just drawn up her own morphine, she wouldn't have become intoxicated with too much. She had had no idea that Tom was so much stronger than he seemed. She had always considered him like a child—nothing of immediate danger to her.

Now, she thought—could he have killed Lucy? He had sickened Tillie with morphine and offered spirits. Perhaps he had offered Lucy absinthe and made her senseless. But how had he gotten her from there to the park? He didn't seem healthy enough to do that. And what about Albert Weber? And that other girl?

A child's scream of laughter drew her to the window.

"Drink your dope! Drink it, drink it!" A little girl in a brown wincey dress was thrusting an empty Keeley's Tonic bottle upon a rag doll she'd pinned to the grass. She stopped when a dark-haired gentleman with a small doctor's bag walked up to the front of the house. When he disappeared, the girl hollered, "Catspaw is here!"

Tillie sighed. How had she gotten here? And more importantly, how could she get out?

A knock on the door made her stand up abruptly. The same man from outside walked in her room and set his black leather bag on the bureau. He had oily black hair, a rosy nose, and tiny dark eyes. His person was thin and proper, but something about his expression immediately put Tillie on her guard.

"I am Dr. Millspaugh." (Catspaw, Tillie said to herself.) "I'm here for your injection."

"What's in it?"

"Bichloride of gold, our special proprietary treatment. It shall not be so foreign to you once you are used to the schedule. Nothing to be afraid of." He took out a syringe, then withdrew three different bottles with tinted liquids inside. Red, clear, blue. He took the red one and drew up a portion into the syringe. "May I see your arm, please? Please push up your sleeve, Miss Pembroke."

Tillie did as she was told. If there was any chance this would make her feel better, or at least as good as the morphine did, then she would try it. Dr. Millspaugh readied the needle. Tillie could have sworn she saw streaks of someone else's dried blood. She opened her mouth to protest, but the thick needle punctured her skin.

"Oww."

It hurt worse when he pushed the medicine in. Without wiping off the needle, Dr. Millspaugh put the syringe back in his bag with the other bottles.

"I shall see you every day at eight in the morning, noon, five in the afternoon, and seven thirty in the evening. One hour later on Sundays." He started to leave, then popped his head back through the doorway. His mouth unkinked from a frown to a flat line. "Oh, and congratulations on your publication, Miss Pembroke."

———※———

Though she asked everyone she saw, no one gave her any further information on "your publication," as Dr. Millspaugh had called it. Tillie stopped asking, thinking it was more dream than truth.

The first two days passed in one long monotonous blur. She was not allowed outside, and Mrs. Ricker guarded the stairs to check any attempt at escape. Tillie's schedule was painfully repetitive.

Wake up, receive shot.

Drink the tonic.

Breakfast of bread and milk.

Drink the tonic. Another shot.

Lunch of boiled chicken and bread.

More tonic.

Supper of overcooked, unseasoned white fish, consommé, and a dish of vegetables so bland it made Tillie want to cry.

Tonic. Shot.

Bedtime.

Repeat.

On the second day, because she had been so utterly bored, she'd called Mrs. Ricker to her room and asked for some whiskey, for her "nerves." Mrs. Ricker had complied all too readily and poured out a jigger of alcohol, which was supposed to help the drunkards from having too severe a time in their first days.

It had tasted foul, like putrid gutter water in medicinal form. Within fifteen minutes, Tillie had been vomiting like a fireman's hose. Mrs. Ricker had smiled sweetly later and asked if she wanted more whiskey. Tillie had said no.

By the third day, she had memorized the pattern of yellow vines on her wallpaper. She grew used to the pain of the large needle and the woozy feeling that the tonics left in her. True, her cravings for morphine had settled quite a bit. Perhaps there really was something to Keeley's Tonic. But Tillie also knew what morphine felt like. It caressed her from within her veins, and when it was gone, her body seemed to crumple upon itself in want. She suspected that Keeley's shots contained some small amount of morphine. Gold? Who knew. The liquid didn't sparkle like gold. How was she expected to get over her habit by using morphine all the time?

She learned that there was another "morphine fiend" in the lady's boardinghouse. Only one. Apparently it was a wealthy woman from the Continent who lived in New York with her sister. She had spent every day in her room for the last year, taking her injections and hardly eating, until her sister had brought her to White Plains to stop using the stuff. The other two ladies in the house were trying to stop their liquor habit. One had managed to escape after lunch and was seen staggering blindly in the center of town and was brought back immediately.

Because of her good behavior, Tillie was allowed visitors. She expected her mother to arrive or possibly Ada. But the first person to show up was James.

Mrs. Ricker accompanied her to the large parlor at the institute across the street. It was two o'clock in the afternoon, so none of the men were lined up for their injections. James was shown in.

"Tillie. You are looking well!" James said. He grasped her hands in his and kissed her cheek. It was an effort not to act as if she'd been kissed by a dead fish. He looked at her hand, then glanced at her, concerned.

"They took away my jewelry. No ornaments for drunks," she lied. She didn't want to say she hadn't been wearing it for days.

"You're not a drunk," he said quietly. A maid came by and poured weak tea for the both of them. "You just need rest."

"I suppose. I'm certainly getting inundated with restfulness here." She paused. "I heard my article was published. Did you bring me a copy?"

"Of course not." James lit a cigarette, and Tillie inclined toward the smoke. He handed it to her and lit another. Smoking was allowed at Keeley's. She actually loathed the habit, but anything to break up the tedious ennui was worth burning out her insides. "Your mother and grandmother," James said between puffs, "are understandably furious."

"Are you?"

"I admit I was surprised. I didn't know it was such a dedicated hobby."

"You never asked."

"People who love each other share things, Tillie." He said the words like an accusation. "I understand you're to stay here for four weeks. I can have you released early, if you promise to comply with the treatments and show progress."

She inhaled deeply, stifling a cough. "I am showing progress, James. Ask Dr. Catsp—Dr. Millspaugh."

"Not just with your treatment here. Ada and John spoke to your grandmother. She knows about your going out after hours. Some weeks, they said you were out every single night. *Every single night.* What were you doing, Tillie?" He looked more hurt than astonished.

"I was researching the article."

"Alone?"

"With Ian." At the expression of alarm on James's face, she put up her hand. "No, it wasn't like that. Ian works for the newspaper. For the *World*. He helped me get access to their archives."

"Well. Now that it's out of your system . . ."

"I thought you encouraged me to have an occupation."

"Something to do, Tillie. Like embroidery or church work. Not a job. You don't really need *employment*."

So that's what he'd meant? What a disappointment. And of course, James wouldn't outright say that Tillie didn't need the money. It was utterly gauche to say the word *money* out loud. "Is that why you were angry with Lucy? Because she was so preoccupied with helping the children at the asylum?"

"That was dangerous work, just as what you've been doing has been dangerous."

Good God, James had a talent for making every argument seem like Lucy and Tillie were in the wrong.

"Still, it made you angry. It made her angry, too, to be told to stop."

James smiled and leaned forward. "I know what you're trying to do. I won't admit to hurting your sister in this squabble, because I did not." He leaned back. "You are remarkably gregarious today. You're usually so quiet and timid. It's not like you."

He was correct; Tillie wasn't the same person she'd been when she'd broken her bone, quaking with fear at every situation that thrust her into societal scrutiny. She also knew this: she wanted to write more. And she still did not have a killer to blame for Lucy's death. She couldn't accomplish a single thing while she was stuck here.

She leaned closer. "James. I would love to leave this place and be back home with my family. I'll do whatever it takes."

"No more leaving the house to meet with that newsie?"

"No more," she lied.

"No more morphine?"

"No more," she lied.

"No more articles?"

"I'm finished with them," she lied again. This was enormously easy. She smiled. "It was helpful for me to get some rest and fresh air to think about everything."

"Did you think about our engagement? I've yet to hear a bona fide yes."

Tillie let a cloud of smoke obscure her face. "I'm not in a good place to consider this right now," she said. Not a lie.

"What if I was to get you out of here? So you felt more like yourself."

"Can you do that?" She mashed out her cigarette in a crystal ash-tray. She had another two hours or so until her next injection. Luckily, Mrs. Ricker came by with her tonic, and she drank that down. It did help her feel better. But it had an odd side effect of making her face feel tense and twitchy and her mouth dry.

"I can. I have an idea too. But I'll have to discuss it with your family." He stood, and Tillie stood too. "It's too bad they couldn't have Ada stay with you. Then at least you'd have your maid to look after you. Your hair is a disaster. But they think Ada was too lenient with your wants."

"When can you visit again?"

"Next week. By then, it'll be ten days you've been here. Enough to show you're dedicated to improving yourself."

Ten days! That would be another week at the institute. She would go mad. But she had a thought. She should write down her experience here in Keeley's. It would be so different from Nellie Bly's article in the *World* five years ago. Nellie had taken only one shot and didn't describe how it really felt. She hadn't even professed to be a drunkard or a morphinomaniac. Tillie *was* one. An article from the perspective of someone who truly didn't want to be here, perhaps looking into whether these tonics and shots were actually helpful or a sham, would be news indeed. Nellie Bly had described the process but couldn't know if it truly worked. Tillie could write an article with a fresh perspective.

First, she had to take notes.

"James? Can you send me paper and ink so I can write you?"

He smiled. "Of course."

Tillie got busy right away. She wrote all sorts of notes, between her doses of medicine and dishes of sand-dry food.

What was in the shots? The tonics? Why the different colors?

How would she manage to get doses so she could have their contents tested? Who would test them?

She wrote to Dr. Biggs at Bellevue to see if he would be able to contact chemists to do this work.

And she wrote to James and Dorothy and her mother and grandmother. Bland letters that spoke of the good fresh air, plain food, and plenty of sleep that allowed her to think clearly. Which they did. And she wrote to Ian, too, but Mrs. Ricker informed her that she'd confiscated that letter. Apparently she was following strict orders about sanctioned communication.

Tillie queried the manager, Mr. Brown, one afternoon (he was so inundated with paperwork that when she offered to organize some files, he accepted). The manager was a quiet bald man who was only strong willed when it came to demanding the hundred-dollar four-week down payment from future clients. Otherwise, he was sweet as a lamb. There was much she learned about fees, the volume of patients, whether the medicines made a decent profit from the mail order, and if the recipes for the mail order were the same.

She was in the middle of writing down her notes in the parlor, when a shadow passed over her pages. She looked up.

It was Ian.

"Ian!" She stood up quickly, nearly knocking over the glass of tonic that sat on the table. "What are you doing—how did you find out I was here? They tore up my letter to you!"

"Oh, I snuck by your house, and Ada told me. Been up here a week, huh?"

"Yes. But," she said, looking over her shoulder, "surely Mrs. Ricker will throw you out in a few minutes. She is attending to Mrs. Porter upstairs, who's having a fit without her morphine."

"How are you?" Ian took off his hat and sat in a chair opposite her. "I'm well."

"Ada told me what happened at Dr. Erikkson's. You cannot go back there, ever."

"But we must go back! What if Tom was the one who attacked Lucy?"

Ian shook his head. "Somehow I think Lucy wouldn't have allowed herself to get in that situation. Why did you take so much morphine there?" Tillie ignored his question. After a long silence, he added, "And you know that you reeked of absinthe when they found you. Ada said so."

"John gave me absinthe," she said. "I don't know why he had it. What happened after he gave it to me? Perhaps I might have been killed if Hazel didn't know that he'd gone to find me. Perhaps—"

Ian looked flustered. "You're ignoring my question. You were out of your mind with that morphine."

"Tom gave me too much!" Tillie said, her voice rising.

"Not just that day. *You* were taking too much, all these weeks. All the time. God, everyone knew it except your family, since you hid it so well. Ada said you kept it in your perfume bottle. They found the whole lot."

Tillie went quiet and cold. She put her pen down, her fingers ink stained from writing so intensely all morning. Her morphine stash was gone. Fine, she could get more. But it felt like an attack. No, it was an attack. She was here, wasn't she? She was off her morphine just fine.

A meek voice inside her spoke: *But you thought yourself, the injections probably have morphine. That's why you're doing so well.*

Ugh. Tillie waved it all away.

"I have a new story idea," she said, ignoring Ian's last words. "It's about Keeley's. I'm gathering information firsthand, as a patient. With a different perspective from Nellie Bly's."

"Not sure what the point of that is. We're all on strike. Didn't you hear?"

For the first time, she noticed that Ian seemed weary. "No. My family told the lady here I wasn't allowed to read newspapers. What strike?"

"It started in Long Island City yesterday, but today, we joined in."

Tillie thought of how hungry Piper, Sweetie, and Pops had been that night on the roof. "Where are they?" She didn't have to say who; Ian seemed to know.

"They're pestering the other kids who are still selling papers to join the strike. It's getting violent already. I told them to stop, to stay out of it. Say, there's going to be a rally at Irving Hall in five days. Maybe you could come?"

Tillie went quiet. Unless James got her out, she'd be here for a full month. At the thought, her belly twisted and rumbled. When was her next dose again?

"Are you listening to me?" He looked at the empty glass at her elbow and frowned. "What is that stuff? Are they just giving you opium in your drinks to keep you happy?"

"That's what I'm going to find out. But I'm not happy being here."

He stared at her. Tillie tossed her head, looking out the window instead of meeting his eyes.

"You're going to keep taking morphine after you leave here, aren't you?" he said.

"I made some mistakes I won't make again. But the morphine made me feel better. All the time. I was hardly able to think after Lucy died."

He shook his head. "There are other ways to deal with grief. Opiates are for broken bones, not broken hearts."

Tillie stood up. She could feel her face burning, and she was so angry everything seemed blurred. "You don't understand anything."

Ian rolled his eyes to the heavens, muttering, "Meshuggener. I understand too much. You need to think with a clear head for once."

"You should probably leave."

"I will." He took something out of his shirt pocket and slapped it on the table. A copy of the *World*. Ian strode to the door and looked back, his face downcast with anger. "It's your article. It's good. Really good. But it would have been brilliant if you'd been sober when you wrote it."

THE WORLD

New York, Wednesday, July 12, 1899

TRUTH REVEALED

ABOUT

"VAMPIRE" KILLINGS

––––––––––

TILLIE PEMBROKE

TRACKS DOWN THE FACTS

––––––––––

Her Heiress Sister Was Brutally Slain

but Not Forgotten

————

MURDERER STILL RUNS LOOSE

————

Other Slayings Ignored by Police

————

WHY THE KILLER

IS NOT "DRACULA"

My sister, Lucy Pembroke, was mercilessly slain on June 8, 1899. Her death haunts everyone who mourns her, not only because she is sorely missed, but because of the brutal nature of her death. The police have told us there is no suspect being held at the Tombs, and we hear no news about leads on her killer. For those of us who demand justice, it is almost harder to bear than Lucy's absence.

We know that she was killed by exsanguination. Her very lifeblood was taken from her, drop by drop, from two puncture wounds to her neck. Anyone who has heard tales of vampires, or read the newest thrilling horror tale "Dracula," by Bram Stoker, is all too familiar with the similarities.

Who has seen this killer? No one. He is a shadow. He leaves no traces, except empty bottles of absinthe that bear no relationship to the folktales or Stoker's vision of the monster. Who has caught this killer? No one. How can one catch that which is inhuman?

The death of a young woman, from a bite to the neck, is terror unto itself. But what is worse is the truth, THIS truth. Lucy Pembroke, my sister, is not the only victim in this very real story that refuses to exist within the pages of fiction.

THREE VAMPIRE DEATHS, NOT ONE

Three deaths have occurred in the span of one month, on the island of Manhattan, that speak to a grisly killer thirsting for victims. And there may be more.

Lucy Pembroke was the second victim. The first victim was Annetta Green, found one and a half months ago by the Croton Reservoir. She was also found with little blood left in her body and puncture marks at the neck on the left side. Her death was blamed on a fall, but a Bellevue Morgue coroner's assistant could not explain why a fall would produce such deep punctures so close together, and nowhere else on the body. She, too, smelled of absinthe.

The third and most recent victim was young Albert Weber, whose death was similar in nature to both Miss Pembroke's and Miss Green's. All three bodies were found somewhere in the vicinity of Central Park. All with exactly the same-size puncture holes, and exactly the same distance apart. One thing seems clear—the similarities indicate a single killer, not many.

THE VAMPIRE VS. THE SCIENTISTS

Why such painstaking care to kill an innocent, if it is not a vampire?

One possibility: to make the murder appear to be caused by vampires. The undead are bloodthirsty, drinking only human blood. From lore and from Mr. Stoker, we know that they prefer night goings; they cannot cast a reflection; they can slip through impossibly small cracks in doors; they cannot enter a household without being invited; they can take the shape of the creatures of the night; they can be killed by beheading and by burning. But these are all "facts" as told to us by creators of fiction and by mothers who intended to frighten their children into their best behaviors.

Speaking on the subject of vampires, we go to the good doctors of this fine island, who were interviewed under anonymity, as good doctors ought not to be consulting on the undead. They are, after all, fairy tales in the professional realm. One doctor noted, "A person who bit and drank human blood might do so to remedy a dietary deficiency. But why prey upon humans? It would be easier to drink the spilled, wasted blood from the beef slaughterhouses."

Another famed pathologist noted, "No pathologic specimens have ever been found of humans having such canines or the ability to bite with such precision."

I had the good luck to interview a well-known zoologist who noted that any animal who wished to drink blood for food would not bite so neatly and without a ragged tearing of the neck, or at minimum without bite marks from the underjaw.

Taken together, the good scientists of this modern day cannot see to a sensible conclusion that a vampire could be the killer. Alternatively, we must go to actual vampire hunters in history.

GALLOPING CONSUMPTION AND INSANITY—ILLNESS, NOT MONSTERS

Within the archives of the newspapers accessible to myself, I found several instances of vampire "hunts" and cases of family members who wasted away under the fear that an undead family member was awaking from the grave to suck their very essence.

There is the story of a Portuguese sailor who was said to have killed his captain and drunk his blood. He assaulted no less than twenty-six others, with witnesses aplenty. He paced back and forth like a "tiger in a menagerie" and was committed to life imprisonment in 1867 for insanity. This is not the type of killer who has killed so cleanly in these instances.

There is the famous case of Mercy Lena Brown, who died of galloping consumption months after her mother and elder sister. When her hapless brother became ill, the townspeople of Exeter, Rhode Island, sought out Mercy's dead body, convinced she was awaking nightly to feed upon him. Her dead body was not decomposed, but her mother's and sister's were. Would that not allude to the undead nature of Mercy?

The truth is, the cold of winter likely preserved her in death, while Mercy's mother's and sister's bodies had ample time and warmer weather to let nature take its course. The final evidence is thus: after her corpse was burned, and her brother Edwin fed her heart's ashes, he died as well. This logic defeats the possibility that Mercy was a vampire.

The true killer in this case? Consumption, which consumes its victims in its own macabre way.

MANHATTAN'S TRUE KILLER

Where is he? And more importantly, why are no further investigations being made to bring to justice the cold-blooded murderer of these innocents?

Blaming their deaths on smoke and shadows is poor detective work, and it is an insult to the scientific discoveries that bloom around us like beacons into the darkness. We must keep searching.

This terrible killer is no "vampire" of lore and popular novels. Let us leave that theory behind, for it does nothing but hinder us. The true killer is still out there, puncturing necks and bleeding victims, using our terror of fairy tales to prevent us from engaging our most valuable organ—our mind—and our most valuable modern asset—our logic.

We must speak for those who can no longer—Lucy Pembroke, Annetta Green, and little Albert Weber. Let us give THEM voices from beyond the grave to demand justice!

CHAPTER 22

The last I saw of Count Dracula was his kissing his hand to me; with a red light of triumph in his eyes, and with a smile that Judas in hell might be proud of.

—Jonathan Harker

Tillie read it, stunned. It was a good article. A great one. What was Ian complaining about?

She reread it carefully, sipping her tonic. Dr. Millspaugh arrived later with his greasy hair and his dirty syringe; she pushed up her sleeve and didn't even stop reading when he slid the needle in her arm.

The article was good. But the strange thing was she didn't recognize herself in it. True, she was a novice writer. She had written and rewritten parts of it several times, trying to get it right. But oddly, she couldn't remember what she'd written. She remembered the gist of it, but the essence of the article—the voice—seemed far away. And now that she read it more closely, there were passages that were a little slipshod, a little heavily drawn. It didn't quite have the energy of a Nellie Bly article.

Had she really written so much of it in a fog that she had forgotten how she'd done it? But it didn't matter. The article was in print, and she was a writer. A journalist! If she could only get out of Keeley's Institute.

Tillie considered escaping during the night, but the lack of money kept her trapped. Good behavior and time were the only other option. Every day, she thought of Ian and the newsies. She begged for information about the strike from Mrs. Ricker, even Dr. Millspaugh, but got only scant details. The date of the newsies' rally loomed closer, arrived, and passed, without Tillie being able to do a thing to help Piper, Sweetie, and Pops. Were they eating enough? What had happened at the rally?

It was so unfair that she was trapped here. But as her hours filled with staring at the dull wallpaper and watching men line up for shots, she thought more about why that was. It was fate, was it not, that she possessed a constitution that needed morphine? Or was it her choice?

She wasn't sure. Her body had needed the medicine. But she had chosen to increase the doses. Placing the blame on her choice or her constitution—both answers led to discomfiting thoughts. What was she able to do, or unable to do, when it came to her own destiny?

And at the end of it all, she was still stuck here.

James returned, but several days later than he'd promised. He arrived with a warm kiss to her cheek. The more she saw him, the less she was alarmed by Lucy's words about James striking her. Those accusatory words were being diluted by James's repeatedly sweet behavior. Today, he wore a smirk like he was hiding a surprise. Which he was.

"I have a solution for you, Tillie."

"To what problem?" she asked. On the veranda, the staff had brought out tea and toast with a scant bit of butter. They were so very mean here with the plain food. Drs. Millspaugh and Keeley must think marmalade was poison.

"Your morphine habit. You've been taking the medicine here, correct?"

"I have. I'm not sure it works, to be honest. They won't tell me the ingredients." This, despite having questioned the cook, Mrs. Ricker, Dr. Millspaugh, and the manager, Mr. Brown.

"I think I have something better. It's a scientific miracle. They say it's not addictive at all, and you only need a fraction of the dose, compared to morphine." He produced a tin from his pocket. Inside were tiny white tablets.

"What is it?" Tillie lifted a pill between her thumb and forefinger. Such an itty-bitty thing. It looked like a saccharin tablet.

"It's called heroin. My doctor says it's perfectly safe. Take them." He handed Tillie the tin. She read the top.

BAYER PHARMACEUTICAL PRODUCTS

HEROIN—HYDROCHLORIDE

1/12 GRAIN

A SEDATIVE FOR COUGHS

BRONCHITIS

PHTHISIS

A cough medicine. That seemed safe enough. She popped a chalky tablet in her mouth, let it dissolve, and smiled.

"You take that and stop those Keeley medicines. When they see you feel fine without them, I'll discuss with your family, and we'll have you discharged."

"Oh. That sounds lovely." How could her sister possibly have felt so terrible about being married to James? She simply couldn't imagine James hitting anyone or anything. "You're brilliant!"

"I'd like to be more than brilliant to you, Tillie." He stood and reached for her hand. After Ian's irritability, James was a balm. She squeezed his hand back.

She understood well enough from the parades of grooms and brides before her that marriage was a maneuver, a dance between warring sides; sometimes it was mortar for joining walls to be built higher. She remembered someone saying—was it Dorothy?—that the union between their families would be one of the century. She thought of everything that James had been to her, done for her. He did not chide her for her habits; he did not seem so scandalized by her writing. Her heart was molding itself to fit what seemed so very fitting.

James left, and Tillie dutifully took her tablets every few hours without saying a word to Catspaw and Mrs. Ricker.

Not only did the pills keep the pain at bay, but she felt impervious. The tablets wiped away all bitterness, regret, and anger that had ever existed. The oppressive heat of summer didn't bother her; she simply noted it and blotted the sweat from her upper lip. If she wasn't careful, she would close her eyes to ponder something and find herself waking up half an hour later. She indulged and took two tablets at bedtime and found she drifted off to sleep on a wave of velvet irresistibility. She was tempted to take double doses during the day but decided not to chance it. She couldn't be caught looking intoxicated.

She ignored the fact that her head felt disengaged from her body or that her mouth was unbearably dry. The discomfort was worse than ever when her dose wore off. She felt profoundly melancholic when she awoke each morning. Her nose ran, and pain resettled into her bones. Yawns nearly cracked her skull open. Before she swallowed her tablet in the morning, disturbing thoughts pressed for attention. Oppressive thoughts that said, I would rather die without these.

Four days later, two and a half weeks into her stay, she was discharged.

"I've never seen a morphine fien—a person like yourself get over everything so quickly," Mrs. Ricker said, handing her folded dresses to put into her trunk. "You must not have been a very constant user.

Some of our other ladies were likely using twenty times what you had been."

Tillie nodded. She had her pastilles in the crevice of her bosom, under her corset. "I would like to buy a bottle of tonic to bring home. Just in case I'm feeling the need to go back to my old ways."

"Of course. With your leftover deposit, we can certainly arrange for a small home supply."

What she needed now was a bottle of the injectable from Catspaw. Then she could bring them both to Bellevue for testing. But how to get one?

"Mrs. Ricker. I should like to meet with Dr. Millspaugh one last time. For a final examination."

"That isn't necessary, my dear. He saw you yesterday."

"Please. It would satisfy my family, and they are the ones who paid for the treatment."

"Very well."

Catspaw was upstairs, it turned out, and came by her room. After his brief examination (he simply glanced at her and felt her pulse), she said, "Doctor, if you please, I would appreciate a written note to my family about my full recovery. They won't believe it from me, but they will from you."

"Of course." He turned to leave, but she pointed to her bureau.

"A thorough note," Tillie added. "I have pen and paper here. If you please."

The doctor seemed surprised but nodded and put his black bag back on the floor, then turned to the bureau and picked up the pen.

"I'll bring my things downstairs. My family is coming for me in about half an hour."

Catspaw hardly said anything as his pen scratched the paper she had left there. He pushed a greasy lock of hair out of his eyes, and it promptly tumbled back. She dragged her trunk closer to the door and, behind the doctor's back, picked up his bag and left the room. He didn't even notice.

Downstairs, she opened the bag and saw the bottles of Keeley's injection liquids—which one to take? There was a clear, a red tinted, and a blue tinted. She'd always received the red one, so she took that. When she was done, she put the bag by the pile with her other possessions in the foyer.

She waited in an armchair by the window until Catspaw came downstairs, a piece of paper fluttering in his hand. He looked alarmed but relaxed when he saw his bag next to hers.

"Oh! There it is. How odd, I thought I'd left it upstairs." He handed her the letter, and Tillie thanked him. It wasn't long before her carriage came with James inside. In less than a minute, she was comfortably tucked in the back seat.

"I'd say the heroin was a marvelous success." James glanced at her disheveled hair and dress. "You'll look more like yourself with Ada tending to you."

"Yes," Tillie agreed, though she wasn't sure what she was agreeing with. As the carriage drew away, she heard a call.

Looking back, she could see Catspaw running from the institute, waving his spidery paw. He must have opened his bag and realized a bottle was missing. Tillie took the tin of pastilles from her corset and popped one into her mouth as the carriage pulled farther away. The doctor frowned deeply but then shrugged and walked back to the institute.

"Did he need to speak to you?" James said.

"Apparently not," Tillie said. With her tongue, she pushed the pastille between her molars and crushed it.

Her mother and grandmother welcomed her home with benign happiness and clasped hands of approval. Her stay at Keeley's was mentioned as a ritual that some ladies on Millionaire's Row had to suffer through.

Tillie was confined to the house again. John had been let go after he'd admitted that she had been running about at night under his nose. This infuriated Tillie. She had no way to contact him and question his behavior with the absinthe. If he had any links to the other murders, that trail was lost.

Ada, thankfully, had kept her job but seemed absolutely heartbroken that John was no longer in the house. She attended to Tillie with a red nose and sniffed into a handkerchief between her duties.

And Tillie dutifully chewed her pastilles.

Dorothy visited with Hazel soon after her return. They were talking about an endless supply of busy nothings. Then suddenly, James was there too.

"Oh. I didn't even hear the doorbell!" Tillie said, blinking slowly.

"I didn't want to disturb you, in case you were sleeping," he said.

"We were going." Dorothy and Hazel stood, and James took Dorothy's chair. Hazel's hand brushed James's shoulder as she passed, and James looked at her with intention. Dorothy was already in the foyer, primping in the mirror. It struck Tillie that they had an understanding, and Dorothy was unaware. Then the moment passed, and just as quickly, Tillie forgot it.

She had a question for James but couldn't remember it. He chatted about the weather, the stocks, and how the hunt cup would miss Tillie next week.

There was a question. What was the question?

Tillie opened her eyes. She hadn't realized they'd been closed.

"Oh! My notes. My papers, from when I was at Keeley's. Do you know where they are, James?"

"I threw them away," James said. His face was neither malevolent nor happy. Just . . . the usual James. A blank expression fixed between a Caravaggio and a Rembrandt. The epitome of a gentleman.

Whereas Ian blazed his emotions like firecrackers, lit from the slightest provocation. She remembered his words.

"Don't give up before you try."

"Why?" Tillie woke up a bit. "They were mine."

"You didn't need them. Keeley's is behind you."

"Dorothy said you had collected letters to bring to me. I don't remember receiving them."

"Because you were still taking those dreadful medicines. There's much you don't remember."

Tillie shook her head. Logic. Where was her logic? The notes. She had been talking about the notes. "But I wanted to write a story. About the medicines, at Keeley's. I think the paper would buy a follow-up story to what was truly in those medicines. I never saw a single glint of gold."

"Don't be silly. You can't see the sugar in tea. Stop thinking so hard." He looked down at her fingers. "I see my ring is back where it belongs."

Tillie looked down. His diamond rosette was back on her finger, as tight as ever. She didn't remember putting it on. There was something else she wanted to ask about. Something that had been nagging at the corner of her memory for days now. Something about the paper.

"Oh. The strike. I haven't read a newspaper since I got home. What happened with the newsies' strike?"

"What? Good God, I have no idea, Tillie. Let Pulitzer and Hearst worry about that." He took something out of his pocket. "No doubt you are running low on these. Here. But don't tell your family. You don't want to have to go back to Keeley's, do you?" He handed her a tin box. This one was twice as big as the first one.

"Thank you." She covered it with her hand, in case her mother passed by.

"You ought to go rest. Tomorrow, I'll come for you. We can take a walk. Perhaps talk about other things."

"Like what?"

"Like setting a date. I'd love for this to all be behind us. Start new, and start fresh." He didn't even wait for an answer. He walked her to the grand foyer. "Up you go. Have a nap. That's a good girl."

Tillie smiled and went up the stairs obediently. She clutched the tin of heroin, and when she reached her bedroom, she stared at it for a full hour before she succumbed to the small animal inside her that yowled in discomfort, and she plucked one from the tin.

She stared and stared at it. And it nearly spoke to her.

It was such a small thing.

She needed it.

It was just for coughs; how could it possibly do her harm?

She lifted it to her mouth, hesitated. If she took it, she knew she would not really be bothered by James's destroying her notes. She would not really be bothered by being married. She would not be bothered by much of anything anymore.

If she took the pill, she would not really mind that Lucy was dead. That her throat had been punctured, that her blood had been forcibly taken, that all the good in the world that she had hoped to do was crushed into nonexistence forever.

Tillie went to the bathroom next to her chamber and washed all the pastilles down the sink. She took the tiny bar of pink rose-scented soap, lathered up her hand, and tugged at James's ring.

If he loved her off of the heroin, then it was real love. She would find out soon enough.

She tugged harder, and the ring flew from her sudsy hands, where it bounced on the wood floor and rolled into a corner behind the porcelain bathtub.

She left it there.

It was a dreadful week.

Tillie's chamber became a sickroom. Ada was at her side nearly the whole time, cleaning the sick, holding her trembling hand, wiping her skin, which sweated so much she drenched her sheets. A doctor visited—a new one. Dr. Turnbull was a stout older gentleman who bellowed, "Less is more!" Grandmama nodded with approval. There was no mention of Dr. Erikkson, and her body was too weak, too occupied by purging itself of its previous habits for her to demand a different doctor.

Her insides roiled with spasms, wanting to squeeze every blessed drop of fluid out of her. She shivered so hard her teeth rattled. Any soup that went down came back up. And yet, the spasms and pain, fevers and sweating, chills and recurrent visits to the toilet lessened in increments day by day.

Dorothy and Hazel visited, occasionally giving Ada a break by holding Tillie's hand and feeding her water by the spoonful.

For some reason, these visits always made her feel better. So much better she felt she might finally get through her trials. But then hours later, she would feel even worse than before. It made no sense.

Once, in a haze of delirium, she could swear that James came to her bedside. Dorothy was nowhere to be seen. Hazel was looking over the bottles of medicine, shaking her head.

"The opium is all gone."

"Well. We'll see how long that lasts." James was chuckling.

Hazel sighed, and he reached for Hazel's soft face. His hand slid to her ivory neck and thence downward, cupping her bosom over her cambric shirtwaist. Hazel gave a muted exhalation of desire.

Tillie fell asleep and later wondered if she'd dreamt it all.

But after several more days, she was sitting up in a chair in the parlor, no longer wearing a soiled nightgown, drinking tea and eating mincing bites of her egg at breakfast. She felt utterly wrung out, but an old and odd sensation had been occupying her body lately.

Her mind was lucid.

Before her broken collarbone, she'd lived in a body full of awkwardness and worry. But her mind had always enjoyed its freedom. If she was curious, she would run after a question, like a kite climbing the heights of a grand wind.

On her medicines, the kite had felt constantly tethered, like it was flying through misty clouds, and at times, through thick syrup. She'd gotten so used to it that she hadn't even recognized the difference.

Now, it was as if a smoked glass had been removed from her vision. Now, Lucy's death loomed larger than ever, as fresh as if it had only just happened. The wound of losing her became brand new, shining and raw. She whimpered at the mere sight of Lucy's chamber door. Sometimes she wanted to scream in rage over nothing, over bitter coffee or frayed boot strings. Ada cried often. In fact, she seemed as sick as Tillie. There were at least three episodes this past week when Ada had vomited into a bin, while Tillie was vomiting into the bathroom sink. They were twin sisters of raging indigestion.

Now that Tillie's worst was over, Ada was still occasionally turning pale and sweaty and darting to the bathroom. At times, she wasn't even making it all the way to the servants' quarters.

Oh.

Oh.

That morning, Tillie was in bed, and Ada had snuck in a newspaper. The strike was over. The newsies were still paying the exorbitant sixty cents a bundle, but at least Hearst and Pulitzer were promising to buy back the unsold papers. Kid Blink, the most vocal and the leader of the newsies, had apparently been disgraced after being accused of accepting a bribe. All of this had happened while her body was twisting and turning, ridding itself of its insistent love of heroin. It infuriated her.

She had completely missed the opportunity to help Ian and those little scamps.

When Ada picked up her empty plate, noting the smear of yolk on the china, she lurched and covered up a dry heave.

"Ada, put that plate down," Tillie ordered. She took the napkin on her lap and hastily covered the yellow smear. After pausing to be sure no one was in the hallway to hear, she pulled her maid closer. "Ada. Are you with child?"

Ada's eyes went huge and glassy. She covered her face with her hands and burst into a sob. She dropped to her knees. Tillie patted her back.

"It's John's, isn't it?"

Ada sobbed into Tillie's lap.

"Have you spoken to him? Does he know?"

Her head shook vehemently. She lifted her eyes. Mucus ran from her nose, and her skin puffed with redness. "He left so quickly we didn't have a chance to say guh-guh-goodbye!" She hiccupped. "He was so angry at being dismissed. So angry! He didn't even look my way when he left. And now I don't know where he is or how to speak to him!" She dropped her voice even lower. "I thought maybe he went back to working at the Metropolitan Museum, but I sent a letter there, and they didn't hire him again."

"Wait. Did you say he worked at the museum? Where Lucy died?"

"Yes. He used to be the night watchman there, but this job paid more, so he left." She sniffled again.

Could John have seen Lucy at the museum? She imagined him striking her, holding her down, an awl raised to pierce her neck. No, no. Why would he choose to work at the house where his victim had lived? It made no sense. Then it occurred to her that John worked at night only. Oh, but she had just convinced herself and all of New York that vampires didn't exist! Ada was still talking, anxiety having drained her peach complexion to a pasty gray.

"Oh, if the missus finds out I'm with child, she'll fire me. She did with the other one. With Betty."

Tillie went still, and the hand stroking Ada's red hair froze. "What did you say? Betty was in the family way too?"

"Yes. Did you not know?" Ada wiped her nose on her apron. "I thought perhaps your sister had said something."

"No. I thought she was fired because of what happened to Lucy. Or for stealing things from the house."

Ada looked up and wiped her tears with her sleeve. "Betty didn't take a thing. It was your sister, Lucy, who was stealing."

CHAPTER 23

It is wonderful what tricks our dreams play us, and how conveniently we can imagine.

—Mina Harker

Lucy. Lucy had been the one stealing, all this time? The food and the linens?

"Why was she stealing?"

"I don't know, but Betty was certainly helping her hide the fact."

It was time to find Betty. John had said she'd been in the Tombs, but where was she now?

"Do you know where I can find her? I have to speak to her."

"Of course I know." Ada had stopped crying, and Tillie couldn't manage to sit still, so she carried the dishes to the kitchen with her. After they put them in the washbasin for the kitchen maids to clean, Tillie looked longingly outside. It was sunny, and the sky was a cornflower blue.

"Of course you knew. And I never bothered to ask you." She was furious with herself for not asking the simplest questions weeks ago. "Can we go outside?" Tillie said. "I'm desperate for some fresh air."

"We can, but Missus says that you need a second chaperone. After Miss Hazel lost you, she doesn't trust that one lady alone can keep you from running off and . . . and . . ."

"And what, exactly?" Tillie raised an eyebrow.

"And writing another article," Ada said sheepishly. "By the way, what a stunner of a story! One of the best I've ever read in the papers."

"Thank you, Ada." Tillie sighed. Had the article even accomplished anything? The unknown truth still tap-tap-tapped at her spine with its insistent, sharp nail.

Where was the killer? And what, really, had happened to Lucy?

"Will you write another article, Miss Tillie?"

"I don't know. I would like to." She stood. "There's still work to be done to bring Lucy's killer to justice. And the worst of it is I'm back where I started. Here, in this cage."

Ada looked around her. "People dream of having such a beautiful home."

"Not if it's the only place you can ever breathe."

"Oh, but once you marry Mr. Cutter, it will all change. Won't it?"

"If I get married. But then my life won't be my own. It isn't now. I don't know what to do, Ada. If I leave this life, I will have no money. No home. No friends. I don't know how to survive."

"Well, I suppose you'd do what I do. Get a job, and work, and find a place to live, and keep going." She put a hand on her belly. "But I should rather you stayed here so I could keep my job. It pays well, and I'll be able to take care of this little one."

Tillie glanced at Ada sheepishly. It was another reminder that there was more to worry about than just herself. Oh, what she wouldn't do for just a tiny sip of laudanum to relax and think things through.

It turned out she was not so trapped as she thought, at least in the small ways. James called on her the next day and invited her out to see a matinee at the Irving Place Theatre. Tillie decided any opportunity to get out was worth the risk. Her suspicions about Tom had never been soothed. He had attacked her, bitten her, and there was nothing to prove he hadn't attacked Lucy the day she'd died. She had to learn more.

And she had to find John somehow. He'd been patrolling the Metropolitan Museum of Art, right around the time Lucy had died. He'd plied Tillie with absinthe, the very same substance found by the three dead bodies. The way he looked at her—it frightened her. And yet the thought of Ada, pregnant Ada, discovering he was a murderer was almost too much to bear.

When James arrived, he kissed her cheek and smiled.

"I was sorry to hear you were so ill. Has the medicine not been working for you?" He led her out to the carriage, and they proceeded downtown. Tillie's dress hung a little loose on her. She wore one of Dorothy's recent purchases, a rather viciously pink gown.

"I stopped taking the medicine. The pastilles you gave me."

"You stopped them?" James said, surprised.

"Yes. And I think it will take quite a while before I adjust to being off them—and the laudanum. And the morphine."

"Too bad. I guess I'll keep these, then." He reached into his pocket and pulled out a fresh tin of heroin tablets.

Tillie inhaled a sharp breath. The tin was shiny and new, the Bayer lettering crisply printed. Her hands itched to reach out, pry the tin open, and toss one down her throat. But she shook her head.

James raised his eyebrows. "Very well, then." He offered the tin to her. "Why don't you just hold on to these. In case you're feeling unwell, in the future."

She couldn't say no. The tin went into her reticule, but now Tillie felt as if there were three people in the carriage. At the matinee—a show about a girl becoming a bright and shining singer on the stages of Paris, while her lover pined for her in the orchestra pit—Tillie sat unsatisfied and irritable. The chair was too plush; her polonaise felt itchy where the lace touched her throat.

All her discomforts and cares would go away if she only took one tiny pastille.

Just one.

She took the tin out, discreetly, and snapped it open. She could feel James's eyes on her. But oddly, she could feel another set of eyes on her too. A prickling on her neck that said she was being watched. She glanced about the crowd in the small theater, but the audience was transfixed by the Parisian singer crooning with a ten-foot wooden Eiffel Tower behind her and an electric crescent moon swinging stage right.

Tillie slowly turned. A man was silhouetted in the door to the theater, tall with broad shoulders. She blinked rapidly, trying to adjust to the backlighting. On her fifth blink, she could make out a face.

John O'Toole.

Tillie turned around. She had to speak to him. She looked down, snapped the pastille tin shut, and grabbed her reticule.

"I'll be back."

"Where are you going?" James whispered.

"The retiring room. It's the heat from the lights. I'll be all right," she whispered back.

Tillie staggered through the row and scurried up the aisle. John was no longer there. She opened the door to the lobby of the small theater. An attendant held a large tray of candy and cigarettes.

"There was a man here, just a moment ago. Did you see where he went?"

He pointed to the front door, and she bolted out into the dazzling sun. She shaded her eyes, and when she was able, she looked about.

John was nowhere to be seen.

Tillie ran west down the block. Union Square opened up before her. It was midday, and people walked here and there with their packages and perambulators. A few pushcart vendors were selling oranges and bags of hazelnuts. The verdant trees of the park were growing lustily in the midsummer's humidity. Everywhere she looked, there were children playing and ladies shopping and men smoking cigars. No John O'Toole.

She'd turned to go back to the theater when she stopped. Slowly, very slowly, she looked about her. She opened her eyes to that blue sky, let her eyes follow the avenue all the way north to where her home was, and southward toward the Battery.

She was outside. She was free and unaccompanied.

Quickly, she checked her reticule. She had only a little money, enough to get her to one location and back, if she took the elevated. She ran back to the Irving Place Theatre and put a nickel in the hand of the closest attendant.

"I have a message for James Cutter. He's in the seat next to this one." She thrust her ticket stub into his gloved hand. "Tell him I had to go. I'll be back home by dinner. Tell him not to worry."

The attendant gave a stuttering nod.

Tillie had a free afternoon and could do anything she wanted, and no one would know. No one. Her first impulse was to go into her reticule and take just a tiny bit of heroin. Maybe just a half tablet to celebrate her freedom. But the impulse was overtaken by the urge to visit Dr. Erikkson's office. Now that she knew the undead were not responsible for Lucy's death, she had to focus on the living.

The Third Avenue el took her up to Fifty-Ninth Street. She walked quickly past Bloomingdale's dry goods store to the next block, where Dr. Erikkson's office was situated. Not too close, but close enough that she could watch. Why did Tom's parents seem to not care that their ill son was capable of hurting women? Whom else had he hurt? She thought about how skittish the maid had seemed. Perhaps Tillie could speak to her, if she left the house.

Across the street, on a small stoop under the arched doorway of an orthopedic hospital, a man perched on crutches. A large bowler hat sat on his head, and he was awkwardly bent over reading a newspaper clutched in one hand. Surely Tillie could stand there a bit and not be noticed. She crossed the street, trying not to make contact with the man. She didn't want to chat with any strangers right now.

He didn't look at her. She took up a position on the other side of the arch and stared at the Erikksons' building. Through the front window, near to the street, she noticed a tall shadow—it must be the doctor. And a shorter person next to him. Too short to be Tom, but soon enough Tillie could see it was Mrs. Erikkson.

"Aren't you at least going to say hello?" the man on the crutches said. He had a strong Eastern European accent. It reminded her of Tobias's voice.

Tillie turned, surprised. He took his bowler hat off, and one of his crutches clattered to the ground.

"Drat. I can't get used to using these," Ian said, scrambling to pick it up. He'd tucked the newspaper under his arm.

"What are you doing here?" she hissed.

He grinned. "Same thing you're doing. Spying on the Erikksons."

Tillie wanted to say so many things—to tell him about her recent illness and how she was no longer taking the medicines. But the memory of his harsh words at Keeley's and her shame at missing the strike stopped her.

"Look!"

She turned back to watch the window across the street. It took a few seconds to readjust to seeing Dr. Erikkson's tall figure gesticulating. Mrs. Erikkson tried to turn away, and he yanked her arm. Her round body jerked toward him.

And then he struck her.

Mrs. Erikkson staggered back and disappeared from view. Tillie put her hands to her mouth. Ian cursed under his breath.

The door to the home opened, and Mrs. Erikkson emerged, face red, eyes swollen from crying, and holding a basket. She pressed a handkerchief to her face as she walked hastily down the street.

Tillie started after her. She turned to Ian. "Let's follow. Maybe we can speak to her away from Tom and Dr. Erikkson."

"Yes. Hold on." Ian abandoned the crutches and paper, hiding them in an alleyway under a pile of loose garbage. "Let's go."

They started walking quickly, but Mrs. Erikkson was a half block ahead. They crossed the street, increasing their speed.

"How long have you been watching them?" Tillie asked.

"At least two weeks. I'm trying to find patterns to see if Tom may be coming across other women. I do know some things. Dr. Erikkson leaves every night to gamble and see some ladies at a saloon near the Metropolis Theatre."

"Not scouting people to bleed to death?" said Tillie.

"It's possible he doesn't go there every night. I asked some of the women there about his schedule. They were quiet as the grave. Refused to say a thing, even when I offered to pay them."

A shrill whistle sounded behind them. Pops was running toward them, a canvas bag filled tightly with newspapers bouncing against his narrow chest.

"Oy, Tillie! Ian!" he yelled.

"Shhh!" Ian said. "Pops, go back to your post. Keep selling, keep a lookout."

"You're using the newsies to do your scouting work?"

"Ten cents for good information! It's woith it," Pops said. "I gotta sell here anyways." He pouted. "Tillie! You don't do midnight picnics wid us anymore!"

"Aw, I will. When I can." She stooped down and hugged the little chum. She fished around in her reticule, pointedly ignoring the medicinal pastilles, and found a peppermint candy. "Here. It's all I have, but I'll get something more later."

"I'd ruther a ham," he said, grinning.

"Get on with you!" Ian said and gently pinched his ear.

"Yeah, all right. Tillie don't pinch me," he opined, running off toward Bloomingdale's, hollering about his paper.

They turned around. Mrs. Erikkson was even farther away, but they could see her bobbing along the street. Ian pointed. "She's turning. Look."

Mrs. Erikkson made an abrupt right into a narrow passage between a home and the alley beside it. It was well swept and clean, and there was a tidy brick building hidden behind a foreshortened house there. She went inside, and they heard the snick of a door lock.

Ian held his hand up to knock but then turned to Tillie.

"Wait. How are you even here? Aren't you still supposed to be at Keeley's?"

"I graduated."

"And they let you meander the city now?"

"I escaped."

"They're going to be furious with you," he said, hiding a grin.

"Can we get back to Mrs. Erikkson?" she snapped.

"No, really—how did you get out this time?"

She rolled her eyes. "I abandoned James Cutter at the Irving Place Theatre."

Ian chuckled. "You really know how to treat your beaus well." He sobered and then said, "By the way, it's nice to have you back."

"Thanks."

"I mean, you. Without the opium or the morphine or what have you."

Tillie stared, agape. "You can tell?"

"Like night and day. Sobriety suits you, Tillie." He smiled gently at her, and the effect was like a hook on a snag, right inside her rib bones. "Now. Should we knock?" He turned to the door of the little brick abode.

Suddenly, the door opened. Mrs. Erikkson held an iron pan in her hand, ready to strike.

"Whoa!" Ian put up his hands. "Don't hit us!"

She lowered the pan. "Oh my! I thought you were someone else. I thought—" Her reddened eyes were still wet with tears. "Miss Pembroke! What are you doing here? Who is this man?"

"May we come in? We were worried about you," Tillie said.

"Worried about me? I was worried about you," she said. "Come in, come in. There are many apologies to be had, on my part. Come in."

They entered the single-room house. Two walls were covered in shelves, each stacked with jars and boxes painstakingly labeled. Strung across the ceiling were bundles of herbs in varying states of drying. Even though it was summer, a stove burned in the corner, keeping the room dry of the city's humidity. Jars of alcohol and brown tinctures steeped on the floor near a worktable. Shelves were loaded with aspirin, bottles of laudanum, and other proprietary formulations for women's pain, lassitude, dropsy. The bottles were wrapped in boxes labeled with an emblem of a leaf and the words

Dr. Erikkson's All-Natural Remedies

Guaranteed Purity

For ALL Symptoms

"The druggists make their own, so my husband started this about seven years ago," Mrs. Erikkson said. "It makes a tidy profit. He sends me to deliver the medicines every day to his patients."

"Why don't you keep these bottles in his office?"

"Oh, we keep some but not most. Goodness, someone broke into our home when we first began and stole everything. Everything! Also, the herbs don't always smell very pleasant, and my husband insisted we keep the pharmacopeia away from the office." Mrs. Erikkson frowned. "What brings you here? Why didn't you call at our house?"

Tillie and Ian looked at each other; then Ian said gently, "We saw him strike you. We wanted to make sure you were all right."

She laughed, but the laugh was a rising ember that extinguished just as quickly. "Everything is quite fine. Sometimes we argue. But never mind that. Miss Pembroke, I cannot begin to express my shame and horror over Tom's behavior. To think that he would take advantage of your delicate health and . . ." She shook her head. "We had to beg the police not to take him away. He isn't right, with being sick all these years. We've paid so much attention to his constitution that we haven't taught him how to be a gentleman. That is entirely upon me and his father. He is being disciplined, I assure you."

"I appreciate your apology," Tillie said. "I wish I'd heard it from Tom himself."

"It's best you don't see him again," she said firmly. Ian nodded in agreement.

"Does he . . . is he able to leave the house?" Tillie asked. "Ever?"

"Of course, he's able. He chooses not to. We've asked him to walk about more to exercise his lungs and his legs. But he likes to stay in his room."

Ian looked at her gravely. "Are you quite sure that he's never tried to hurt another woman or one of your husband's patients?"

"No. Well, yes. That is to say . . . he and the maid, Beatrice. I've caught him with her. She's terrified of him now and keeps her distance." She wiped her face, and when she dropped her hands, she appeared utterly exhausted. "But I simply didn't imagine he would have the strength to take it this far. He spends most of his days taking his morphine and sleeping. And reading." She smiled faintly. "He feeds his mind, because he chooses not to enter society."

Tillie thought about what she'd said. She was busy delivering medicine all the time. She couldn't possibly watch Tom all day, or even all night. Her words did not completely dispel the possibility that he was far more violent than she knew.

"Has he ever hurt you?"

"Goodness, no! He is sweet as a child could be to his mother."

"Your husband . . . has he ever hurt Tom?"

"I think that's enough talk for one day." Mrs. Erikkson turned around, putting several bottles into her basket and cushioning them with crumpled newspaper. "If I don't fetch these deliveries on time, there'll be more fighting." She sniffed and headed for the door. When it opened, the bright sunlight sparkled over the dust motes that arose from their movement. "Thank you for your visit. And thank you for allowing me to apologize."

They thanked her and left. Walking slowly, they saw Mrs. Erikkson, her basket heavy with goods, glance at a paper list and sigh before starting her rounds.

"She seems miserable," Tillie said.

"No less miserable than a lot of people on this island," Ian noted.

The sun was beginning to sag near the horizon. "I said I would be home by dinner. They'll be furious with me. I may never get out of that house again, not until I'm married off."

"I'll marry you, and then you can cause whatever mischief you'd like," Ian said, grinning.

"Would you?" Tillie asked seriously.

"In a heartbeat," he said and winked. But his voice was so light-hearted that it was obvious he didn't mean it. "Say. I'll walk you home, and I'll make sure no one sees me when we get close."

"Thank you."

They said nothing while they walked up Lexington Avenue, past Beth El Synagogue, past the convent and St. Vincent Ferrer church on Sixty-Fifth Street. The silence between them stretched out while the rattle of wagon wheels, the honking of an occasional Klaxon, and the storekeepers chatting with patrons filled the void. Suddenly, Tillie said, "You know, there is one thing we've forgotten. All three victims had just recovered from an illness. An infectious illness. We know Lucy visited Dr. Erikkson the day she died, but what about the others?"

"You don't still think he's a vampire, do you? After that article you wrote?"

"No, I don't. But we've seen that Dr. Erikkson has a violent streak. He became enraged when I asked about my sister. And I'm fairly sure this isn't the first time he's hit his wife."

"What if . . . what if you were right earlier, and it has more to do with the illnesses themselves? The recovery? I can't imagine why, but it's the one thing the victims all had in common. If only we knew of a patient who got sick with an infection of some sort and went to visit Dr. Erikkson . . . then we could watch and see if he or Tom tried to hurt them."

"If only," Tillie said. "You can't predict who's going to be sick or not."

"True." They were silent for a long while again. Tillie liked how Ian would slow his long-legged stride to match hers, and once in a while their shoulders bumped, and their hands swished against each other's as they crowded closer to avoid other pedestrians. Tillie wished for more collisions like this, but to her disappointment, the sidewalk opened up as they neared Sixty-Eighth Street. The Foundling Hospital and its attached asylum was to the right. Home was only two avenues away.

Tillie stopped suddenly. "This is where Lucy used to do her charity work. I haven't been by to visit them. I wonder if the sisters know that she died." A sudden idea ignited in her, a plan. She felt it rush to her fingertips, but it also turned her stomach into a quivering mass. She turned to Ian. "You should stop here. I'm close to home."

"All right." He looked troubled and kept kicking a dent in the sidewalk. "Say, I want to apologize. I wasn't very nice to you up in White Plains."

"You spoke the truth. I probably haven't heard much of it lately." She smiled sadly. "I guess we're even. I wasn't truthful to you about all that medicine I was taking, and you weren't truthful to me about the article."

"No more lies, eh?" he said.

Tillie bit her tongue and nodded but said nothing. Was it lying to not say what you were thinking?

"I think it may be a very long time before I ever see you again. I've an article I'd like to work on, but I have no idea how long it will take."

"The street rats'll miss you. I'll let them know you'll send a ham when you can." She laughed, and Ian shoved his hands deeper into his pockets. He mumbled something.

"I'm sorry. What did you say?"

"Nothing."

She cocked her head. "Ian."

"I said I missed you. When you were in White Plains, and we weren't talking. I missed our nights researching."

"I did too." She stepped a little closer. "Do you remember our picnic on the rooftop with the kids?"

He grinned a yes.

"I think I may have kissed you that night. And I don't really remember it."

"Well, you did," he said seriously.

"I should like to have one to remember you by. Not that one down at Newspaper Row, either." She cleared her throat. "Uh. If that's all right with you. Sober this time."

Ian swallowed. He seemed nervous all of a sudden. He dragged his fingers through his thick hair and swallowed again.

"S'all right," he croaked.

Tillie came closer, ignoring the passersby on the street, and rose to her tiptoes. She lightly kissed his lips, swaying when she lost her balance. Ian steadied her with hands on her waist. She leaned in closer and let the light kiss blossom into something with intention and strength.

"Indecent!" hissed a lady who walked by. "For *shame!*"

They separated. For a change, Ian was the one who seemed slightly drunk.

"That I'll remember for the ages," Tillie said, blushing. "Off with you now." She waved him down the street, and Ian turned in the direction from which they'd come. He seemed in a hurry to go, but she recognized it as embarrassment. Tillie rounded the corner onto Sixty-Eighth Street and found the entrance to the Foundling Hospital.

She knew exactly how to find this "vampire," and the answer lay within these walls. If there was one similarity between the victims, it was that they'd had a disease and recovered.

Surely, there was an illness here that could bring Tillie to her knees and lure the killer as well.

"Time to catch a vampire," she whispered as she walked up to the gates.

CHAPTER 24

It is only when a man feels himself face to face with such horrors that he can understand their true import.

—Jonathan Harker

The New York Foundling Hospital took up much of Sixty-Eighth Street between Lexington Avenue and Third. Tiny crosses adorned the iron railing skirting its border, and marble window lintels contrasted with the imposing redbrick walls. An enormous, drooping willow tree swaying in the breeze seemed to gesture for Tillie to enter.

She passed through the marble columns and just inside the heavy doors was greeted by a nun in a simple black-and-white habit. The nun was about her mother's age, spindly, with spectacles and a smile that was doled out in a very limited quantity.

"I'm very sorry, but we are about to close for the evening. Perhaps come back tomorrow?" she said.

"Please. My name is Mathilda Pembroke. My sister was Lucy Pembroke."

"Miss Pembroke!" The nun put her hand to her mouth. "Oh! We have heard about the loss of your dear sister. What a terrible tragedy."

"Yes. And I . . ." The next words seemed to materialize from nowhere, but she meant them with all her heart. "I would like to continue the work that she did. I haven't much time. It may be a very long while before I have another opportunity to return here. I'd like to speak to whomever my sister worked with, if I may."

"Of course. That would be Sister Cecilia. She is monitoring the preparations for supper. Come with me."

They strode through the great hall and up the stairs to the second level. The place was clean and simple, devoid of decoration. A room was open to the right—a long corridor with tiny tables and bins of toys. Several nuns watched over children playing quietly while others listened to one of the sisters reading a book. Another room had a seemingly endless number of cribs lining two sides and tiny children occupying small rocking chairs or splayed out on the floor, warring with tiny wooden figurines. The children were dressed in neat but well-worn clothing.

Another nun, plumper than the one who led Tillie, came toward them and, at the sight of Tillie, stopped, a look of astonishment on her face.

"Sister Cecilia," Tillie's guide said, "this is Miss Pembroke, the sister of our dear Lucy. She wished to speak to you."

"You are a version of your sister, and it took my breath away to see you. Why, you have the same smile!" Sister Cecilia came forward, the crucifix she wore bouncing against her chest. "What brings you here at this time of day? We are readying for supper, and the children will go to bed soon after."

"I am interested in continuing my sister's work. Can you tell me where she—can you show me where she used to work?"

"Of course. Perhaps we could do a full day tour tomorrow, or later this week when the children aren't so tired."

"I'm afraid I may not be able to come again anytime soon. I'm so sorry for the imposition."

"Not at all. We are used to the call of duty at all hours."

"All hours?" Tillie asked.

"Yes—picking up babies in the middle of the night, when the bell is rung and they're left in the basket on the street. It has been our way since 1867. We have taken in over twenty-seven thousand children since then. Sixty years ago, infanticide was rampant. It is no longer."

Tillie was shocked at the numbers. Those children could fill a city. "How awful that their mothers did not want them."

Sister Cecilia smiled kindly. "They are often very much wanted, but poverty prevents their mothers from keeping them. Or madness. Or sickness and death. They despair that their children will suffer with them, so they leave them here. Some families are able to retrieve their children when their circumstances improve." Tillie followed her down a long corridor; the smell of antiseptic and lemon oil filled her nostrils. "Here we are. You'll want to see the hospital wing, of course."

"Yes, I understood she liked to work with the ill children."

"And it got her sick! It was no surprise. She was here nearly every day. But I thought she had recovered," Sister Cecilia said, unlocking a door. It opened into a hallway where several nuns wearing long white aprons and white caps were busy rolling small trolleys filled with medicine bottles in and out of rooms.

"She did," Tillie said, peeking through the windows. Some contained hospital beds covered in gauzy netting; others, tiny cribs with wailing infants. "She was so happy being here."

Tillie could almost see her sister's ghost in the hallways, her heart full of all the things she could do to help the children. These were wants and desires unknown to Tillie—as much a crime as Lucy's death—but she wanted to know them now.

"And she was so generous with her time and her resources." Sister Cecilia had stopped; she clasped her hands together. "These are our hospital rooms. We opened the hospital wing about twenty years ago."

"Resources?" Tillie asked. Could her grandmother have been that generous as to give them money?

"It wasn't much, but it mattered." The room they stood outside was tiny, and there were only two children. A caretaker, not a nun, was feeding a baby with a rubber teat connected to long tubing. The tube led to a glass bottle half-full of milk in the woman's hand. The woman looked familiar. Tillie peered closer, trying to see her face better. She looked up, saw Tillie's face in the window, and promptly dropped the bottle.

"Oh!" Tillie said.

"Do you know that child?" Sister Cecilia asked.

"No. But I know the nurse. It's Lucy's maid—"

"Betty Novak. Why, yes. She was the one who was always bringing extra food and medicine for the children."

"She was?" Tillie said, confused. But wasn't Lucy the one who was really doing the "stealing"?

"I would say that you could ask her yourself, but she's in a quarantine room with the smallpox patients."

Tillie's heart thrummed fast and warm. Smallpox. She'd been a child when their old doctor, Dr. Peterson, had come by the house to administer the vaccine. She had watched her father, her mother, and Lucy receive theirs. Sleeves rolled up, they were pricked with a tiny double-tipped needle filled with fluid from an ampoule of vaccinia virus. There had been an outbreak in the years before, and Dr. Peterson had been pressing all his patients to get vaccinated.

"Not Mathilda," her mother had said. "She is far too young."

"Which is exactly why she should get the vaccine. At her tender age, the illness could ravage her."

Her mother and father had argued about it viciously, Tillie remembered. Coming from a household where science wrote the rules, her father had been at a loss. He did not know how to address his wife's dogmatic reasoning.

"I know of women who have gotten the vaccine and still been infected," Mama had said. "Are you sure it will work?"

"I can assure you, you are far less likely to die or to have a disfigurement if it does pass through the family. You cannot say the same for your daughter if she is not vaccinated." The doctor looked at Tillie severely, as if it were her fault that her mother was refusing.

"Next year," her mother had said. "When she's six, I shall allow it."

Her father had already rolled down his sleeve and gone back to his study. Tillie remembered watching the vaccine area on her sister's arm grow red and pustular, then change to a large dark scab that left a telltale dime-size scar. Her mother had decided to employ a new doctor after that. And another, and another. Dr. Erikkson had been their most recent, and he had been fired, too, after what happened with Tom.

Tillie never had received the vaccine.

"May I go inside to speak to Betty?" Tillie asked.

"I cannot allow it."

"I've been vaccinated," she said, hoping the lie would sound true.

"I'm sorry, Miss Pembroke. We mustn't disturb her. There are other rooms where you can visit. I can give Betty a message for you."

Tillie listened to Sister Cecilia go on about the history of the Foundling Hospital, about how they were ever expanding and in need of funds and donations. They were on the cusp of leaving the hospital wing, when one of the younger nuns came up to Sister Cecilia and whispered something in her ear.

"Can you not take care of it? Isn't Sister Evelyn there to attend to this?"

"No, Sister."

She sighed and turned to Tillie. "There's a situation in the infant room. I'll be back in a moment. Wait here." They exited the hospital wing, but as the two nuns walked away on their silent black boots, Tillie let her hand catch the edge of the door before it could lock shut. When the sisters were out of view, she slipped back into the wing and paused outside the smallpox quarantine room. Betty was back to nursing the child, who was clutching at the tubing with her chubby hands. Tiny round welts dotted the child's skin every inch or so.

Tillie put her hand on the door. Going in meant she would risk getting the infection. She might infect others too. She could start an epidemic, but that was less likely. Everyone in the house was vaccinated. The servants who weren't she would demand be sent away until their own vaccines were completed. She could make sure no one else entered the house. She would warn others.

Lucy had been infected with typhus and Albert Weber with cholera. Annetta Green had been sick with consumption. Whether they were all tied to Dr. Erikkson or had been identified another way, she didn't know, but she had no other avenues to try.

Succumbing to smallpox would be no minor event. Her smooth skin would be forever scarred, possibly terribly so. Tillie had always rested comfortably in the knowledge that she was not visually arresting, like Lucy had been. Yet she had enjoyed the privilege of the appearance of health, of skin that was unmarred by illness.

But to stop the slayings, once and for all? It would be worth the scars. Lucy had risked her life too. She would borrow her sister's bravery tonight, wear it like a shield.

Tillie opened the door and shut it behind her.

"Miss Pembroke!" Betty exclaimed and nearly dropped the bottle again. "I thought that was you! What are you doing here? You must leave. These children are very sick. It's not safe."

"I've been vaccinated," Tillie said. Ruefully, she thought, *Opium taught me how to lie. I might as well use it for good.* She walked over to the child Betty was holding, who eyed her with curiosity and wide blue eyes. She was perhaps a year old. "May I hold her?"

Betty, in a state of shock, handed the child over. As the bottle was now empty, Tillie fed her spoonfuls of milk and oats until the girl fell asleep. She let her fingers run across the sores on her little arm as she slept, thumb in mouth. It reminded her of Piper. She would tell Ian to bring the newsies to the nearest dispensary to have them vaccinated, and soon.

"I wanted to speak to you," Betty began, "but I was in the Tombs for ever so long."

"We found out you had stolen from us. And then, Ada told me it was Lucy, not you."

"Yes," Betty said, somewhat miserably.

"Yes to which truth?" The child stirred, and Tillie rocked her in her lap. She was a bit surprised by how naturally it came to her. Perhaps Lucy had been good with children too. If only she had Lucy's diary back; it was still with the police.

"I am not a thief. Miss Lucy had set aside baskets of food and goods for me to bring to the asylum every week. The cook saw it and said nothing, but neither did my mistress. In the end, I was the one blamed, and Miss Lucy was dead, and she had no voice to tell anyone the truth."

"Well, I know now. And I can tell anyone who needs to hear what happened."

"It won't matter. I am content to work here now. The nuns knew me well, and Miss Lucy knew I would be fired once she was married. Mr. Cutter didn't want me in the house."

"Why on earth not?"

Betty suddenly scrunched up her face and frowned. "I don't want to say. I heard that you and he—that he's your betrothed now. Is that true?"

"It isn't. Everyone would like it to be."

"Are you so sure?"

"Absolutely. He has been very kind to me, but . . ." She couldn't finish her sentence. She couldn't put her finger on it, but Lucy's voice in her diary continued to speak a warning to her.

The toddler had fallen asleep, mouth slack. A few times, she coughed, and Tillie did not turn her head away. She would be certain she caught the virus, no matter what. Finally, she laid the child back in the crib and smiled. Sister Cecilia would be looking for her. "Time to go."

Tillie headed to the door, but Betty stopped her. "Wait. In case you aren't fully sure about marrying Mr. Cutter, you must know one thing. She had an argument with him, you know. Over me."

"You?"

"He was kind to me. Almost like a brother at times. I thought it sweet and a sign that he would treat your sister well, if he could treat the servants like family." Her face soured. "But I saw him once with that lady's maid who's with Miss Harriman all the time."

"Hazel!"

"Yes. Once, when they were all riding together on Long Island, Hazel kept back, and James said he'd twisted his ankle. I saw them in the stables together. He had her skirts over her head, and they were . . ." Her face contorted with disgust. "Like goats."

Tillie put her hand over her mouth. Hazel and James? "I had no idea."

"It's no surprise. That woman's been wanting James to marry Dorothy all this time. Keep him closer and keep her job. Why, she's the one who told James that Lucy was always going to the Foundling Hospital. Them fighting was her dearest wish." She waggled a finger. "You see, if Dorothy marries someone else, Hazel might get let go. But James would always keep her under their roof, wouldn't he?"

Tillie thought about Hazel caressing James's arm, of the intimacy between them that she thought had been a dream—and now she knew she had imagined neither. Hazel had seemed so kind. Could this be why she was always offering opium and morphine to her? To ruin her chances with James? Or to keep her pliant, unaware, too clouded to notice what was happening right before her eyes?

"Did my sister know about this?"

"Oh yes. She suspected it. And she tried to keep him away from me too."

Betty was near to Lucy's age of twenty-one, but she had large elfin eyes and a tiny frame. Tillie had always thought she looked barely sixteen, even younger in a certain light. But now that worry and care had aged her a little, she looked like she was approaching thirty. Exhaustion blanketed her like an invisible smothering cloth.

"What happened, Betty?" Tillie asked slowly.

Betty's gray eyes reddened. "There was a baby. Mr. Cutter's baby. Your sister knew. We were returning in the carriage after bringing her to visit a friend, and in the carriage . . ." She passed a hand over her eyes. "He was stronger, and I felt that I'd put myself in the situation. I thought it was my fault."

"Oh, Betty!" Tillie covered her mouth. "Good God, no, that was not your fault."

"It doesn't matter anymore. Lucy cared for me as best as she could, lightening my load." Her mouth twisted. "I miscarried around the same time as your sister died. She was going to call the wedding off. Did she not tell you?"

"No," Tillie said. "I wish she had. I wish I'd asked her."

"She kept too much to herself. That was a terrible week. But it got worse, because Mr. Cutter told your grandmother that I was stealing silver, and the police came. I wanted to warn you, Miss, but it took months for the sisters to help me out of the Tombs."

The footfalls grew close, and Sister Cecilia's shadow darkened the window of the door. She looked alarmed and began knocking at the door. When they didn't open it, she began trying different keys in the lock, one after the other.

"He promised me he'd help if I stayed quiet. He would give me money, more than I was making as a maid. I didn't know what to do. The day your sister died, she'd decided to call off the wedding. I remember that day. She liked to write down her thoughts in a little book sometimes, but she'd forgotten it at home. She begged me to give her time alone to think. Away from me, and away from everyone. I was angry at her, because I was afraid I'd get in trouble for not accompanying her. We fought at the doctor's office, but in the end she got her way, and I went back to the house by myself. And then . . . then I lost everything!"

Betty finally broke into tears and snatched her apron to her face.

The door burst open, key ring jangling. Sister Cecilia was red in the face, almost redder than Betty. "Miss Pembroke! I thought I had lost you!"

"I'm not lost," Tillie said, turning around and heading for the door. She looked at Betty, who was trying desperately to regain her composure before the nun. They nodded to each other, an acknowledgment of so many things, and more to come. "I'm not lost at all," Tillie said.

<hr/>

The illness arrived slower than expected, but it came with an inevitability that frightened Tillie.

In one week, she succumbed to a fever. Tillie coughed and ached, and her head throbbed with a severity she had not known before. Her mother called for Dr. Turnbull, but Tillie asked for Dr. Erikkson, and only Dr. Erikkson.

"Why? That man—that family. We cannot allow him in here," her mother said.

"Dr. Erikkson," Tillie said again. "He knows this illness well. He'll know how to care for it."

Tillie begged relentlessly, even when her mouth grew sore with a rash that spread to her tongue and palate. Between bouts of vomiting, she asked for only Dr. Erikkson.

As she knew what would be coming, she'd banished Ada from the house. When she'd come home the night after her visit to the Foundling Hospital, she'd instructed Ada to remain at a distance.

"Don't come near me. In fact, leave the house, Ada. Leave your things and just go. I'm sick, and I can't have you or the baby get sick. Go to your family, and I'll send for you when it's safe to return."

"Sick?" Ada cradled her belly. "But you look so well!"

"It's smallpox," she warned. "Leave right now." Ada picked up her skirts, turned, and left the room.

Tillie questioned the rest of the servants through one of the older maids, whom she remembered had also received a vaccine all those years ago. All the unvaccinated servants were sent away on Tillie's command, and fear drove them away before even receiving word from her mother or grandmother.

Days after her mouth erupted, the fever subsided only to return when her skin broke out in a rash. The rash started as flat red dots the size of a small button. They rose to blisters a few days later, filled with pus a few days after that. They dotted her skin, from her face and neck down her trunk. She'd heard of children getting the smallpox so badly that hardly any normal skin showed through. Tillie could see swaths of normal skin, but looking in the mirror, dizzy and feverish, she knew. She would never look the same again. She cried a little at this—saying goodbye to a version of herself she had taken for granted her whole life. Planned as this was, there was still shock and mourning to be done. But she also knew that she would survive this. Purpose thrummed strongly in her heart.

This would be worth it.

Wouldn't it?

A letter from Ian arrived well into her second week of sickness. One of the newer maids, already vaccinated, didn't know the policy to destroy them first.

> *Tillie,*
> *I heard from Ada about your illness. I sincerely hope that*
> *you haven't done what I think you have. If this is your*

plan, you're mad to have put yourself at risk. I'm furious. Do I even have a right to be furious? I don't know but I am.

Since I know you'll worry, I've brought Piper, Pops, and Sweetie to the dispensary on Eldridge Street to get them vaccinated. I'm vaccinated too. Say, we should do an article on vaccination rates in the city. Wouldn't that be swell?

I hope you get well soon. I would visit you, but no doubt I'd be turned away.

Stay off the dope, will you? I know you can.

Yours,

Ian

"I can't be kept away from my chum, even if she does look like a raisin muffin," said a voice from her doorway.

Tillie looked up. "Oh. Dorrie. You have a way with words. What are you doing here?"

"Says the lady who writes articles for the newspaper. My family was against my coming, but I've been vaccinated, and I don't care." As if smallpox were an occurrence as irritating as a canceled theater show. Dorothy settled herself in a chair by Tillie's bed and withdrew some needlepoint from her reticule. "Well, all right. You look like a currant bun, then." She glanced at Tillie, her smile faltering. "Are you uncomfortable? Can I get you anything?"

"Really, Dorothy. I don't need the laudanum anymore," Tillie said, adjusting her pillow. Well, that wasn't completely truthful. The longing for opium had sewn itself into her very being. She could not simply loosen the stitches and pull it out for good. It took every ounce of effort to refuse it, but refuse it she did.

"Ah, good. Wretched stuff, laudanum. Hazel wanted to know if you needed any, so I shall tell her no."

"About Hazel," Tillie said. There was no proper way to say it, so she just blurted it out. "I heard that Hazel and James have . . . they've . . ." Her face was aflame. "I know on good authority that they've had an affair. I thought you should know."

Dorothy stabbed a red flower in her needlepoint. She yanked the needle through, but the thread knotted on the fabric, and she frowned. "Damn. I don't know why I bother. I do hate needlework."

"Dorrie. Did you hear what I said?"

Dorothy looked up and smiled, a beatific expression on her face. "Hazel would never do such a thing. It simply isn't true."

Tillie tried to press on, but Dorothy began to relentlessly gab about some new play in the Tenderloin district. Her friend tackled the embroidery with gusto for the next hour with fingers that trembled ever so slightly. Not a single stitch was added that wasn't ruthlessly snipped and undone.

Tillie had tried. Later that day, when two boxes of exquisite roses arrived from James, Tillie had them thrown out with the kitchen garbage.

⚬

Ian's letter wouldn't leave her mind. Tillie had the typewriter brought up to her bedroom and placed on a table by the window. When she had the energy to be out of bed, she started making notes for two different articles—one on the truths about living through smallpox and one on the experience of having lived through Keeley's Institute as a real patient. Just that morning, she'd had a maid send off her Keeley's medicine samples (those, James hadn't taken) to Dr. Biggs to have them tested. She couldn't wait to find out the contents.

Though her grandmother and mother hadn't forgiven her reckless abandonment of James at the theater and the unexpected visit to the sickrooms of the Foundling Hospital, they were so terrified that she would die from the illness that they relented and allowed Dr. Erikkson to visit once. Only once. Both Pembroke matrons insisted on being in attendance.

"Classic smallpox," Dr. Erikkson announced, a surprise to no one. "Bed rest and aspirin. I'll prescribe a salve to rub on the pockmarks once they heal to minimize the scarring. She's very lucky she didn't get one of the more malignant cases or the hemorrhagic type." He left several bottles of his proprietary medicine and was gone. After such a perfunctory visit, they weren't sure what to think.

"Very professional," her mother noted.

"He seemed like he was ready to bolt as soon as he could. Only the guilty act in such a way," Grandmama said. "Are you satisfied, Mathilda? Can we finally remove that dreadful man and his family from ours?"

"Yes."

"And will you promise not to write anything about it?"

Tillie pressed her lips together.

"Why this need to write to the world?" her mother inquired.

"It's a fever, a passion. We all had them. We all left them behind," her grandmother said.

"And was it worth it, leaving it behind?" Tillie asked. Her mother seemed frozen into speechlessness, perhaps terrified that Tillie would ask her the same question.

"Yes. Of course!" her grandmother nearly boomed. "It always is. We have our fortune. We have our name. It is always worth the sacrifice. Some mistakes are best left in the past."

A month ago, Tillie would have stayed silent, wretched and afraid under her grandmother's gaze. But she couldn't contain her anger.

"Lucy. Lucy is the mistake you'd like to leave in the past," she said.

"Mathilda!" her mother gasped.

Grandmama rose and headed for the door. "Go on and tell her. She's good at finding answers; she'll find out anyway," she said to her daughter, and then to Tillie: "You're clever, Mathilda. It's a blessing and a curse." She looked at the medicines Dr. Erikkson left. "Put that salve on your scars. How will we ever get you married looking like that?" She shut the door.

Tillie would have waited for her mother to speak. But she was coming to realize that her mother was perfectly comfortable evading difficulty—for centuries, if possible.

"Lucy never did look much like me. The hair, the eye color. Papa is not her papa, is he?"

Her mother shook her head, staring at her lap.

"Who was he?"

"I can't say. I won't. But I loved him, and he didn't want me. He was . . . is . . . already married and refused to divorce and marry me."

"And Papa?"

Mama looked up, her eyes shiny with tears. "Oh, he loved me for years. I was already showing when he offered marriage. He didn't mind. He took to Lucy like she was his own child. But Grandmama always feared that someone would tell the truth and our shame would be thrust upon all of New York."

Clarity entered Tillie's mind. "Lucy knew, didn't she?"

"She saw him—her father—at a ball. He was visiting from Europe. I'll say that much—he's not American. She saw the resemblance immediately." Mrs. Pembroke inhaled and hiccupped at the same time, the sound of a sob being swallowed. "She was going to tell James. She didn't want to lie about who she was."

"Did she? Tell James?"

"I don't know. I don't think so."

"And so Lucy died, and you and Grandmama were fine with that. Leaving the secrets behind."

"We didn't wish her any harm. We would never! But the investigation and the newspaper articles—it had to stop. The more our family is in the public eye, the more likely the truth will come to light. We cannot have that."

330

Her mother rose, smoothing her skirt.

"Others have died, Mama. Not just Lucy. Your secrets aren't more important than preventing the deaths of more innocents."

But her mother seemed to have retreated back into her careful composure. "When you are better, things will be back to normal. No more writing, no more running around."

"I'll never stop writing," Tillie said. "The house, the carriages, the money. It's always been enough for you and Grandmama, but not for me. I want to learn things outside of myself and bring more thought and knowledge to the world. Why is that so very terrible?" She sat up.

"Mathilda," her mother said. "Grandmama has made it clear to me. If you continue to write, we shall cut you off. No money, no dowry, no inheritance."

"Then I shall get a job, and I may even gain a living writing," Tillie said with equal gravity.

"Ugh. Working? Like your other grandparents?"

Tillie tried not to look hungry, but she couldn't help it. "They did? Tell me."

Her mama hesitated but seemed resigned to speaking. "They took care of the sick. Your grandfather was a doctor in Philadelphia. And your grandmother was a druggist. Can you believe that?" She shook her head. "A woman pharmacist! She had dark hair and eyes, like your father. Both poor as paupers."

Tillie grabbed her mother's hand. "There is honor in having a profession, in not being idle. They had no money; there is no dishonor in being poor. I am glad you told me about them."

The color in her mother's cheeks had disappeared, leaving her looking like an ink-and-pencil drawing on white paper. A whisper of wind might blow her away. "I suppose those memories belong to you, too, whether I like it or not." She smiled uncertainly, then left the room without another word.

Visions of her grandparents and her father swirled in her mind. Somehow, she could imagine them smiling at her from far away. Tillie had meant what she'd said, hadn't she? She'd be perfectly content in a boardinghouse. And she would learn to cook soup. Right now, all she could do was butter her toast. She was fairly sure she could live on soup and toast.

One of the maids knocked on the door. "You've a visitor, Miss."

"I don't want to see James," Tillie said.

"It isn't Mr. Cutter, Miss. Your grandmother says to send them up."

A few minutes later, a woman entered the room. She wore a simple dress of brown poplin and a matching hat decorated with cream ribbons. She was older than Tillie, younger than her mother, with light-brown eyes that were large and steady. A tiny circlet of pearls was pinned at her throat.

She looked about the room; looked at Tillie in her sickbed, the reddened but healing marks on her face; and sat down on the chair that her mother had recently vacated. Finally, she swelled her breath to speak.

"Baked mud."

Tillie's mouth dropped open in confusion. "I'm sorry?"

"Baked mud. You wanted to know what elephants smell like. That and elephant feces. Really, they smell like a barnyard, though in the wild, I can imagine their odor is different."

"You . . . you're Nellie Bly."

"Yes. I've only just received all your letters. I was in Europe, but I am back now." A spasm of sadness constricted her eyes. "My sister died suddenly, and I had to come home."

"I'm so sorry," Tillie whispered.

"It looks like we have suffered the same loss, though yours was more nefarious. Mine was just due to nature."

Tillie nodded. She was a little starstruck, sitting before the most famous female journalist in the world. Nellie Bly was right here, in her bedroom.

"When I arrived, your grandmother asked me to speak to you about my life as it is now," Nellie said matter-of-factly.

"She did?"

"Yes. To let you know that I have been married now for many years and am quite financially comfortable due to my advantageous match."

Tillie was taken aback at the disclosure of such personal information. Famous as she was, Nellie was still a stranger.

"I see."

"Writing for a living is a perilous undertaking, Miss Pembroke. The work is hard, the pay is poor, and there is no guarantee that your editor will want your ideas."

Tillie's shoulders drooped. "Then you think I should give it up, like you did? And marry?"

"I didn't say that." Nellie leaned forward. "I kept writing after I married. I covered the National American Woman Suffrage Convention in Washington during my newlywed year. Granted, when we first were married, my husband gave me no sense of security. If he died, not a penny would come to me. That has changed since, but back then—I knew I had to take care of myself." She leaned back.

"But now that you have that security—"

"I am not retired from my journalistic career, Miss Pembroke. In fact, I am far from done. There are some organizational items I must attend to in my husband's business. I've been in Europe far too long. I may even try my hand at inventing."

Nellie rose to her feet. "I came here for three reasons," she said. Tillie got the feeling, both from her articles and her current presence, that Nellie did not beat about the bush. "One, to make sure you weren't dead. And here you are: you are quite alive. Your last letters were a bit worrisome. Two, to ask if you've found the monster who killed your sister."

"Oh. I have not. But I have an idea as to how to find them."

"I see. I assume I'll read an article about that when it happens. Don't get yourself killed in the process. The stunts these young journalists do to sell a paper!" She shook her head.

"But weren't you afraid to do some of these things you did?" Tillie asked.

"There are stunts, and there is immersing yourself for the sake of gathering information for the public. Know the difference between them." Her voice softened. "I have done some things because I hadn't the courage to say I was afraid. And I learned more about myself in the process. Safe does not make for a good story."

"So . . . you didn't come here to convince me to stop writing? Grandmama—"

Nellie straightened, looking like a thousand-year-old tree, ever impervious to the wind. "I have told you the facts of my circumstances. As in the newspaper business, it is up to the reader to decide for themselves what to think. I think for nobody but myself, Miss Pembroke, and I suggest you do the same." She turned, and her skirts swept the carpeted floor as she left.

"Wait! What was the third thing?" Tillie asked.

She paused at the door. "Oh. For the love of Pete, *stop writing to me*. Four letters to all my residences and my editor? It's a waste of paper, and I shan't write back. I'm too busy. Good day to you, Miss Pembroke."

CHAPTER 25

But this night our feet must tread in thorny paths; or later, and for ever, the feet you love must walk in paths of flame!

—Van Helsing

All at once, just a week after the lesions had begun to erupt, they scabbed over, and Tillie's reflection resembled a raisin-studded vanilla cookie. And then the scabs fell off, leaving shiny, reddened marks that sank into her skin, as if a tiny bite of flesh had been taken in the process. A hundred greedy bites, all over her body. A payment for sickness, as if the sickness were not payment enough as it was.

"It's not so bad," Ada said. She had returned after Tillie's lesions were deemed fully healed. "With a little powder, they're less noticeable."

"Ada, they are as noticeable as a fly doing the backstroke in a bowl of cream soup." She sighed. It didn't bother her that much; what bothered her was how melancholy her mother had become, fussing over her situation. How everyone's eyes would land on her and think the cruelest things, and those words would make their way to her mother's ears. It was common knowledge that Tillie was once considered "a fine girl," which was a euphemism for "not quite pretty but not absolutely ugly either." Now, they feared she was intolerable.

One good effect of her illness was that leniency had entered the household. Perhaps the fear of losing Tillie altogether had made them loosen their grip; perhaps since her prospects had plummeted as her pockmarks settled in permanently, they decided that all hope was lost anyway. No matter what the reason, it felt as though the giant's fist around her had begun to uncurl. Tillie could breathe again. She could write letters and receive them, uncensored, and she had begun, with Ian's help, to plan the final test of her hypothesis—the reason why she'd sickened herself.

Accompanied by Ada, and with Ian secretly watching from a distance, she took three separate walks outside, sometimes in the daytime, when Lucy had disappeared, sometimes later. Twice, she walked in Central Park, hoping that being in the vicinity of where the victims had been found might incite an attack. She'd even convinced Ada to remain a good distance away. Ada would rub her growing belly and glance around, still looking and longing for John.

Nothing happened.

Somewhere after her fifth attempt in two weeks, she stopped trying. And then a letter arrived.

It was from Tom Erikkson.

Tillie's fingertips went numb at reading his name on the envelope.

Dear Miss Pembroke,
If you have not already burned this letter, then call me blessed. There is no excuse for my actions. I have asked myself countless times why I acted so monstrously, but all the reasonings behind my behavior do not lessen what I have done. I am deeply sorry. My family have attempted to make excuses upon my behalf to prevent me from heading to the Tombs and being locked away at Sing Sing, which is where I belong. They were successful, for good and for bad.

I am hoping that I can apologize in person. A letter can be written by anyone, and it can too easily become a mask obscuring true sentiment. I realize you owe me nothing, less than nothing, but I am begging for a chance for forgiveness. I dare to hope to become a better example of what God had intended me to be.

I will be at Bryant Park on Thursday at four o'clock p.m. I hope to see you then.

Yours in regret,

Tom E.

Tillie dropped the letter on the floor.

Her first thought was to burn it.

Her second thought was that an outdoor area at Bryant Park was an absolutely abysmal place to set up her murder. Public places were inconvenient in that respect. But perhaps it was chosen as such, a good distance from his home and away from the sites of the other murders, so she might feel safe. And she did, now that she considered it.

I could see what he has to say and question him further about his father, Tillie thought. Ada could watch her from afar. And Ian.

The next day, Tillie spoke to her mother. Tillie no longer woke up after noon; she was up by seven in the morning, tapping away at her typewriter after breakfast.

"I'm to meet Tom Erikkson today," she said. She and her mother had taken to walking together once the morning rush had sped by on the avenues.

"That's an absolutely wretched idea. You mustn't." Her mother held an umbrella above them both. She shunned the sunlight, but Tillie always ducked aside to absorb the warmth and light when she could.

"Ada will be with me. So will Ian."

"Please stop communicating with that person, Mathilda."

"He's just a friend, Mother."

337

"Womenfolk do not befriend men. It is exceptionally scandalous when both are unmarried."

Exceptionally scandalous. Tillie would like to embroider that on her lapel.

"Well, it's not like James Cutter is a better option," Tillie said. "He hasn't visited me once since I recovered." Amongst his other terrible attributes, like having affairs under his fiancée's nose and impregnating the maids against their consent.

Her mother sighed. "Perhaps it's for the better." She tightened her grip on Tillie's arm. "I should tell you. There are rumors that he's setting his sights on Dorothy. He's been to her home to visit nearly every day this week."

"He has? That's terrible!" Even after she'd told Dorothy about James and Hazel?

"Terrible? Well, for us, perhaps. It would be wonderful for Dorothy, though the Cutter family doesn't get so much out of the match. The Harrimans' fortune has taken a turn for the worse these last few years."

"You're sad for me, Mama. Don't be."

"I don't want you to be alone in life," she said. "Being alone is terrifying."

"Are you so terrified, now? You have me, and you have Grandmama."

"I'm not speaking of myself," she said. "I had my time. I *was* married. I'm speaking of you."

Tillie reached for her mother's hand. It had gone thinner of late. The tendons showed more clearly, as if a reminder to all that a Pembroke was flesh and bone, after all, not just gilt clocks and large mansions.

"Mama. Do you miss him?"

Mrs. Pembroke looked almost terrified at the question. She smiled, a plastic smile, and said, "I'm very happy, Mathilda."

"That's not what I asked." Tillie waited, letting the silence stretch out thin as skim milk. Mrs. Pembroke suddenly inhaled sharply, as if she'd been holding her breath for a decade.

"I do. I miss him." She covered her mouth and looked away, her eyes tearing. "He was a good man, Mathilda."

"Then why, *why* is the mere mention of him such an atrocity under this roof?"

"He was poor, and—"

"He had an occupation. He was only poor by your standards!"

"And his heritage . . ." She trailed off.

"He had a Chinese grandfather, is that not so?" Her mother nodded. "Which means that I have a Chinese great-grandfather. Ought I to be ignored too? Do you love me less for that fact?"

"God, no! Oh, Mathilda, I never meant for you to feel that way!" They stopped in the middle of the sidewalk. "It's not him. It never really was him. He loved me despite everything. Oh God! It was him that tolerated Grandmama, not the other way around. She despised him! But I wanted to stay in this house, so he agreed. She knew he thought very little of her money, our wealth. And she hated him because he reminded her of my mistakes."

"But you had me. And Lucy. Was that wrong?"

Her mother grabbed Tillie's hand. "No. Never. But we Pembroke women have always had to push aside our passions for what was right, for the sake of safety and propriety."

"And has it made you happy?"

This time, her mother didn't answer.

"I know what Grandmama would say. Happiness isn't important, but family is."

Her mother nodded. "We Pembroke women are a long succession of broken hearts. Even your grandmama wears her pain like armor. It is and always has been."

"There's a story there too," Tillie said. "And one day I'll learn it. Stories are how the world evolves." She smiled. "I like to hear about my father and his family. It's part of my evolution."

"You really want to write?" her mother asked after blotting away the rest of the moisture from her cheeks.

"I do. I have a mind to keep myself occupied. So long as I can learn about this precious, extraordinary, and occasionally heartless world, I can be content."

In the end, Mama agreed to let Tillie meet with Tom. When the hour arrived, Tillie was more nervous than Ada. Ian had said he'd meet them at Bryant Park, and Tillie felt a terrible wanting the entire morning. She found herself looking for spare heroin pills on the floor of her bedroom and sniffing her perfume jars to see if they still perhaps held a little morphine.

It was times like this, when she was distraught, that she felt unwhole. There was no other way to explain the feeling. It seemed that opium called to her wherever it was in the world. She knew it was waiting for her at the druggist on Third Avenue and Sixty-Eighth Street. That the opium dens near Canal Street issued clouds that would lure her to dreams mired in numbness. Going to meet Tom, who might invite her for another afternoon of morphine intoxication, she feared she might not be strong enough to say no.

"It's time. Let's go," Ada said. "The carriage will wait on the corner, in case we have to leave quickly."

"Perhaps I shouldn't go," Tillie said. She sat back down on her bed and clutched the bedpost. "I'm not feeling well."

"You said yourself this was a good idea. You'll be safe." Ada smiled, a little too brightly. Why was she pushing so? "Even your mother agreed! Come now. Let's get this over with."

Ada cajoled her to let go of the bedpost, then the bedroom doorknob. She practically pushed Tillie down the stairs and into the carriage. Tillie clung to the window, her head halfway out, for fear she would not get enough air, all the way down Fifth Avenue. She didn't notice the nimbus clouds crowding the sky or the light rain hitting the ground, giving rise to a moist, muddied street smell. People were rushing indoors to restaurants and stores, ducking into carriages. A few prepared citizens deployed black umbrellas that bloomed darkly along the sidewalks.

"Let's go back. No one will be there," Tillie said.

"It's only a light rain," Ada said. "I've a stout umbrella for you." It was as if she had prepared for any excuse.

They arrived at Bryant Park at last. The grounds for the new library were still an awful mess, with piles of rubble slowly being carted away chunk by chunk. It was hard to believe that only last year, those massive Egyptian-style walls had held twenty million gallons of good Croton River water.

The carriage parked on Forty-Second Street, just adjacent to the park. A slight fog had risen, but a single figure was visible on a bench near the main circle of greenery inside the park.

"There he is," Tillie said. She shivered. "I guess I ought to go."

"I'll be here, within sight. You'll be all right. Where is that Ian fellow?"

"I don't know. He may be waiting for me to show up."

"We'll drive around the park so it's not obvious we're waiting for you," Ada said. She rubbed the small round of belly beneath her waist, patting it like an old friend.

Tillie exited the carriage with the help of the driver, but the step was narrow and slick with rain. She slipped, twisting her left shoulder. Her bad shoulder. She bit down on her tongue instead of crying out in pain.

"Upsy-daisy! Are you all right?" Ada asked.

"I'm fine," Tillie said. She rubbed her shoulder and followed the shining sidewalk into the park.

It was quiet. The carriages had slowed in the rain, and the usual chatter of people was absent. Even the birds in the trees were close beaked. She stopped before entering the circular walkway inside the park and turned to see Ada and the carriage driving down the street and out of view as they turned the corner. Ada had said she'd stay in sight. Would they turn around soon and come back?

A hand touched her shoulder, and Tillie inhaled sharply and turned.

It was Ian. His hair was sodden, and tiny raindrops clung to his eyelashes. She had the strangest urge to lick them off.

Stop that, she thought.

"I'm sorry I'm a little late," he said in a rush. "There was a problem with the elevated, and then I had to skip one because it was packed with passengers escaping the rain."

"That's all right." She lowered her voice. "I think that's Tom over there."

They looked together. Sure enough, Tom Erikkson, looking oddly out of place wearing a long black woolen cloak, sat on a bench. He was peering at a pair of birds who kept hopping close, then away, then close. They seemed to have an eye on a biscuit in his hand.

"He hardly looks like someone who would murder all those people," Tillie said.

"One way to find out. Ask." Though it seemed a laughable suggestion, Ian didn't smile.

"Are you serious?"

"I am. Where is your maid?"

"I don't know. Ada said she was going to wait—oh, there she is. Wait, they're driving off again. Why does she keep doing that?"

"Well, I'm here. Come on." They walked together toward the bench. Tillie felt like she could breathe again. She realized she'd been holding her body stiffly and clenching her fists on and off all morning. With Ian next to her, her body loosened. It wasn't so much that she assumed he'd fight for her if something happened. It was that when Ian was nearby, the landscape around her immediately felt familiar and comforting, no matter where they were.

Tom turned his head at their approach. His eyes lit with pleasure at seeing Tillie but quickly darkened when he saw she was not alone.

"Hello, Tom," Tillie said, trying not to clench her teeth. Seeing him again gave her the unexpected and intense urge to strike him in the face with a brick.

"Hello. Who's this?"

"This is Mr. Metzger. He's a friend. Ian, this is Tom Erikkson."

Tom nodded, and Ian nodded back. Tom began, hesitant at first. "I thought . . . I assumed you'd be here alone."

"That's an awfully big assumption, after what you did. You wanted to speak? Go ahead." She folded her arms together in front of her.

Tom shifted uncomfortably and spoke more to his feet than to Tillie. "This is hard for me, but I suppose it should be. You're probably wondering why I'm even here, in this park. Well, I'm trying to get out of the house more. I've been living in that one room most of my life. I can't change that I'm not well, but I can change some things." He rubbed his head, as if he were kneading a headache away. He let go and tried to smile. "Would you believe I've taken more of a keen interest in my health? I've been choosing my foods carefully, working on my strength. This is my fifth time out of doors."

Tillie wasn't so sure it was doing any good. He looked visibly ill, like he might close his eyes and fall asleep for a week.

"I know," Tom continued, "that my mind hasn't been right. What happened with you—I've had nightmares where I've done that to people—to women. But I didn't think I would do such a thing while awake. Strange thoughts I've had, and violent ones, but what makes a gentleman is one who knows right from wrong, no matter what thoughts reside within this." He tapped his skull. "I was having trouble knowing the difference between what was real and wasn't."

Tillie said nothing. He still hadn't apologized.

"I just want to say I am sorry. I'm so, so very sorry. It was wrong, and I should be in the Tombs, and . . ."

As he was searching for more words, movement caught her eye. Tillie saw a man walk behind a grouping of trees in the corner of the park. He wore a black bowler hat and a light-gray coat. The clothes were ordinary enough, but his gait and the tilt of his head were unmistakable.

"Did you see him?" Tillie hissed to Ian. Tom looked, too, but he seemed a little too forlorn at the moment to care.

"I did. Who was that?" Ian said.

"I think it was John O'Toole. The man we hired to guard the house. He and Ada—" Tillie stopped. This was an interruption she didn't want to have. Was Ada close by? Would she try to speak to him about her condition? Why, why was John always afoot and watching when she did not wish him to be? "I have to speak to him," she said, moving away.

"Where are you going?" Tom asked.

"Stop," Ian said, jarred by the sudden change in Tillie's focus. "Let me speak to him. Ask him why he's here." He leaned close and murmured in her ear, "This fellow here couldn't hurt a fly. He looks to be on his deathbed. You'll be safe for a minute, out here in the open. I'll be back soon." Ian took off in a light run toward the exit of the park, where they'd last seen John.

Tom sighed, as if such interruptions were an inevitability in his life. "As I was saying—I am sorry," he continued. He was rather white in the face, and he had started to perspire. His hand grasped the lapel of his coat. He tugged at the collar of his shirt. "God, why is it so hot?"

"Are you quite all right?" Tillie said.

"I think the exercise of being outside has been too taxing." He stood, and his eyes suddenly unfocused. "My heart is beating so fast. So fast. I should go home."

Tillie grabbed his arm, alarmed. She helped lower him to the bench. "You do need to go home."

"I was feeling well yesterday, when I wrote you. I had even made my own breakfast. Though perhaps the cook's seasoning has been too harsh. Oh God." He turned his head to the side, and a waterfall of oat gruel poured out of his throat onto the paved stones. It stank like rotten apples.

"Ian!" Tillie yelled, turning her head in the direction where he had run off. "Ian! Ada! He needs help!"

A carriage had stopped only thirty feet away. It was a hansom cab, not the Pembrokes' carriage, and it wasn't Ada inside. Mrs. Erikkson stumbled out, her face bright red, as if she'd been crying for the last hour.

"Is that you, Miss Pembroke? Have you seen Tom? He ran off this morning, and I can't find—oh, goodness gracious, God in heaven. What's happened to him?"

"I don't know," Tillie said. She looked around, frantic. Where was Ian? "Ian!" she hollered again. The rain had started up again, this time a torrent of gray that shrouded the park. The park was deserted except for them. Tillie's hair began to droop around her eyes, obscuring her range of vision. Her dress grew heavy from all the wet.

"Help me. We'll get him into the hansom, and I'll bring him home. I'm so sorry, Miss Pembroke. After all that's happened—and now this. He knows better. He ought to have left you alone."

Mrs. Erikkson had grabbed Tom around his torso, under his arms. Tillie cringed at the thought of standing close to Tom, but she couldn't let him stay here in the rain. Luckily, it was her good shoulder that she was able to slip under Tom's other arm. Tom wobbled the necessary steps to the hansom, as she and Mrs. Erikkson struggled and slipped on the slick pavement. Mrs. Erikkson opened the door to the carriage as Tillie struggled under Tom's weight, which had suddenly gotten heavier. She heaved his arm around her back and looked at his face.

Tom was slack jawed, in a dead faint.

"Sir!" Tillie yelled. As quickly as she could without dropping Tom, she pounded on the door. "Driver! Help us!"

"Not worth a penny, these drivers!" Mrs. Erikkson croaked as she pushed and pulled Tom's limp body into the carriage. She pushed her skirts aside and pulled Tom in by his armpits. She exited the other door and came around to Tillie's side, where she was struggling to maneuver his feet inside.

"What happened to him?" Tillie asked.

"I don't know. He never should have left the house—his heart is too weak. Please, help me get his legs in, and we won't bother you again."

Tillie looked back through the rain but could not see Ian or John or Ada. Where had everyone gone?

Mrs. Erikkson was pushing Tom's legs, but the weight of his torso was making her efforts ineffectual. She was wheezing. With a determined breath, Tillie squeezed herself in the cab and pulled his body all the way in. Mrs. Erikkson leaned in the door and felt Tom's face.

"He'll be all right. He needs more medicine. We've run out."

"Surely you can get more," Tillie said. "You have that entire little house full of medicines."

"Not this one, we don't," Mrs. Erikkson said and pulled out a brown jar.

"You can't give it to him—he's not awake yet," Tillie said, patting Tom's unconscious face. "He'll choke on it!"

"Oh, this isn't *his* medicine. This is for you."

Tillie looked up, confused. Mrs. Erikkson had covered her own nose and mouth with a cloth. She had already unscrewed the top of the jar, and now she thrust the container forward. A clear liquid hit Tillie square in the face. Some of it splashed into her mouth, which filled with a pungent bitterness. Her tongue felt like it was dissolving away, numbed almost instantly.

The liquid burned her eyes and blurred everything. Tillie began to cough uncontrollably. She wiped her face and neck, but the liquid seemed to turn almost instantly into a vapor cloud that she could not escape. Every breath, every gagging cough, she inhaled more of it. Her mind instantly became befuddled, and she could not sit up in the carriage. She lurched forward, coughing, gagging, on top of Tom's prone body. She couldn't seem to use her arms, to tell her legs to kick, to get up, to run away.

Mrs. Erikkson shut the carriage door, then went to the other side.

"It's so nice to use ether on a rainy day. No chance of explosions or fire." She unscrewed another jar and poured it into the back of the carriage. "There. It'll stay close to the floor and keep you two asleep for quite a while."

She shut the door and went to drive the carriage. Tillie tried to lift her arm again to smack the side of the carriage to warn someone that she needed help. But there was no one there, no other driver, no one to hear. Her blurred eyes saw that her hand wasn't lifted, and in the next moment she couldn't remember why she was here or why she'd ever needed to call for help.

CHAPTER 26

The blood is the life!

—R. M. Renfield

Tillie saw the world as if through a kinetoscope. A broken kinetoscope.

There was a carriage around her, and a warm body beneath her. There was the pungent odor of that terrible stuff that Mrs. Erikkson kept dribbling over her mouth. It made her choke on nothing. It burned her lips and tongue and made her gag. Pink-tinged froth spewed from her throat when she coughed. Holes punctured her vision and thoughts, as if someone were shooting bullets through her memory, over and over again.

She was being dragged out of the carriage, laughing. Coughing. She spit up a wad of mucus into a dirty alleyway, tasting blood, and two strong arms went around her chest to drag her into a darkened room.

"Don't let him touch me," Tillie tried to say. She spoke the words over and over, but they were garbled, like *Donna donna toe* or some such. Sometimes she saw the words emerge from her face, the letters twisting into a sinewy white line that floated up into the air and dissolved into smoke.

A few coherent thoughts emerged from her garbled brain.

This wasn't like morphine. Morphine made her feel like she belonged in her own body. This stuff—did Mrs. Erikkson say it was ether?—this made her feel like a piece of a puzzle dropped into a stew full of shoestrings and potatoes. None of it made sense. She was not herself. She was not content.

She was not.

At some point, the fog of disorientation lifted. She found that she was in a darkened room that smelled of musty herbs and sharp spirits. A damp, muddy scent hung like a curtain around her, as if she were deep within an earthen hole. Tillie went to rub her nose and found her arm was tied near her side. So was her other arm, and her ankles were restrained.

Her whole body was bound to a table of some sort. She wriggled but could not pull away from her bonds. A thick rag muffled her mouth. Her voice box felt sore and swollen when she tried to produce a cry. Frothy, metallic secretions collected at the back of her throat, and she gagged and coughed.

There were footsteps nearby. Not nearby—above her. She opened her eyes. Above her, a ceiling made of thick wooden planks. Crumbs of dried dirt gently rained down as someone paced. The pacing ceased, and all went quiet.

A squeaking hinge issued, and somewhere a door shut. Bright light nipped at her eyes as the ceiling seemed to yawn open in the corner. She blinked several times before she could focus again.

Mrs. Erikkson came down a ladder, her skirts gathered in one fist. She jerked closed the trapdoor. A tiny lamp in the corner was lit, and she picked it up to bring it closer. Her face brightened with a pert smile when Tillie's eyes met hers.

"Awake, are we? Good. That means the ether will be gone from your blood soon. We can begin. I couldn't have a fire before. The ether might have exploded. I could have used morphine, but morphine won't subdue without a needle and, well"—she shivered—"I greatly dislike needles."

Tillie mumbled through the gag.

"I'm sorry to say I cannot answer your questions, but I appreciate the company." She smiled again. "It's so nice to be able to talk to someone with intelligence. The boy was just too young to understand. Your sister and the other girl, too afraid. But you—you understand. You know all about what I am not!" She smiled and turned toward a workbench laden with large bowls and flasks. Mrs. Erikkson bent to the fireplace, and there was a spark of light. The kindling crackled and snapped as it caught fire.

Two large bottles of absinthe rested on the corner of the table. Mrs. Erikkson poured out a tumblerful and began to drink. She winced as it went down and poured more into the glass. Her hand shook a little, spilling some onto the table. Tillie could smell the herbaceous liquor in the air.

Mrs. Erikkson moved a pile of journals from a chair and sat down. She lifted one, licked her thumb, and turned the pages. "Patterns in infectious protection in smallpox patients." She nodded and smiled at Tillie. "That's you, my dear." She flipped to another page. "Those vaccines are a good idea, but I wish to protect my Tom the best way possible. Most diseases don't have vaccines yet. The more we can give him, the better. You'll help."

The fire in the brick hearth was now burning merrily. A cauldron Tillie hadn't noticed before had begun to simmer. As the fumes rose, she crinkled her nose at the acrid, unrecognizable odor.

Mrs. Erikkson caught her looking. "That was extracted from a boy who suffered from a leg infection that cured beautifully under my husband's care. His blood has been cooking down for nearly three days now. When it's done, I'll divide it up and dry it down. Tom has not been taking his medicines for far too long."

Tillie mumbled against the rag. Mrs. Erikkson shook her head and closed her eyes for a moment. She sighed. "Ah, good. The absinthe is working. And now, I can give you some morphine to help with the discomfort." She opened a syringe kit and drew some medicine up. "I get so dizzy at the sight of sharp instruments. But like all womenfolk, I manage because I must." Tillie cringed and tried to wriggle away from the needle, but there was no escaping. Mrs. Erikkson didn't bother to lift up her sleeve or skirt, simply touched Tillie's leg with one hand and jabbed the needle in with the other.

"There. You're looking a little purple, my dear. Let's get some oxygen into that good, thick blood of yours before we begin. Now, if you scream, I'll just say it was me, and then I'll cut out your vocal cords with this." She held up a short curved knife that shone in the firelight.

She loosened Tillie's gag a little, and Tillie was able to breathe. She gasped, wild eyed.

"Please don't do this! There are people looking for me. They'll come soon, I know it."

"Oh, they came by already. They found nothing. And they'll find nothing until I'm done." She busied herself organizing some metal instruments on the table.

"Tom will know!"

"Tom is sleeping, and he thinks you've gone home safely." Mrs. Erikkson turned and smiled, looking around the tiny dark room. "I love my little oubliette. You know that word, do you not? It comes from the French word 'to forget.' No? You don't know the word? What about abattoir, then? Another pretty French word."

Tillie knew that word. Abattoir. Slaughterhouse.

Mrs. Erikkson continued. "From the verb *abattre*. 'To strike.' Though I think *oubliette* is a bit more pretty." She tucked a stray gray hair into the knot on her head. "I've learned a bit from reading your article. I can't have all my marks look like vampires. This last one, I sawed off his head after I was done. With you, I'll tear your throat out after, like you were attacked by a dog. I thought the fear of vampires would be a wonderful way to lead them away from a person like me, but no longer. I have to be more careful. And I can't be pretending to be a candy seller either! That only worked once, with that Weber boy. Anyway. There are other ways to bleed and be unseen."

"Why are you doing this?" Tillie began to whimper. "My sister too?"

351

"That's just a bad happenstance. Your family will get over it, just like I've gotten over my regrets in life. But I must work to take care of my Tom until the treatments begin to take effect."

"Treatments? What treatments?"

"The blood. After certain sicknesses, it protects people from getting sick. And it will protect my Tom too. My harvests have nourished his stews and soups and drinks, though he doesn't know it. His stomach is like mine, very delicate. He shall get so strong. But in the meantime, he doesn't even know what he needs." She patted a bottle next to her. Fowler's solution—Tillie had seen it at the druggist. "The arsenic in it keeps him quiet and gentle. It's not good on the stomach, and Tom dislikes it so, but he doesn't need to know."

Tom had said he'd been fixing his own meals and had felt stronger. Until today.

"You gave him some this morning, didn't you?"

"I did! And then he ran off before I could sedate him with a good fat dose of morphine."

"You're not helping him. You're keeping him sick to make him better? I don't understand."

"You wouldn't know. You haven't a mother's feeling," Mrs. Erikkson said tartly. "Tom is all I have. We lost the first child, and I shan't lose the second. And his father pays no attention to the new findings in the medical news every day." She lifted up a journal and shook it. "I couldn't be a doctor. There was no money, and my impediment."

"Impediment?"

"The needles," Mrs. Erikkson said. She picked up the bottle of absinthe and poured herself another tumblerful, drinking it quickly. She shivered. "This is the only thing that keeps my neurasthenia at bay."

"You're careless. You keep leaving bottles behind when you leave your victims."

"Nobody cares, nobody knows," Mrs. Erikkson singsonged. She was getting drunk.

"Does your husband know that you've murdered people to grind them into a pharmacopeia?" Tillie said.

Mrs. Erikkson pounded her hands on the table, and Tillie winced in astonishment.

"Don't you judge me! Tom is my *life*." She wiped her mouth, hand shaking. "My husband is a dolt and vastly insufficient as a parent and a husband. But he's been supplying me nonetheless."

She meant Lucy. And Albert Weber. And Annetta Green. They'd been Dr. Erikkson's patients too.

"I've seen him strike you," Tillie said. She was having difficulty keeping the panic out of her voice. She ached to be free of her bonds and sit up.

"Yes. Like I said, insufficient. He is a weak and frightened man, but he knows he is nothing without me." She poured herself one last tumblerful of absinthe. She put down the empty bottle but misjudged the edge of the table. The bottle fell off and bounced on the hard dirt floor. Mrs. Erikkson kicked it into the corner. "On occasion, I speak back, and he dislikes it. But I need his income to help Tom. My husband spends enough time between the thighs of those whores he visits every night, and his guilt keeps him in check."

"I thought he—I thought Dr. Erikkson was the killer."

Mrs. Erikkson hooted a laugh. "My husband? He can hardly function! He won't eat in public or in front of me. A proponent of the great Reverend Sylvester Graham. He thinks by eating purely, he won't succumb to impure thoughts. He hasn't touched me as is a husband's right in years. At night, he succumbs to all his sins with those whores and starts fresh in the morning." She straightened up. "Enough. It's time to proceed. My, you're still quite alert. I'll give you some more morphine."

"No, it's quite enough—"

"Don't be silly. You want to be quiet when this all happens. It's better this way! It is kindness itself. Excitement in the blood could cause too much excitement in Tom when he takes the medicine. I like them to be quiet as lambs when they go."

Mrs. Erikkson readied another dosage of morphine, when a loud knocking came from above.

"No doubt my husband wants me to do another delivery." She wiped her hands on her apron and smiled. "I shall be back." She replaced Tillie's gag and climbed the ladder. The trapdoor over the chamber closed tightly, and she heard Mrs. Erikkson's footsteps crossing the floor. There was that same creak of the door opening and more voices.

Tillie tried to yell and scream, but the gag muffled her sounds too much. She looked around. The fire, the needle and syringe, and then next to them on the table—an unrolled leather case that held several sharp-pointed lancets and what looked like ice picks of graduating thicknesses.

So these were the vampire teeth used to bore into people's necks. These would be the instruments of Tillie's own death. Her eyes widened in terror, imagining Lucy pinned to this very table. Her sister had intended to change the course of her life, to leave James, to provide security for Betty. This was not how Lucy had wanted her life to end. This was not how Tillie wanted this story to end.

Not like this.

She wriggled in her bindings. They were tight, and she could gain no purchase to pull free from them. She could feel the morphine working within her, too, a coming tidal wave that promised that everything would be fine and peaceful, and why was she struggling so anyway? It buffed her consciousness into apathy, and the last thing she needed was to be complacent.

But interestingly, it wasn't very potent. Tillie had been used to such high doses, and those tablets of heroin she had been taking before had been deceptively strong. She was still quite awake. She recalled that even as her morphine use had progressed, she had been needing larger and larger doses to keep herself satisfied. But Mrs. Erikkson did not know how much she had been using. Tillie worried, though. Perhaps she would not be quite as tolerant of high doses now that she had not taken any opiates for weeks. She could not chance that Mrs. Erikkson would give her more.

The door upstairs shut again, and Mrs. Erikkson was soon back downstairs in the chamber. Tillie feigned sleep, watching her from under nearly closed eyelids. Mrs. Erikkson opened up a second bottle of absinthe and poured a small glass. Her eyes shut as she swallowed it down.

She removed a small section of the table from just under Tillie's neck and hung a pail beneath it. She spread an oilcloth under Tillie's shoulder and neck, then turned her head to the side so it faced the fire and the table of instruments. Tillie knew she would pierce her neck, and the blood would spurt directly down into the bucket. Clean and neat. It explained why Lucy hadn't been drenched or splattered in blood. Mrs. Erikkson's setup put cow milking to shame.

"Already sleeping, eh?" Mrs. Erikkson murmured. "Very well."

She loosed the gag from around Tillie's head, where the cloth obscured parts of her neck. There was yet another knock on the door upstairs.

"Confound it! Why do they keep bothering me?" Mrs. Erikkson hissed. "I'll not answer them this time."

Tillie listened carefully. There were murmurs and a peculiar flitting, light musical sound from outside. A tiny voice could be heard through the floorboards. Faint, ever so faint.

"Pape!" the tiny voice said. It was yelling, but the strength was diluted through layers of wood doors and floors, distances. "Get your *World* today!" Dim, high-pitched whistles sounded, a rising trill of insistence.

It was Piper. There was no doubt. In seconds, he would be too far to hear her.

Tillie quickly licked her lips and whistled her birdlike pips in quick succession, before screaming with all her might. "Help! Piper, it's me, Tillie! Help!"

Mrs. Erikkson rushed to Tillie's side quickly and brought both fists down like hammers onto her face. The blows made Tillie gasp, her head ringing with pain.

"Be silent!" she hissed. She went to her table and picked up the syringe, fumbling for the morphine. But the absinthe had done its job, and the woman's hands were clumsy. In her rush, she knocked over the small bottle; liquid gushed over her worktable and instruments.

"Damn it!" she said, her voice rising in panic.

Tillie, meanwhile, was whistling as loudly as she could despite her eye swelling rapidly from being struck. She yelled and hollered, banging her head against the table. Mrs. Erikkson abandoned the syringe and mashed her meaty hands over Tillie's mouth. Tillie bit down hard, tasting salty, iron-tanged blood in her mouth. Mrs. Erikkson screeched in pain, reeling back and holding her hand.

"Very well! I'll silence you one way or the other." She grabbed the short curved knife from the table, but before she could reach her mark, Tillie lunged, trying to bite her hand again. She spat blood into Mrs. Erikkson's face. The knife's aim was untrue; as it drew against Tillie's neck, it pierced the skin at the wrong angle.

Tillie felt warm blood drizzling from her neck, heard it dripping into the bucket. But she didn't stop struggling. Despite the dizziness clouding her mind, she whistled, yelled, screamed while Mrs. Erikkson dried her hands to get a better grip on her knife.

"Stop struggling!" she hissed. "Be still!" She pushed Tillie's temple down against the table. Tillie shook her head left and right, her head slipping stickily beneath Mrs. Erikkson's grip. Mrs. Erikkson abandoned her effort to keep Tillie still. "You broke your clavicle here, did you now?" she said, touching the angle of bone that slightly tented the skin near her right shoulder. "Yes, you did." Mrs. Erikkson fetched a brick from a pile by the hearth. She lifted it high over her head and brought it crashing down onto the newly mended bone.

The pain was even worse than when Tillie had first broken it riding. White light exploded behind her eyelids, and she heard and felt the bone crunching into shards. Tillie screamed silently, open mouthed, incapable of even making sound. She froze in the maelstrom of pain, doing everything within her power not to move.

"There. Now I can work in peace." Mrs. Erikkson propped the brick back on the hearth, calmly gathered the knife and one of the ice pick–like tools.

"You . . . ," Tillie gasped. She managed to pry her good eye open to stare at Mrs. Erikkson. "They'll know what you did." She licked her dry, cracked lips and whistled shrilly again.

Mrs. Erikkson's face suffused red with irritation. "That's enough from you." Knife raised, she stepped closer to Tillie's body. Tillie inhaled, as deeply as the pain allowed, and let out one last whistle. Above the oubliette and from the street, it was silent. It was too late.

Tillie sagged against the table. She closed her eyes in resignation.

And then a single whistle sounded. It came from above the floorboards.

Mrs. Erikkson paused with the knife over Tillie's neck. The surety of her expression warped into a pang of fear.

Suddenly, the trapdoor opened, and light flooded the tiny chamber. Piper, with his curly black hair, peered down, alongside John O'Toole and Ian.

"Stop!" John roared. Mrs. Erikkson, her face splattered with crimson, hands dripping in Tillie's lifeblood, staggered back from the table, still holding the knife. She looked at all of them, saw what they saw— Tillie, bound to the table; the friendly hearth with its fire burning; the instruments laid out before her. Her lower lip quivered, and her eyes bulged. She looked like she was gagging on air.

"No . . . ," she murmured. Her hand reclenched around the sickle knife. "You'll take him away. You don't know how to care for him. I'll have nothing!"

John had already started to make his way down the ladder, when Mrs. Erikkson lifted her fist. With the assurance of someone who knew anatomy intimately, she touched her neck with one hand as a guide, right over the pulsing artery. Her other drew the knife closer to carve her own flesh.

A different voice rang out. "Stop, Mother!"

Tom's ashen face was there in the trapdoor. He reached a hand down to the chamber.

"Tom?" Mrs. Erikkson faltered, her knife poised in midair. It was all the interruption needed. John had jumped past the last rungs of the ladder, dropping to the floor. He sprang forward to knock the knife out of her hand. Ian jumped down next, and together they tackled her to the floor.

"You'll kill him!" she shrieked. "You'll kill him! No one knows how to care for him. No one! Stop!"

She was stronger than any of them had imagined. Ian finally tied her arms together behind her back, and John had to kneel on her legs to keep her still. Piper had scrambled down the stairs to start untying Tillie. Ian wiped the sweat from his eyes and came to her side.

"It's done. It's over," he said, stroking her hair as Piper loosened the last of her bonds.

Tillie looked at Tom, still peering through the door into the oubliette. He had an otherworldly look on his face, a mixture of relief, confusion, and utter shock. She saw him sit down with a bump and cover his face with his hand.

Tillie's neck was still bleeding at a steady clip, and Ian pressed a cloth against the wound. She closed her eyes from equal parts dizziness and relief. She wasn't sure her heart had the strength for one more beat. But even if it stopped, she would know, with a tiny smile, that she was not broken.

CHAPTER 27

But we are strong, each in our purpose; and we are all more strong together.

—Van Helsing

"Is she dead?"

"Stuff it. She's just sleeping."

Tillie stirred. Her neck was terribly sore, but that was the least of her problems. Her left shoulder hurt more than she had ever remembered. This pain was so livid and alive it felt like a creature was stabbing her from the inside of her body with tongs and torches and knives.

She opened her eyes.

Peering at her closely were Piper, Pops, and Sweetie. Pops looked like an old man in the body of a ten-year-old. He held a wilting bunch of daisies in his fist. Piper was chewing rather aggressively on a thick rind of bread crust.

"Oh, ow." Tillie groaned.

"You're awake. Sooner than I thought," Ian said. He was farther away, sitting in a chair that had been placed in the corner of the bedroom.

"Oh goodie. You're not dead. Can we have cake now?" Sweetie asked. She ran to the door, which was open. In the hallway, Tillie could see Ada and John talking. They turned to the sound of voices with lit eyes and smiled. Ada rushed to her side. It seemed like her belly had grown since Tillie had last seen her.

"You're awake! I promised they could come in so long as they were quiet, but . . ."

"You promised cake if we were quiet!" Piper shouted.

"Ugh, these *boytshiks*," Ian said affectionately.

"You need to teach me more Yiddish," Tillie said. "I don't understand half of what you say. It's all scandalous, I'm sure."

"It's not. And I'll teach you." Ian suddenly started picking at a loose thread on his sleeve, but he was smiling.

"Scamps. Let's go," John said at the doorway. "Not that they'll be quiet. They all scattered to find you after you went missing. To your house and the doctor's street, Central Park. Whistling like mad birds." He inclined his head into the room. "Are you sure you'll be fine without me?" he asked Tillie, though perhaps he was asking Ada.

"I'm fine, John!" Ada made a shooing gesture with her hands. The three newsies and John left, their chatter dissipating as they thumped downstairs.

Tillie struggled to sit up. Her arm, with its broken clavicle, was again bound against her chest. Oh God, everything hurt. Her wrists were sore. She pushed up the sleeve of her nightgown and saw the ligature marks and cuts from where she had been tied down. Memories of being in Mrs. Erikkson's oubliette flooded her.

"Oh." She looked at Ian. "What happened after I fainted?"

"Well, the police came and took Mrs. Erikkson away, but they took Tom and Dr. Erikkson too. They didn't know how extensive their involvement was."

"Were they? Involved?" Tillie asked.

"I don't think so. I think their worst crimes were being a monstrous husband and a son who thought it was acceptable to attack young women, intoxicated or not."

"It's on the front page of the paper," Ada said.

Tillie hadn't seen Ada since she had driven off in the carriage. "Ada. What happened to you when we were at the park? I thought you were going to be nearby."

"I was. And then—I saw John around the corner. I just lost my senses. I started arguing with him because he had left me, and then I told him about the baby—" She held her belly. "He had been following you. Of all the times! He would ruin everything, and I told him to be off, but he wouldn't listen."

"Well, why on earth was he following me?" It hadn't just been that time either. There'd been that night she'd seen him outside her window, watching her. Other times too.

"Why don't you ask him yourself?" Ian said. John had returned and stood in the doorway. As usual, he had that somewhat perpetually angry look about his face. Ada strode forward and pulled him into the room. He kept his hand in hers.

"I apologize. I didn't mean to scare you. Your grandmother had paid me two months in advance for my service, and when they let me go, well. I had a job to do for which I was paid, and I don't take that lightly."

"But then why did you give me absinthe in the carriage? After Tom attacked me?"

"I confess I stole it from the Erikksons' home. I figured you might need something to calm down. They had a case of it by the door. I knew you wouldn't drink it if you knew where it came from." He was peering at her the way he always did. Even that one time, when Ada and John had been in each other's arms, having a midnight tryst, he'd always stared. Tillie looked away, embarrassed.

"John, you're doing it again," Ada said quietly.

"Oh." He rubbed his eyes. "I'm sorry." He pulled a pair of brass spectacles out of his pocket and put them on.

"He's terrible about his spectacles. He thinks they'll make his eyes weak if he wears them, but then he can't see past ten feet if he doesn't. So he ends up squinting and staring all the time."

"I loathe them," he mumbled. "They make me look like an old man." Ada smiled up at him with the unabashed incandescence of someone so in love that even spoken gibberish would bring on a fit of romantic sighs. She reached for his hand, and John's angry eyebrows unfurled and his face lit when he looked at Ada.

"We're to be married this week. If you're well, I hope you'll come with us to the church," Ada added. She patted her belly. "The sooner the better."

"Oh, Ada! I would love to!" Tillie touched her face, feeling the indented scars over her cheeks. "I'll have to wear a veil. I don't want to be bad luck, looking like this."

"You look fine. You have battle scars. We all do, but some show more than others," Ian said quickly. He stood. "I have something for you." He reached down to a satchel and pulled out a book. He laid it on Tillie's lap. It was Lucy's diary.

Ada and John had retreated to the hallway.

Tillie touched the leather binding. She was tempted to open it and start reading from the first page, thirsty to hear her sister's voice. Lucy had written this for herself and perhaps had had no intention of sharing it with anyone. Hence the locked drawer. Reading it would bring back currents of memories, sweet and bitter. Lucy was gone, and her tormenter would no longer hurt anyone else. There was satisfaction in this fact, relief. But there was no serenity to accompany the relief. It did not quell the tempest that was Tillie's loss. She thought of Nellie Bly's recent visit and how, despite the woman's matter-of-fact way of speaking and acting, Tillie had spied a shadow in her expression, like a bruise on her soul. She'd recognized it in herself—the mark of someone who has lost a loved one so dear.

"Aren't you going to read it?" Ian asked.

"I don't know," Tillie said. She looked up at Ian, her face stricken. For the first time since Lucy died, Tillie cried.

December 1, 1899

Dear Lucy,
I have decided to start writing in a diary, just as you did. This is my first entry. One must start somewhere, don't you think?

You will be satisfied to know that Mrs. Erikkson will never hurt another soul again. She is currently awaiting trial, but everyone believes that she will end up in Sing Sing and meet her fate via "Old Sparky." A terrible way to die, but her fate is no longer in anyone's hands but the law's now.

Dr. Erikkson and his son were released, having been found innocent of the charges of conspiring with her to kill all those people. They found that she had killed at least ten others in the preceding year as she perfected her technique of cooking down blood from her victims and methodically spoon-feeding it to Tom. This, all in the name of improving his constitution, which rapidly improved once he stopped taking all the medicines she constantly fed him. Apparently, the arsenic and mercury in the Fowler's solution and calomel were doing more harm than good.

I believe she drew a deep happiness from keeping him sick and dependent on her, though I cannot imagine why any parent would want that for their child. It is confounding, as a concept. Tom wrote to me one last time, promising to be a better man, to respect the fairer sex. I have hope he will succeed but care little about waiting to see what happens. That is between him and society, and his God. He deserves to be in Sing Sing.

I am working on more articles. One, on the results of the chemistry analysis of Keeley's formulas and my time at the institute. Do you know that none of Keeley's Gold Cure contains gold? It's scandalous!

I am also writing another with Ian, on the working situation of children in this city. Children ought to be in school, not working in the factories and on the streets. It's quite horrible, but you knew this, I am sure. You never had the chance to meet Ian Metzger, but I believe you would approve. Aside from those absurdly long eyelashes of his, he is quite respectable. Well, aside from the one serious lapse on his part regarding that article about you. I suppose we have all made our grievous mistakes at some point in our lives. Mine were learning about the world without being in the world, and not being in your life enough. But now, with a pen as my sword, I am listening, and I am watching, and I am unafraid to confront the truth.

Ian has tried to make his earlier omission up to me by being forthright about all his thoughts, at all times. It is quite irritating. He has told me that my pockmark scars look like the constellation Cassiopeia. He said that was fitting, until I stumbled upon some research by Henry Bryant Bigelow, who has named an upside-down Caribbean jellyfish "Cassiopeia." That I have such a creature splattered across my face pleases me. Ian laughed and said that is just like me, to be enthralled over being associated with such a fantastical creature. I told Mama this, and she clucked her tongue, which is all she can do lately to keep me well behaved.

Speaking of Mama and Grandmama, they miss you. They do not say this aloud, but I hear them sigh when they pass by your room.

Grandmama has not changed much, but Mama has. When I demanded to go to the Foundling Hospital to continue your work or said I would write all day on my typewriter, Mama defended me. She and Grandmama yelled like cats over a fishbone for nearly a week, but Grandmama has finally gotten over her shock that her female descendants do, in fact, have as much backbone and fire as she has. As a result, she no longer forces me to go to balls and has not refused my plans to organize a fundraiser for the Foundling Hospital with Dorothy.

Hazel is helping, too, though I see her far less than I used to. She is married, and her husband is already away in California. I am sure James is happy about this situation. Dorothy too. Dorothy is pleased that her companion is still by her side. Hazel is pregnant already! I have said nothing about who the father must be. It is not my place to say anything. She seems to know she will have a girl. "It's our lot in life," she said, "for women like us to have girls that end up as companions to ladies in high society." She said she would name the girl Birdie because she liked the idea of a child feeling free in a world where so much keeps us tethered. I think it's a beautiful name, though I am relieved not to see much of her lately.

Speaking of Dorothy—she is to be married!

You'll never guess to whom.

Yes, you will.

She is to be married to James. I am not surprised, nor is Hazel, nor is Mama, but the news is stirring neverthe-less. I only just heard yesterday when Dorothy came to visit. Their wedding is to be in one month. She told me that she hopes to be with child as soon as possible so that she and Hazel can have children close together. She says she wishes for a girl, too, and that the child will unfortu-nately be named after one of the Cutter grandmothers or great-grandmothers. It's some name that sounds vaguely chemical, like Chlorine, or Allene, I cannot remember.

I sat Dorothy down and told her everything I knew about James. About his forced tryst with Betty, about hit-ting you, about rumors between him and Hazel. I told her he seemed to want to keep me subdued with heroin. She shrugged and said all husbands are imperfect; it is up to their wives to keep the sheen of perfection well polished. And she did not believe a whit about Hazel and James. I believe she will be truly unhappy, but I cannot alter her decision. She is steadfast, but more importantly, she is poorer than I realized. Her father's fortune is woefully dwindled, and James promises a life she is used to living. She will not be swayed, and it breaks my heart.

We get along as if my previous engagement to James were nothing, and it is nothing, because I will support her no matter what. But I feel she is pushing me away, in increments. At some point, I would not be surprised if I have no mention in her life. She asks me about my prospects, and I find I am shy to speak of them.

But she did urge me not to rely on Grandmama's word on the family fortune. I spoke to the family lawyer, who said that even though I am not a male heir, I am due my dowry whether I marry or not. They never told me this. It is not a gargantuan sum, but it does mean I will not be penniless, with careful management. It also means I can marry whomever I choose. Grandmama was angry that I sought out that information, and Mama had no idea. Nellie Bly was right about one thing—one must take care of oneself. I can secure my own future and the future of those I care dearly for.

Speaking of which, with the money, I have secured a better living situation for Piper, Pops, and Sweetie. They live with Ian now, and he has pulled them out of their daily work to keep them in school. They love it, especially Pops, who wishes to become a college professor someday, but Piper and Sweetie torment their teachers as much as the passersby they used to solicit with their papers. I have wishes to keep them closer to me. Adoption would be wonderful, but in many ways, I am very old fashioned. I should like to be married before I have children. I am only waiting to be asked.

Then again, perhaps I should write an article about what happens when a lady asks a man for his hand in marriage. I should think that would be quite a scandal. However, I can weather scandals, as I know now.

It's only a matter of time before he asks, or I ask first. I wonder which shall happen first.

Can you guess who the lucky gent is? I shall give you a hint.

(He thinks I have a jellyfish splattered across my face.)

I have mentioned it to Mama and Grandmama, and Grandmama accuses me of being intoxicated with opium again and out of my senses. I have assured them that I am intoxicated with an altogether other entity that cannot be bottled or sold.

When I was recovering from the attack, I returned James's ring to him with a note. He never visited me while I was ill, nor after. Ada tells me that she heard from one of the Cutter maids that he was horribly disappointed to hear that I had scars on my face after my illness, and that I continued to shun the heroin tablets. That was that.

When I returned the ring, I enclosed a note. Do you want to know what it said?

⟞⟝

Dear James,
Please find enclosed your gift. Thoughtful though it was, I do not believe it fits me very well.

As for your offer to build me a grand library that would house all the stories I should ever wish to read, thank you, but I must decline.

I prefer to write my own.
Sincerely,
Tillie Pembroke
He never wrote back. Fancy that.

AUTHOR'S NOTE

Book ideas are very odd things. They attack you in the middle of the night and cause insomnia; they pop up while you're stalled in traffic and then make you miss a turn. I've ceased being surprised when weird ideas come to me from wherever. However, this time, there were several glimmers of inspiration that are responsible for making *Opium and Absinthe* come alive. They're all over the place, so stay with me.

First of all, there is Francis Ford Coppola's 1992 movie, *Bram Stoker's Dracula*. It featured Winona Ryder, Gary Oldman, Keanu Reeves (Keanu! My heart!), and Anthony Hopkins. I was a junior in college when that movie came out, and it cast a spell on me. It was a grotesque, passionate, eerie, twisted fairy tale of sorts that left an indelible mark (bite?) on my memory. In particular, there is a scene when Dracula and Mina share absinthe together. The scene does not occur in the original novel, but I forever remembered the ritual of it as a token of a time, place, and era that was both romantic and brutal. More recently, I got my hands on the annotated version of Stoker's *Dracula*, by Leonard Wolf—an amazing compendium of illustrations, photos, and notes that brought an incredible depth to the original story.

Then there was this book: *Quackery: A Brief History of the Worst Ways to Cure Everything*, cowritten by me and my journalist friend Nate Pedersen only a few years ago. Writing this book was an experience like none other. We researched some of the wackiest, weirdest, and grossest methods that people have tried to heal themselves over the last several centuries. People often ask me what my favorite chapters were to write, and my answer is usually thus: the chapter on cannibalism and corpse medicine.

Egyptian mummies were once used as a cure-all. Human blood was once drunk from fallen gladiators to tame epilepsy. And human fat was a salve that was touted to treat rabies. Let's face it. Sitting here in the newish twenty-first century, we think nothing of liver transplants and blood transfusions. Even face transplants are not so shocking anymore. But actually consuming parts of a dead person, for the sake of a cure? Unthinkable. Unless—it occurred at a time when medicine was still blossoming with truths.

Some of my research also took me into the history of opium and opiates. I learned that in the late 1800s, when syringes were invented, they enabled a new legion of people to inject morphine (identified in 1804, but then available as an injection toward the middle of the 1800s). The interesting thing was that the syringes were expensive. Morphine addicts, also called morphinomaniacs, were oftentimes wealthy women being treated for all sorts of ailments. When heroin came on the market at the end of the century, it was thought not to be addictive. The original manufacturer was Bayer (as in the Bayer that makes aspirin today). These snippets of medical history were both fascinating and sadly still timely, given our opioid addiction crisis today.

Finally, the last piece of this bookish pie came in the form of a musical—*Newsies*. My daughter became entranced with the musical and the story, and our whole family listened to the music countless times. I did a little research into the newsies' strike and found out that all those events occurred in 1899, just before the new century.

And then I found out that Bram Stoker's *Dracula*—the original book—was released in the United States in 1899.

I thought, Huh. What if someone was killing someone, and the murders looked like vampire deaths? And a newsie helped solve the murders? These were the questions that started the entire process. *Opium and Absinthe* was born.

Tillie is near and dear to my heart, and I have done my best to portray her as a very imperfect person who became a victim to opiates in the way that any ordinary person might. Addiction does not just affect one section of society. It is a very complicated thing. It is physiology, psychology, social mores, pharmaceutical power—and it is pain. It is anything but glamorous, and it kills in its own right. If you or someone you know suffers from addiction, please do reach out for help. If you can, call your doctor for guidance. Here are more options:

- Substance Abuse and Mental Health Services Administration Help Line:
  1-800-662-HELP (4357)
- NIH: National Institute on Drug Abuse Step by Step Guides:
  https://www.drugabuse.gov/publications/step-by-
  step-guides-to-finding-treatment-drug-use-disorders/
  table-contents
- For teens, check out https://abovetheinfluence.com/

Thank you again for reading my book. It is always an honor and a privilege to share my imagination with you. As I spent so much time with all the characters in *Dracula* and in *Opium and Absinthe*, I found there was much to be learned about human nature, inhuman nature, and all the facets of humanity itself, both beautiful and terrible. We all have the capacity for much love in the face of cruelty. Remember Van Helsing's words:

"There are darknesses in life and there are lights; you are one of the lights."

Go forth and shine.

—Lydia

ACKNOWLEDGMENTS

As always, a huge thank-you to my family. They have remained support-ive and enthusiastic, no matter how many characters I murder off every year. To all my readers, who keep supporting my books—I am endlessly grateful. Thank you to Kate Brauning, Angela Hawkins, and Sarah Kosa for your early feedback and friendship. Thank you to Felicity Bronzan, who has helped keep my life from turning into utter chaos, and to Sarah Simpson-Weiss for being such a kick-ass assistant! To Dana Kaye and her team—thank you again for your awesome publicity support.

Thanks to Eric Myers, my wonderful agent. And a deluge of grati-tude to the entire team at Lake Union, including Jodi Warshaw, Caitlin Alexander, Ashley Vanicek, Nicole Pomeroy, Laura Barrett, Kathleen Kent, and Edward Bettison, who helped make this strange, twisted idea come to fruition and brought it to readers around the world.

ABOUT THE AUTHOR

Photo © Chelsea Donoho

Lydia Kang is an author and internal medicine physician. She is a graduate of Columbia University and New York University School of Medicine, and she completed her training at Bellevue Hospital in New York City. She lives with her family in the Midwest. Follow her on Twitter @LydiaYKang and Instagram @LydiaKang.